SHARP dialogue

锐对话

著

（汉英对照）

北京出版集团
北京人民出版社

图书在版编目（CIP）数据

尖锐对话：汉英对照 / 刘晓明著. — 北京：北京
人民出版社，2022.9
ISBN 978 - 7 - 5300 - 0573 - 6

Ⅰ．①尖… Ⅱ．①刘… Ⅲ．①新闻采访—作品集—中
国—当代—汉、英 Ⅳ．①I253

中国版本图书馆 CIP 数据核字（2022）第 166600 号

BBC 对出版此书不持异议，对书中内容不承担责任。

Sharp Dialogue
Copyright © 2022 Liu Xiaoming
All rights reserved.
ISBN：978 - 7 - 5300 - 0573 - 6 （Paperback）
Published By Beijing People's Publishing House
First printing edition 2022

The BBC is not responsible for the transcription and translation of this content.

▲ 2010 年 5 月 26 日，在白金汉宫向英国女王伊丽莎白二世递交国书。女王生前曾接受 12 位中国大使递交国书，我是最后一位当面向她递交国书的中国大使

▲ 2011 年 11 月 10 日，与英国议员等共同启动大熊猫伙伴关系网站

▼ 2012 年 1 月 23 日，接受英国 BBC《新闻之夜》栏目主持人帕克斯曼现场直播采访

▲ 2012 年 1 月 23 日，接受英国 BBC《新闻之夜》栏目主持人帕克斯曼现场直播采访后与其交谈

▼ 2012 年 3 月 14 日，接受英国 BBC 广播四台《今日》栏目主持人戴维斯现场直播采访

▲ 2012 年 12 月 21 日，接受英国 BBC《新闻之夜》栏目主持人艾斯勒现场直播采访

▼ 2014 年 1 月 5 日，接受英国 BBC 世界新闻台主持人库马拉萨米现场直播采访

▲ 2014年1月5日，接受英国BBC国际广播电台主持人沃里克现场直播采访

▼ 2014年1月8日，接受英国BBC《新闻之夜》栏目主持人帕克斯曼现场直播采访

▲ 2014 年 1 月 14 日，接受英国天空新闻台《杰夫·兰德直播间》栏目主持人兰德现场直播采访

▼ 2015 年 9 月 3 日，接受英国 BBC《新闻之夜》栏目主持人佩斯顿现场直播采访

▲ 2015 年 10 月 14 日，接受英国《电视四台新闻》栏目主持人斯诺现场直播采访

▼ 2015 年 10 月 15 日，接受英国独立电视台《十点新闻》栏目国际主编奥马尔采访

▲ 2015 年 10 月 9 日，与 BBC 新闻总监哈丁、主持人、编辑、记者 30 余人座谈

▲ 2015 年 10 月 16 日，接受英国 BBC《新闻之夜》栏目主持人戴维斯现场直播采访

▼ 2015 年 10 月 18 日，接受 BBC《安德鲁·马尔访谈》栏目主持人马尔现场直播采访

▲ 2015 年 10 月 18 日，接受英国天空新闻台《莫纳罕访谈》栏目主持人莫纳罕现场直播采访

▼ 2017 年 1 月 6 日，在英国 BBC 广播四台接受奥尼尔勋爵采访

▲ 2017 年 6 月 26 日，在庆祝香港回归祖国 20 周年招待会上讲话

▲ 2017 年 6 月 29 日，接受英国 BBC 广播四台主持人汉弗莱斯现场直播采访。采访后，
与汉弗莱斯交谈

▲ 2017 年 11 月 19 日，接受英国独立电视台《佩斯顿星期日访谈》栏目主持人佩斯顿现场直播采访

▼ 2019 年 6 月 21 日，接受英国天空新闻台《政治新闻综述》栏目主持人博尔顿现场直播采访

▲ 2019 年 8 月 15 日，在中国驻英国大使馆就香港问题举行中外记者会

▲ 2019年10月1日，接受英国天空新闻台《今夜天空新闻》栏目主持人莫纳罕现场直播采访

▼ 2019年11月26日，接受英国BBC《尖锐对话》栏目主持人萨克现场直播采访

▲ 2020 年 2 月 9 日，接受英国 BBC《安德鲁·马尔访谈》栏目主持人马尔现场直播采访

▲ 2020 年 4 月 28 日，接受英国 BBC《尖锐对话》栏目主持人萨克在线直播采访

▼ 2020 年 5 月 14 日，接受英国天空新闻台《新闻时间》栏目主持人奥斯汀在线直播采访

重磅推荐

Highly Recommended

我了解刘晓明战友。他祖籍广东，从小就知道三元里老乡们爱国反帝的传统；年轻时就敬佩老一辈革命家毛主席、周总理；在大西北挂职省长助理时，虚心学习老革命根据地的党史；后来出任驻友好邻邦朝鲜的大使，不负韶华。1999 年美空军悍然轰炸我驻南联盟使馆，我驻美使馆在中央指挥和国内外舆论支持下，迫使美国时任总统写下道歉词时，他作为公使挺立在我身旁。

晓明同志在驻英期间，永记祖国天安门城楼上"中华人民共和国万岁""世界人民大团结万岁"的口号和习主席"以人民为中心"的理念，特别注重与民间和新闻界交流……《尖锐对话》不妨说是真诚对话，记述了他为推动和平、正义和人类发展事业做的大量工作。

日前，他约我推介此书并谦虚地说，不用"吹捧"，写"三百字"就行。我欣然从命。我想说的很简约：此书难得，广大中外朋友读后会颇受启迪，愿为构建人类命运共同体多干实事。

——李肇星

外交部原部长

第十一届全国人大外事委员会主任委员

《尖锐对话》反映了我国工作在一线的外交官在国际舞台上面对西方媒体诸多不确定性的挑战，充满自信，从容应对，发出中国声音的现实故事，看后印象深刻。有此经历和体会的人都清楚，每一次接受西方媒体新闻采访或面对面访谈，甚至电视直播，对被采访者的政策水平，以及其对国内外形势的了解和判断力、所涉专业知识的熟悉程度和水平、语言表达和应变能力，是一次真刀实枪的考验。刘晓明大使驻英 11 年，接受采访 170 多次，其中，电视、电台采访 53 次，经常会面对很多不确定性或刁钻问题，甚至不友好的挑衅，但他都能够用事实、数据、法律、历史、案例睿智地代表国家回答问题、申明立场、发表评论，讲好中国故事，彰显了中国外交官不惧挑战、迎难而上、敢于斗争、善于斗争的责任担当，彰显了文明古国的大国风范。尤其面临当前复杂的形势，特别推荐《尖锐对话》。

——解振华
中国气候变化事务特使
国家环境保护总局原局长
国家发展和改革委员会原副主任

刘晓明大使多年来活跃在中国外交舞台上，为世界外交界和政策研究界所瞩目。我本人关注刘大使已经多年，这不仅仅是因为他在讲好中国故事、做好国际传播方面的国际影响力，更是因为我在思考这样一个重要的问题：中国的崛起是如何赋能我国的外交官在国际舞台上展现中国风貌的？呈现在读者眼前的这本书收录了刘大使在任职驻英大使期间（2010—2021年）接受电视和电台采访实录30余篇。书中重点回顾了21世纪第二个10年中英两国共同关心的所有重大双边和国际事件，包括习近平主席访英、新时代的中国、香港问题、新冠肺炎疫情、中日关系等丰富内容。通读下来，我的感受是：这无疑是一部"活"的中国外交史，不仅是专注中国外交崛起和外交话语权构建的学者的重要参考书，更是关心中国复兴和中国走向世界舞台中心的所有读者的必读书。

——郑永年
前海国际事务研究院院长
香港中文大学（深圳）教授

如何清晰有力地向国际社会表达中国立场、形象生动地向世界讲好中国故事，是中国外交和对外传播在"百年未有之大变局"中的一道必答题。刘晓明大使的新著《尖锐对话》为这一难题提供了一个堪称经典的答案。

　　刘大使在书中所涉及的重大国际、外交和内政问题上，坚定把握政治原则及政策立场，运用高超的叙事和应答技巧，充分阐释中国看待上述问题的视角、制定政策的原则和采取行动的逻辑，既敢于斗争、不回避尖锐问题，又善于斗争、不掉入话语陷阱。

　　英国是传媒业最为发达、新闻集散最为活跃、舆论传播能见度最高的西方国家之一，也是中国外交和对外传播工作的重点与难点。刘大使在驻节英伦十一载的岁月中，为增进西方社会对中国国情和政策的全面真实了解，破解西方舆论对中国形象的曲解误导，与当地媒体广泛交流、持续发声，在西方新闻传媒业最为发达的心脏地带成就了一系列精彩的对外传播篇章。他与BBC节目主持人之间充满睿智和机敏的唇枪舌剑，已经成为诠释大国形象的经典场面；他将日本军国主义形象地比作"伏地魔"等也已作为经典桥段而广为传播。《尖锐对话》一书不仅以采访实录的方式再现了这些经典场景，展现了作者与英国顶级媒体之间的精彩互动，具有强烈的现实场景感，而且充分展示了中国外交的丰富内涵，帮助我们从一个侧面了解到国际形势的风云激荡、中国和平崛起的外部效应以及外交工作者对祖国的忠诚奉献。本书将成为新时代中国外交和对外传播的一个生动写照。本书内容均为刘大使亲身经历，具有口述史的宝贵价值，可以成为深入研究国际形势变化、中国外交、对外传播以及对英外交等专题的重要参考资料。

——崔洪建

中国国际问题研究院欧洲研究所所长

刘晓明在担任中国历史上任期最长的驻英国大使期间曾发表一系列演讲，并结集出版。现在他又将任内接受英国电视和电台采访的内容汇编成册，以《尖锐对话》为题出版。和他演讲中的表现一样，刘晓明在采访中立场坚定、毫不留情。他的访谈直率、尖锐，具有说服力；他擅长反驳，对那些针对中国的虚假主张和指控做出回应，甚至可以用《帝国反击战》[1]给他的系列采访加上诙谐的副标题。

　　采访的主题从新冠肺炎疫情到香港，再到中国与英国的关系，涵盖范围广泛。刘大使在采访中与大多数英国最著名的电视主持人唇枪舌剑。值得称赞的是，他从不回避挑战，这使他在电视和媒体上的曝光率远远超过任何一位外国驻英大使，因此获得了表达中国观点前所未有的机会。

　　虽然他和他的中国同事谨记"每个人都有权拥有自己的观点，却无权拥有属于自己的事实"这一格言，但是他展现出能言善辩者的智慧和斗志，实在令人敬畏。他的语言能力非常出众，反映出他在英国文学方面的深厚底蕴。他在一次采访中曾告诫主持人："我希望人们能多一些'理智与情感'，少一些'傲慢与偏见'。"[2]

　　总之，读罢此书，人们对一位杰出的外交官应对媒体的专业能力，不能不表示钦佩。

——查尔斯·鲍威尔勋爵

英国议会上院议员

英国前首相撒切尔夫人外事顾问

---

　　[1]　《帝国反击战》又名《星球大战2：帝国反击战》，是美国著名导演厄文·克什纳1980年执导的太空歌剧史诗片，获多项影视大奖。

　　[2]　《理智与情感》和《傲慢与偏见》均为英国著名女作家简·奥斯丁的名著。

Following on his book of speeches delivered during his unprecedentedly long term of office as China's Ambassador to the United Kingdom, Ambassador Liu Xiaoming has now published a compendium of his interviews with British television under the title "*Sharp Dialogue*". As with his speeches, he takes no prisoners. The interviews are characteristically incisive. They are also concentrated on rebuttal, responding to what he regards as false claims and allegations levelled at China. Indeed the sub-title to the collection might humorously be "*The Empire Strikes Back*".

The interviews cover a very wide range of subjects from Covid, to Hong Kong, to China's relations with the UK. They pit Ambassador Liu against most of Britain's best known television interviewers. It is to his credit that he never shied away from a challenge. This gave him far greater exposure to television and the media generally than any other foreign ambassadors, and thus unrivalled opportunities to put across China's views.

He emerges as a formidable debater and someone who relishes a battle of wits, although he and his Chinese colleagues should not forget the adage that everyone is entitled to his own opinions but not his own facts. His is also a considerable achievement linguistically, reflecting a serious knowledge of English literature. "I hope we can have a bit more sense and sensibility rather than pride and prejudice." he reproves one interviewer at one point.

In short, one cannot but admire the professional media skills of a remarkable diplomat.

Lord Powell of Bayswater
Foreign Policy Adviser to Prime Minister Margaret Thatcher

刘晓明大使的书是对过去 10 年中英关系发展史的独特贡献。刘大使是在英国任职时间最长的中国大使，他长达 11 年的任期与戈登·布朗、戴维·卡梅伦、特雷莎·梅和鲍里斯·约翰逊等 4 位首相领导的英国政府执政、英国脱欧公投以及最终退出欧盟的整个历程重叠。在英国的这段特殊时期，刘大使的长期任职使他对英国的政治、社会和经济动态有着非凡的洞察力。他热情广泛地接触各界人士，经常通过大众媒体和多媒体讲述中国故事。刘大使的做法非常有效——他从不回避棘手和复杂的问题，总是以建设性的方式以及极具个性的雄辩和礼貌去应对这些问题。这本书是刘大使在英国期间的珍贵访谈录，它代表了在这个关键的历史节点，缩小中西方"了解赤字"的非凡努力。

——诸立力

英国伦敦大学学院理事会主席

世界经济论坛国际商务委员会联席主席

Ambassador Liu Xiaoming's book is an unique contribution in the history of the evolving Sino-British relations over the last decade. Ambassador Liu was the longest serving Chinese Ambassador in Britain and his extended tenure of 11 years overlapped with the administrations of four prime ministers—Gordon Brown, David Cameron, Theresa May and Boris Johnson—as well as the whole journey of the Brexit referendum leading to Britain's eventual exit from the EU. During this special period in Britain, Ambassador Liu's long tenure enabled him to gain exceptional insights in the country's political, social and economic dynamics. He reached out enthusiastically to a broad spectrum of stakeholders to present the China story, oftentimes via mass media and multimedia communications. Ambassador Liu's approach has been highly effective—never one to shy away from difficult and complex issues, he would always confront them constructively, with typical articulacy and courtesy. This book is a treasurable collection of Ambassador Liu's interviews during his time in Britain—they represent a remarkable effort to mitigate the "understanding deficit" between the West and China at this crucial juncture of history.

Victor L.L. Chu
Chair of Council, University College London
Co-Chair, International Business Council, World Economic Forum

刘晓明于2010—2021年担任中国驻英国大使，这11年是中英关系非同寻常的时期。2013—2016年，两国享有有史以来最热烈的关系。这个时期的亮点是2015年英国不顾奥巴马政府的反对，决定加入亚洲基础设施投资银行，这一决定鼓励了许多欧洲国家也采取同样的行动。习近平主席于当年晚些时候访问英国，这被广泛认为是一次重大的成功访问。这一时期在当时被称为中英关系的"黄金时代"是有充分理由的，但是它并没有持续下去。2016年，卡梅伦首相输掉了脱欧公投并辞职，随后中英关系开始恶化，直到2019年支持脱欧的鲍里斯·约翰逊政府上台，两国关系达到了一个新的低点。"黄金时代"让位于针对中国的越来越大的敌意和在香港问题上日益升级的紧张关系。刘晓明的文章和访谈为我们观察这一时期中英关系的高潮和低谷提供了非常有价值的真知灼见。他一直是中国立场的有力支持者和能言善辩者，这使他成为英国政界非常知名和受人尊敬的人物。

——马丁·雅克
英国著名学者
政治评论家、作家

Liu Xiaoming's period of service as China's ambassador to the United Kingdom from 2010 until 2021 covered an extraordinary time in China-UK relations. Between 2013 and 2016 the two countries enjoyed the warmest ever relationship between the two countries. The highlight was the UK's decision to join the AIIB in 2015, despite opposition from the Obama administration, which in turn encouraged many European countries to act likewise. President Xi Jinping's visit to the UK later that same year was widely regarded as a major success. This period was described at the time as a golden era in China-UK relations and for good reason. But it did not last. Prime Minister Cameron lost the Brexit referendum, and with his resignation in 2016, relations between China and the UK began to deteriorate and reached a new low point with the election of the pro-Brexit government of Boris Johnson in 2019. The golden era gave way to growing hostility towards China and rising tensions over Hong Kong. Liu Xiaoming's collection of articles and interviews provide us with a very valuable insight into the highs and lows of this period. He was at all times a powerful and articulate proponent of China's views and became a very well-known and respected figure in British politics.

Professor Dr. Martin Jacques
Political commentator & author

《尖锐对话》抓住了两种文化和两种体制之间的差异。刘晓明大使利用英国媒体帮助英国政府领导人、官员、商界和金融界了解中国，了解快速崛起的中国经济和社会体系。

由于 19 世纪划定的分割线，许多西方人认为俄罗斯和中国的社会主义者致力于推翻资本主义。但事实并非如此。中国也拥有庞大的民营部门，同样面临与英国诸多相同的治理和共享问题。

在《尖锐对话》中，读者可以了解到中国如何寻求共赢的成果，而英国的一些关切使取得这些成果变得困难。

《尖锐对话》表明，它不是在宣传，而是在帮助人们看清事实，了解中国的历史、中国的方式和中国的计划。刘大使是在海外最早与西方媒体打交道的人之一，交流内容包括管控分歧甚至利益冲突。

只有打破繁文缛节，你才能触及真正的问题。刘大使是来到英国愿意以这种方式开展接触的为数不多的中国人之一。

让我们享受阅读这些媒体访谈，跟随刘大使穿越中英之间数百年缺乏交流的历史，去真正了解彼此在关键问题上的立场。

——斯蒂芬·佩里
英国 48 家集团俱乐部主席
"中国改革友谊奖章"获得者

Sharp Dialogue captures the difference between two cultures and the two systems. Ambassador Liu used the media in the UK to help officials, leaders, business and finance to understand China and the fast emerging Chinese economic and social system.

Because of fault lines laid down in the 19th Century many in the West have the opinion that Socialists from Russia and China are committed to the downfall of capitalism. But that is not the case. China has large private sector and China faces many of the same problems of governance and sharing that are also evident in the UK.

In Sharp Dialogue you can see how the Chinese approach is to find win-win outcomes but the UK has concerns that make outcomes difficult.

Sharp Dialogue shows that this is not about propaganda, but it is about helping others see the facts and understanding the Chinese history and ways, and plans. Ambassador Liu was one of the first Chinese overseas to engage with the Western media systems and manage differences, and even sometimes, clashes of interest.

It is only through breaking from simple politeness that you can get to the real issues. Ambassador Liu is one of the few Chinese who have come to live in the UK who has been prepared to engage in this way.

Enjoy reading the media moments as Ambassador Liu travels across hundreds of years of few contacts to achieve real understanding of each other's position on key matters.

Stephen Perry
Chairman, 48 Group Club
Awardee of China Reform Friendship Medal

与媒体公开交流的能力和意愿，是刘晓明担任中国驻英国大使期间的突出特点。正如《尖锐对话》书名所示，当中国问题以及后来的涉港、新冠肺炎疫情等问题成为全球关注的焦点时，刘大使认识到与BBC等新闻媒体进行公开对话的重要性。作为一个乐观主义者，刘大使对全球化和中英双边关系等复杂问题有其独到见解，这也是他在中国驻英国大使的岗位上取得巨大成功的重要因素。当前，中国在世界上的地位和影响几乎占据新闻头条，《尖锐对话》一书让我们有幸聆听刘大使与不断刨根问底的媒体进行交流时的雄辩口才。

——里士满公爵
全英赛车俱乐部主席

Liu Xiaoming's ability, and willingness, to communicate openly with the media was typical of his tenure as China's Ambassador in Britain. As his book's title suggests, he recognised the importance of an open dialogue with the BBC, and other news outlets, when China, Hong Kong, and latterly the Covid pandemic, were the focus of interest worldwide. Ever the optimist, Liu's understanding of complex issues such as globalisation and China-UK bilateral relations were a significant factor in his huge success as his country's Ambassador. His book *"Sharp Dialogue"* gives us further insight into how he was able to communicate so eloquently with an ever-inquisitive media at a time when China's position in the world was rarely far from the headlines.

The Duke of Richmond and Gordon
President of the British Automobile Racing Club

21世纪地缘政治的核心挑战之一，是"让世界听到中国的声音"。习近平主席自 2012 年担任中共十八大报告起草组组长以来就认识到了这一需要。报告中包含推进如何"让世界听到中国的声音"的政策。《尖锐对话》的巨大价值在于，它提供了一个独特的案例研究：刘晓明大使如何在中国驻英国大使馆做出最有价值的开创性努力，从而为"让世界听到中国的声音"发挥最佳影响。刘晓明大使 2010 年抵达英国时，已在多国积累了丰富的交流经验。他在美国担任中国大使馆公使（副馆长）的经历使他深刻认识到，中国需要在沟通方式上进行创新。仔细研究《尖锐对话》这本书中的采访，可以看出他努力以最地道的英式英语在英国进行交流的价值。此外，他以一种对英国媒体产生最佳影响力的方式进行交流的技巧也令人印象深刻。从他接受如此之多的电台和电视采访，以及撰写的大量媒体文章中，人们能够体会到他为"让世界听到中国的声音"而不断探索新方式的热情。我希望这本访谈录有助于读者研究这位 21 世纪具有极高造诣的中国传播者刘晓明大使。

祝贺刘晓明大使！

——麦启安
英国东亚委员会秘书长
全球化智库国际理事会主席

In the geo-politics of the 21st century one of the core challenges is to "Let the world hear the voice of China". This need has been recognised by President Xi Jinping since he was Chairman of the Committee that produced the 18th Congress Political Report in 2012. Embedded in that Report were policies to advance how to "Let the world hear the voice of China". The huge value of this book is it provides a unique case study of how Ambassador Liu Xiaoming made most valuable pioneering efforts from the Chinese Embassy in UK to make optimal impact to "Let the world hear the voice of China". When Ambassador Liu Xiaoming arrived in UK in 2010, he had gathered wide experience of communicating in many nations. His experience in the USA as the Deputy Chief of Mission had impressed on him the need for China to innovate in how it communicates. A careful study of the interviews in this book "*Sharp Dialogue*" will show the value of his great efforts to communicate in the best possible native English style used in the UK. Also, what comes across is the skill of Ambassador Liu Xiaoming to communicate in a style that has optimal impact in UK media. The passion of Ambassador Liu Xiaoming to explore new ways to "Let the world hear the voice of China" can be grasped by reading these many radio and TV broadcast interviews he made and the large number of media articles he wrote. I hope this collection of interviews provides a catalyst for the study of the approach of one of the most consummate of China's communicators in this century—congratulations Ambassador Liu Xiaoming!

Alistair Michie
Secretary General, British East Asia Council
Chairman, International Council, Centre for China and Globalization

刘晓明大使于 2010—2021 年担任中国驻英国大使 11 年。在中国 5000 多年历史的背景下，他的任期恰逢中国历史及中英关系发生非凡的变革和进步。

自 1949 年中华人民共和国成立以来，中国国家利益得到显著推进，包括经济和金融地位加强、基础设施投资增加、对全球贸易的重要性提升、人民更加富足且吃苦耐劳、教育水平提高、军事力量增强。我们见证了中国在全球市场上的惊人竞争力，以至于它在世界贸易中的份额已经上升到与美国相当。

此外，中国用 40 年奇迹般地使 7 亿多人摆脱了贫困，医疗保险覆盖率几乎达到 100%，人均预期寿命更长，人民生活更幸福。中国境外旅游人数已增至 1 亿左右。正是在此期间，刘晓明担任中国驻英国大使，他以多种方式参与了这些进步的各个方面。正如时任英国首相戴维·卡梅伦所说，这一时期是"黄金时期——中英关系的黄金时代"。

在他担任大使期间，中英之间的商品和服务贸易翻了一番，中国来英投资则增加了 3 倍。2015 年底，习近平主席对英国进行国事访问之前，刘大使在 2015 年 10 月接受英国独立电视台（ITV）采访，他表示，中国的崛起带来的机遇远大于威胁。两国认为这个时代已经超越了浮华、客气话和口号。人们希望并致力于深入发展两国之间的关系。困难总是难免的，但总而言之，在刘大使任职期间，中英两国关系迎来了黄金时期。英国应当感谢刘大使所取得的所有成就，特别是使中英关系基础更加牢固和稳固。

——雅各布·罗斯柴尔德男爵

英国著名银行家

英国科学院荣誉院士

Ambassador Liu Xiaoming served as the Ambassador of China to the United Kingdom for eleven years from 2010 to 2021. Within the context of Chinese history of over 5,000 years, his period of office coincided with one of exceptional change and progress in the history of China and its relationships with the United Kingdom.

Since the founding of the People's Republic of China in 1949 there has been a period of remarkable advance for China's interests including a strengthening of its economic and financial position, its investment in infrastructure, its importance to global trade, the self-sufficiency of its people and a strong work ethic, combined with a high level of education and the strengthening of its military power. We have witnessed China becoming astonishingly competitive in the world market; so much so that its share of world trade has risen to being comparable with the United States.

In addition, China has miraculously elevated some seven hundred million people out of poverty within forty years. Medical care now covers nearly one hundred percent of the population whose life expectancy has become longer and happier. The number of people travelling outside China has risen to about one hundred million. It was during this period that Liu served as Ambassador and he was, in one way or another, involved in all these areas of progress. It was a period which our then Prime Minister, David Cameron, referred to as "a Golden Time—a Golden Era in China/UK relations".

In his years here as Ambassador, trade between China and the UK in goods and services doubled while investment from China tripled. At the time of President Xi Jinping's state visit to the United Kingdom at the end of 2015, the Ambassador said in an interview with ITV in October 2015, that the rise of China presented an opportunity significantly more than a threat. The two countries saw the era as going beyond pomp, kind words and slogans. There was a wish and commitment to develop profoundly the relationship between the two countries. Inevitably there would be difficult moments but, in the round, during the Ambassador's term of office, China and the United Kingdom enjoyed a golden period in their relationship. The United Kingdom owes the Ambassador an immense debt of gratitude for all that he achieved and indeed for putting the relationship between China and the United Kingdom on a much stronger and secure footing.

Baron Jacob Rothschild
British Banker
Honorary Fellow of the British Academy

《尖锐对话》汇集了刘晓明担任中国驻英国大使期间，广泛接受英国主流电视台和电台的采访。他在采访中思维敏捷、幽默风趣，有时还带有火药味，突显了一位成就卓著的外交官的气质。他就当今世界一系列重要问题解释中国的立场，使人们了解中国和西方国家在一些问题上并不总是意见一致。然而，要解决这些困难的问题，坐下来讨论是非常重要的。阅读本书，可以更好地了解中国，了解中国对当今世界问题的立场。

　　　　　　　　　　　　　　　　——保罗·纳斯爵士
　　　　　　　　　　　　　　弗朗西斯·克里克研究所所长
　　　　　　　　　　　　　　英国皇家学会前会长
　　　　　　　　　　　　　　诺贝尔生理学或医学奖获得者

Sharp Dialogue is the second volume of Liu Xiaoming's series "Tell China's Story" based on the speeches and interviews he gave whilst he was China's Ambassador to the UK. This second volume covers a wide range of interviews he gave mainly on mainstream UK TV and radio. Quick, witty, on occasion combative, these interviews show him to be an accomplished diplomat explaining the position of China on a range of topics important for the world today. They give insights into a number of issues over which China and Western Nations do not always agree and the discussions are important if some these difficult problems are to be resolved. Read this book and get better informed about China and its position in today's world.

Sir Paul Nurse
Chief Executive of the Francis Crick Institute
Former President of the Royal Society
Nobel Prize Laureate in Physiology or Medicine

我很高兴就刘晓明大使的系列采访集谈谈感想，尤其是因为阅读采访集把我带回到共同缔造的激动人心的中英关系"黄金时代"的那些日子。记得是在 2015 年秋天，来自英格兰"北部振兴计划"包括商业和其他名流在内的各界领军人物，对中国进行了旋风式正式访问。随后，英国接待了习近平主席激动人心的国事访问。作为曼联的球迷，我直到今天仍无法理解为什么我当时未能阻止习近平主席访问曼城俱乐部。为了给自己的懒惰寻找借口，我总是说刘大使要为此负责。与刘大使会面总是一件令人高兴的事，尤其是回忆起我就全球化中存在的问题对刘大使进行了采访，这一期 BBC 广播访谈节目内容也收录在他的采访集中。对于这次访谈我想谈两点。一个是访谈中刘大使在我和 BBC 的脑海中播下了一颗种子：我本可以沿着"丝绸之路"长途旅行并拍摄一部纪录片，可惜这个绝妙的想法没有实现。另一个更为重要：如果当初决策者们能够听取我和多位接受我访谈的人士关于全球化弱点的总体建议，那么世界是有可能避免当前的一些混乱问题的，包括全球缺乏团结的问题 —— 希望这种问题只是暂时的。

——吉姆·奥尼尔勋爵

英国议会上院议员

"金砖之父"

英国财政部前商务大臣

英国皇家国际事务研究所前主席

It is pleasure to say a few words about this collection of interviews, not least as it brings back sentimental thoughts for me of the brief exciting days of the Golden Era that I was part of. I recall the formal UK visit to China in Autumn 2015 where we took civic leaders from across the Northern Powerhouse along with an array of business and other civic figures on a frantic tour of the country, and of course, so after, the UK hosted President Xi here for his exciting trip. I still , to this day, cannot fathom , how I didn't manage to stop him visiting Manchester City instead of Manchester United—my own sporting obsession—and I will hold Ambassador Liu responsible for that as my lazy excuse. It was always a delight to meet with the Ambassador and I also reflect on that interview I did with him for my BBC documentary on the failings of globalisation that is featured in his collection. Two things spring to mind, firstly, he sowed the seeds in my and the BBC's mind for a possible long travel documentary that I might have done, travelling along the Silk Road, which alas didn't materialise, but would have been wonderful. And secondly, and more seriously, if policymakers would have heeded the general advise from my various interviewees as well as myself about the weaknesses of globalisation, we might have avoided some of the issues and mess the world seems to find itself in today, including the weaker state of global togetherness that seems to- hopefully, only temporarily- exist.

Jim O'Neill, Baron O'Neill of Gatley

The Man Who Coined BRICs

Former Commercial Secretary to the Treasury

Former Chairman of the Royal Institute of International Affairs

我于 2010 年至 2021 年担任中国驻英国大使。使英 11 年使我在中国外交史上至少创造了两项纪录：一是中英关系史上任期最长的驻英使节；二是中华人民共和国成立以来连续在一国驻节时间最长的大使。然而，最让我感到骄傲的是另外三项纪录：驻外一个任期内发表了 700 多场演讲，在主流报刊撰写了 170 多篇文章，接受主流媒体采访 170 多次。

大使是一国的代表，全称是"特命全权大使"，足以显示其使命光荣、责任重大。大使的主要职责是执行国家外交方针政策，维护国家主权、安全和发展利益，促进本国与驻在国的关系。国家之间的关系涉及方方面面，大使的工作也可谓千头万绪。千头万绪抓什么？怎么抓？我们常说，国之交在于民相亲，民相亲在于心相通。使两国民众"心相通"，可以说是大使的重要职责，也是做外交工作的最高境界。因此，我抓住各种机会，利用各种平台介绍中国的内外政策，讲中国的故事，促进两国"民相亲""心相通"。

在国外讲中国故事与国内有很大不同。特别是在西方国家，讲好中国故事更不容易。首先是西方民众对中国的了解非常有限，他们获得中国有关信息的主要渠道是西方媒体，包括电视、电台、报刊、网络、新媒体等。其次是一些民众对中国存在固有的"傲慢与偏见"。再次是西方媒体对中国片面、歪曲的报道和恶意炒作。最后是一些反华势力蓄意抹黑中国的形象。面对这样的舆论环境，是知难而退，还是迎难而上？我没有别的选择，只有挺身而出。有的朋友问我，对于你的每次演讲、撰文、采访，国内是否都有指示？我回答，有，也没有。国内的指示既原则又明确，就是积极主动发声，讲好中国故事。但怎么讲、对谁讲、什么时候讲，则需要使节本人来把握。在讲中国故事、传播中国声音方面，我始终提醒自己要敢于担当、不辱使命，要对得起"特命全权大使"这个称号。

怎样让世界听到中国声音？我通过演讲、撰文、采访三位一体模式，积极主动开展公共外交，形成全方位立体效应。演讲、撰文、采访各有优势和短板。演讲的优势是以我为主，主场效果好，答问环节也可有效控场；短板是受众少，局限于现场听众。撰文的优势是传播范围大，读者群广泛，特别是对精英阶层有较大影响；短板是篇幅受限，而且主动权在报社，能登不能登，登多少字，登什么版面，甚至连文章标题都由报社来定，据称这是西方媒体的"行规"，也是"报社特权"。采访分报刊采访和广播采访。报刊采访的优势和短板与撰文大同小异。广播采访分电视采访和电台采访，细分有直播采访和录播采访，还有各大电视台直播或录播的记者会。电视和电台采访的优势是直观、生动，覆盖面大，时效快；短板是时长有限，采访者或主持人掌握发问权和控场节奏。

三种传播方式不仅优劣势不同，而且难易差别很大。我把演讲、撰文比作"小考"，把记者会比作"中考"，把电视和电台采访特别是现场直播采访比作"大考"。之所以叫"大考"，是因为每次现场直播采访都如同一场"高难度、高强度、高烈度"的博弈。

所谓"高难度"是因为难以掌控。现场直播采访的主动权完全掌握在主持人手里。采访前，对方一般给一个采访议题范围。但谈起来，主持人可以问任何问题，许多问题与事先商议主题毫无关系。如2014

年初英中贸易协会举办中国商业大会，当天英国天空新闻台主持人兰德邀请我做客该台访谈节目《杰夫·兰德直播间》谈谈大会情况。结果，整个访谈没有问一个关于中国商业大会的问题，而是不断纠缠新闻自由和网络监管。在这类采访过程中，主持人还有意提各种刁难甚至挑衅性问题，有时还搞"突然袭击"，当场播放几段编造的视频，让你作答。因而，准备一场现场直播采访是很难的，你不知道对方会问什么问题，挖什么"坑"。

所谓"高强度"，是指直播采访时间短、节奏快、高度紧张。除了个别节目，直播采访时长一般为5~10分钟。这样短的时间内，要谈好几个问题。主持人不停地问，被采访者抓紧答。主持人经常打断对方，以掌控对话。被采访者只能分秒必争地阐述自己的观点。

所谓"高烈度"，是指采访交锋激烈。西方电视节目主持人与国内的有很大不同。他们不仅把直播采访看作是讨论问题，还看作是斗智斗勇的博弈。他们把被采访者当作对手，准备了各种刁钻问题，设计了各种陷阱。他们往往对对手的回答并不感兴趣，而是刻意让对手难堪，以显示他们的智慧和本事，特别是在镜头前，他们更是当仁不让。这就决定了直播采访必然是针锋相对，唇枪舌剑，充满火药味。英国广播公司（BBC）有一档旗舰直播访谈栏目，干脆就叫 *Hard Talk*（可译为《艰难对话》或《尖锐对话》）。由此可见现场直播采访的"高烈度"。

在我接受的170多次主流媒体采访中，53次是电视和电台采访，其中33次是英美媒体采访，现场直播采访29次。对于这29次"三高""大考"我都高度重视、认真准备。每次我都召集专门会议，集思广益。据说，西方公认的"沟通大师"——美国前总统克林顿和英国前首相布莱尔，每次接受直播采访前，都召集助手假设各种问题，包括模拟现场问答。

他们作为谙熟西方媒体运作的西方政治家，又讲母语，尚且如此，我们中国外交官更要为之付出几倍的努力。

为什么要上电视？为什么还要选择现场直播采访？2020 年新冠肺炎疫情发生不久，以美国为首的西方势力编造各种谎言和谣言，对中国进行污名化、妖魔化，企图把病毒源头扣在中国头上。我于当年 4 月接受 BBC《尖锐对话》栏目主持人萨克直播采访，就中国抗疫阐明立场，澄清事实，激浊扬清。据 BBC 称，此次采访在英国国内播放 2 次，向全球 200 多个国家播放 5 次，受众 4 亿多人。这就是我为什么选择现场直播采访，为什么明知山有虎，偏向虎山行。为了让世界上更多的人听到中国声音，再难、再苦、再累也在所不惜，"三高"挡不住，"大考"难不倒。

本书收录我使英期间 32 次接受英美电视和电台采访实录，其中 24 次为现场直播采访。我不敢说每次采访都圆满成功，回过头看，的确有不少可以改进的地方，有的可以说得更好些、更全些、更准些。虽然我的能力和水平有限，但我努力了、尽力了，可谓不辱使命，对得起"中国特命全权大使"的称号。

刘晓明

2022 年立春

目 录
Contents

香港问题
Hong Kong

新冠肺炎疫情
Covid-19

习近平主席对英国国事访问

President Xi Jinping's
State Visit to the UK

2015年10月19—23日，应英国女王伊丽莎白二世邀请，习近平主席对英国进行国事访问。这是中国国家主席10年来首次对英国进行国事访问，也是在中英建立全面战略伙伴关系第二个10年的开局之年，我国新一届领导人对英国的一次重要访问，具有承前启后、继往开来的重大意义。中英双方决定通过此访构建面向21世纪的全球全面战略伙伴关系，共同开启持久、开放、共赢的中英关系"黄金时代"。英国社会各界对习近平主席此访翘首以待，期待访问为中英关系确定新的定位，树立新的目标，制订新的规划。英国媒体从电台到电视台，从报纸到杂志再到新媒体，高度关注、广泛报道此访，在英国掀起一股强劲的"习旋风"。同时，也出现了一些不和谐的声音。少数反华势力鼓吹"中国威胁论"，一些媒体跟风炒作，编造与中国经贸合作给英国带来的"安全风险"，并对中国的人权状况说三道四。

针对这一形势，我积极主动开展公共外交，广泛做各界工作，增信释疑，扩大共识，增进正能量，抑制负能量。除广泛接触英国王室、政府、议会、工商、智库、高校等各界人士外，我还重点做英国媒体工作。我在使馆举行中外记者会，在英国主流大报和习近平主席将访问的城市地方报纸上发表文章，为西方著名智库英国皇家国际事务研究所刊物撰文，推动在英国主流社会有较大影响的《名流》《外交家》等刊物出版专刊，介绍习近平主席访问的重要意义。我还对英国广播电视媒体实现了全覆盖，与英国广播公司（BBC）新闻总监、主持人、编辑、记者等座谈，4天接受英国各大电视台5场采访，其中1天2场，都是现场直播。采访中，我介绍了习近平主席访问的目的和意义，阐述中方在中英关系、人权、网络安全等问题上的原则立场，澄清事实，批驳谬论。这一系列公共外交活动为习近平主席国事访问营造了有利的舆论环境。

接受英国电视四台《电视四台新闻》栏目主持人斯诺现场直播采访

作者手记

2015年10月14日，在习近平主席对英国国事访问前夕，我接受英国电视四台现场直播采访。采访在该台《电视四台新闻》（*Channel 4 News*）栏目演播室进行，由该栏目主持人乔·斯诺（Jon Snow）主持。

电视四台是英国第三大公共服务电视机构。《电视四台新闻》是该台旗舰新闻节目，以国际报道和深度访谈著称，观众超过100万。斯诺是英国著名媒体人，在电视四台担任主持人近30年。

斯诺一上来便单刀直入，问习近平主席远道而来，希望从英国得到什么，并用典型的英式幽默自嘲英国为中等欧洲国家。他接着就中国的经济前景、政治制度、人权、司法，英国工党领袖对华态度等，提出一连串问题。我向他介绍了习近平主席对英国国事访问的目的和重要意义，回答他的有关提问，重点引导他正确看待中国，特别是正确认识中国共产党。

采访实录如下：

斯诺： 习近平主席远道而来，专程访问英国这样一个中等欧洲国家，希望从英国得到什么？

刘晓明： 习主席访英是为了促进中英两国关系。你把英国称为"中等国家"，我们并不这样看。我们认为英国仍是一个拥有全球影响力的国家，是世界经济增长的动力源之一。中英之间可以合作的地方很多，英国是中国在欧盟内第二大贸易伙伴，中国是英国在欧盟外第二大贸易伙伴，英国是中国在欧洲最大投资目的国，过去3年间中国在英投资迅速增长。

斯诺： 但中国经济形势不容乐观，进口下降了20%，股市灾难性下跌。习主席是否能够说这些情况现在都已经过去了？

刘晓明： 当你观察中国经济时，应当关注全局，应从长远的角度看待中国经济。从根本上说，中国经济仍然基本运行良好。今年上半年，增长速度达到7%，中国经济增长速度仍然在世界上领先。

斯诺： 难道你不认为这些情况表明，共产党国家和自由市场经济这两种理念在一定程度上存在矛盾吗？两者之间能成功结合吗？

刘晓明： 你把中国称为"共产党国家"是不对的，中国的国名是中华人民共和国，是由中国共产党所领导的，正如英国的执政党是保守党一样。

斯诺： 但在中国没有人能选举一个非共产党的政党来管理中国。

刘晓明： 中国共产党提供了强有力的领导，得到人民的拥护，人民支持共产党带领中国由贫穷走向繁荣。这样好的领导，为什么要更换？你只需看看中国过去30年的发展。中国从一个较为贫困的国家一跃成为世界第二大经济体，这是一个奇迹。

斯诺： 英国是不是在中国人权问题上说得太多了？你认为英国应该停止讨论中国的人权问题吗？

刘晓明： 我认为人权问题是可以探讨的。没有哪个国家是完美的。但你们刚才播放的视频给我留下一种印象，就是一说到中国的人权问题，你们往往只关注负面。要讨论人权问题，就必须有全面的观察，弄清楚人权到底是什么。我认为，人们有追求更好的生活、更好的教育、更好的工作机会的权利。我想所有人都会同意，中国人民的生活条件比以往更好，人均寿命比以往更长，人们享受幸福生活。

斯诺： 但是令人担忧的是死刑和拘留问题，有很多人被拘留。

刘晓明： 你说有"很多人"，你们刚才放的短片说有上百人被拘，但要知道中国有13亿多人口……

斯诺： 也许不止上百人。

刘晓明： 我不知道英国有多少囚犯……

斯诺： 但英国的囚犯都是经过法律审判的。

刘晓明： 在中国，也是要通过正常法律程序进行审判的。中国是一个法治国家，任何人违法都必须承担法律责任，所有法治国家都应该尊重法律。我们也许在国家治理方法上有所不同，但在厉行法治方面我想我们看法应是一致的。

斯诺： 你看过皇家美术学院举办的艾未未艺术展吗？

刘晓明： 说实话，我对他的作品不感兴趣。英国有这么多博物馆，我都挤不出时间去欣赏……

斯诺： 但他是国际上最知名的中国艺术家。

刘晓明： 我不这么认为。我认为他之所以在西方出名是因为他对中国政府的政策持批评态度……

斯诺： 他到底有什么问题？中国政府跟他有什么过节？

刘晓明： 他曾因涉嫌经济犯罪被警方依法调查，被限制出境。但现在有关限制已经取消，他可以出国搞展览，这恰恰说明了中国很开放。

斯诺： 最后一个问题，新任工党领袖科尔宾最近抨击中国的自由市场理念，他特别提到了最近天津发生的火灾，造成许多消防员和工人死亡，他特别批评中国搞自由市场，导致了这场灾难。你对这位左翼领导人是否感到失望？

刘晓明： 事实上，我今天下午刚和他见过面……

斯诺： 噢，这很有意思。

刘晓明： ……我们商讨了他即将和习主席举行的会见。我们谈了很多，谈到了工党对中英关系所做的贡献，也讨论了中国共产党与英国工党的党际交流，谈得很融洽。

斯诺： 这么说关系很好？

刘晓明： 是的，关系很好。至于你刚才提到的事故，这是一场很不幸的悲剧，中国政府正在调查此事，相关的责任人将受到惩罚，决不姑息。

斯诺： 非常感谢刘大使接受采访。

刘晓明： 不客气。

A Live Interview with Jon Snow on *Channel 4 News*

On 14th October 2015, I was invited to a live interview with *Channel 4 News* hosted by Jon Snow. I stressed the significance of the forthcoming state visit of President Xi Jinping, and answered questions about China-UK bilateral relations, bilateral economic cooperation and China's economy. The full text is as follows:

Snow: I'm joined now by China's Ambassador to Britain, Liu Xiaoming. He is with us right now. President Xi Jinping is coming all the way to the middle ranking European nation and nowhere else, and then going home. What's he hoping to get from Britain, Ambassador?

Liu Xiaoming: He will be here for promoting relations between China and the UK. You regard UK as a middle ranking country. We do not think so. We still believe the UK is a country with global influence. It's one of the powerhouses, and China and the UK have a lot to cooperate about. The UK now is China's second largest trading partner within the EU, China is the UK's second largest trading partner outside Europe, and UK is the largest recipient of Chinese investment. So in the past three years, China's investment is booming here in the UK.

Snow: But the backdrop in China is not an easy one: a 20% reduction in imports and of course this catastrophic fall in the stock market. Will the President be able to say that's all behind us now?

Liu Xiaoming: When you look at China's economy, you have to focus on the big picture. You have to see China's economy in the long-term view. I think fundamentally and basically China's economy is still sound and good. For the first half of this year, the growth rate of the Chinese economy is 7%. China is still a leading country in the world, in terms of the growth of its economy.

Snow: But don't you think these events have told us about a degree of tension between the idea of a Communist state and a free market economy. Can you really have that marriage?

Liu Xiaoming: I don't think your definition of China as a Communist state is a right one. China has its official name, People's Republic of China, and it's led by the Communist Party of China. Just like here in this country. Your ruling party is Conservative Party, does this…

Snow: But nobody could elect a non-Communist Party to run China.

Liu Xiaoming: But the Communist Party provides a strong leadership and enjoys the people's support. The people support the Communist Party as their leader to lead China from poverty to prosperity. So why should we rock the boat? And you just look at the past 30 years, China, turning from a relatively poor country to the second largest economy. It's a miracle.

Snow: So do you think Britain has talked too much about the human rights in China? Do you think they have stopped talking about human rights in China?

Liu Xiaoming: I think we can talk about human rights. No country is perfect. But I think in your earlier video clips you gave the impression that once you talk about human rights in China, you always talk about the negative side of China. When you talk about human rights, you have to have a comprehensive view. What are the human rights? I think people have a right to a better life, a better education, a better job. I think everyone would agree that Chinese people live better, live longer. They enjoy their lives.

Snow: But the things which exercise people are executions and detentions. And there are detentions of very large numbers of people.

Liu Xiaoming: Very large numbers of people? Your video clips talk about 100 people.

You have to remember China's population is more than 1.3 billion.

Snow: It might be rather more than 100 people.

Liu Xiaoming: I don't know how many prisoners here in the UK…

Snow: But they've all been tried.

Liu Xiaoming: They've all been tried through normal legal process. China is a country ruled by law. For those people who violate the law they have to be held accountable. So all countries ruled by law have to respect the law. We might be different with regard to how countries are run, but I think we agree that country should be governed by the rule of law.

Snow: Have you been to the Royal Academy to see Ai Weiwei's art exhibition?

Liu Xiaoming: To be frank with you, he is not my taste. There are so many beautiful museums here in the UK. But I've been so busy. I have to find time to …

Snow: But he is the most famous Chinese artist in the world.

Liu Xiaoming: I don't think so.

Snow: And his show is …

Liu Xiaoming: I think he is famous here because he is critical of Chinese Government's policy…

Snow: Why do you bother with him? Why is he a problem? Why does the Chinese state have a problem with him?

Liu Xiaoming: He was under investigation because of fraudulent accounting. He had been denied an exit to leave China. But now he can leave and put up his exhibition. That shows how open China is.

Snow: Let me ask you a final question. The new Labour leader, Jeremy Corbyn, has attacked China's free market philosophy, particularly regarding what happened to the victims of the fire in which a lot of firemen died and a lot of workers died. He specifically blamed China's free market for that disaster. Are you disappointed in this new apparently left-wing leader of the Party?

Liu Xiaoming: In fact, I just had a meeting with him this afternoon ...

Snow: Oh, that's very interesting.

Liu Xiaoming: ... to prepare for the meeting that he is going to have with the President. We talked quite a lot. We talked about the contributions made by the Labour Party to the development of China-UK relations. And we talked about the party-to-party exchanges, the Labour Party and the Communist Party.

Snow: So the relation is good?

Liu Xiaoming: The relation is good. The incident you are talking about is a bad incident. It's a tragedy. And the Chinese Government is investigating this. Those who are responsible will be held accountable and will be punished. There is no mercy about that.

Snow: Thank you very, very much.

Liu Xiaoming: It's my pleasure.

Channel 4 News is a flagship news programme of Channel 4, the third largest public television broadcaster in Britain. It is known for its international coverage and in-depth interviews, and has an audience of more than one million. Jon Snow is a senior presenter of Channel 4, having served as the broadcaster for nearly 30 years.

接受英国独立电视台《十点新闻》栏目
国际主编奥马尔采访

作者手记

2015年10月15日，我接受英国独立电视台（ITV）《十点新闻》（*News at Ten*）栏目国际主编拉吉·奥马尔（Rageh Omaar）采访。采访中我着重介绍了习近平主席对英国国事访问的重大意义和中英关系进展情况，并回答了有关中英经贸合作、全球化、人权、野生动物保护等问题。奥马尔对中英关系的"黄金时代"特别感兴趣，我向他详细介绍了"黄金时代"的由来。

英国独立电视台设立于1955年，是英国历史最悠久、规模最大的商业电视台，拥有多个频道，观众达400万。《十点新闻》是该台强档新闻节目。

10月19日，在习主席抵达伦敦当天，独立电视台在黄金时段播放对我采访的主要内容，并在该台网站播放采访实录视频。

采访实录如下：

奥马尔： 为什么说中英关系进入了"黄金时期"，你的这一认识和信心从何而来？

刘晓明： 我的信心来自于同英国各界的接触，来自于英国首相和财政大臣对中国的访问。英国首相和财政大臣都表示，英国希望成为中国在西方最好的伙伴，希望成为中国在西方最坚定的支持者。事实上，"黄金时代"的表述最初来自于卡梅伦首相本人。考虑到今年将迎来中英关系一系列重要事件，我在年初出席英国议会庆祝中国春节活动时，发表了今年第一场公开演讲，我用了"大年"一词来形容2015年。在这一年，习主席将对英进行国事访问。威廉王子于3月份访华，此访是继女王1986年访华后，英国王室成员近30年对中国进行的一次重要访问。卡梅伦首相在春节贺词中使用了"黄金年"的表述，他将今年视为双边关系的"黄金年"。在唐宁街举行的春节招待会上，我见到了卡梅伦首相。我对他说，你的"黄金年"比我的"大年"好，我们于是就今年是中英关系"黄金年"的表述达成共识。卡梅伦首相在今年5月大选后提议，中英双方为打造中英关系的"黄金时代"共同努力。这一说法得到中国领导人的认同。所以我们不仅在讲"黄金年"，也在讲中英关系的"黄金时代"。

奥马尔： 但是不久之前你还公开讲，英国在发展对华关系方面落后于其他欧洲国家。你的看法为什么出现这么大的变化？

刘晓明： 事实上，当我说英国在对华关系方面落后于其他欧洲国家时，主要指的是政治领域，媒体没有完整报道我说的话。当时，有英国媒体问我如何看待中英关系及中法、中德关系。我表示，每一对双边关系都各有优势。我列举了中英合作在至少五六个领域的优势，同时表示双方政治互信和政治关系还有待加强。政治关系是双边关系的基础。英国媒体没有报道我讲话的积极面，而只关注消极面。

奥马尔： 尽管如此，你还是认为英国在发展对华政治关系方面落后了，现在你已发生了巨大转变。

刘晓明： 那是一年多以前的事了。你知道，在那以后双方高层交往频繁。英国首相实现访华，财政大臣两度访华。英国大选刚刚结束，中国外交部部长旋即到访，在第一时间同英国新政府建立联系。今年6月，两位中国领导人访问英国。中英关系有三大支柱或机制作为支撑：中国国务委员和英国外交大臣共同主持的中英战略对话；中国副总理和英国财政大臣共同主持的中英经济财金对话；中国副总理和英国卫生大臣共同主持的高级别人文交流机制会议。今年9月，三个机制均举行了新一轮对话，双方高层交往非常频繁。这些都为习主席的国事访问做好了铺垫。可以说，中英政治关系十分有力，政治互信不断增强。

奥马尔： 国事访问期间，人权问题，中国的人权问题将被提出来。据我所知，工党领袖科尔宾表示，他将向中方提出人权问题。针对英国对中国人权记录的批评，中国如何回应？

刘晓明： 正如我在中国大使馆举行的习主席访英中外记者会上所说，中国对讨论人权问题持开放态度。我们不回避讨论人权问题。我们需要全面看待人权问题。一些西方人、政客和媒体只盯着一些个案，却忽视中国人权进步。30年来，中国发生了翻天覆地的变化，中国在人权领域取得了巨大进步，任何不抱偏见的人对此都会认同。什么是人权？当我们谈论人权问题时，我们谈论的是人们拥有更好的生活、教育、就业机会，更多的言论、结社和旅行自由。有一些人谈起人权却只知道纠缠个案，认为这就是人权问题的核心。为什么不看一看中国用短短30年时间使7亿人摆脱贫困？这是一个奇迹，在世界上前所未有。中国医疗保险现在覆盖了几乎全部人口，每年出境的中国游客数量达到1亿，中国人民人均寿命不断延长，生活更加幸福。我认为这才是基本人权。

奥马尔： 但总会有人提出与"异见分子"有关的个案。既要提出个案，又想与中国保持良好的经贸合作，这种关系有没有可能？

刘晓明： 双方要求同存异。我认为，国际关系准则需要各国共同遵守，其中一条基本准则就是不干涉别国内政。如果我认为你的制度不完美，对一些个案不满意，于是将整个双边关系绑架，试问这符合中英两国的利益吗？我们有就人权问题开展对话的渠道。我说过，没有任何国家是十全十美的。双方都有各自的关切。英国和美国人权也谈不上完美，关于中方对英国和美国人权状况的关切，我可以给你拉一个单子。但我认为高层交往的主要目的、驻英国使馆和我作为大使的主要职责并非单单关注人权领域，人权只是双边关系中的一个领域。中英在开展合作方面拥有广泛利益。我认为，英国民众更关心自己的就业、生活和教育。中国民众也是一样。中英两国政府需要努力寻求共识，共同增进两国人民的福祉。我们可以就人权问题展开辩论，但不能一叶障目。即使我们把所有的时间用来辩论，恐怕也不会争出胜负。

奥马尔： 我想问一下中英关系"黄金时代"非常重要的一部分——双方不断发展的经贸关系。中国参与欣克利角核电站项目协议的签署意义重大。中国企业是否希望更深入参与英国核电项目？

刘晓明： 我认为，中国企业对所有能够产生良好效益、有利于公司发展的项目都感兴趣。相信英国企业在中国也是一样。

奥马尔： 就是说，中国企业对各个领域都感兴趣，包括核能、房地产等？

刘晓明： 当然。还有基础设施、酒店。

奥马尔： 中国企业拥有希思罗机场10%股份。

刘晓明： 拥有希思罗机场10%股份、泰晤士水务8%股份，还有维他麦、曼彻斯特空港城等，中国企业在英国有一系列投资。

奥马尔： 会有大型商业代表团随访吗？

刘晓明： 商业代表团会单独抵达英国，不作为习主席代表团的一部分。国事访问和其他访问十分不同。各界都希望利用访问加深各自领域的合作，希望习主席和英国首相见证合作协议的签署。这对企业来说是一种殊荣。

奥马尔： 你将此访称为"超级国事访问"，似乎中英关系要重新开启，或说是重振中英关系。这是不是说得过头了？

刘晓明： 我确实说过这将是一次"超级国事访问"，意思是双方要在现有基础上将双边关系提升到新的高度，给双边关系一个新定位。这也是为什么我认为访问是承前启后、继往开来的新里程碑。过去几年双方没有谈到"黄金时代"，而这次，双方首次达成开启中英关系"黄金时代"的共识。

奥马尔： 中国对国事访问的报道多不多？中国人怎么看这次访问？

刘晓明： 中国人民对访问有很高期待。中英两国人民对彼此抱有好感。几个月前我看到一项调查，显示在对中国的好感度上，英国要高于许多其他欧洲国家。我想这在中国也一样。当英国政府决定率先加入亚洲基础设施投资银行时，我刚好在国内。英国此举得到广泛好评和欢迎。中国人民认为英国领导人具有远见，他们看到了英国视中国崛起为机遇，而非威胁。中英两国把彼此视为真诚伙伴，看到了双方合作的机遇。这不仅是隆重的场面，也不是空谈的口号，而是实实在在的行动。

奥马尔： 近期英国国内关注的焦点之一是雷德卡钢铁厂因来自中国的廉价钢铁竞争而被迫关闭的问题。英国曾是一个钢铁制造大国。在英国，钢铁产区的民众是否有理由对来自中国的竞争表示担心呢？

刘晓明： 我们生活在全球化的时代，每个国家都需要不断推进经济转型。在中国拥有优势的一些领域，其他国家需要调整转型，反之也是一样。你知道，中国曾在服装、鞋和玩具制造方面拥有强大的优势，一度生产了全世界80%～90%的玩具。但现在一些东南亚国家在这些领域的优势逐渐凸显，低廉的劳动力成本使它们具有更强的竞争力。这时就需要我们做出调整。如果还是一味固守缺乏竞争力的产业，就会丧失发展的机会。这就是中国积极推进经济转型的原因。一些人担心中国经济增速放缓，实际上这种放缓是健康的调整过程。即使增速由之前的两位数降至8%或7%，中国经济增长速度仍居世界前列。中国经济正在转型，英国经济为什么就不能转型呢？

奥马尔： 威廉王子录制的关于野生动物非法贸易的电视短片即将在中国播出。中英是否会在该问题上合作？

刘晓明： 没错。中国是国际打击濒临灭绝物种非法贸易和保护野生动物的坚定支持者。中国在这一问题上的态度积极主动。我曾陪同威廉王子访华，习主席会见他时我也在座。双方谈到中英如何开展合作，保护野生动物，打击非法贸易。习主席介绍了中国做出的努力，包括销毁5吨象牙。这显示出中国政府的决心。中国还是许多动物保护国际会议的积极参与者。威廉王子和查尔斯王储共同倡议召开了伦敦打击非法野生动物贸易峰会，中国派出大型代表团参会。中国还举办了保护野生动物相关论坛。相信中英在该领域合作潜力巨大。

奥马尔： 谢谢大使先生接受采访！

刘晓明： 不客气。

An Interview with Rageh Omaar
on ITV *News at Ten*

On 15th October 2015, I gave an interview to International Affairs Editor of ITV News Rageh Omaar on *News at Ten* programme. The full interview is as follows:

Omaar: What gives you the confidence and the feeling that this is indeed a golden period of China-UK relations?

Liu Xiaoming: My confidence comes from my contact with the British people from all walks of life, from top down. For example, from the Prime Minister's visit to China, the Chancellor's visit to China. They both said Britain wants to be the best partner for China in the West. Britain wants to be the strongest supporter for China in the West. In fact, the expression "Golden Era", the word "golden", was first used by Prime Minister David Cameron. At the beginning of this year, I expected a series of important events in China-UK relations. In my very first public speech in the Parliament for celebrating the Chinese New Year, I said that 2015 will be a "big year" in China-UK relations. We were expecting the visit by President and the visit by Prince William to China. This will be the most important royal visit to China in 30 years since Her Majesty's visit to China in 1986. Then when we celebrated the Chinese New Year, Prime Minister Cameron in his new year message used the word "golden year". He sees this year as a golden year. When I met with him in No.10 for the Chinese New Year Reception, I told him, Prime Minister, I think your "golden year" is better than my "big year", so we reached the consensus that this year is a "Golden Year". After the election, Prime Minister Cameron proposed that we should work together for the "Golden Time" for China-UK relations. And that idea was endorsed by Chinese leaders. So now we're not only talking about a "Golden Year", we are talking about a "Golden Time"and a "Golden Era" for China-UK relations.

Omaar: But it was only a short time ago that you were publicly saying that Britain was lagging behind other European countries in their relations with China. Has it really changed so much?

Liu Xiaoming: In fact, when I said the UK lagged behind the other European countries, I was talking about the political relations. I think my comment was not fully reported. The question put to me was about how I see China's relations with the UK, and China's relations with France and Germany. I said, each bilateral relationship has its strengths. I listed five to ten areas where China-UK relations are strong. But I said, we are still weak when it comes to political trust and political relations. Political relations are really the foundation of the overall relationship. The media however were interested in the negative side rather than positive side of my comments.

Omaar: But the positive side comes into this—even though you felt that a short time ago Britain was lagging behind in its political relations with China—that seems to have changed dramatically?

Liu Xiaoming: That was more than one year ago. Within this year there were a series of high-level contacts. The Prime Minister went to China. The Chancellor went to China twice. Immediately after the British election, the Chinese Foreign Minister was here to set up early contact with the new government. Then in June, two senior Chinese leaders came here. Between China and the UK there are three pillars or mechanisms, what we call, to support this relationship: the Strategic Dialogue co-chaired by a State Councilor of China and the UK Foreign Secretary, the Economic and Financial Dialogue co-chaired by a Chinese Vice Premier and the British Chancellor and the High-level People-to-People Dialogue co-chaired by a Chinese Vice Premier and the UK Secretary of State for Health. All these three mechanisms had a meeting in September. This was a very intense exchanges of visits. All these lead up to this state visit of President Xi. So political relations between China and the UK are very strong and political mutual trust has very much been strengthened.

Omaar: The issue of human rights, China's human rights will be raised. I understand that the leader of the Labour Party Jeremy Corbyn has said that he is going to raise it. How does China react to criticism of its human rights record?

Liu Xiaoming: I think we are open to discussions about human rights as I said in the recent press conference. We don't shy away from discussing human rights. As I said, the important thing is to have the big picture. When talking about human rights, you have to approach this issue from a comprehensive perspective. Some westerners, politicians and media people, they only focus on some individual cases, but missed the big picture of the progress of China's human rights. In the past 30 years, there are enormous changes in China. I think any people who holds no bias would agree about the great advancement on China's human rights. What are human rights? When you talk about human rights, you talk about people's right for better living, better education, better job, freedom of speech, freedom of assembly and freedom of travelling around. When some people talk about human rights, they try to dig out some individual cases which they think are a focus on, or concerns about human rights. What would you say about China elevating 700 million people out of poverty just within 30 years of time? It's a miracle. No country has done that. The medical care in China covers almost 100% of the people. Each year now, the number of Chinese people travelling outside China is about 100 million. The Chinese people are living longer and happier. They are enjoying their lives. I think that's a basic right of any human.

Omaar: But there will always be these cases of dissidents that are raised. Is it possible for China to have good relations with a country economically and otherwise, whilst at the same time these individual cases are raised? Can you have that relationship?

Liu Xiaoming: We can only agree to disagree. I think there are international norms countries should follow. The basic norm is non-interference in each other's internal affairs. If I see your system as not perfect, if I see you have cases I'm not happy about, then I hold the whole relationship hostage. Will that be in the interest of the UK or China? We have a channel to discuss our differences over human rights. As I said, no country is perfect. You have your concerns and we also have our concerns. I can give you a list of concerns of cases where we don't think human rights are perfect in the UK and US. But I think the whole purpose of a high-level visit and the main mission of the Embassy and Ambassador here is not to focus on human rights only. Human rights are one of the areas in relations between China and the UK. We have broad interests for collaboration. I think people in the UK care more about their jobs, about a better life, about their education. That's the same for the people in China. The government leaders have to find common ground how we can work together for common good. We can debate but we should not miss the big picture. If we spend all our time debating, I don't think you will have a winner from this.

Omaar: Can I talk about the growing economic relationship, which is an important part of this golden era of UK-China relations. The agreement for China to be involved in the Hinkley nuclear power project was a significant moment. Is that a field where Chinese companies would want to be involved more in the UK?

Liu Xiaoming: I think Chinese companies are interested in all projects where they think they can get good returns and help promote their businesses. In China, your companies have the same aim.

Omaar: So they are looking at all different areas, nuclear power, housing?

Liu Xiaoming: Yes, of course. Infrastructure, Hotels.

Omaar: And Heathrow Airport, 10%, Chinese ownership?

Liu Xiaoming: Heathrow Airport, 10%, Thames Water, 8%, Weetabix, the City airport in Manchester, and ...

Omaar: And there'll be a big business delegation coming with the President?

Liu Xiaoming: They will be here separately. They are not part of the entourage. When you have a state visit, which is quite different from other visits, it is really a big event that all sectors from both sides focus on, they want to use this visit to promote collaboration across the board. They want the President and the Prime Minister to witness the signing ceremony. It's a kind of pride and honour for their businesses.

Omaar: When you talk about it, describing it as a super state visit, it's almost like a restart of the relations between China and the UK. Would it be too much to say that? Not a restart, but sort of re-energisation.

Liu Xiaoming: Yes, that's exactly the word I used, to re-position, how we move from here to a higher-level. That's why I call it a "new milestone". It's a landmark linking the past and the future. So this is an important visit. We haven't talked about "Golden Time" or "Golden Era" in previous years. This is really the first time both sides have this consensus that we work towards the "Golden Era" for China-UK relations.

Omaar: Is it being reported widely in China, the state visit? How is it being seen there?

Liu Xiaoming: The Chinese people have high expectations for this visit. The Chinese people like the British people, just as the British people like Chinese people. I read a poll several months ago, that in the West, in Europe, the percentage of liking for China among Britain people is higher than many other European countries. I think the same can be said in China. When the British government decided to take the lead to join the AIIB, I was in China. It was well received and widely welcomed. They see that the British leadership has the vision. They see that Britain sees the rise of China as an opportunity, not a threat. The two countries see each other as partners earnestly. They really see opportunities for cooperation, not just for pomp, words or slogans. We really mean business.

Omaar: One of the issues that has been high on the agenda in the UK recently is that Britain used to be a very big steel-producing country. The Redcar steel mill has closed down because of the availability of cheap steel from China. Should communities in steel-making areas be worried about China?

Liu Xiaoming: When we are in the age of globalisation, every country has to make adjustment. In some areas where China is strong, others need to make adjustment, vice versa. China used to be very strong in processing of clothes, shoes and toys. I think China provides 80% ~ 90% of the toys in the world. No more that is the case now. Some Southeast Asian countries are now very strong in these areas. Low cost of labour has made them more competitive. So you have to make adjustment. If you continue staying with your old and traditional business, you are losing money and opportunities. That's why China makes its own adjustment. That's why some people are concerned about the slowdown of the Chinese economy. In fact, it's a healthy slowdown. Even with the slowdown from double-digit to 8% or 7%, China is still the leader in terms of growth. China is making adjustment. Why not Britain?

Omaar: Prince William is making a television speech shown in China, talking about the illegal trade in wildlife. Is China cooperating with that?

Liu Xiaoming: Very much so. China is strongly supportive of the international efforts to fight against illegal trade in endangered species and to protect wildlife. In fact, China has taken its own initiative in this area. When Prince William was in China, I traveled with him. I also sat in a meeting he had with the President. They talked about how China and the UK can cooperate in protecting wildlife and fighting against illegal trade. President Xi told him about the efforts China has made, including destroying five tons of tusks, which shows the determination of the Chinese government. China has been an active participant in many international conferences. When Prince William and the Prince of Wales sponsored an international summit here for the protection of wildlife, China sent a large delegation to attend this conference. China is also hosting its own forums for the protection of wildlife. I believe there is a great potential of cooperation between China and the UK in this area.

Omaar: Thank you very much, Ambassador!

Liu Xiaoming: My pleasure.

ITV is the oldest commercial network in the UK. *News at Ten* is ITV's flagship news programme and one of the most watched evening news programmes in the UK with an audience of 4 million.

接受英国BBC《新闻之夜》栏目主持人戴维斯现场直播采访

作者手记

2015年10月16日，我在英国BBC《新闻之夜》(*Newsnight*) 栏目演播室接受该栏目主持人埃文·戴维斯 (Evan Davis) 现场直播采访，介绍习近平主席对英国国事访问有关情况。

《新闻之夜》是英国BBC电视二台旗舰时政访谈栏目，以深度分析和激烈辩论著称，在英国政界和知识界影响较大，全球受众广泛，英国及世界政要、商界领袖、社会名流、知识精英经常接受该栏目采访。

戴维斯是经济学家，在BBC多个栏目担任主持人，以提问犀利、刁钻、咄咄逼人闻名。我们围绕中英经贸和投资合作、中国"机遇论"和"威胁论"、网络安全、人权、民主等问题展开了激烈讨论。

采访实录如下：

戴维斯： 我们今天邀请到中国驻英国大使刘晓明先生。大使先生，晚上好。感谢你来到我们的演播室。

刘晓明： 感谢邀请。

戴维斯： 如果中英位置互换一下，你认为中国会允许英国的承包商在中国建设核电站吗？

刘晓明： 我想问一个问题，你们有资金，你们有技术在中国建核电站吗？

戴维斯： 假如有，你认为我们可以得到允许吗？

刘晓明： 假如有？我不太确定。我认为，英国希望中国来英投资建设核电站，是因为英国需要中国的资金和技术，中国拥有先进的核电技术，中国的核电站数量比许多国家都要多。

戴维斯： 所以中国建造了许多核电站，而英国可以从中受益。但我认为中国不会允许英国投资中国的核电站。我从中国的政府网站上找到一份限制或禁止外商投资的产业目录，比英国限制得更为严格。目录6，包括放射性矿产品勘探开采；目录9，放射性矿产品冶炼加工和包装，核燃料生产等。中国禁止外国投资其核电行业，你是不是认为我们允许中国投资英国核电站的做法很愚蠢？

刘晓明： 你们一点也不愚蠢。事实上，你们很聪明，懂得用中国的资金来建造你们的核电站，让英国人民获益。可以的话，我们也想这么做。

戴维斯： 好吧。这是双赢的局面。

刘晓明： 我同意你的说法，双赢。

戴维斯： 很多其他行业是英国的强项，但中国却禁止外商投资。比如航空交管。英国一家实力很强的空管公司就不能进入中国。还有邮政、拍卖、古董店、高尔夫球场建设等等。为什么中国禁止外商投资高尔夫球场？

刘晓明： 事实上，有一些外商在中国投资高尔夫球场。你最近一次去中国是什么时候？

戴维斯： 这份禁止外商投资产业目录上是这么规定的，这份规定是不是过时了？

刘晓明： 事实上，中国企业和外国企业有很多合作，中国有不少合资企业……

戴维斯： 为什么是合资形式？为什么外商进入中国不能……

刘晓明： 他们可以进入中国，建立合资企业。这样，中国的合资伙伴就可以帮助他们的外国伙伴了解中国市场。你要知道，中国和英国处于不同发展阶段。正如你们刚才的短片所说，英国在很多方面都比中国先进。中国还是一个发展中国家，我们必须一步一步来。我们要借鉴英国的经验，避免英国曾经犯过的错误。因此我们在一些领域要谨慎小心。

戴维斯： 这是双赢的事情，我们欢迎中国来投资，允许中资进入各个领域。可是有时候看起来不太对等。

刘晓明： 我不这么认为。如果不对等的话，英国怎么能成为欧盟内仅次于德国的第二大对华投资国？而且，英国对华投资还在不断增长。所以我认为这是双赢的。

戴维斯： 再问一个问题。英国有很多安全关切，今天《泰晤士报》引述了安全部门对核电站合作的关切。有人担心中国在核电站计算机系统中植入"后门"，这样一旦英中两国发生外交争端，中国可以绕过英国对核电站进行管控。在核电站的安全清洁方面以及核电站的管控问题上，中国如何让英国人放心？

刘晓明： 中国将严格遵循国际标准。你们的情报部门不会笨到不知道这些事情。中国到英国来是为了双赢的合作，我们不是为了控制英国的核电站。控制英国的核电站对中国有什么好处呢？如果双方要成为伙伴，相互之间应有一个基本的信任。如果任由这种负面言论发展，中国企业可能就不敢来英国投资了。如果这样，那么就与财政大臣奥斯本所说的"英国是对中国投资最开放的西方国家"背道而驰了。

戴维斯： "基本的信任"，但这种基本的信任存在吗？据说在上海，有一座中国人民解放军61398部队的大楼，发出大量的网络攻击，这是瞎说吗？

刘晓明： 这不过是谣传、炒作。首先我要告诉你，中国政府坚决反对这种行为。不久前，习近平主席对美国进行国事访问的时候，中美两国就共同打击网络犯罪达成共识。中国的任何政府部门都不会参与网络间谍活动，中国政府也不会支持任何这样的行为。这是中国政府的承诺。

戴维斯： 我们不会相信这一点，这是一种承诺吗？

刘晓明： 如果你们都不相信我们，又怎么能共同建设伙伴关系？

戴维斯： 但一份泄露出来题为《军事战略科学》的手册中承认，中国有网络攻击部队。这个网络攻击部队是怎么回事？

刘晓明： 我不相信有这样的事情。我不认为中国有网络攻击部队。中国是开放合作的国家。事实上，中国本身就是网络攻击的受害者。

戴维斯： 是的。

刘晓明： 孔子有一句名言。很抱歉，我要把你带回到2000多年前。孔子曰："己所不欲，勿施于人。"这就是中国人的哲学，中国人信奉这一哲学。我们不会去攻击任何人，因为我们自己是黑客攻击的受害者。

戴维斯： 简要问一个关于人权的问题。假如下周英国大张旗鼓地谈论人权问题，比如进行抗议，假如反对党领袖或首相大谈人权问题以及英国的人权观，英国会在对华经贸和投资合作方面付出代价吗？

刘晓明： 首先，我想问你两个问题：第一，你认为英国的人权状况完美吗？第二，你认为英国的模式在全世界看来是完美的吗？我认为每个国家在如何改善人权、如何保护人权的问题上都有自己不同的国情。你同意我的看法吗？

戴维斯： 我同意。

刘晓明： 你怎么定义人权？

戴维斯： 我不是在批评中国的人权。我的问题不是关于中国的人权状况。我的问题是，如果英国批评中国的人权状况，当然中国也可以批评英国的人权，我们将为此付出代价吗？

刘晓明： 难道这是习主席对英国进行国事访问的目的吗？大家相互批评对方的人权状况？

戴维斯： 不是，当然不是！但如果英方提出人权问题，英国是否会为此付出代价而失去中国投资？我想，如果习主席访问英国的时候批评英国的人权……

刘晓明： 这不是中国人做事的方式。

戴维斯： 我知道习主席不会这样做。

刘晓明： 我们尊重他国国情。中国宪法保障人权，而且人权说到底是一国的内政问题。我希望你们以全面的眼光看待中国的人权事业。你知道……

戴维斯： 我不是要争论人权问题。我的问题是关于贸易。中国是否会用贸易手段阻止我们谈论人权问题？

刘晓明： 当然不会。

戴维斯： 那么就是说，如果英国谈论中国人权问题，不会付出代价，贸易和投资……

刘晓明： 你认为我们会把贸易当成武器去争取我们要得到的东西吗？这种想法绝对是错误的。贸易是双赢的。我们出口你们需要的东西，进口我们需要的东西，这是双赢的。

戴维斯： 那就是说如果有时我们在人权问题上有不同看法，双方还可以继续进行经贸合作？

刘晓明： 中英两国的社会制度，包括政治制度和经济制度，以及历史、文化有很大差异，双方处于不同的发展阶段，我们之间有不同，这很正常。但我们仍然可以合作，我们可以求同存异。你同意我的观点吗？

戴维斯： 我同意。我很高兴我们看法一致。最后一个简短的问题，我们的卫生大臣谈到他的华裔妻子以及亚洲人的工作观念。他说，希望英国人民能像亚洲国家人民那样勤奋工作。你认为英国人勤劳吗？还是享受了太多福利？

刘晓明： 中英两国可以相互学习。中国人民很勤劳，英国人民富有创造性，两国人民可以相互学习。

戴维斯： 你的意思是说英国人不够勤劳？（笑声）

刘晓明： 应该说中国人民更勤劳。中国之所以能创造奇迹，在30年的时间里，把一个相对落后的国家发展成为世界第二大经济体，我想这应该归功于勤劳苦干的中国人民。

戴维斯： 你认为再过40年，中国会像英国一样吗？可以民主选举国家主席吗？

刘晓明： 这又回到了我们之间的根本差异问题。你们认为英国的制度是民主的，而我们认为中国的制度是民主的，我们称之为中国特色的民主。英国的领导人并不是直接选举产生的。中国的领导人也是通过间接选举产生的。我们选举产生县级人大代表，之后逐级选举产生市级、省级和全国人大代表，再由全国人民代表大会选举产生国家主席。

戴维斯： 这是一个很大的议题。我们还要请你回来，再讨论这个议题。

刘晓明： 我们可以花整个晚上的时间来讨论民主问题。

戴维斯： 大使先生，非常感谢。

刘晓明： 不客气。

A Live Interview with Evan Davis
on BBC *Newsnight*

On 16th October 2015, I was invited to a live interview with BBC *Newsnight* hosted by Evan Davis. I talked about the significance of the forthcoming state visit of President Xi Jinping, and answered questions about China-UK bilateral relations, bilateral economic cooperation and China's economy. The full text is as follows:

Davis: Well, I'm glad to say I am joined by the Chinese Ambassador to this country, Liu Xiaoming. Very good evening to you, Ambassador. Thank you for coming in.

Liu Xiaoming: Thanks for having me.

Davis: Do you think your country, if the tables were turned, do you think China would let a British contractor build a nuclear power station in China?

Liu Xiaoming: I would ask, do you have the money, do you have the technology to build nuclear power stations in China?

Davis: Suppose we did? Do you suppose the UK would get access?

Liu Xiaoming: Suppose? I am not sure about that. I think the reason why China is here, why you want China, is that you need Chinese investment. And also in term of technology, China is very advanced in terms of nuclear technology. I think China has more nuclear power stations than many other countries.

Davis: You are building lots of them and we can benefit from that. But I don't think we would. I mean, on your Government website there is a catalogue of sectors prohibited for foreign investment industries. It is more restrictive than ours. I mean, No.6, exploring, mining and dressing of radioactive mining products. No.9, smelting and processing of radioactive mineral products; production of nuclear fuel. You wouldn't let us go anywhere near your nuclear industry. I wonder whether you think we are stupid to let you come near ours?

Liu Xiaoming: No, I think you are not stupid. In fact you are very smart, you know, using Chinese money to build your nuclear power station, and the British people will get benefit. If we can do that, we would love to do it.

Davis: All right. It is win-win.

Liu Xiaoming: It's win-win. I quite agree with you.

Davis: But there are lots of other things you don't do which we are really good at. I mean, air traffic control. We've got a great air traffic control company prohibited from foreign investment in China. Companies in postal services, auction companies, antique shops engaging in antique, construction of golf courses. Why can't we build golf courses...?

Liu Xiaoming: In fact there are several foreign investors building golf courses in China. What was the last time you were in China?

Davis: Well, I just got this catalogue of prohibited foreign investments industries...Is this an out of date one?

Liu Xiaoming: In fact there are many cooperations, joint ventures, between Chinese and...

Davis: Ah, joint ventures. But they can't go in, they can't go in and ...

Liu Xiaoming: They can go in, as a joint venture...

Davis: Why don't you...

Liu Xiaoming: …so that the Chinese partners can help foreign business to get a feel of the market. But you have to remember that China and the UK are at different stages of development. Just as your video clip said, you are more advanced in many areas and China is still a developing country. So we have to do things step by step. We have to learn your lessons. We try to avoid the mistakes you have made. So we have to be more cautious, when it comes to some of the areas of business.

Davis: But I mean, it is a win-win trade and that's why we welcome you in. And we will let you do all sorts of things here. Sometimes it looks like it's not reciprocal.

Liu Xiaoming: I don't think so. If we do not reciprocate, how could the UK become the second largest European investor in China, after Germany only? And your investment is also coming more and more. So I think it is win-win.

Davis: Let me ask you this one. There are a lot of concerns, security concerns. In fact, *The Times* newspaper today quoted security sources mentioning some of them, in relation particularly to nuclear power. There are fears that trap doors or back doors could be inserted into computer systems which might allow the Chinese to bypass British control of a nuclear plant, in the event of a diplomatic row. Now, how…is there any way the Chinese can assure those people in Britain who worry about that? Look, your plant is going to be safe and clean, but we won't have control.

Liu Xiaoming: We will do all this by following international standards. I think your intelligence people, your security people are not that stupid not to know all these things. You know, we are here for win-win cooperation, we are not here to try to control your nuclear power station. What will China get by controlling a British nuclear power station? I think you'd have to see there is a basic trust, when you are forging partnership. So I think if this bad media keeps playing up, China's business might be scared away from entering the UK. It would just be opposite to what your Chancellor has been saying the UK will be the most open western country to Chinese investment.

Davis: But basic trust? Is there a basic trust? I mean what about this People's Liberation Army Unit 61398 building in Shanghai, out of which a very large portion of the cyber crime reaches out of China…Is this nonsense?

Liu Xiaoming: I think that is a hyped rumour. First of all, I want to let you know that the Chinese Government strongly opposes this kind of practice. During President Xi Jinping's visit to the United States, the two Governments reached consensus that the two countries will work together to fight against this cyber crime. We are committed that none of the Government agencies will be engaged in cyber espionage, and none of the Government agencies will be in support of such activities.

Davis: We won't believe this. Look, I mean, it's a commitment…

Liu Xiaoming: If you don't believe us, how can we work together and build partnership?

Davis: But I have been reading your own book, the Science of Military Strategy, the PLA's own manual 2013 version, which was leaked out. This book did acknowledge that China has network attack forces. I mean, what is the network attack force?

Liu Xiaoming: I don't believe this. I don't think we have any cyber attack forces. China is more open for cooperation. In fact China itself is a victim of hacker attack.

Davis: Yah.

Liu Xiaoming: And in China, we have a saying, This is Confucius philosophy. I'm sorry to drag you more than 2, 000 years back. Confucian said: "Do not do to others what you don't want them to do to you. "That is our philosophy. We follow this philosophy. Since Chinese are victims of hacker attack, we don't want to inflict the same attack onto others.

Davis: Look, very briefly, human rights. If Britain makes a big fuss about human rights next week—if there is a big protest, suppose the opposition leader, suppose the Prime Minister talks a lot about human rights and our version of it—will we have a price to pay in trade and investment?

Liu Xiaoming: First of all, I would ask you this: do you think human rights are perfect in the UK? That's number one. Secondly, do you think UK's model is perfect worldwide? I think every country has its own conditions——how to improve human rights, how to protect them. Do you agree with me?

Davis: Yeah, I do.

Liu Xiaoming: What is your definition of human rights?

Davis: I am not criticising your human rights. Sorry, my question wasn't about your human rights. The question was, if we criticise your human rights, and you can criticise ours, will we pay a price…?

Liu Xiaoming: Is that what our President is here for, criticising each other on human rights?

Davis: No, no. If it came up, would there be a price to pay in terms of investment? 'Cause, I tell you why. I think if your President came and criticised our human rights, I think…

Liu Xiaoming: That is not our way of doing things.

Davis: He is not gonna do that, I know.

Liu Xiaoming: We respect the conditions of other countries. We think human rights are basically guaranteed by Chinese constitution, protected by the constitution, and it's really an internal matter to begin with. Of course, I hope you would have a big picture of human rights in China.

Davis: I am not getting into an argument about human rights. My point is about trade, and whether you use trade as a way to stop us talking about human rights.

Liu Xiaoming: No, we…

Davis: So there will be no price to pay if we spoke about human rights, and trade and investment…

Liu Xiaoming: So you think we use trade as a weapon to get things we want? That is absolutely wrong. Trade is win-win. We export what you need, and import what we need. I think it is a win-win.

Davis: So we should carry on trading even if we sometimes have a disagreement over human rights.

Liu Xiaoming: I agree. China and the UK are so different in social systems, both political and economic, in history and in culture, different stages of development. We differ. That is natural. But we can still do business. And we can reserve our differences and seek common good. Do you agree with me?

Davis: I do agree with you, I do. I am glad we agree. Just one, very quick last one. Our Health Secretary spoke about his Chinese wife, and the working values in Asia. He said we want to be a country that can work hard in the way the Asian economies do. Do we have a good work ethic here or do we have benefit levels that are too high…?

Liu Xiaoming: I think the two countries can learn from each other. The Chinese people are working very hard, but the British people are very creative. So the two peoples can learn from each other.

Davis: We are not hard-working (laughing) …

Liu Xiaoming: Not as hard as the Chinese people. So that's how China can make a miracle, just in 30 years, to turn a relatively poor country into the second largest economy. I think we should give a credit to the hard-working spirit of the Chinese people.

Davis: In 40 years time do you think China will look more like Britain? Do you think there may be a democratically elected President?

Liu Xiaoming: So that's where we come to some of the basic of differences between us. You believe the UK is a democracy. We think our system is a democracy. We call it democracy of Chinese characteristics. When other people look at the UK, your system, the way you elect your national leaders, it's not a direct election. In China, it is also indirect election. We elect the county deputies, the county deputies elect the provincial deputies, then the national deputies, then the national leaders.

Davis: This is a bigger conversation…We'll get you back…We will discuss that one another day ...

Liu Xiaoming: We can spend the whole evening talking about democracy.

Davis: Ambassador, thanks for coming.

Liu Xiaoming: Thank you. My pleasure.

Newsnight is a popular BBC 2 programme which specialises in in-depth analysis into current affairs and robust cross-examination with senior politicians.

Evan Davis, economist, is *Newsnight*'s lead presenter and economics editor, the most senior economics post at BBC.

接受英国BBC《安德鲁·马尔访谈》栏目主持人马尔现场直播采访

作者手记

　　2015年10月18日，我接受英国BBC《安德鲁·马尔访谈》（*The Andrew Marr Show*）栏目主持人安德鲁·马尔（Andrew Marr）现场直播采访。

　　《安德鲁·马尔访谈》是BBC旗舰直播栏目，也是英国最有影响力的时政访谈节目之一，每周日现场直播1小时，收视人群约有500万。该栏目每次邀请4~5位嘉宾，就不同的议题与主持人一对一交谈。英国首相、内阁大臣、各政党领袖、社会名流、学术精英等经常接受该栏目采访。

　　栏目主持人马尔是英国知名媒体人、专栏作家、政治评论员、历史学家，写过10多部历史专著，多数被评为畅销书；获多项新闻大奖，包括两次被评为"年度专栏作家"。曾多次采访英国政要和外国领导人，包括俄罗斯总统普京、美国总统奥巴马等。他创办《安德鲁·马尔访谈》栏目，并担任该栏目主持人达16年，直至2021年底离开BBC。

　　我使英11年，曾先后4次接受马尔现场直播采访，这是第一次。我们围绕习近平主席对英国国事访问、中英经贸关系、人权等问题展开了讨论。采访结束时，马尔预祝习主席对英国国事访问取得圆满成功。

采访实录如下：

马尔： 中国国家主席习近平即将对英国进行国事访问。在访问前夕，我们邀请到中国驻英国大使刘晓明。欢迎你，大使先生，很高兴你能做客我们的栏目。

刘晓明： 谢谢。

马尔： 首先提一个关于英中关系的问题。你是否认为，就中国而言，英国就像一个经济"乞丐"，没资格向中国提人权问题？

刘晓明： 首先，中国和英国是伙伴关系，我们称之为全面战略伙伴关系。两国都是具有全球影响力的大国，有广泛领域可以进行合作，实现双赢。你谈到人权，这当然也是我们可以讨论的领域，关键在于以什么方式讨论。谈论人权问题时，人们应以全面的眼光看待中国的人权事业，应该看到中国人权事业所取得的巨大进步。

马尔： 也就是说，情况已经发生变化。英国工党领袖科尔宾表示要提人权问题。如果他在女王为习主席举办的国宴上提出人权问题，这不会冒犯习主席吧？

刘晓明： 你觉得科尔宾会在女王举办的国宴上提出人权问题吗？我不这么认为。习主席对英国进行国事访问是为合作和伙伴关系而来，不是来争论人权问题的。我们都知道，中英两国存在很多差异。两国历史、文化不同，处于不同发展阶段，双方有不同看法是很正常的，在人权问题上也是如此。在中国，我们更关心的是人民有权享有更好的生活、更好的工作、更好的住房。我认为中国人民现在过着幸福的生活。另一方面，中国人民也享有……

马尔： 但在中国，有很多"异见人士"因为表达自己的观点而被投入监狱。

刘晓明： 这种说法不对。在中国，所有违法者都要通过正常的司法程序进行审判。

马尔： 但他们因为批评中国政府而入狱，在英国，我们不认为这是犯罪。

刘晓明： 没有人因为批评政府而入狱。服法入狱的人是因为他们从事犯罪活动，包括煽动、从事或组织推翻合法政府。在英国，如果有人从事危害英国国家利益、危害英国人民安全的行动，我想他们也会受到法律的惩罚。也许我们双方看法不同，我们可以进行讨论。

马尔：　大使，我给你举一个具体的例子。英国皇家美术学院正在举办一个非常重要、令人兴奋的艺术展，伦敦很多年都未举行这样的艺术展，这就是艾未未艺术展。艾未未是一个国际化的中国人，他是个爱国者，为自己是中国人感到自豪。他的父亲和毛主席等老一辈关系密切，而他却曾被短暂地关在监狱里。你认为艾未未是"异见人士"，或是危险分子，还是爱国公民？

刘晓明：　我不知道你对这个所谓"艺术家"了解多少。我曾接受BBC另一个节目采访，我告诉主持人，我对艾未未的"艺术"不感兴趣。中国有很多才华出众的艺术家，比艾未未更有才华。艾未未之所以出名，是因为他批评中国政府。事实上，艾未未从未被关入监狱。他因为涉嫌经济犯罪，包括做假账、故意销毁会计凭证等，而依法受到调查。如果是在英国，一个艺术家也同样涉嫌经济犯罪，你们不会对他进行调查吗？

马尔：　我只能说，我们俩在这个问题上的看法不同，我认为艾未未是一个伟大的艺术家，他的展览非常精彩。我们意见可以不同，但还是可以继续谈论下一个话题。查尔斯王储决定不出席女王举行的国宴，这是否会冒犯中国政府？

刘晓明：　查尔斯王储将在多个场合与习主席会面。如果他不能出席女王举行的欢迎晚宴，一定有自己的原因。据我所知，查尔斯王储为接待习主席做了很多努力。他为了与习主席会面，甚至调整了原先的日程安排。据我所知，查尔斯王储至少将与习主席会面3次……

马尔： 抱歉打断一下，我能不能再问一个问题。英国的安全和情报专家警告英国政府，中国正通过核电站建设合同来接近英国国家安全的核心。换句话说，英国正在打开大门，让中国接触到一些包括中国在内的其他国家绝不会对外开放的领域。

刘晓明： 我不知道那些人从哪儿搞到这些信息。我可以告诉你，中国到英国投资是为了双赢合作，这符合英国的利益，也有利于中英合作伙伴关系。英国需要中国的投资，英国人民希望过上更好的生活，希望拥有清洁能源。据我所知，今后10多年里，英国将淘汰不少旧的核电站，因此需要找到新的能源供应。

马尔： 英国当然需要资金和技术。但中国政府肯定不允许外国在中国投资建设核电站吧？

刘晓明： 我曾被问到同样的问题，而我反问了几个问题：你们有资金吗？你们有技术吗？你们有管理经验吗？如果你们都有，我们当然希望与你们合作。比如法国，中国和法国在核电领域有一些合作，因为法国在核电方面拥有先进的技术。我认为英国在其他领域更有优势，为什么眼睛总盯着在中国建核电站呢？

马尔： 人们期待下周英中将签署一个关于核电的大合同，你认为会签吗？

刘晓明： 我当然希望如此，因为这是两国的重大合作项目。

马尔： 最后一个问题，你刚才说不认为科尔宾会在女王举办的欢迎晚宴上向习主席提出人权问题，但科尔宾的助手说他要提。如果科尔宾真的提出人权问题怎么办？

刘晓明： 我想，这个欢迎晚宴是女王举办的，女王是主人。不管是科尔宾还是其他人，都是女王的客人。英国是礼仪之邦，英国人很聪明，他们知道在这样的场合应该如何做。我们并不回避讨论人权问题。上周，我见到了科尔宾，我们谈得很好。我希望……

马尔： 那你的建议是，不要在这种公开的场合提人权问题？

刘晓明： 我们对"麦克风式外交"不感兴趣，对"镜头外交"也不感兴趣，我们更愿意坦诚地交换意见。如果他有关切的问题，我们可以讨论。

马尔： 大使先生，非常感谢你接受采访。预祝习主席对英国的国事访问取得圆满成功。

刘晓明： 谢谢。

A Live Interview
on BBC *The Andrew Marr Show*

On 18th October 2015, I was invited by BBC Andrew Marr to give a live interview. I talked about the significance of the forthcoming state visit of President Xi Jinping and answered questions about China's investment in nuclear power stations in the UK and human rights. The full text is as follows:

Marr: Ahead of the State Visit by the Chinese President, I am joined by the Chinese Ambassador to the UK, Liu Xiaoming. Welcome, Ambassador, very nice to have you here.

Liu Xiaoming: Thank you.

Marr: First of all, about Britain's relationship with China. Are we in essence now a begging bowl economy, as far as the Chinese state is concerned, which doesn't have the right to raise issues like human rights?

Liu Xiaoming: First of all, I think China and the UK are partners. We call it a comprehensive strategic partnership, because our two countries are very important countries with global influence. We have so many areas for cooperation, for win-win. When you talk about human rights, I think that is also an area where we can talk. But the important thing is how to approach human rights. When you talk about human rights, you should not miss the big picture in China. I hope people would realise how much progress China has made in the area of human rights.

Marr: So this is a changing picture, and the President won't be offended if it is brought up, for instance, at the state banquet by the Labour Leader Jeremy Corbyn, who says he will bring it up?

Liu Xiaoming: You think the Labour Party leader will raise this issue at a state banquet? I don't think so. I think President Xi is here for cooperation, for partnership. He is not here for debate about human rights. We all know that China and the UK differ very much because we have different histories and different cultures. We are in different stages of development. It's natural we have differences, even with regard to human rights. In China we care more about the rights for better life, for better jobs, for better housing. I think the Chinese people enjoy their happy life. On the other side, I think the Chinese people enjoy…

Marr: But there are a lot of dissidents who are in prison for expressing their views.

Liu Xiaoming: But I wouldn't say there are a lot of dissidents. All criminal are tried through a normal legal process.

Marr: But there are people who express criticism of the Chinese government and the state, whom we would not regard as criminals, who end up in prison in China.

Liu Xiaoming: No one would be put behind bars simply because they are criticizing the government. The criminals are put behind bars because they have a criminal record. They either incite or engage in organization to overthrow the legitimate government. Here in this country, I think, once you are involved in some activities that work against the interests of Britain and endanger the safety of the people, you will be put behind bars. Maybe we have some different opinions. In that case, we can talk to each other.

Marr: Well, let me give you a specific if I may, Ambassador. The most important and exciting art exhibition we've had in London for a very, very long time is the Ai Weiwei's exhibition at the Royal Academy. Here is somebody who is a global Chinese figure. And he is a Chinese patriot, very, very proud of his Chinese origins, and his father was close to Chairman Mao and all the rest of it. Yet he ended up in prison for a while. Do you regard him as a dissident, as a dangerous figure or as a patriotic important Chinese citizen?

Liu Xiaoming: I don't know how much you know about this so-called "artist". I was interviewed on one of your programmes. I told the presenter, he is not my taste. There are so many talented Chinese artists. Yet…and many are much better than him. Why is he so famous here? The reason is that he is critical of the Chinese Government. He has never been put behind bars. He was under investigation because he was suspected about a crime. He was suspected of fraudulent accounting, destroying accounting documents. What about...if the same happens here in the UK, surely you investigate comparable criminal activities?

Marr: The only thing I could say is that we disagree about this. I think he is a great artist. I'll have to say it's a great exhibition. We can disagree about that and move on. Is the Chinese Government offended by the Prince of Wales' decision not to attend the state banquet?

Liu Xiaoming: He will be with the President on several occasions. He might have a good reason if he is not available. But I know the Prince of Wales has made a lot of efforts. He even has to change his original schedule in order to meet the President. I think he will meet the President at least on three occasions…

Marr: Can I ask, I am so sorry to interrupt you, can I ask about the stories that British security and intelligence experts have warned our government that China is getting very, very close to the heart of state security through this nuclear contracts. And in a sense, they are opening the door to things that most governments, including the Chinese government, wouldn't allow.

Liu Xiaoming: I don't know where they get this information. I can only tell you that Chinese are here for win-win cooperation. We think it is in the best interests of Britain and also in the interest of partnership between China and Britain. I think that the UK needs Chinese investment here and UK people want to have a better life, want to have clean energy. I know you have to close the old nuclear power stations in the next dozen of years. You have to find resources for the new energy supply.

Marr: We certainly need the money, we need the expertise. But China wouldn't allow a foreign power to build her nuclear power stations surely?

Liu Xiaoming: Recently I was put the same question. I ask, do you have the money? Do you have the technology, do you have the expertise? If you have all these, we certainly would want to have cooperation with you. Like France, you know, the French nuclear services, we have some cooperation with France, because they have the technology. I think the UK is strong in other areas. Why do you always focus on building nuclear power stations in China?

Marr: We're expecting a big contract to be signed next week. Do you think it will be?

Liu Xiaoming: I certainly hope so, because it is a very important project between our two countries.

Marr: And finally, you said earlier on that you didn't think that Jeremy Corbyn would raise human rights at the state banquet. I mean, his people have been briefing that he will. If he does, what happens?

Liu Xiaoming: I think a state banquet is Her Majesty's banquet, it's her show. Either Jeremy Corbyn or others are there as guests. I think British people are very polite, very smart. They know how to behave on occasions like this. We do not shy away from discussions about human rights. In fact, I had a good meeting with Jeremy Corbyn last week. And I do hope…

Marr: So your advice is not to do this in public?

Liu Xiaoming: We are not interested in microphone diplomacy, just like we are not interested in TV camera diplomacy. We are more interested in candid discussion. If he has his concern, we can talk about it.

Marr: Yes. Ambassador, thank you very much indeed for joining me. And good luck with the State Visit.

Liu Xiaoming: Thank you.

The Andrew Marr Show is one of the most influential political programmes on BBC, where the UK's Prime Minister and other Cabinet ministers give interviews. It has a TV rating of 5 million audiences.

Andrew Marr is a well-known British presenter who has interviewed many state leaders including US President Obama and Russian President Putin.

接受英国天空新闻台《莫纳罕访谈》栏目主持人莫纳罕现场直播采访

作者手记

2015年10月18日，我就习近平主席对英国国事访问，接受英国天空新闻台（Sky News）《莫纳罕访谈》(Murnaghan Programme)栏目主持人德莫特·莫纳罕(Dermot Murnaghan)现场直播采访。

英国天空新闻台是除BBC新闻台之外英国唯一一个24小时滚动播放新闻的有线电视频道，拥有750多万观众。该台在海外对138个国家和地区播放新闻节目，约有1.15亿用户。《莫纳罕访谈》是该台旗舰时事访谈节目，以深度辩论著称。莫纳罕是该台资深主持人，曾担任BBC和英国独立电视台主持人。

我向他介绍了习主席访问英国的重要意义，回答了他有关网络安全、中英经贸合作、人权等问题的提问。

采访实录如下：

莫纳罕： 中国国家主席习近平下周将对英国进行国事访问，卡梅伦首相形容两国关系将进入"黄金时代"。两国可能将签署一系列重要协议，包括核能合作。今天，我们有幸邀请了中国驻英国大使刘晓明参与我们的节目。早上好，刘大使。首先，请问英国是否应该对中国感到担心？

刘晓明： 没有什么好担心的。中国是个爱好和平的国家，习主席访问旨在促进合作，巩固两国伙伴关系。两国有很多领域可以开展合作。作为具有全球影响力的国家，中英两国携手合作可以共同建设一个更美好的世界，促进世界繁荣，维护世界和平。

莫纳罕： 我问这个问题，是因为英国军情五处网站上开设了一个公众互动栏目，并进行了一次关于国家安全最大威胁的问卷调查，来自中国的网络恐怖主义被列为第二大威胁。我想，你也可能看到了这个问卷，军情五处对中国感到担忧。

刘晓明： 中国坚决反对网络犯罪，中国自己就是黑客攻击的受害者。

莫纳罕： 这些攻击来自何处？

刘晓明： 来自各个方面，网络空间不是一个安全的地方，各国应共同合作，而不是相互指责。习主席对美国国事访问期间，他与奥巴马总统达成共识，中美两国政府均反对任何网络犯罪活动，也不支持任何组织参与网络犯罪活动。

莫纳罕： 这一共识说得十分清楚明了，但为什么军情五处分析认为中国在网络犯罪问题上是全球最大威胁之一？

刘晓明： 听到这样的分析，我感到很遗憾。我听到不少关于对核电站安全的担心。中国企业是应英国政府和企业的要求前来建设核电站的，他们来不是为了所谓控制核电站，而是为了开展双赢的合作。他们的活动将严格遵循国际标准和规则，是透明的。英国的安全监管部门不会笨到让中国企业控制英国的核设施。我认为这些担心是一些媒体炒作的结果，有些人不想看到……

莫纳罕： 媒体和安全部门会说，这是军情五处网站问卷调查得出的结论。

刘晓明： 你应该去问军情五处。中国企业来英国不是当间谍的，不是来刺探英国的核设施的，他们有重要的事情要做，他们来英国是为了合作，为了双赢的合作，这是中国企业投资的唯一目的。

莫纳罕： 听说习主席来访期间将与英方深入讨论"北部振兴计划"，听说这个词很难翻译成中文。

刘晓明： 没那么难，中文词汇十分丰富。你会说中文吗？

莫纳罕： 对不起，不会。

刘晓明： 是有几个不同的译法，最终我们选定了一个比较贴切的。

莫纳罕： 很高兴听到这一点。但是，人们对英格兰北部地区的发展有不少忧虑，特别是钢铁产业。中国是个钢铁大国，人们对此很担心。有人批评中国将自己过剩的钢铁倾销到世界各地，你能接受这种批评吗？今早英国有家媒体称，与其说你打造一个"北部振兴计划"，不如说制造一个"北方贫困带"，你对此有何评论？

刘晓明： 在全球化时代，每个国家均需进行相应的产业调整，中国也是一样。中国过去一直是个加工业大国，生产大量玩具、服装等，英国和美国80%～90%的玩具来自中国。现在，我们面临来自东南亚国家的竞争，它们的劳动力成本远低于中国，竞争力强，许多工厂都转移到那些国家去了。所以，中国也在努力从加工业大国向制造业大国转型，每个国家都需进行调整。中国企业到英国来了，要努力适应，寻找中英两国的共同点。我们肯定会考虑到英方的关切，考虑当地民众的关切。

莫纳罕： 作为中国大使，你一定听说不少关于中国人权记录的关切，尤其是对中国大量死刑人数的关切。卡梅伦首相曾表示，英国反对死刑，哪里有死刑，英国就会抓住一切机会提出这一问题。假如英国首相向中国主席提出这一问题，你是否觉得很无礼呢？

刘晓明： 我在英已任职5年，我经常听到人们谈及人权问题。然而，人们往往看不到中国人权的整体情况。什么是人权？

莫纳罕： 就是公正司法的权力，不被轻易判处死刑。

刘晓明： 基本的人权就是让人们生活得更好。在我看来，有些人谈论人权时，往往看不到中国在仅仅30年的时间里就使7亿人脱贫，没有哪个国家能在这么短的时间里取得这样的成绩。中国人现在生活得更好，寿命更长，享受着幸福生活。在政治生活中，中国人民享有前所未有的尊严和自由。你谈到死刑问题，中国是个大国，治理一个13亿多人口的国家与治理一个6400万人口的国家自然是不一样的。中国在死刑问题上十分慎重，死刑数量在逐年下降，而且要经过最高人民法院的严格复核程序。

莫纳罕： 最后问一个有关工党领袖科尔宾的问题。前一段时间你一定在密切关注工党领袖选举。关于习主席将与英国的在野党即工党领袖科尔宾谈什么，你们是否进行过实质性探讨？

刘晓明： 国事访问期间，习主席将在白金汉宫会见工党领袖科尔宾，我们期待习主席与科尔宾进行一次富有成果、有意义的会见。

莫纳罕： 中国与科尔宾能搞好关系吗？科尔宾是个社会主义者，而你们是共产主义者。

刘晓明： 社会主义者之间可以辩论，社会主义者和共产主义者之间也可以进行辩论，但我们来英国是为了寻求共同点。事实上，我上星期会见了科尔宾，为习主席与科尔宾的会见做准备。我们的会见很有意义，工党曾为发展中英关系做出了重要贡献。现在，我们与保守党及工党均保持良好的党际关系。我真诚地希望，在科尔宾的领导下，工党继续为发展这一重要双边关系做出积极贡献。

莫纳罕： 大使阁下，我们采访时间到了，非常高兴见到你，也非常感谢你。预祝习主席访问取得圆满成功。

刘晓明： 谢谢。

A Live Interview
on Sky News *Murnaghan Programme*

On 18th October 2015, I was invited to a live interview with Dermot Murnaghan on Sky News *Murnaghan Programme*. The full text is as follows:

Murnaghan: I am joined by the Chinese Ambassador to the UK, H. E Liu Xiaoming. A very good morning to you, Ambassador.

Liu Xiaoming: Good morning.

Murnaghan: A broad question first of all. Does UK have anything to fear from China?

Liu Xiaoming: Nothing to fear about China. China is a peace-loving country and the President will be here for cooperation and partnership. And I think China and the UK have a lot to cooperate about and we believe China and UK are two important countries of global influence. By working together, the two countries will help to build a better world, to promote prosperity and uphold world peace.

Murnaghan: Okay. I ask that question because I am sure you have had a look at it as well: Our security service, MI5, has opened an accessible website talking to the British public and that it has a question and answer page about the current biggest threats to national security. And then we have, at number two, Chinese cyber terrorism. MI5 are concerned about China.

Liu Xiaoming: China is very much opposed to cyber crime. China itself is a victim of hacker attacks.

Murnaghan: From where? Where do they emanate?

Liu Xiaoming: Everywhere, I would say. Cyber space is not a safe place. Countries should work together rather than criticising each other. During President Xi's state visit, he and President Obama reached consensus that the two governments will not support any cyber crime and we will not be supportive to any organisations to engage in cyber crimes.

Murnaghan: Well, that's loud and clear. But why would MI5 have come up with this analysis that China is one of the biggest global threats on cyber crime?

Liu Xiaoming: I'm sorry to hear this analysis. I heard quite a lot about these concerns about the nuclear power station. I think Chinese companies are here to build nuclear power at the request of the British business and government. We are here not for the so-called control of your nuclear power station. We are here for win-win cooperation. We will play by the international standard and follow the international rules. It is transparent. I think your security authorities, regulation authorities are not that unwise to let the Chinese companies control your nuclear facilities. I think these are things that have been hyped up by some media, by some people who do not want to see…

Murnaghan: The media and security services say, there it is on the MI5 website.

Liu Xiaoming: I think you should put this question to your MI5. But we are here, we are not spying on your nuclear facilities. I think we have more interest in doing something else: we are here for cooperation, for win-win. That is the whole purpose of Chinese investment here.

Murnaghan: And I know that President Xi Jinping is going to have long discussions about the Northern Powerhouse, which I understand doesn't translate very easily into Chinese.

Liu Xiaoming: Not that difficult. The Chinese language is very rich. I think Northern Powerhouse…do you speak mandarin?

Murnaghan: No, I am afraid not.

Liu Xiaoming: There are several translations, but at the end of the day we have found a very appropriate one.

Murnaghan: Okay. That's good to hear. But there are concerns about what's going on in the northern parts of Britain at the moment. When it comes to the steel industry, again, there are big concerns about China as a huge producer of steel. Do you accept criticisms of China that China has now got massive overcapacity in steel and is dumping it on global markets. Instead of a Northern Powerhouse, you are creating, as one of our newspapers says this morning, a "northern poorhouse"?

Liu Xiaoming: I think every country has to adjust itself to globalization, even in the case of China. China used to be a processing power for clothes, for toys, in the past. I think China exported maybe 90% or 80% of toys to this country and to the United States. But we are now faced with very competitive neighbours in Southern Asia and Southeast Asian countries. As their labour forces are more competitive and cost lower, business moves from China to those countries. So we have to adjust from processing to manufacturing. I think any country, every country, has to adjust itself. And we are here and, we should accommodate, looking for common ground between China and the UK. We certainly will address concerns here. We certainly will address concerns of your local communities.

Murnaghan: Don't you believe there is reason for, you must have seen it, you are the Ambassador, concerns about Chinese human rights records. Particularly things about the mass number of people executed in China and things like that. The Prime Minister said we oppose the death penalty everywhere and anywhere and we will raise it at all opportunities. Presumably the Prime Minister is going to do this with the President. Do you think that is rude?

Liu Xiaoming: I have been here for five years and I have heard a lot of comments about human rights in China. But I think more often than not, people miss the big picture of human rights in China. What are human rights?

Murnaghan: The right for a fair trial and not to be summarily executed.

Liu Xiaoming: The basic right is for people to have better living. I think people sometimes, when they talk about human rights, they miss the picture that China, in only 30 years, elevated 700 million people out of poverty. No other country has done that within such a short time. And Chinese people are living better, living longer and they enjoying their happy lives. Even in their political life, I think never before in the history of China did people enjoy the unprecedented dignity and freedom they do today.

You are talking about death penalty. China is a large country. To run a country of 1.3 billion will be naturally different from running a country of 64 million. The penalty has been handled in a very careful way, and the number reduced with each passing year. And it has to be approved by the Supreme Court so that such punishment comes through a very careful process.

Murnaghan: Last question: About the Labour leader Jeremy Corbyn. You will have viewed his election with interest. Have you had any substantive discussions between your President and the leader of the Labour Party, the leader of the Opposition?

Liu Xiaoming: President Xi will have a meeting with Jeremy Corbyn during the state visit at Buckingham Palace. We look forward to a productive and meaningful meeting between the President and Jeremy Corbyn as the Leader of the Labour Party.

Murnaghan: And do you think you will get on well with him? He is a socialist and you are a communist.

Liu Xiaoming: You know, socialists can debate. Socialists and communists can have a debate. But we are here for common ground. In fact last week I had an interesting meeting with Jeremy Corbyn, to prepare for the President's meeting with him. I think the Labour Party has made its important contributions to developing relationship between our two countries. And currently we have very strong party-to-party exchange relationship, with both the Conservative Party and the Labour. And I sincerely hope the Labour Party, under the leadership of Jeremy Corbyn, will continue to make its positive contributions to this important relationship.

Murnaghan: Your Excellency, we're out of time. It's great to see you. Thank you very much indeed. Here is to a successful visit.

Liu Xiaoming: Thank you.

Sky News is the second largest broadcaster after the BBC, providing 24 hours news broadcasting in the UK, with more than 7.5 million audiences in the UK and 115 million worldwide. *Murnaghan Programme* is the flagship current affairs programme known for its in-depth debate and discussions. Dermot Murnaghan is a senior presenter of Sky News.

如何认识中国

Understand China

英国是最早承认中华人民共和国的西方大国，也是最早同中华人民共和国开展经贸往来的西方大国之一。时至今日，两国交流覆盖各个方面，涉及各个领域，广度和深度均今非昔比。但令人遗憾的是，中英之间仍然存在"了解赤字"和"认知赤字"。英国电视台、电台、报纸、网络关于中国的报道，仍有不少偏见、误导，甚至假消息。在这样的舆论环境里，英国民众难以了解真实的中国，他们对中国的认知有很多误区，特别是对中国共产党存在很大误解。一些人听到"共产党"和"共产主义"就产生心理障碍，因而也就难以客观地看待共产党领导下的中国。针对这种现象，我在英国讲中国故事时，重点讲中国共产党的故事，讲中国共产党带领中国人民实现中华民族伟大复兴的故事，使英国民众了解中国共产党是什么，要干什么；从哪里来，到哪里去。我多次在英国电视台、电台接受现场直播采访，介绍中共十八大、十九大、人大、政协"两会"。针对BBC主持人对中国共产党的误解，我指出，中国共产党将马克思主义理论与中国国情相结合，建立了中国特色社会主义制度。这一制度符合中国实际，给中国带来了发展与进步，取得了巨大成功，造福了广大人民，得到了广大人民的拥护。在英国独立电视台的现场直播采访中谈到中共十九大，我指出，习近平总书记将带领中国人民开启中国特色社会主义的新时代，到2020年中国将彻底消除绝对贫困，全面建成小康社会。

接受英国BBC广播四台主持人多德采访

作者手记

2011年12月20日，我在英国BBC广播四台（BBC Radio 4）演播室接受知名主持人菲利普·多德（Philip Dodd）的采访。

多德是英国著名学者、作家、记者、编辑、企业家、节目主持人，著有多本专著，创办多种杂志，担任BBC顾问兼主持人，曾担任伦敦现代艺术学会会长。他也是国际知名策展人，推动举办国际民间博物馆峰会，创办创意产业公司"中国制造"，促成英国维多利亚与艾尔伯特博物馆落户广东深圳。

此次采访正值大熊猫"阳光"和"甜甜"刚刚抵达苏格兰爱丁堡，这也是我第一次接受英国广播电台采访。采访主要围绕大熊猫来英国的意义及中英关系。

采访实录如下：

多德： 为什么大熊猫对中国非常重要？大熊猫是否是中国送给英国的"厚礼"？

刘晓明： 大熊猫是中国的"国宝"，也是世界濒危物种。由于大熊猫发情难、受孕难、育幼难，所以野生大熊猫数量很少。为了拯救和保护大熊猫，中国政府在政策制定、法制建设、资金投入等方面采取多项措施，大熊猫保护状况呈现不断向好趋势。但即使如此，大熊猫野生种群数量也只有约1600只。

我想强调，大熊猫来英国不能简单被定性为"赠礼"，而是中英双方一个重要科研合作项目，涵盖野外生态学、大熊猫人工繁殖和育幼、大熊猫认知演化和行为研究等多个领域。虽然历史上来英国的熊猫不少，但是从未在英国产崽，希望在中英两国科学家携手合作下，大熊猫"甜甜"和"阳光"能尽快产下熊猫宝宝，为中英大熊猫联合研究带来新成果，为人工培育的大熊猫重返大自然提供更多帮助。

多德： 大熊猫作为中国派出的"形象大使"，将向外界传达什么信息？中国是否认为大熊猫来英国有助于提升中国软实力？据估算，2020年，中国中产阶层将达到6亿人，中国将成为一个名副其实的超级大国。随着欧洲深陷债务危机，中国是否认为西方国家喜爱大熊猫源自对开拓中国市场的兴趣？

刘晓明： 大熊猫体态黑白分明，憨态可掬，备受中国人民和世界人民的喜爱。大熊猫来英国传达的信息可以用3个P概括，即Panda Conservation（熊猫保护）、Public Awareness（普及知识）、Peoples Friendship（民间友好）。在国外开展大熊猫合作首要目的和任务是促进在人工和自然环境下的熊猫繁衍和生存研究；其次是普及熊猫的知识，让国外民众近距离、直观地了解熊猫，更加喜爱熊猫，支持熊猫保护工作；再者是以熊猫为使者，增进人民之间的友谊。

"甜甜"和"阳光"落户爱丁堡将成为中英增进了解、深化友谊、扩大合作的纽带，为两国人民友好交往谱写新的佳话。

了解大熊猫，必然离不开了解它们的故乡——中国，了解中国的风土人情、经济社会；了解今天的中国走和平发展道路，愿与世界互利共赢；了解中国人民热情善良，愿与各国人民友好相处。

为推动两国青少年友好交往，中国驻英国使馆与英国的一些大学合作，正在全英百所中小学开展大熊猫主题演讲和绘画比赛，特等奖得主将有机会访问大熊猫的故乡——中国四川。

中国对加强对外经济合作持开放和欢迎态度。中国过去30多年来取得了举世瞩目的发展成就，但中国的中产阶层将于今后10年达到6亿人的说法似乎有些夸大。中国人均GDP仍排在世界100位以后，1亿多人还生活在联合国界定的贫困线以下。中国在相当长的时间内仍将是发展中国家，中国的发展还有很长的路要走。中国改革开放已经30多年，中国入世也已满10年，中国的市场越来越开放，今后中国愿与包括英国在内的世界各国扩大互利合作，实现共同发展。

多德：　你是否认为西方对中国不够了解？

刘晓明：　坦率地说，西方确实存在对中国不了解，甚至误解的情况。中西方文化不同，处事风格迥异。中国人讲究谦逊平和，不喜张扬。比如，西方人送礼物时会说："我的礼物有多好，希望你喜欢。"但中国人即使送很昂贵的礼物，也只说："这点薄礼不成敬意，请笑纳。"

我还想指出，增加了解是双向道。中国人应更多地向外界讲中国故事，与世界分享成功经验。同时，西方媒体应该全面客观报道中国，向西方公众展示一个真实的中国。让西方公众看到，中国取得的成就不仅限于经济，而是包括政治、社会、文化等全方位的发展进步。希望中西方能共同努力，增进西方公众对当代中国的全面认识。期待BBC为此做出积极努力。

多德： 我完全赞同。

An Interview with Philip Dodd on BBC Radio 4

On 20th December 2011, I gave an interview to Philip Dodd, a well known presenter, at the studios of BBC Radio 4. I talked about the meaning of the giant pandas in Britain and the China-UK relations. The full text is as follows:

Dodd: Why are giant pandas so important to China? Are the giant pandas a "big present" from China to Britain?

Liu Xiaoming: Giant pandas are China's "national treasure" and an endangered species in the world. The reasons are they do not impregnate easily and are not good at taking care of their cubs. So wild giant pandas are small in number. To save and protect giant pandas, the Chinese government adopts many measures in policy making, legal construction and capital investment. These have helped to constantly improve the protection of this species. But even so, the population of wild giant pandas is only about 1600.

The coming of giant pandas to the UK cannot be simply regarded as a "present". It is an important scientific research project of China-UK cooperation and covers various fields such as field ecology, artificial breeding and rearing of giant pandas and study in cognition evolution and behaviour of giant pandas. Although many giant pandas came to Britain in the past, they never gave birth to a baby in this country. I hope that the cooperation of both Chinese and British scientists would help Tian Tian and Yang Guang to produce baby pandas as soon as possible, bring new results in the China-UK giant panda researches and further facilitate the release of artificially raised giant pandas into the wild.

Dodd: What is the message given by the giant pandas to the rest of the world as

China's "image ambassador"? Does China believe that the coming of giant pandas to the UK will help to enhance China's soft power? It is estimated that by 2020, China will have 600 million middle class people and will become a true superpower. As Europe is deeply mired in the debt crisis, does China think that the affection of the western countries on giant pandas is out of their interest in expanding the Chinese market?

Liu Xiaoming: With their distinctive black and white colours and lovely look, giant pandas are very popular among the people both in China and in the world. The messages brought by the giant pandas to the UK can be summarized with 3 Ps: Panda Conservation, Public Awareness and Peoples Friendship. The first aim and task of the cooperation on giant pandas abroad is with the study in the reproduction and survival of giant pandas in artificial and natural environments; The second purpose is to disseminate the knowledge on giant pandas, so that people of other countries can have a close look at them and directly learn about them, and then love giant pandas more and support the protection work; And third, it is to enhance the friendship between the peoples with the pandas as a messenger.

Tian Tian and Yang Guang's settlement in Edinburgh will be a tie for China and the UK to enhance mutual understanding, deepen friendship and expand cooperation, and will be a new story of the friendly exchanges between the two peoples.

It is impossible to learn about giant pandas without understanding their home country—China, China's culture, history, economy and society, the path of peaceful development pursued by China today, the country's will of achieving mutual benefit and win-win results with the rest of the world, and the enthusiasm and kindness of the Chinese people who are ready to get on with the people of other countries.

To promote the friendly exchanges between young people, the Chinese Embassy is working with some British universities to organize speech and painting contests revolving around giant pandas in 100 primary and secondary schools across Britain. The top prize winners will have an opportunity to visit the hometown of giant pandas—Sichuan, China.

China welcomes foreign businesses with open arms. It is true that China has made remarkable achievements over the past 30 years, but it is quite an overestimation to say that there will be 600 million people in middle class in China in 10 years. China's per capita GDP is still ranked over 100th in the world and there are 100 million

Chinese people still living under the poverty line defined by the United Nations. China will remain a developing country for quite a long time and the country has still a long way to go in its development. It has been over 30 years since China's reform and opening up and 10 years since its WTO accession. China has an increasingly open market, and in the future, China is willing to expand the mutually beneficial cooperation with the rest of the world including Britain to achieve common development.

Dodd: Do you think the West does not know China well enough?

Liu Xiaoming: Frankly, there is indeed a lack of understanding or even misunderstanding of China in the West. With different cultures, China and the West handle things in quite different styles. The Chinese people emphasise modesty and peace and do not like taking a high profile. For example, when presenting a gift, a Westerner would describe how good the gift is and say "I hope you like it. " But in the case of a Chinese person, even if his gift is very expensive, he would still say "This humble gift is not enough to show my respect. Please kindly accept it. "
Enhancing understanding is a two-way street. The Chinese people should tell more about China to others and share its success story with the rest of the world. At the same time, the Western media needs to have a comprehensive and objective coverage on China and display China as it is. They need to let the Western public see that China's achievement is not limited to economy. Our success owes much to an all-round development and progress in politics, society, culture and other aspects. China and the West should work together to encourage a more comprehensive knowledge on China, and the BBC could make active efforts to this end.

Dodd: I fully agree.

In the UK, Philip Dodd is an award-winning broadcaster, writer, curator and cultured enterpreneur.

接受英国BBC《新闻之夜》栏目
主持人帕克斯曼现场直播采访

作者手记

　　2012年1月23日是农历大年初一，我来到英国BBC《新闻之夜》（*Newsnight*）栏目演播室，接受该栏目主持人杰里米·帕克斯曼（Jeremy Paxman）现场直播采访。

　　主持人帕克斯曼是英国著名记者、作家、评论家，在BBC旗舰时政栏目《新闻之夜》担任主持人25年。他采访风格直率、犀利、咄咄逼人，英国舆论界对其褒贬不一。褒者称赞他知识渊博、头脑清晰、提问尖锐，特别是对政客毫不留情，常把对方逼到墙角。贬者认为他居高临下、傲慢偏激、目中无人、言辞尖刻，甚至使被采访者感到恐惧，因此引起不少争议。

　　这是我出任驻英国大使以来，第一次接受电视直播采访。当时国际上没有突发事件，中英关系也没有突出问题。BBC称，帕克斯曼想跟中国大使结识一下，随便聊聊，谈什么都行。这的确是一个介绍中国的机会，但也存在很大风险。一是没有主题，无从准备；二是帕克斯曼的采访风格令许多英国政客，包括内阁大臣，望而生畏。我第一次上来就面对一个"狠主"，多少感到有些紧张，但责任感呼唤我必须迎战。

　　果不出所料，帕克斯曼一上来就咄咄逼人，问："你是共产党吗？"我知道来者不善，他并不是要搞清楚我的身份，而是要给中国贴标签。在西方，特别是在冷战时期，"共产党"是个贬义词，"共产党国家"便成了专制的代名词。美国有位参议员至死不叫中国的全名"中华人民共和国"，张口闭口"红色中国""共产党中国"。20世纪50年代，周恩来总理在会见美国青年代表团时，曾纠正美国记者的提问，告诉他中国的国名是"中华人民共和国"，不是"共产党中国"；就像美国叫"美利坚合众国"，不叫"共和党美国"。周总理说，国家是人民的，人民选举代表来领导这个国家。时至今日，冷战残余未消，"共产党中国""共产党国家"仍不时挂在西方政客嘴边，出现在西方各种媒体上。我抓住帕克斯曼这个提问机会，批驳冷战思维，为我们的党和国家正名。

　　接着，我们围绕中国的对外政策和国际作用、中国经济实力、伊朗核问题、人权问题等进行了讨论。他给我留下的印象既是一个善辩者，也是一个倾听者。我给他留下的印象，用他的话说是能言善辩、有说服力。他希望我今后有机会再次做客《新闻之夜》。我的第一次现场直播采访，即第一次"大考"算是通过了。

　　采访实录如下：

帕克斯曼： 大使先生，新年好！

刘晓明： 谢谢。

帕克斯曼： 让我们先搞清一个名词。你是共产党吗？

刘晓明： 中国共产党在中国是执政党，拥有超过8000万名党员。但是中国有13亿人口，因此不能说中国是"共产党国家"，就像不能说英国是"保守党国家"一样。

帕克斯曼： 但可以说英国是资本主义国家。

刘晓明： 中国是社会主义国家，实行的是中国特色社会主义。

帕克斯曼： 我不久前去北京采访，与不少年轻人交谈。给我留下深刻印象的是，他们对中国在国际上发挥的作用很有信心，认为中国将成为21世纪一支不断崛起的重要力量。你也这么认为吗？

刘晓明： 中国一定会为世界和平和繁荣做出越来越大的贡献，但我们不认为中国是一个超级大国。应该说，中国是一个国际影响力和国际责任都在不断扩大的最大的发展中国家。

帕克斯曼： 但人们不理解中国在联合国安理会的所作所为，如中国反对制裁伊朗和叙利亚。人们在问，中国的目的是什么？

刘晓明： 这种看法不对。事实上，中国4次投票支持联合国安理会涉伊核问题决议。我们明确反对伊朗拥有核武器。但另一方面，中方认为，通过外交手段和平解决伊核问题才是最佳途径。和平解决的代价最低，而且有利于维护地区的和平稳定。

帕克斯曼： 中方是否认为一个拥有核武器的伊朗会对世界和平构成潜在威胁？

刘晓明： 是的，一个拥有核武器的伊朗不利于地区和平与稳定。所以中方从一开始就明确反对伊朗发展核武器。中国总理不久前访问海湾国家时再次重申了这一立场。

帕克斯曼： 那么为什么不能制裁伊朗？

刘晓明： 现在已有制裁措施在实施之中。我们不赞成为了制裁而制裁，这样做徒劳无益。我们鼓励各方与伊朗通过外交谈判以和平方式解决有关问题。

帕克斯曼： 你认为中国在世界上能够发挥道义作用吗？

刘晓明： 我认为，中国在维护世界和平、构建和谐世界方面能够发挥自己应有的作用。

帕克斯曼： 中国在国际上想推动实现什么？比如美国为了推行民主不惜发动战争。中国想推行什么？

刘晓明： 中国致力于构建和谐世界。我们主张国与国相互尊重、相互包容，而不是把自己的价值观和社会制度强加给别人，这样的世界才更加和平，更加繁荣。我们主张世界各国携手努力，保障各国共同安全与福祉，维护世界和平与稳定。我们坚决反对在国际事务中诉诸武力。

帕克斯曼： 现在我们来谈谈中国的经济实力。中国现在拥有数万亿美元的外汇储备，这么多钱干什么用？

刘晓明： 中国仍然是一个相对不富裕的国家。虽然中国的经济总量仅次于美国，居世界第二，但中国人均GDP在全球仍排在100位以后。中国仍有近7亿人生活在农村。按照联合国每天1美元的贫困线标准，中国仍有1.5亿人生活在贫困线之下。脱贫致富、改善民生仍是中国政府的重要职责。

帕克斯曼： 现在谈谈人权这个棘手问题。知名艺术家艾未未曾说，缺乏言论自由的世界是蛮荒之地。你是否能理解他在说什么？

刘晓明： 艾未未并不缺乏言论自由，否则，你怎么知道他讲了什么？

帕克斯曼： 不幸的是，他的言论使他遭受牢狱之灾。

刘晓明： 你的说法不对。事实是，他曾因涉嫌逃避缴纳税款、故意销毁会计凭证等犯罪行为而受到调查。在任何法治国家，公民都需要尊重、遵守法律，没有人可以凌驾于法律之上，即使所谓"知名"艺术家也不例外，触犯了法律，就要受到法律的制裁。这在中国如此，在英国恐怕也是一样。

帕克斯曼： 但艾未未应该有自由表达言论的权利。

刘晓明： 如果艾未未没有自由表达言论的权利，你怎么会知道他的言论？

帕克斯曼： 好的，大使先生，非常感谢你接受采访。

刘晓明： 感谢你的邀请。

A Live Interview with Jeremy Paxman on BBC *Newsnight*

On 23rd January 2012, I had a live and one-on-one interview with Jeremy Paxman on BBC 2's *Newsnight* programme. The transcript of the interview goes as follows:

Paxman: Happy New Year! Mr. Ambassador.

Liu Xiaoming: Thank you.

Paxman: Let's try to define our terms. Are you a communist?

Liu Xiaoming: In China, the ruling party is the communist party. The communist party now has more than 80 million party members. But you have to remember China is a country with 1.3 billion people. So I don't think you can call China a communist country, just as you can not call the UK conservative UK.

Paxman: But you could call the UK a capitalist country.

Liu Xiaoming: And we say China is a socialist country. We could call China a socialist country with Chinese characteristics.

Paxman: Talking to the young people, in particular in Beijing, I very strongly got the impression that they were pretty optimistic about China's international role. They saw this as a century which was developing very much in a way that was going to make China a much more significant force in the world. Do you think that?

Liu Xiaoming: China will certainly contribute its part to maintaining peace and

prosperity in the world. But we do not see China as a superpower. I would characterize China as the largest developing country with increasing international influence and responsibilities.

Paxman: But people look at what China does on the UN Security Council, for example, over the question of—you opposed the sanctions on Syria, sanctions on Iran, and they wonder, you know, what you are trying to achieve?

Liu Xiaoming: That's not the right impression. In fact, China voted four times with other members of the Security Council on the issue of Iran. China is strongly opposed to the Iranian nuclear weapon programme. But on the other hand, we believe diplomatic and peaceful solution is the most beneficial solution to the problem. It costs less and it's in the interest of maintaining peace and stability in the region.

Paxman: But do you accept that Iran is a potential threat to world peace, a nuclear armed Iran?

Liu Xiaoming: I would say, yes, Iran with nuclear weapons is not in the interest of peace and stability in the region. So that is why China made it very clear from day one that we are strongly opposed to Iran developing nuclear weapons. That has been reaffirmed by the Chinese Premier in his recent visit to the region.

Paxman: So why not impose sanctions, then?

Liu Xiaoming: There are already sanctions in place. But we don't think sanction for the sake of sanction serves the purpose. We also encouraged peaceful negotiations to engage Iran for a peaceful settlement of this issue.

Paxman: Do you think China has a moral role in the world?

Liu Xiaoming: I think China has a role to play, in terms of building a more peaceful, harmonious world.

Paxman: But what do you try to promote? The United States, for example, says it promotes, and will go to war, to promote democracy. What do you try to promote?

Liu Xiaoming: We are promoting a harmonious world. We believe the world will be more peaceful, prosperous, if all countries respect each other, rather than imposing their own ideas and systems onto others. We believe mutual respect, mutual accommodation and working together for the common good, common security is in the interest of peace and stability of the world. So we are strongly opposed to any military solutions.

Paxman: What about economic power? China sits on this mountain of trillions of dollars worth of foreign exchange. What's that for?

Liu Xiaoming: China is still a relatively poor country. Though China now is number two in terms of GDP, after only the United States. But in per capita GDP, China is still behind 100 countries. There are still about 700 million people living in the countryside. And there are about 150 million people living under one US dollar a day, that is the UN poverty line. So there is an enormous responsibility for the Chinese government to improve livelihood of those parts of the population of China.

Paxman: And let's talk a little bit about that difficult matter of human rights. Ai Weiwei, the well known artist, says that without free speech, you are living in a barbaric world. Do you understand what he's getting at?

Liu Xiaoming: I think Ai Weiwei has his freedom to express his view. Otherwise how could you get his opinion on this?

Paxman: Unfortunately, he has been in prison of course, isn't it?

Liu Xiaoming: No, he was under investigation on suspicion of evading tax, destroying his accounting books. In any country of rule by law, you have to respect and abide by the law. Nobody in a country ruled by law should be above the law. So even a so-called well-known artist has to abide by the law. When he violates the law, he should be punished. There's no doubt about that in China, I guess it's the same in Britain.

Paxman: He should be free to say what he likes, shouldn't he?

Liu Xiaoming: If he is forbidden to voice his opinions, how could you get to know them?

Paxman: All right, Mr. Ambassador, thank you very much.

Liu Xiaoming: Thank you for having me.

Newsnight is a weekday BBC 2 current affairs programme which specialises in analysis and often robust cross-examination. Jeremy Paxman, a well-known British journalist and commentator, has been its main presenter for over two decades.

接受英国BBC广播四台《今日》栏目
主持人戴维斯现场直播采访

作者手记

2012年3月14日，我在英国BBC广播四台《今日》（Today）栏目演播室，接受主持人埃文·戴维斯（Evan Davis）现场直播采访。当天，十一届全国人大五次会议闭幕，BBC邀请我谈谈中国"两会"。

《今日》栏目是BBC广播四台旗舰节目，每天早上6—9点播放时政要闻、访谈、座谈，以深度新闻分析和激烈辩论著称，在英国被誉为对设置政治议题最具影响力的节目，是英国首相、大臣、议员、政党领袖、社会精英必听的节目，每周听众达1100万人次。前文已介绍过主持人戴维斯，这是我们第一次见面。采访主要围绕"两会"、民主、选举、中国政治体制改革以及朝鲜等问题展开。

采访实录如下：

戴维斯： 中国"两会"刚刚闭幕。中国的全国人大是世界上最大的议会，有近3000名代表，每年会期两周左右。在今年人大会议闭幕记者招待会上，温家宝总理发表了一些有意思的讲话。他说中国将推进经济和政治体制改革，促进财富共享，同时将允许人民币汇率更大幅度自由波动。

今天我们很高兴邀请到中国驻英国大使刘晓明来到我们的演播室。早上好！

刘晓明： 早上好！

戴维斯： 感谢你接受采访。我们能谈谈民主吗？你认为中国正在走向拥有更加公开、自由选举的西方式民主吗？现在中国的全国人大并不是选举产生的吧？

刘晓明： 中国的全国人大代表是选举产生的，我认为这样的选举体现了中国式的民主，即有中国特色的民主体制。西方舆论很关注温总理关于政治改革的讲话，我认为温总理的讲话是重申中国政府在这一问题上的基本立场。对中国过去30多年来的改革开放，西方一些人只看到经济改革，而看不到中国的改革是全方位的，不仅有经济改革，也有政治体制改革。

戴维斯： 你认为中国的政治体制改革能走多远呢？

刘晓明： 我想如果拿现在的中国和30年前相对比，你会发现中国取得了长足进步。中国改革开放的总设计师邓小平先生在开启改革开放之初，就将政治改革作为一项重要任务。中国过去实行了几千年的封建统治，直到中华人民共和国成立后才建立了社会主义民主制度。这个制度并不尽善尽美，我们在持续不断地探索如何加强中国政府的问责制，使其运作体制更为高效和民主。但是看看今天中国的变化，恐怕只能用"天翻地覆"来形容。

戴维斯： 但是中国有这么一群人，他们已跻身中产阶级，比上一辈人富裕很多。你认为他们是否希望在国家事务中多一点发言权、能够拥有对领导者不好的做法进行反抗的权利？他们可能会说："我们不想处处听人指挥，我们要发言权。"你认为你刚刚所描述的渐进式改革能否满足公众的需求而不带来严重危机或社会动荡？

刘晓明： 我认为，中国的政治改革正处于进行时。任何制度都不是完美的。我们取得的进步是巨大的，但仍有改进空间。中国政府做了很多努力确保中央和地方政府更好地对人民负责，打击腐败，使人们享有公平获得信息的渠道。举个例子来说，最近中国全国人大改革了代表选举办法。过去城镇代表要多于农村代表，现在城镇和农村可按同一比例选举人大代表，这就是要赋予所有人平等发声的权利。

戴维斯： 你是《今日》栏目的听众吗？

刘晓明： 是的。

戴维斯： 当你听到我的同事们在访谈节目中痛斥政客或对他们态度强硬

时，你会怎么想？这是好事还是坏事？

刘晓明： 这也许不是坏事。我发现一个很有趣的现象，它也许反映了东西方文化的不同。中国和不少亚洲国家的民众比西方民众更尊重他们的领导人。究其原因，不知是你们的政治家干得不好，还是中国和亚洲国家领导人工作更出色。总而言之，亚洲领导人更受到他们国家人民的尊重。

戴维斯： 要谈的东西太多了，比如叙利亚、朝鲜。你曾经在朝鲜工作，对吗？

刘晓明： 是的，我在那里常驻了三年半。

戴维斯： 虽然我应该谈叙利亚，但我还是想问朝鲜问题。中国什么时候采取行动？因为那里的形势最终取决于中国。朝鲜的情况很糟糕，2500万人被一个"疯狂的"家族劫持着。中国想什么时候结束这种情况，说"够了，我们需要朝鲜也进行改革"？

刘晓明： 朝鲜是我们的近邻，我们希望他们经济发展、繁荣。在我们看来，当务之急是保持朝鲜半岛的和平稳定。因此，我们希望与朝鲜保持良好关系。朝鲜人民应当有美好的未来。我们认为，确保朝鲜半岛稳定的最佳办法是与朝鲜接触，而不是孤立他们。中国一直与朝鲜保持积极接触。现在朝鲜有了新的领导人，应当为他执政提供良好的外部环境。朝鲜新领导人上台以来，已经有了一些积极的变化，朝鲜和美国在核问题和援助方面达成了一些协议。如果有关国家都能相向而行，共同努力，朝鲜半岛的未来必将更加美好。

戴维斯： 但重要的是要帮助朝鲜人民。据我们所知20世纪90年代一场饥荒就饿死了数百万人。我们要让朝鲜，或者说鼓励、强迫朝鲜领导层进行中国式的改革。

刘晓明： 中国一贯奉行不干涉内政的原则。我们认为，应当由一国的人民自己决定国家的未来。

戴维斯： 我真希望我们的采访能一直谈下去。大使先生，我现在知道你也是我们节目的听众了，以后可以邀请你再次接受采访，谈更多的问题。谢谢你。

刘晓明： 不客气。

A Live Interview with Evan Davis
on BBC Radio 4 *Today* Programme

On 14th March 2012, following the closing of the annual NPC and CPPCC sessions in Beijing, I did a live interview with Evan Davis on BBC Radio 4's *Today* programme. The transcript of the interview is as follows:

Davis: As you've heard, China's National People's Congress has just finished its annual sitting. It is the world's biggest parliament, has almost 3, 000 members and tends to meet a couple of weeks a year. This year Chinese Premier Wen Jiabao closed the congress with a press conference where he made some rather interesting comments about stepping up economic and political reforms to spread wealth wider. He also said that Beijing would allow the currency the yuan to float more freely.
With us in this studio, I am pleased to say we have the Chinese Ambassador to the UK, Mr. Liu Xiaoming. A very good morning to you!

Liu Xiaoming: Good morning!

Davis: Thank you for coming in. Can we talk about democracy? Do you think China is on a path to more western style democracy with more open elections, freer elections? I mean the parliament doesn't actually have any elections at the moment, does it?

Liu Xiaoming: Yes, we do have elections. But I think that's Chinese democracy. That means democracy with Chinese characteristics. I think many people focus on what Premier Wen has said about political reform. But Premier Wen basically reiterated the position of the Chinese government with regard to political reform. For the past 30 years, China has engaged in reform and opening-up, but some people in Western world only pay attention to economic reform. In fact this reform is all-round reform. It is not only about economics, but also about political reform.

Davis: How far can it go, do you think?

Liu Xiaoming: I think China has come a long way, if we compare China today with China 30 years ago. When Mr. Deng Xiaoping started this reform and opening-up, one of the top priorities on his agenda was political reform. China had been ruled by emperors for thousands of years. It was not until after the founding of the People's Republic that we adopted what we call a socialist democracy system. But it is not perfect. So it is always on the road of practicing, searching for new methods, how to make our system more effective, more accountable, more democratic. But if you look at China today, it is quite changed, and is what we call "tremendous transformation".

Davis: But there are people in China, who perhaps are a little more middle-class, a little more affluent than they were a generation ago. Do you think they will like a little more say in the way the country is run? We had commune rebellion against bad actions of their leaders. People are beginning to say, " Look, we don't want to be bossed around and we're not going to be told. We like to have some say. " Do you think you can deliver that to the public on this gradual path that, as you said, has been changing already, without great crisis, rupture, or social disruption?

Liu Xiaoming: I would say political reform is already an ongoing process. No system is perfect. We have made tremendous progress and achievements, but there is still a lot of room to improve. I think the government has made a lot of efforts on how to make the government, both central and local, more accountable to the people and how to fight corruption, how to make people have access to information. For instance, the recent National People's Congress you mentioned has reformed the way people elect their deputies. In the past, the cities had more deputies than the countryside. Now we have it more evenly, more balanced. So, people will have their equal voice.

Davis: Now tell me this. Do you listen to *Today* programme in your role as Ambassador?

Liu Xiaoming: Yes.

Davis: What do you think when you hear my colleagues sitting next to me here berating a politician or interviewing him very toughly? Do you think that is a good thing or a bad thing?

Liu Xiaoming: It might not be a bad thing. That is a different culture. In fact I find it very interesting. I find Chinese people, Asians in general, show more respect to their leaders than the Western public. I am still trying to find out the answer, whether your politicians did a good job or maybe Chinese leaders and Asian state leaders have done a better job. But, they earned more respect from their public.

Davis: There are so many things we can talk about, because, there is Syria, there is North Korea. Your were based in North Korea, I think?

Liu Xiaoming: Yes, for three and a half years.

Davis: I just want to ask you about North Korea, but I know I should talk to you about Syria. When is China going to — because it is all down to China. North Korea is a country where 25 million people have been held hostage, more or less, by a mad family. When is China going to pull the plug on that and just say, "Look, enough is enough. We need reform in North Korea as well?"

Liu Xiaoming: We see the DPRK as our close neighbour. We certainly would like to see them enjoy prosperity and economic development. And peace and stability are our top priority. So we want to have good relations with the country. We believe their people deserve a better future. So we think the best way to ensure stability in the Korean peninsula is to engage with them, rather than isolate them. That is why China engages very actively with what we call the DPRK. Now they have a new leader. We believe that he should be given the opportunity to carry out his duties. It seems to me there are good signs since the coming of the new leadership. The United States and the DPRK reached agreement on the nuclear programme, and on aid programme. We believe that if all countries work together, we will have a better future for the Korean peninsula.

Davis: It's about helping the people in North Korea though. We know a famine killed a couple of million people in the 1990s. It's about letting and encouraging, or indeed imposing reform on the leadership there, domestic reform of the kind China has engaged in so the population can have a …

Liu Xiaoming: China has always followed the principle of non-interference in the internal affairs of other people. We believe it is up to the people to decide the future of their respective countries.

Davis: We could talk for ages. Ambassador, we know now you listen to the *Today* programme. We can get you on and grill you again on many issues. Liu Xiaoming, thank you very much for coming in.

Liu Xiaoming: Thank you for having me.

Today, colloquially known as the *Today* programme, is a long-running BBC early-morning news and current-affairs radio programme on BBC Radio 4. It is the highest-rated programme on Radio 4 and one of the BBC's most popular programmes across its radio networks. Evan Davis joined the presenter team on *Today* in April 2008 following a six-and-a-half year stint as the BBC's economics editor.

接受英国BBC《新闻之夜》栏目
主持人艾斯勒现场直播采访

作者手记

2012年12月21日，我在英国BBC旗舰栏目《新闻之夜》（*Newsnight*）演播室，接受该栏目主持人加文·艾斯勒（Gavin Esler）现场直播采访。

艾斯勒是英国知名作家、记者、评论员，担任《新闻之夜》栏目主持人长达11年，并兼任BBC多个栏目主持人，曾采访多国政要。从2014起，担任英国肯特大学名誉校长。其采访风格以稳健、专注、深邃著称。

当时正值中共十八大闭幕不久，采访围绕十八大展开。我向他介绍了十八大选出的新一届领导集体和十八大为中国未来5年乃至更长时间绘制的新蓝图。我们还谈了反腐败、互联网、新闻自由、民主、人权、中国的大国作用、中日关系、叙利亚等问题。

在他要宣布采访结束前，我指出演播室背景中国地图的错误，说它缺少中国领土十分重要的一部分，那就是台湾。中国人民十分珍视领土完整。艾斯勒说，我确信这一点，看来我们还要请你回来接着讨论这个话题。

采访实录如下：

艾斯勒： 大使先生，谈到高层换届，我们首先想到的是选举，大规模人事调整和新领导人当选。外界对中共十八大领导人换届并不太明白。你认为这次换届重要吗？

刘晓明： 我认为中共十八大对中国未来发展至关重要。十八大选出了新一届领导集体，他们将在今后5年乃至更长的时间领导中国。他们年富力强、作风务实，基层经验丰富。他们中有的人有农村工作经历，有的在厂矿工作过。十八大还为中国未来5年甚至更长时间描绘了新的蓝图，那就是全面建成小康社会。我们的目标是到2020年实现GDP在2010年的基础上翻一番。

艾斯勒： 10年内GDP翻一番？

刘晓明： 对。不仅GDP翻一番，而且人均收入也翻一番。

艾斯勒： 中国共产党的新领导人习近平谈到打击腐败问题，他很清楚腐败引发了民众的不满。中国必须整治腐败，否则老百姓会更加不满。但中国将如何打击腐败？

刘晓明： 我认为腐败不是中国独有的问题。中国现在处在社会转型时期，总会出现这样那样的问题。邓小平先生在中国改革开放初期曾说，窗户打开了，清新的空气会进来，同时苍蝇和蚊子也会进来。关键是看党如何面对问题，如何采取措施解决问题。我认为，中国领导人对打击腐败问题，决心是坚定的，态度是坚决的。

艾斯勒： 你认为互联网是苍蝇、蚊子吗？互联网是否让中国感到棘手？我们不理解中国为什么要控制公众交流信息，中国在担心什么？

刘晓明： 我认为这是对中国互联网发展的误解。事实上，中国在互联网问题上是很开放的。我们拥有世界上最多的网民。

艾斯勒： 但我们的记者在中国就用不了脸书、推特等西方社交网站。情况和你所描述的不完全一致。

刘晓明： 每天，在中国，博客们在网上发表成千上万条评论，66%的中国网民在网上经常发表评论。政府的职能是管理规范互联网使用，使网民获得有益的信息，对不健康及有害的内容予以清除，以确保互联网健康有序运行。

艾斯勒： 但这应该由普通民众决定。中国有数千年的发明创造史。我们认为信息自由是创造力的源泉。西方人认为中国因为不喜欢某些观点而采取严厉压制措施，这影响了信息流动，是非常不利的。

刘晓明： 如果你在中国上网，你会接触到各种观点，非常开放。包括政治、经济、文化的各种议题都可以讨论。你应该对中国互联网有更加全面的认识。

艾斯勒： 大使先生，有一个重要观点能否帮我们解释一下？这就是中国希望在2020年GDP翻一番，成为世界上最大的经济体，中国希望在世界上发挥什么样的作用？

刘晓明： 中国当然希望发挥一个负责任的大国作用。我们称自己为负有全球责任的最大发展中国家。我们希望为世界和平与稳定做出贡献，因为我们需要一个和平的国际环境发展自己。

艾斯勒： 因为没有和平，经济发展无从谈起。

刘晓明： 确实如此。另一方面，中国的和平发展也将对世界和平与繁荣做出贡献。同时，中国的经济发展也会推动世界经济的增长。

艾斯勒： 但与此同时，如何理解一些看似小问题但可能会演变成大问题的事态，比如中日围绕海上一些礁石的争端就可能引发冲突。

刘晓明： 我们当然愿与日本保持良好的关系。我知道你是在说钓鱼岛，事实上，钓鱼岛自古以来就是中国的领土。

艾斯勒： 但日本好像并不这样认为。我们对此感到担心。

刘晓明： 日本借1895年中国在甲午战争中战败之机，非法窃取了钓鱼岛。1943年，英美中三国领导人丘吉尔、罗斯福、蒋介石在开罗开会，发表了《开罗宣言》，明确要求日本无条件将所有窃取的领土归还中国。

艾斯勒： 中国是否能够和平解决这一问题？

刘晓明： 中国当然致力于通过和平方式解决钓鱼岛问题。

艾斯勒： 另一个中国可以发挥作用同时也很具有争议的问题是叙利亚。俄罗斯总统普京表示并不关心阿萨德政权的命运。中国政府关心阿萨德政权的命运吗？

刘晓明： 我们关心的是叙利亚人民的命运。我认为，应当由叙利亚人民来决定谁是他们的领导人。中国之所以反对西方国家在联合国安理会提出的一些涉叙决议，就是因为这些决议主张政权更迭。

艾斯勒： 你认为阿萨德倒台是件坏事吗？

刘晓明： 我想这要由叙利亚人民来决定。叙利亚人民认为符合自身利益的选择，中国都会赞同。由谁来担任叙利亚的领导人，叙利亚应建立什么样的政权，不应由中国来决定，而应由叙利亚人民自己来决定。

艾斯勒： 但很明显，大多数叙利亚人民希望阿萨德下台，期待获得外国帮助，这才是问题所在。

刘晓明： 这要看你同叙利亚哪一方说话。当前叙利亚正陷于内战状态，国内既有反对派，也有政府的支持者。现在重要的是立即停火止暴，早日启动政治过渡进程。

艾斯勒： 我们西方人需要明白的一点也许可以用英国作家鲁德亚德·吉卜林的一句话来概括，这就是"东方与西方永远无法完全理解对方"。你是否认同这一说法？

刘晓明： 在我看来，西方未能很好地理解中国。在西方一直存在着严重的对华偏见。一谈到中国，一些人总是摆脱不掉冷战思维。他们不喜欢共产党，所以往往以观察苏联的视角来看中国，从而无法了解真实的中国。我希望人们能多一些"理智与情感"，少一些"傲慢与偏见"。

艾斯勒： 这的确又是另一位英国作家的名言。可以说，自邓小平时代以来，中国发生了翻天覆地的变化。"中国共产党"这一称谓已经很难帮助外界理解中国的发展道路。现在听起来，中国共产党已经不是一个真正意义上的共产党了。

刘晓明： 我认为，这是对中国共产党的误解。在中国，中国共产党坚持走中国特色社会主义道路。中国共产党将马克思主义理论与中国国情相结合，建立了中国特色社会主义制度。这一制度符合中国实际，给中国带来了发展与进步，并取得了巨大成功。对于这样一种行之有效、造福广大人民、得到广大人民拥护的制度，为什么要改旗易帜呢？

艾斯勒：　你非常明确地指出西方对中国存在误解。但中国是不是对西方也有误解？当我们谈论人权、互联网等西方十分看重的问题时，并不是要试图占上风，而是相信指出这些问题有助于提升中国的创新能力。

刘晓明：　我们欢迎善意的批评。同任何一个国家一样，中国并不完美，还有很多需要改进的地方。但我们坚决反对别国干涉中国的内政，反对以人权为工具企图改变中国的政治制度，企图抹黑中国，这是我们不能接受的。

艾斯勒：　大使先生……

刘晓明：　在我们结束之前，我还想指出一点来说明中西方之间的不同。在你们演播室，我身后这张背景中的中国地图就有错误。它缺少中国领土十分重要的一部分，那就是台湾，它比这张地图上海南省的面积还要大。我们中国人民十分珍视领土完整。

艾斯勒：　我确信这一点。看来我们还要请你回来，下次我们再接着讨论这个话题。感谢你，大使先生。

刘晓明：　不客气。

A Live Interview with Gavin Esler on BBC *Newsnight*

On 12th December 2012, I gave a live interview to Gavin Esler on BBC *Newsnight*. I answered questions about the 18th National Congress of the Communist Party of China and China's development, cyber space governance and foreign policy. The full text is as follows:

Esler: Ambassador, when we think of a change at the top, we think of elections, we think about a whole lot of people swept away and completely new people coming in. This doesn't look like such a big deal to those outside your country. Has it been a big deal?

Liu Xiaoming: With regard to the 18th Party Congress, I think it's a big deal in terms of China's future development. I would say it's significant because it elected the new leadership which will lead the country for the next five years and even beyond. And this new leadership is young, energetic, and down-to-earth. They have a lot of experience with the grassroots, some of them even worked in the countryside and factories. And also this congress produced a new blueprint for China for the next five years and even beyond. That is to build China into a well-off society. The target is to double the GDP of 2010 by 2020.

Esler: So in 10 years you'll double GDP?

Liu Xiaoming: Yes, in 10 years, not only double the GDP, but also double the per capita income of the people.

Esler: What about that specific point that the new leader Mr. Xi made about corruption, which he knows really angers ordinary people? And you've got to crack

down on it. But how you are going to actually do that, deliver, because it will make these people even angrier if you don't do it in these five or ten years.

Liu Xiaoming: I think corruption is, not a problem for China alone. Once you are in a period of social transformation, it's unavoidable you have all kinds of problems. Just like Deng Xiaoping once said at the beginning of the opening up in China. He said "when we open the window and let in the fresh air, it is unavoidable that flies and mosquitoes will come in. " But the important thing is how the party faces up to it and adopts measures to deal with this problem. I think the leadership is resolute and determined.

Esler: Do you see things like the Internet as being like flies and mosquitoes? I mean do you see it as a bit of an irritation. Because again, from our side, we don't understand what you are worried about, when you want to control how people exchange information.

Liu Xiaoming: I think there is a misperception about the Internet development in China. In fact, China is much more open in terms of the Internet. China has the most number of internet users.

Esler: But our correspondent can't even get onto Facebook when he's in China. I mean you can't get onto Twitter. It's not quite as you presented.

Liu Xiaoming: In China, every day, there are hundreds of thousands of comments made by bloggers and 66 percent of Chinese internet users make comments online. It is up to the government to regulate the use of internet in protection of the safety of the internet to ensure that healthy content is available and unhealthy content should be removed.

Esler: But isn't that really up to the ordinary people to decide. Looking at the history of your country, you've had thousands of years of creativity and we see creativity is based on the free exchange of information. And part of the reasons why people in the West think your crackdown has been very hard on bloggers and is very difficult for some people because you don't like certain ideas.

Liu Xiaoming: If you are in China and get connected to the Internet, I think you can get all kinds of opinions. It's much more open than you suggest and a lot of things can be debated including politics, economic, cultural affairs. I think you have to have a big picture of the internet development in China.

Esler: Ambassador, can you help us with the main point? China may become, with the ambition of doubling the GDP by 2020, the world's biggest economy, but what world role does China want to have?

Liu Xiaoming: China certainly wants to play a role as a responsible country. We call ourselves the largest developing country with global responsibility. We want to contribute to peace and stability of the world because we need a peaceful environment to develop our own country.

Esler: Because you couldn't have that economic development without peace.

Liu Xiaoming: That's right. And China's peaceful development in turn will contribute to peace and prosperity of the world. And I think China's growth is also a big contributor to the world economic growth.

Esler: How does that square with what seem to us as quite small problems which could become very big problems, for instance the potential for conflict with Japan over a bunch of rocks in the sea?

Liu Xiaoming: We certainly would like to have good relations with Japan. I know you are talking about the Diaoyu Islands. In fact, these islands have belonged to China since ancient times.

Esler: You know this is not quite how the Japanese see it. We are worried about it.

Liu Xiaoming: It was not until 1895 when China lost the first war with Japan that Japan illegally seized these islands. It was in 1943 when Churchill, Roosevelt and Chiang Kai-shek met in Cairo. They issued the *Cairo Declaration*. And in this *Cairo Declaration*, it declared in explicit terms that all territories seized by Japan from China

should be returned to China without any conditions.

Esler: Does that mean you can resolve it peacefully, you think.

Liu Xiaoming: Of course, we want to resolve this peacefully with Japan.

Esler: One other issue which China has had a role which has been very controversial, which is the question of Syria. We've got President Putin saying that we are not concerned about the fate of the Assad regime. Is the Chinese government concerned about the Assad regime?

Liu Xiaoming: We are concerned about the fate of the Syrian people. I think it's up to the Syrian people to decide who will be their leaders. So the reason why China opposed some of the resolutions tabled by Western countries in UN Security Council is because these resolutions called for regime change.

Esler: Do you think it will be a bad thing if Assad went?

Liu Xiaoming: I think it's up to the Syrian people. If the Syrian people believe what is good to them, we will agree with them. It's not up to China to decide who should be their leader and what kind of the regime should be in place. I think it's up to the Syrian people.

Esler: But isn't it kind of obvious that most Syrian people want to rid of him and they would like help from outsiders. And that is a problem.

Liu Xiaoming: It depends on which side of the Syrian people you are talking to. I think Syria is in a civil war situation. You have opposition and you also have the people behind the government. So the important thing is to bring about a ceasefire and to immediately start this political transition process. I think that's the most important thing: to stop violence.

Esler: One of the big things we in the West have to get our head around is perhaps summarized by British writer Rudyard Kipling, who said that the East and the West will never completely understand each other. Do you think that's true?

Liu Xiaoming: I think there's a problem for Western countries to understand China. There's a strong bias against China. When it comes to China, some people are still haunted by this cold war mentality. They do not like communist party, so whenever they see China, they see China through the lens they use to look at the former Soviet Union. And that really prevented them from having a big picture of China. So I do hope that we have more sense and sensibility rather than pride and prejudice.

Esler: Right. It was a quote from another famous English author. I mean in terms of that, so much has changed since the Deng Xiaoping era, even the phrase Chinese communist party does not sound to outsiders as if it sums up where China is going. It sounds like a very uncommunist communist party.

Liu Xiaoming: I think there's a misunderstanding about the communist party in China. In China, the Communist Party still upholds the path of Chinese socialism. We call it socialism with Chinese characteristics. It has combined the Marxist theory with realities of China. The system suits China. It can deliver. It's successful. So why should we change this system when it's still effective and it can still deliver benefits to its people and is welcome by its people.

Esler: You've been very clear on how we might misunderstand you. Do you think you sometimes misunderstand us, which is in saying that when we talk about human rights issue, the internet, all those kinds of issues which seem quite important to us, it's not to be triumphant about that, it is to suggest actually you will be a more creative country if you have some of these?

Liu Xiaoming: We welcome criticism with good intention. Because we don't think China is perfect. Just like any countries, there's much room to improve. But we are strongly opposed to interference in China's internal affairs and the use of human rights as tools to change China's political system, to humiliate China. That is something we can not accept.

Esler: Ambassador ...

Liu Xiaoming: Before we finish, I just want to mention one thing about how we have differences. Like the map behind me. There is one mistake. There is one important part of China that is missing. That's Taiwan. It's much bigger than the Hainan Island. We Chinese people hold territorial integrity dearly.

Esler: Indeed. Perhaps you'll come back and we can talk again about this. Thank you.

Liu Xiaoming: My pleasure.

Newsnight is one of the best known current affairs programs on BBC TWO. It has built a reputation for the depth of its analysis and intensive cross-examination, with strong influence across the broad spectrum of politics and intelligentsia. Being a prominent author and correspondent, Mr. Gavin Esler joined the *Newsnight* in 2003 and has interviewed a broad range of world leaders.

接受英国天空新闻台《杰夫·兰德直播间》栏目主持人兰德现场直播采访

作者手记

　　2014年1月14日，我在英国天空新闻台（SKY NEWS）演播室，接受该台访谈栏目《杰夫·兰德直播间》(*Jeff Randall Live*)主持人杰夫·兰德(Jeff Randall)现场直播采访。

　　《杰夫·兰德直播间》是天空新闻台财经和时事旗舰访谈栏目，主持人邀请英国和外国政要、商界领袖、知识精英等，就国内外热点问题进行一对一对话。每周一至周四晚7—8点黄金时段播出，观众100多万人次。

　　兰德是英国著名专栏作家、记者，曾在BBC担任商业主编。2007年创办《杰夫·兰德直播间》栏目，直至2014年3月。也就是说，我是做客《杰夫·兰德直播间》的最后几位嘉宾。

　　采访当天，英中贸易协会在伦敦举行"中国商业大会"，卡梅伦首相发来贺信，我在会上发表主旨演讲。天空新闻台提出，兰德希望邀请我谈谈"中国商业大会"。但整个采访过程，兰德没有提一个关于"中国商业大会"的问题。针对他对中国的一些误解，我介绍了中共十八届三中全会和中国特色社会主义。我们

还谈了中国的网络管理、中英经贸合作、东西方交流、中日关系
等问题。

采访实录如下：

兰德： 下面接受采访的是中国驻英国大使刘晓明。见到你很高兴，感谢
你接受采访。

刘晓明： 感谢你的邀请。

兰德： 在我看来，今年对中国领导人来说是决定成败的关键一年。2013
年，中国领导人推出了财政、土地和商业等一系列改革计划。而
今年，落实计划的时候到了。

刘晓明： 没错。去年对中国来说是十分重要的一年。中国共产党召开十八
届三中全会，中国新一届领导集体推出了全面深化改革的总体计划。
这一计划涵盖五大领域，不仅包括经济改革，也包括政治、社
会、文化和生态环境改革，这些改革将给中国带来翻天覆地的变化。

兰德： 在我看来，为了保持人们的信心，中国必须对私营资本竞争开放
更多领域。用不了多久，中国将成为一个由共产党领导的资本主
义国家。

刘晓明： 这种看法是不对的。我们现在建设的是中国特色社会主义。正如邓小平所说，市场和计划都是经济手段。计划经济不等于社会主义，资本主义也有计划；市场经济不等于资本主义，社会主义也有市场。中国取市场和计划两者之长，最大限度发挥制度优势。

兰德： 显而易见，中国希望进入高端产业并成为全球商业领军者。当今世界，发展最为强劲的产业之一当数媒体。我们今天都看到了时代华纳有线电视公司招标的消息。然而，《纽约时报》、彭博社、脸书、推特在华均被屏蔽。中国想要掩饰什么？

刘晓明： 中国依法管理媒体。重要的是，无论是中国媒体还是外国媒体都必须遵守中国法律，服务于人民的利益。我们关注的是信息健康以及是否有利于增进中外相互了解。

兰德： 你的意思是说，中国要的是"宣传"，而非"事实"？

刘晓明： 这种说法是错误的，我们一直讲的就是事实。

兰德： 但是彭博社、脸书和推特究竟会发表什么损害中国利益的信息？

刘晓明： 这个问题你应该去问他们。我们希望他们在中国依法从业，遵守职业道德，而不是散布诋毁中国的谣言和偏见。这不利于促进中外相互了解。

兰德： 随着中国日益成为全球经济的重要力量，这种秘密封锁总有一天会被打破。随着中国人日益走出国门，人们最终会发现真相。

刘晓明： 中国的开放程度远远超出西方人的想象。如今，中国人足迹遍布世界各地，中国人十分了解国外的情况。遗憾的是西方却缺乏对中国的足够了解。两者之间存在巨大不平衡。西方总有一些人抱着冷战思维，戴着有色眼镜和陈旧的思维定式看中国。我认为，西方媒体和记者尤应以更加广阔的视野全面看待中国。

兰德： 关于双边贸易，中国公司在英国表现强劲。他们收购了许多英国著名企业，包括维他麦、地产公司、时装品牌、罗孚汽车等。但英国公司却不能赴华收购中国公司。这种情况是不是应该结束了？这方面应该是双向的才行。

刘晓明： 的确应当如此。贸易是双向的。事实上，英国在对华贸易方面做得很好。

兰德： 可英国还是不能收购中国公司。

刘晓明： 为什么不能？本周初，我出席了中英首只在伦敦发行的RQFII投资基金发起仪式。任何个人投资者都可以对其进行投资。说到贸易，英国去年在对华出口方面表现出色。英国对华出口增长13.8%，远远超出中国其他欧盟贸易伙伴。

兰德： 最后一个问题是关于你们"家门口"的外交问题。中国与日本之间在一些无人居住的小岛问题上存在争端。许多人认为中国正在展示军事实力、清算旧账。不是这样吗？

刘晓明： 不是这样。事实是，日本首相悍然参拜供奉有甲级战犯的靖国神社，甲级战犯就是日本的纳粹。试想如果德国领导人参拜希特勒或其他纳粹战犯，英国人民将做何感想？将心比心，就能更好地理解中国人民的感受。

兰德： 大使，很高兴与你交谈，感谢你拨冗接受采访。

刘晓明： 谢谢邀请。

A Live Interview with Jeff Randall on Sky News

On 14th January 2014, I gave a live interview on *Jeff Randall Live* on Sky News. I answered questions from Jeff Randall on a wide range of issues, including the Third Plenum of the 18th Central Committee of the Communist Party of China, China's economic reform, China-UK economic cooperation and trade, media and internet management, exchanges between the East and the West and China-Japan relations. The transcript of the interview goes as follows:

Randall: Joining me now is China's Ambassador to the UK Liu Xiaoming. Ambassador, lovely to see you. Thank you for coming in.

Liu Xiaoming: Thank you for having me.

Randall: It strikes me that this is a make-or-break year for the leadership in Beijing. In 2013, the President set out plans for fiscal reform, land reform, business reform. This year, he has to deliver.

Liu Xiaoming: That's right. Last year was very important for China. As a result of the Third Plenum of the Communist Party of China, the leadership launched a master plan on what we call "comprehensively deepening reform". In fact, the plan covers all the important areas of the economy. Not only economy, it includes the following major areas: economic reform, political reform, social, cultural and environmental reforms. So I think the country will be completely changed as a result of these reforms.

Randall: It seems to me that in order to maintain the confidence of the people, many more sectors will have to be opened up to private competition. Very soon, this is going to be a capitalist country run by a communist party.

Liu Xiaoming: No. That's not true. In fact, we call it socialism with Chinese characteristics. Just as Deng Xiaoping said, market and plan are just tools of the economy. In a socialist economy, you have a market. And in a capitalist market, you have plan. So I think it's a combination of the two. We try to make the best of the two systems.

Randall: Clearly China wants to be in cutting-edge industries, wants to lead the way in global business. One of the world's booming businesses is media. We saw that bid today for Time Warner Cable. And yet in China, the *New York Times*, Bloomberg, Facebook and Twitter are all blocked. What do you have to hide?

Liu Xiaoming: We manage the media according to law. The important thing is the media, whether foreign or Chinese, have to follow the law of China. And they have to serve the interests of the people. What we are concerned about is healthy content and whether it is in the interest of improving mutual understanding between China and the world.

Randall: Are you saying what you want is propaganda rather than the truth?

Liu Xiaoming: No. That's not true. We are looking for truth.

Randall: But what Bloomberg, Facebook and Twitter possibly publish that would damage your interests?

Liu Xiaoming: You should ask them. We would expect them to be a good citizen in China, rather than spreading rumours and biased stories against China. We don't think that serves the purpose of increasing mutual understanding between China and the outside world.

Randall: As China becomes increasingly a global force in the global economy, this sort of hermetic seal around the country will dissolve, will it not? Because Chinese people will travel increasingly to foreign countries and they will find out the truth.

Liu Xiaoming: China is a much more open country than you can imagine. Chinese people are all over the world. They know the outside world. But unfortunately, it is Western countries who don't know enough of China. There is a big imbalance between how much the Chinese people know the outside world and how much the outside world knows China. Especially in Western world, there are still some people haunted by the "Cold War" mentality. They see China through tinted glass and they see China through stereotyped mindset. I think especially for the Western media and Western journalists, they have to wide open their eyes to see a comprehensive picture of China.

Randall: What about two-way trade, that is part of this deal, the implicit deal? Chinese companies have done very well in the UK. They bought the famous businesses such as the Weetabix, property companies, fashion names, Rover the car company. We in Britain cannot go and buy Chinese companies. That has to end, does it not? It has to be a two-way street.

Liu Xiaoming: Yes, very much so. Trade is a two-way street. In fact, Britain is doing very well in terms of trade.

Randall: But we can't just go and buy a Chinese company.

Liu Xiaoming: Why not? Earlier this week, I was attending an inaugural ceremony, the so-called "ring the bell" for the first RQFII launched here in the UK. All British individual buyers can invest in these shares, in this fund in China. Talking about trade, I think Britain last year did very well in terms of export to China. Your exports to China increased by 13.8%, much higher, way higher, than the other EU partners of China.

Randall: Finally, what about foreign affairs as it were closer to your home. You have this dispute with Japan over uninhabited islands. Many see it as China flexing its military muscles and settling old scores. That is true. Isn't it?

Liu Xiaoming: That's not true. It is the Japanese Prime Minister who visited this war shrine where they honour Class A war criminals of Japan. That is Japanese equivalent of Nazi in Germany. What the British people will feel about if German leaders pay respect to Hitler and other leaders of Nazi? By comparison, you may have a better understanding of the feelings of Chinese people.

Randall: Ambassador, it's been a pleasure. Thanks for coming in. We appreciate your time.

Liu Xiaoming: Thank you for having me.

Jeff Randall Live is one of the most watched evening financial and current affairs programmes in the UK and reaches elite audience from the British political, business and financial circles.

接受英国BBC《新闻之夜》栏目
主持人佩斯顿现场直播采访

作者手记

2015年9月3日,我在英国BBC总部演播室,接受BBC旗舰访谈栏目《新闻之夜》(*Newsnight*)主持人罗伯特·佩斯顿(Robert Peston)现场直播采访。

佩斯顿是英国著名政治评论员、记者、编辑、作家,在多家电视台担任过主持人,曾获多项新闻大奖,包括皇家电视学会年度人物奖。

采访当天正值北京举行纪念中国人民抗日战争暨世界反法西斯战争胜利70周年大会,采访就从纪念大会开始。我向他介绍了习近平主席在10多分钟的讲话中,18次提到"和平",强调这就是中国发出的信息。

我们讨论了中国的军费开支、中国经济、言论自由等问题。

采访实录如下:

佩斯顿： 我们今天邀请到中国驻英国大使刘晓明先生。大使先生，当我想到中国时，我想到的是一个国土辽阔、正迈向现代化、逐渐富裕的国家。但我们今天看到的令人震撼的阅兵场面，会使有些人觉得中国又回到了"毛泽东时代"。中国是否再次向世界发出这样一个信息，即中国是一个危险且令人生畏的国家？

刘晓明： 我认为你得出的印象是错误的。事实上，中国发出的信息响亮而明确，这就是和平。和平来之不易，和平应当珍爱，和平应当维护。中国将为维护世界和平和地区稳定做出自己的贡献。习近平主席在10多分钟的讲话中，18次提到"和平"。这就是中国发出的信息。

佩斯顿： 今天，美国总统奥巴马访问阿拉斯加时，几艘中国军舰正好出现在靠近阿拉斯加的公海上。这是巧合吗？

刘晓明： 我想，我们还是先谈谈今天的纪念大会，之后我再回答你的问题。我说和平来之不易，在西方很少有人了解中国人民为抗日战争做出了多大牺牲。事实上，第二次世界大战发端于中国。中国人民抗日战争开始时间最早、持续时间最长、伤亡人数最多。中国军民伤亡3500万人，占世界各国伤亡总人数约1/3，是二战中伤亡人数最多的国家。因此中国人民把抗日战争和世界反法西斯战争胜利70周年视为一个庆祝胜利、缅怀为国捐躯英烈们的重要时刻。

佩斯顿： 但和平需要中国军费保持如此之快的速度增长吗？去年12%，今年10%。这是一笔巨大的开支。

刘晓明： 请不要忘记，中国是一个大国。中国的面积是英国的40倍，人口是英国的20倍。而中国的人均军费仅是美国的1/22，是英国的1/9。而且中国军费占GDP的比例逐年下降，今年是过去5年来最低的。正如你所知，中国有辽阔的国土需要保卫，此外，中国军队承担着多重任务。

佩斯顿： 考虑到当前中国经济的增长速度，我认为中国军费占GDP的比例事实上略有上升。你谈到中国要维护稳定，美国共和党总统参选人特朗普说中国人想要饿死美国人，你对此有何评论？

刘晓明： 我不认为他此番言论代表美国主流民意。在美国，你总会听到某种声音，但……

佩斯顿： 但如果特朗普当选美国总统呢？你认为问题会有多严重？

刘晓明： 这是一个假设性的问题，我不知道你会怎么回答假设性的问题，我是不会回答假设性问题的。但我可以肯定地告诉你，中国愿意和美国建立良好关系。在访谈开始前播出的节目中，你说中国想挑战美国的主导地位，甚至挑战美国的世界领导地位。这不是中国的立场，我们无意这么做。中国在实现自身发展方面已经面临足够多的挑战，我们无意去挑战美国的主导地位。我认为中美在亚太地区应该成为好伙伴。

佩斯顿： 中国举行阅兵式是为了展示军力，转移人们对中国经济下滑的注意力吗？很多经济学家认为中国经济面临严重问题。

刘晓明： 我认为西方观察家们夸大了中国经济面临的困难。中国经济确实面临一些困难和挑战，这在中国发展过程中是正常的。

佩斯顿： 中国股市市值蒸发了5万亿美元，这是小数目吗？

刘晓明： 我认为股市有其自身的运行规律。股市有起有伏，美国股市也是如此。我们要看中国经济的全貌。中国经济的基本面是好的。今年上半年中国GDP增长了7%，增量相当于世界第二十大经济体瑞士的GDP总量。

佩斯顿： 习近平主席表示希望中国经济更加现代化，市场更加自由化。自由市场的一个重要组成部分就是，人民应该能自由地表达对市场的意见。而在中国，一些记者和基金经理因为涉嫌制造股市恐慌而被逮捕。这对西方人来说是十分令人震惊的。

刘晓明： 中国人民享有言论自由。在你所说的案件中，那些人违反了法律。中国是法治国家。

佩斯顿： 我说过关于英国市场很可怕的话，比那些人说中国市场的话要可怕得多。你觉得英国政府应该逮捕我吗？

刘晓明： 那些人不仅仅是发表"可怕"的评论。他们制造谣言，引起市场恐慌。中英两国国情不同，法律制度也不尽相同。一些行为在英国可能不违法，而在中国则不同，如果违法，就要受到法律的惩罚。

佩斯顿： 非常感谢，大使先生。

刘晓明： 感谢邀请。

A Live Interview with Robert Peston on BBC *Newsnight*

On 3rd September 2015, I was invited to a live interview with BBC *Newsnight* hosted by Robert Peston. I elaborated on the significance of the Commemoration of the 70th Anniversary of the Victory of the Chinese People's War of Resistance Against Japanese Aggression and the World Anti-Fascist War, and answered questions about China's military expenditure and China's economy. The full text is as follows:

Peston: Joining me now is the Chinese Ambassador to the UK, Liu Xiaoming. Ambassador, I think of China as this fast modernizing country-a fast enriching country. But we've seen this extraordinary military display today, which takes some of us back to the era of Mao. Is this China again sending a sort of message to the world that, you know, you are fierce and dangerous?

Liu Xiaoming: I think the impression you had is not correct. In fact, the message is loud and clear, that is peace. Peace was hard won and peace should be cherished and maintained. And China will make its due contribution to maintaining world peace and regional stability. You know, in his ten minutes speech, President Xi Jinping used the word "peace" 18 times. So, that's the message.

Peston: So these gunboats that sailed off the coast of Alaska when President Obama was there today, was that just a sort of accident?

Liu Xiaoming: I think we are talking about this commemoration first, then I'll come back to this naval fleet. When I say peace was hard won, not many people, especially in the West, realize how much sacrifice China has made during the war against

Japanese aggression. In fact the war, the Second World War, started in China, started earliest, lasted longest, and China suffered the largest casualties. We paid the price of 35 million casualties, and that is the most among all the sufferings of the world in Second World War. It's about one third of the casualties of the world. And so Chinese people see this 70th anniversary as a big occasion for us to celebrate the victory, to honor the fallen soldiers who, sacrificed for their motherland.

Peston: But this peace require defense spending to go up this extraordinary way, 12% last year, 10% this year? Enormous money you're spending.

Liu Xiaoming: You have to remember that China is a large country. China, in terms of territory, it's about 40 times the sige of UK. In terms of population, it's about 20 times. Yet in terms of per capita military expenditure, China is only 1/22 of the United States and 1/9 of Britain. And also in terms of proportion of expenditure with regard to GDP, the growth is decreasing. This year, in fact, is the lowest of the past 5 years. And you know China is, as I said, a large country to defend; the Chinese military has a lot of commitments.

Peston: I think it's the share of the GDP that's actually gone up a bit, given the rapid growth of the economy. But you talk about obviously your desire for stability. What do you think when you hear the leading Republican Presidential Candidate Donald Trump talking about how he thinks that Chinese want Americans to starve?

Liu Xiaoming: I don't think it represents the majority view in United States. You always have some voice in the US, but I don't think….

Peston: But if he became President, how serious would that be?

Liu Xiaoming: I think it's a very hypothetical question. I do not know how you would answer that. But I certainly will not answer this hypothetical question. But I can assure you that we want to have good relations with United States. And you mention in your film before this interview, that China wants to challenge the dominance of the United States, and even want to challenge the US leadership. That is not our position, not our intention at all. I think in China, we have a lot of challenges to deal with in our domestic development, and we have no intention to challenge US dominance. And we believe that the US and China should be good partners in the Asia-Pacific region.

Peston: Now is this display of military strength a distraction from the slowdown in the Chinese economy which many economists think is quite serious?

Liu Xiaoming: I think China's economic difficulties have been exaggerated by Western observers. I think we have some difficulties, challenges, that's for sure. But they are the natural outcome…

Peston: Five trillion dollars lost of the Chinese stock market. Is that trivial?

Liu Xiaoming: No. I think the stock market has its own rule of the game. It has ups and downs, like in the United States. We have to focus on the big picture of China. I think the basics and fundamentals of the Chinese economy are still good and sound. We achieved 7% increase for the first half of this year. That 7% increase is about the same size of the total GDP of the 20th largest economy in the world which is Switzerland.

Peston: And very briefly, your president has said he wants a modernized economy and see markets liberalized. A really important part of free markets is that people should be free to say whatever they like about those markets. Now journalists, hedge firm manager have been arrested for allegedly scaremongering about the stock market. To us in the west, that is very shocking.

Liu Xiaoming: I think Chinese people enjoy, freedom of speech. The cases you have mentioned are those who involve in violation of law. China is a country ruled by law. And…

Peston: But I said much scarier thing about British markets than they said about Chinese market. Do you think the British Government should arrest me?

Liu Xiaoming: No. It's not only about the scary comment about the market. It's also about, making and spreading the rumors, causing disturbances in the market. And

you know, China and Britain are run by different rules of game. And maybe in some of the cases in Britain, it's not a violation of criminal law. But in China, you know, it constitutes a wrong-doing. So they have to be held accountable for their wrong-doings.

Peston: Ambassador, many thanks!

Liu Xiaoming: Thank you for having me.

接受英国BBC广播四台
奥尼尔勋爵采访

作者手记

　　2017年1月6日，英国BBC广播四台（BBC Radio 4）播出专题节目《全新世界：改变全球化》（*The New World: Fixing Globalisation*）。我在该节目中接受了英国议会上院议员、著名经济学家吉姆·奥尼尔（Jim O'Neill）勋爵的采访，就中国经济发展成就、中国对全球贸易的贡献、中国经济结构改革及社会收入平等、"一带一路"建设等与全球化密切相关的议题阐述了看法。奥尼尔因首创"金砖国家"的概念，被誉为"金砖之父"，他曾担任美国高盛集团负责资产管理事务的主席、英国财政部商务大臣、英国皇家国际事务研究所主席，长期研究全球化议题。奥尼尔在专题节目中还采访了时任世界银行行长金墉、英国前首席大臣兼财政大臣奥斯本、哈佛大学全球化问题专家罗德里克等世界政治、经济、金融、学术界知名人士。

　　BBC广播四台是英国最有影响力及最受欢迎的广播电台，是BBC最重要和投入资源最多的金牌旗舰电台，以新闻、时政、科教、历史类节目为主。听众人数超过1100万人次，主要在英国国内，同时覆盖爱尔兰、法国和北欧地区。

　　我接受奥尼尔采访实录如下：

奥尼尔： 谈论全球化不可能忽略中国。我本人因创造了"金砖四国"
（BRIC，巴西、俄罗斯、印度和中国）概念而为世人所知。在
"金砖四国"中，中国经济总量超过其他三国总和。即使中国经济
仅以6.5%的速度增长，略低于印度7%以上的增长率，到2020年
中国经济总量将相当于数个"新印度"加起来的总和。为更好地
理解中国对世界的巨大影响，我采访了中国驻英国大使刘晓明。

刘晓明： 中国取得的发展成就堪称奇迹，在人类历史上没有先例。在30年
时间里，中国7亿人口摆脱贫困，超过1亿人进入中产阶级，人
均预期寿命大幅提高，达到76岁，远高于世界平均水平，也远高
于其他任何一个发展中国家。

奥尼尔： 经历了这一非凡历程，从很多方面来看，中国已成为世界贸易最
重要的国家。

刘晓明： 中国已成为世界上120多个国家和地区的第一大贸易伙伴。

奥尼尔： 120多个，覆盖了全球一半以上人口。

刘晓明： 是的。中国也是70多个国家和地区的最大出口市场。每年，中国
进口商品总额近2万亿美元，这为许多国家提供了巨大市场。预
计未来5年，中国商品进口总额将达到8万亿美元。这些都表明
中国对世界经济已经做出并将继续做出重要贡献。

奥尼尔： 全球化带来的挑战不光是如何培训新兴产业的工人，更重要的问题是如何帮助那些技能已经被淘汰的产业工人。刘大使对中国政府如何应对这一困境进行了说明。

刘晓明： 在中国也有同样的问题。由于经济结构调整和转型，一部分人感到被落在了后面。但是我们必须解决产能过剩问题。例如，许多人都在谈论钢铁产业。事实上，当我看到英国媒体报道一些英国钢铁厂关闭导致4000人失业的消息，我完全理解这些钢铁工人的处境和感受，因为我们也面临同样的挑战，需要重新安置大约200万钢铁工人。

奥尼尔： 什么才是最好的解决办法呢？

刘晓明： 我们需要对这些工人进行培训，同时要鼓励他们自主创业。一方面，我们有大量下岗钢铁工人；另一方面，服务业又存在巨大的需求，包括家政、物流等。因此我们可以培训这些钢铁工人从事此类工作。

奥尼尔： 也许西方国家的政策制定者需要考虑在增加工人收入方面做得更多。我认为，过去10年中国在这方面下了很大功夫，并且一直是这么做的。

刘晓明： 确实如此。工人的工资水平提高了，中国政府还设定了最低工资标准，以确保工人收入。在改善城市农民工生活方面，政府也做了巨大努力。每年约有1亿农民工进城务工，所以政府要采取大量措施，包括为农民工建造廉租房等。中国的口号是："不让一个人掉队。"

奥尼尔：　"不让一个人掉队"，但我们不能想当然地认为市场会自动均摊全球化的巨大好处。如果我们能解决这一问题，全球化将继续带来好处，也不会很快止步。实际上，中国计划建设的"一带一路"将进一步提升全球化水平。

刘晓明：　我把这看作是"新全球化"。有人反对全球化，是因为一部分人、一部分国家感到被甩在了后面。所以中国"一带一路"倡议的主旨是包容性，让尽可能多的国家受益。

奥尼尔：　比如像哈萨克斯坦？

刘晓明：　对，还有俄罗斯、阿富汗、巴基斯坦以及丝绸之路经济带沿线的许多欧洲国家。例如，过去3年来，中欧班列取得了很大成功，运行了2000多趟，将中国商品一路输送到欧洲国家。

奥尼尔：　途经维也纳，如果我没记错的话。

刘晓明：　对。新海上丝绸之路则将中国同菲律宾、印度尼西亚及其他东南亚国家连接起来。虽然中国经济增长有所放缓，但仍然是世界经济的引擎。中国希望同其他国家分享中国经济增长的好处。同样，只有同其他国家加强互联互通，中国的发展势头才能得以延续。

An Interview with Lord Jim O'Neill on BBC Radio 4

On 6th January 2017, BBC Radio 4 broadcasted an episode of *The New World: Fixing Globalisation*, in which I was interviewed by the renowned economist Lord Jim O'Neill and shared my views on China's economy and globalisation.

The transcript of the interview is as follows:

O'Neill: As I said, when talking about globalisation, it's kind of impossible to ignore China. I've become well-known for creating the acronym of BRIC which refers to Brazil, Russia, India and China. China is bigger than the other 3 put together. Even growing by just 6.5 percent, slower than India's rate of more than 7 percent, China will be the equivalent to several "brand new" Indias before this decade is over. For further flavor of the staggering impact China has on the world, I've met with Chinese Ambassador to the UK, Liu Xiaoming.

Liu Xiaoming: The achievement China has achieved is really a miracle that has never been seen in the history of humanity. China has pulled 600 million people out of poverty just within 30 years. China has developed into a country which has more than 100 million middle-class population with the life expectancy tremendously increased to about 76 years. It is much higher than the world average and also much higher than any other developing country.

O'Neill: Through this remarkable journey, China has become in many ways the most important country in world trade.

Liu Xiaoming: As a matter of fact, China is the largest trading partner with over 120 countries and regions.

O'Neill: 120, so more than half of the world's population.

Liu Xiaoming: Yes, very much so. China is also the largest export market for more than 70 countries and regions. Every year China imports about 2 trillion US dollars of goods, so it is a huge market for many countries. For the next 5 years, China will import more than 8 trillion US dollars of goods from the rest of world. That shows what kind of contribution China is making and China is going to continue to make.

O'Neill: But the challenges brought up by globalisation is not just about making sure people are trained and ready for new industries. What about those whose skills are no longer needed? The Chinese Ambassador explained how the Chinese government approaches this dilemma.

Liu Xiaoming: We also have people in China who felt left behind in this economic, structural transformation, and you have to do away with over capacities. For instance, there is a lot of talk about the steel industry. In fact, when I read news that 4, 000 people have to be laid off in this country, I fully understand their feelings because we also face the same challenge to re-allocate about 2 million steel workers.

O'Neill: What's the best way of doing that?

Liu Xiaoming: You have to train these workers, and you have to create new start-up business. So on the one hand, we have redundant steel workers, on the other, there is still big demand for services, domestic care, logistic services, etc. So we can train these steel workers to work in these sectors.

O'Neill: Maybe western policy makers need to consider doing more to boost the income for workers. This of course is something I think China has been deliberately doing in a significant way in the past decade.

Liu Xiaoming: Very much so. The wages of workers have been increased. Our government has also set the minimum level of basic wages that you have to guarantee. And lots of efforts have been made to improve the livelihood of migrant workers in the city. Every year, around 100 million migrant workers settle in the big cities. So the government made a lot of efforts, such as building affordable houses. The slogan in China is, "do not let a single person be left behind."

O'Neill: "Not a single person left behind. " But one can't just assume that markets will be able to spread the considerable benefits of globalisation on their own. If we could solve this, globalisation has got lots of good to spread it to all, and it's not stopping anytime soon. In fact, the Chinese are planning a new Silk Road that is gonna take it up to another gear.

Liu Xiaoming: I regard this as new globalisation. One of the reasons why there's resentment towards globalisation is that some people feel left behind and some countries feel left behind. So the purpose of the Belt and Road, or the main theme of it, is "inclusiveness", to include all countries.

O'Neill: So we are talking about countries like Kazakhstan.

Liu Xiaoming: Yes. And Russia, Afghanistan, Pakistan and also many European countries along the Silk Road. For instance, in the past three years, the Eurasia Express railway has been very successful. Over 2, 000 trains have been in operation, transporting goods from China all the way to European countries.

O'Neill: Going through Vienna, if I am not mistaken.

Liu Xiaoming: Yes. The other road we are talking about is the new maritime Silk Road linking China to Southeast Asia, including the Philippines, Indonesia, etc. Though China's growth slows down a little bit, China is still an engine of the world economy. So China wants other countries to share the benefits of its growth. China believes it can only continue this momentum by linking with other countries.

Lord Jim O'Neill is British but an outstanding global thinker and opinion leader. After a career with Goldman Sachs as its Chief Economist he was Commercial Minister in the UK Treasury with Chancellor George Osborne.Following that he became Chairman of the world famous think tank Chatham House.

接受英国独立电视台《佩斯顿星期日访谈》栏目主持人佩斯顿现场直播采访

作者手记

2017年11月19日，我在英国独立电视台《佩斯顿星期日访谈》(*Peston on Sunday*)栏目演播室，接受该栏目主持人罗伯特·佩斯顿现场直播采访。

英国独立电视台《佩斯顿星期日访谈》是该台政治主编佩斯顿主持的旗舰时政类栏目，主要就英国政治、经济、社会、外交和重大国际问题，进行一对一的现场直播采访。被采访者包括英国和外国政要、议员、企业家、作家、社会名流、知识精英等。该栏目于2016年5月开播，很快在英国社会受到广泛关注，产生较大影响。当天，在我前后参加该栏目访谈的还有英国财政大臣哈蒙德、前外交大臣米利班德等。

2015年他在BBC《新闻之夜》栏目担任主持人时，曾采访过我，给我留下较深刻的印象。他的采访风格直率、专注、兴趣广泛、历史纵深感强，熟悉国际事务，提问跨度大，可以从亚洲一下跳到非洲，从朝鲜核问题一下转向中国与津巴布韦的关系。

这次采访正值中共十九大召开不久，我们围绕中共十九大、

中国特色社会主义、贫富差距、脱贫攻坚、朝鲜核问题、中国与
津巴布韦的关系等问题进行了讨论。

采访实录如下：

佩斯顿： 刘大使，很高兴见到你。你刚从北京回来，出席了极为重要的中国共产党第十九次全国代表大会。外界普遍认为，中共十九大习近平主席成为自毛泽东之后最有权威的中国国家领导人，是这样吗？

刘晓明： 习近平主席在中共十九大再次当选中共中央总书记，他将带领中国人民开启中国特色社会主义新时代。

佩斯顿： 说到中国特色社会主义，我注意到，和英国一样，中国社会也有着巨大的贫富差距。中国是一个社会主义国家，能够接受这样的贫富差距吗？

刘晓明： 中国是有贫富差距问题。但同其他发展中国家相比，不能说今日之中国贫富差距是"巨大的"。

佩斯顿： 有许多亿万富豪，不是吗？

刘晓明： 事实上，减少贫困、缩小贫富差距正是中共十九大的重要议题。我们已经意识到，中国存在发展不平衡、不充分问题。习近平主席在十九大上指出，我们将尽一切努力消除贫富差距，满足人民对日益增长的美好生活的需要。我们将尽一切努力打赢脱贫攻坚战。中国现在仍有4000多万贫困人口。过去30年，我们已经使7亿贫困人口脱贫。

佩斯顿： 真是了不起的成就！

刘晓明： 中国共产党和中国政府的目标是，到2020年中国全面建成小康社会之时，使这4000多万人口全部脱贫。这意味着按照中国的贫困线标准，全面消除贫困，在中国全面建成小康社会。

佩斯顿： 今天要谈的内容很多。你曾担任中国驻朝鲜大使相当长的时间……

刘晓明： 三年半。

佩斯顿： 西方关切的是，中国没有对朝鲜施加足够压力，迫使其放弃核试验。你怎么看？

刘晓明： 这不是事实。事实是，中国已经尽一切努力劝说朝鲜放弃核试验。我担任中国驻朝鲜大使时，一直努力劝说朝鲜，发展核武器不符合朝鲜的国家利益。

佩斯顿： 那它为什么还是要发展核武器？

刘晓明： 因为它也有自己的合理诉求。朝核问题事关信任与安全。朝鲜与美国之间缺乏互信，这是问题的根源。因此六方会谈积极致力于推动实现朝鲜半岛无核化，寻求全面综合解决这一问题的办法。我们还推动实现关系正常化……

佩斯顿： 难道不应该加大制裁力度吗？许多人认为中国应该对朝鲜实施更严厉的制裁。

刘晓明： 从2006年开始，那时我还担任中国驻朝鲜大使，中国就一直参与联合国的相关决议。联合国前后通过了11项决议。中国不仅投了赞成票，而且一直严格遵守这些决议，履行自己的义务。重要的是，国际社会应该认识到不能为了制裁而制裁。制裁只是一种手段，而非最终目的。我们的目的是要促使朝鲜坚持半岛无核化方向，因而应该与朝鲜进行接触。联合国决议不是只有制裁（佩斯顿插话："当然不是。"），而且还包括谈判和外交解决……

佩斯顿： 当前，你对朝核问题的前景感到悲观吗？

刘晓明： 不，我仍持谨慎乐观的态度。我始终相信，只要各方保持接触，鼓励朝鲜重返谈判，我们就能够找到解决危机的外交方案。

佩斯顿： 我想再问一个国际问题。中国在津巴布韦有着巨大的经济利益。

如果穆加贝下台，中国会感到高兴吗？

刘晓明： 中国始终奉行不干涉别国内政的外交政策。津巴布韦是中国的友好国家，中国曾支持津巴布韦人民争取国家独立，后来一直支持津巴布韦发展经济。中国绝不会干涉津巴布韦的内政……

佩斯顿： 我想追问一下，有许多报道称，如果没有得到中国的支持，津巴布韦军方不会对穆加贝采取这样的行动。

刘晓明： 这不是事实。我们从未干预津巴布韦的内政。津巴布韦的前途和命运应当由津巴布韦人民决定。我们当然希望局势能够得到和平解决。

佩斯顿： 很高兴再次见到你，大使先生，与你交谈总是令人十分愉快。

刘晓明： 感谢邀请。

A Live Interview on ITV *Peston on Sunday*

On 19th November 2017, I gave a live interview on ITV's *Peston on Sunday*, in which I shared my views on the 19th National Congress of the Communist Party of China. I also answered questions about the DPRK nuclear issue and the latest developments in Zimbabwe.

The transcript of the interview is as follows:

Peston: Very nice to see you, Mr. Ambassador. You are just back from that incredibly important Congress in Beijing. Is it right — it was widely reported as establishing President Xi as perhaps the most powerful leader China has had since Mao — is that right? Is he now the most powerful Chinese leader since Mao?

Liu Xiaoming: I would say, he has been re-elected as the General Secretary of the Party and he will lead the country into a new era of building socialism with Chinese characteristics.

Peston: You use the phrase socialism with Chinese characteristics? One of the things that is very striking about China, as it is in this country, is that there is a big gap between rich and poor in China. Is that acceptable in a socialist country?

Liu Xiaoming: There is a gap. I wouldn't say a big gap, if you compare China today, the gap between rich and poor, with some other developing countries.

Peston: A lot of billionaires?

Liu Xiaoming: That is exactly what the Party Congress is trying to address. We realize there is unbalanced and inadequate development in China. A lot has to be done to

address the ever-growing needs of the people for a better life. That includes, as the President said during the Congress, we will do everything possible to address this gap between poor and rich. We will do everything we can to elevate the poor population. In China right now there are still 40 million. In the past 30 years we have elevated 700 million people out of poverty.

Peston: That's a remarkable achievement.

Liu Xiaoming: The target for the Party and the government is to get those 40 million people out of poverty by the year 2020. That means we will wipe out poverty, according to the poverty line in China, when we successfully build a moderately prosperous society in China.

Peston: There's a lot to talk about. You were Ambassador to North Korea for quite some time?

Liu Xiaoming: For three and a half years.

Peston: In the West, there's concern that China isn't putting enough pressure on North Korea to abandon its nuclear tests. What do you say to that?

Liu Xiaoming: That's not true. As a matter of fact, China has done everything we can. We tried to dissuade the DPRK from developing their nuclear weapons programme. When I was Ambassador there, I did my best to convince them that it would not be in their interest to develop nuclear weapons.

Peston: Why have they gone ahead?

Liu Xiaoming: Because they have their legitimate concerns. The DPRK nuclear issue is an issue of trust and an issue of security. Because of the distrust between the DPRK and the United States, it is the root cause of this issue, so that's why from day one we set the goals for the Six-Party Talks to make sure that Korean peninsula will be nuclear free and address this issue with a comprehensive approach. We are also calling for the normalization process…

Peston: Shouldn't there be tougher sanctions? Many say China should impose tougher sanctions.

Liu Xiaoming: We have voted consistenlly in the UN since 2006, when I was the Ambassador. Since then, there have been 11 UN resolutions on the DPRK. China voted along and China abided by the resolutions strictly and implemented our obligation. The important thing you have to realize is you can't impose sanctions for sanctions' sake. Sanction is a means but not the purpose. The purpose is to get the DPRK to Keep committed to denuclearization. So you need to engage them. So the UN resolution is not only about sanctions.

Peston: No, no.

Liu Xiaoming: It is also about negotiations, about diplomatic solutions… .

Peston: Are you pessimistic about North Korea at the moment?

Liu Xiaoming: No, I am still cautiously optimistic. I still believe that if all parties could engage each other and we encourage the DPRK to return to the negotiation table, we can still find diplomatic solution to this crisis.

Peston: Can I ask one other question about the international picture? China has big economic interests in Zimbabwe. Is China pleased with seeing the end of Mugabe?

Liu Xiaoming: It has always been China's policy not to interfere into the internal affairs of other countries. Zimbabwe is a friendly country to China and we supported the Zimbabwe people in their days for independence, and later on for their development. We will never interfere into their internal affairs…

Peston: Can I press you on that, because there are widespread reports the army would not have taken the action against Mugabe without the support of China?

Liu Xiaoming: No, that's not true. We never interfere into their internal affairs. This is up to them, the Zimbabwean people, with regard to what to do with the future of their

country. We certainly hope that things will be resolved peacefully.

Peston: Very nice to see you again, Mr. Ambassador. As always it is a great pleasure talking to you!

Liu Xiaoming: Thank you for having me.

Peston on Sunday is the flagship political discussion programme on the British television network ITV. The programme is presented by Robert Peston, the Political Editor of ITV News.

接受英国天空新闻台《政治新闻综述》栏目主持人博尔顿现场直播采访

作者手记

2019年6月21日，我在英国天空新闻台演播室，接受该台时政栏目《政治新闻综述》（*All Out Politics*）主持人亚当·博尔顿（Adam Boulton)现场直播采访。

《政治新闻综述》是天空新闻台旗舰时政栏目，聚焦英国政治和国际上的重大事件，邀请英国和外国政要、议员、政治评论员、国际问题专家与主持人举行一对一的对话，英国首相、内阁大臣和各政党领袖是该栏目常客。

博尔顿是英国著名的政治评论员、专栏作家、主持人，担任天空新闻台政治主编和新闻总编长达32年，采访过9位英国在任首相，主持过英国大选主要政党候选人电视辩论。

这次采访正值中英第十次经济财金对话举行，我们围绕英国脱欧、中英关系、中英美关系、中国政治制度、华为、香港、英国保守党领袖候选人等问题进行了讨论。

采访实录如下：

博尔顿： 这里是天空新闻台《政治新闻综述》栏目，我们从威斯敏斯特——英国政治的中心发布消息、开展辩论提出见解。本周，中国高级别代表团到访英国，双方签署了价值超过5亿英镑的贸易协议。但由于围绕华为和香港游行示威等问题引起的争论，英中关系未来发展仍然存疑。我们邀请了中国驻英国大使刘晓明先生，非常欢迎你！

首先谈谈贸易问题，就双边贸易关系而言，你认为脱欧会给英国还是中国带来更大机遇？

刘晓明： 我希望对双方都是如此。你刚才提到的来访十分重要。近日，中国国务院副总理率领高级别代表团访问英国，与英国政府举行第十次经济财金对话。访问期间，双方达成了69项合作成果。过去10年来，中英每年举行一轮经济财金对话，两国商品和服务贸易额翻了一番，中国对英投资额增长了3倍。"沪伦通"的启动是本次对话的亮点之一，意义重大。

博尔顿： 这意味着两国股票可以相互交易吗？

刘晓明： 是的。英国的上市公司首次可以在上海股市出售股票，英国投资者也能购买在上海股市上市公司的股票。

博尔顿： 英国脱欧之后，估计需要同中国谈判达成新的贸易安排吧？

刘晓明： 我们对此持开放态度。当然，英国必须首先完成脱欧。中英双方就新的贸易安排一直保持密切沟通。中方愿意同欧盟和英国都保持良好伙伴关系。

博尔顿： 我从报纸和杂志上了解到，中国对英国脱欧的决定感到困惑，是这样吗？

刘晓明： 我不这么认为。首先，这是英国与欧盟之间的事情。对中国来说，挑战和机遇并存，我们希望能够抓住机遇，妥善应对挑战。第十次中英经济财金对话的另一个亮点就是中国对英国牛肉开放市场。我不知道你是否喜欢吃牛肉。过去23年，因为"疯牛病"，中国禁止从英国进口牛肉。现在限制解除了。

博尔顿： 这对英国农民来说是个好消息。

刘晓明： 中国国内对牛肉的需求很大，每年进口超过100万吨牛肉。英国是牛肉出口国，中国访客与游客来英都想品尝一下安格斯牛肉和威尔士黑牛肉。因此，我认为中国对英国牛肉需求量很大。

博尔顿： 鉴于特朗普的美国与中国之间的关系，你认为英国需要在美国和中国之间做选择吗？

刘晓明： 我们希望与英国、美国都发展良好关系。我相信，英国将独立做出符合英国自身利益并有利于中英合作的决定。

博尔顿： 中英之间存在意识形态差异。中国是一党制国家，而我们实行西方传统民主制度，两者必将冲突。

刘晓明： 中国存在了5000多年，中英两国有不同的制度。70年前，中国共产党领导中国革命，成立了中华人民共和国。中英之间一直存在一些差异，但这些差异并未阻止两国携手合作，实现共赢。我不同意你所说的中国是一党制国家，中国有8个参政的民主党派，准确地说，中国是共产党领导的国家，如同英国是保守党领导的国家。我们实行中国特色社会主义民主制度，通过自己的方式选举国家领导人。中英两国应该彼此尊重。

博尔顿： 中国政府利用先进技术和通信设备对公民进行严密监控。在这样的情况下，英国还能允许华为深度参与5G网络建设吗？

刘晓明： 中国政府从未利用科技监控老百姓。而在英国，你们在很多地方安装了监控设备。中国在一些地方安装监控设备是为了国家安全和防范恐怖主义。华为是一家优秀的企业，在英国经营18年，为英国电信产业发展做出了贡献。华为是5G技术的领军者，我希望英国能够继续与华为合作。

博尔顿： 如果新任英国首相决定拒绝华为，会有什么后果？

刘晓明： 这将不仅对华为而且对中国企业发出十分错误和负面的信号。英国被认为是最开放、最具良好营商环境的国家。过去5年，中国在英国投资迅猛发展，对英国在过去10年间的投资额增长了3倍。如果英国拒绝华为，肯定将对外发出十分负面的信号。

博尔顿： 英国政府是否已就香港形势向中方交涉？

刘晓明： 双方有接触。英方表达了自己的关切，中方向英方阐明香港特区政府修例决定的合法性和必要性，表明中央政府支持特区政府的决定，包括修例和暂缓修例的决定。中方同时也就一些外部势力企图利用此事干涉中国内部事务表达了关切，我们告诉英国政府，香港问题纯属中国内政。

博尔顿： 市民反抗的场面很大，据说有1/4的香港人上街游行。你认为怎样解决这个问题？比如说，林郑月娥辞职？

刘晓明： 大多数英国媒体只关注上街的示威者。它们忘记了有80万香港民众签名支持特区政府修例。特区政府就修例征求了民众的意见和建议，收到的4500份反馈中，3000份支持修例，只有1500份反对。我希望事态平息下来。我们对特区政府有信心。香港特区政府已经决定暂停修例，愿花更多时间倾听民众的声音。我希望民众对林郑月娥特首和特区政府做出积极回应。

博尔顿： 英国末任港督彭定康认为修例破坏了香港回归之时英中达成的协议。

刘晓明： 这种说法不对。我认为恰恰相反，修例正是为了把香港建设成为一个更加美好的地方，而不是"避罪天堂"。

博尔顿： 谈谈你对保守党领袖候选人约翰逊的看法。

刘晓明： 我们很熟。他在担任伦敦市长期间有力促进了伦敦与中国城市之间的经贸关系。他担任外交大臣期间曾多次访问中国。我与另一位保守党领袖候选人亨特外交大臣也很熟。我祝他们两人好运。

博尔顿： 谢谢刘大使接受采访。

刘晓明： 不客气。

A Live Interview with Adam Boulton on Sky News *All Out Politics*

On 21st June, 2019, I gave live interview on Sky News' *All Out Politics* hosted by Adam Boulton. I talked about, among other topics, China-UK relations in the context of the just concluded 10th round of the China-UK Economic and Financial Dialogue. The transcript is as follows:

Boulton: This is *All Out Politics*—news, debate and opinion from the heart of Westminster. A high-level Chinese delegation was in the United Kingdom this week to sign a trade deal worth more than £500 million. But questions remain about the future of the UK-China relationship, given the row over Huawei and the continuing protests in Hong Kong. Joining me now is Chinese Ambassador to the UK, Liu Xiaoming. Welcome to you, indeed!

Let's talk about trade. First of all, Brexit. Does it offer greater opportunities to the UK or China in their trade relationship?

Liu Xiaoming: I hope both. You mentioned this high-level visit by the Chinese Vice Premier. It was very significant. During the visit, 69 outcomes have been signed. This is the tenth Economic and Financial Dialogue, co-chaired by Chinese Vice Premier and the Chancellor of the UK. So, in the past 10 years, each year we had one round of dialogue. The trade between China and the UK in goods and services doubled, and investment from China tripled. What is significant of this round of Dialogue is that there is the launch of the Shanghai-London Stock Connect. That was very significant.

Boulton: This is basically selling each other's stocks.

Liu Xiaoming: Right. For the first time UK listed companies can sell their shares in

Shanghai Stock Market. The UK investors can buy directly from Shanghai.

Boulton: Presumably the United Kingdom is going to need a new trade arrangement with China as we leave the European Union.

Liu Xiaoming: We are open to this, but first you have to complete your Brexit. We have been very actively engaged with the UK side in discussing about new arrangement. We want to have partnership with both the EU and the UK.

Boulton: I read in newspapers and magazines that China is bemused by the decision to leave the European Union. Would that be fair?

Liu Xiaoming: I don't think so. China will leave it to the UK and the EU to decide. There are both challenges and opportunities. We want to seize the opportunities and try to handle the challenges in an orderly way. The other thing I should mention about this latest round of the Dialogue is the beef. I do not know if you care much about the beef. There has been a ban on import of UK beef for the past 23 years because of the mad cow disease. Now the restriction is lifted.

Boulton: Something for British farmers there.

Liu Xiaoming: There is a big demand in China for beef. Every year we import one million tonnes of beef. The UK is an exporter of beef. Each time when the Chinese visitors are here — and tourists — they are all looking for Angus beef and Welsh black cattle beef. So, I think there is a big demand for UK beef.

Boulton: Given the relations between Donald Trump's America and China, do you think the UK's gonna have to choose basically?

Liu Xiaoming: We want to have good relations with both the UK and the US. I trust that the UK will make its decision independently, in the UK's national interest and in the interest of UK-China cooperation.

Boulton: There is a sort of ideological divide. China has a one-party state. We have a western tradition of democracy. In the end, it would seem that those may be strained.

Liu Xiaoming: China has been around for 5, 000 years. We have had different systems. 70 years ago, the Communist Party led China's revolution and established the People's Republic. I think there have always been differences, but these differences have not prevented our countries from working for the common good. I can not say that we have a one-party system. In China, we have eight democratic parties. Of course the country is led by the Communist Party of China, just like the UK is led by the Conservative Party. We have a Chinese democracy, or democracy of Chinese characteristics. We have a different way to elect our leaders. But we need to respect each other.

Boulton: Yeah, if you take for example tech or communications, China has used tech for surveillance of its citizens. Therefore, should Huawei be allowed to gain a significant foothold in our 5G system here?

Liu Xiaoming: I don't think the Chinese government use tech for surveillance of its citizens. Here in the UK, you have a lot of CCTV. For us, it is for the security of the country to prevent terrorist attacks and so on. Huawei is a good company. They have been here for 18 years，and they have made their contribution to the telecom industries in this country. They are the leader in 5G technology. I do hope that the UK will keep Huawei for the benefit ...

Boulton: What would be the consequences if the new prime minister did not admit Huawei?

Liu Xiaoming: I think this would send a bad signal, a negative signal, not only to Huawei but to Chinese businesses. The UK is regarded as the most open, most business-friendly. That's why in the past 5 years, you have seen a soaring of Chinese investment here. In the past 10 years, Chinese investment here tripled. If the door is shut on Huawei, it will send a very negative message.

Boulton: Have you had any representations from the British government about the situation in Hong Kong?

Liu Xiaoming: We do have a talk. They expressed their concerns. We explained to them why the decision is legitimate and necessary. And why we support the Hong Kong government in their decision, both to start the amendments and also to suspend the decision. We also expressed our concern that some foreign countries try to use this to interfere into the internal affairs of Hong Kong. We told the British government that Hong Kong is entirely an internal affair of the Chinese.

Boulton: These are extraordinary scenes of civil disobedience. People are talking about a quarter of the Hong Kong population taking to the streets. How do you think that this situation is going to be resolved? Would, for example, the removal of Carrie Lam be the answer?

Liu Xiaoming: Most British media focus on the people on the street, the demonstrators. They overlooked that there are 800, 000 people signing up to support the Hong Kong government to amend the Ordinance. When they sent out the amendment to solicit opinions, they got 4, 500 replies, and 3, 000 of them support the amendment. Only 1, 500 made their observations opposing it. I do hope things will calm down. We have full trust in Hong Kong SAR government in resolving this matter. The SAR government has decided to suspend the amendment and they want more time to listen to the people. I hope the people will respond positively to Carrie Lam and her administration.

Boulton: Lord Patten, the last British Governor of Hong Kong said this is a clear breach of the agreements that were reached at the time of the handover.

Liu Xiaoming: We don't think so. I think it is just the opposite. I think the decision to amend the ordinance is just for the purpose of making Hong Kong a better place and not a safe haven for fugitive criminals.

Boulton: What do you think of Boris Johnson?

Liu Xiaoming: I know him very well. When he was Mayor of London, he did a great job to promote business relations between Chinese cities and London. When he was foreign secretary, he visited China on several occasions. I also know Jeremy Hunt very well. I wish best luck to both candidates.

Boulton: Ambassador, thank you for joining us.

Liu Xiaoming: My pleasure.

Adam Boulton is a British journalist and broadcaster who was formerly editor-at-large of Sky News, and presenter of *All Out Politics*. He has interviewed every British Prime Minister from David Cameron back to Alec Douglas-Home.

接受美国全国广播公司商业频道
记者威斯巴赫采访

作者手记

2019年11月14日，我在出席"法国巴黎银行全球市场大会"并发表主旨演讲后，接受了美国全国广播公司商业频道（Consumer News and Business Channel, CNBC）资深记者安奈特·威斯巴赫（Annette Weisbach）的采访。

CNBC是全球三大财经电视媒体之一，每天24小时通过有线电视、卫星电视和互联网向全球90多个国家播放财经新闻，在美国拥有9360多万收费家庭用户，占全美收视家庭总数的80%以上。

威斯巴赫是该台资深记者、经济学家，曾采访多国政要和商界领袖。我们的采访围绕华为、中欧关系、中美关系、知识产权保护等问题进行。

CNBC将这次采访在该频道《欧洲财经论坛》（*Squawk Box Europe*）等栏目播出，并在其网站和推特同时刊登。

采访实录如下：

威斯巴赫： 关于华为及其设备在5G网络中的作用，有许多不同的看法。对此你怎么看？你能否向欧洲和美国的消费者保证，华为设备不存在任何问题？

刘晓明： 我认为，华为和其商业合作伙伴之间没有什么问题，华为的确是一家很好的企业，它不仅为英国的电信业发展做出巨大贡献，而且很好地履行了企业责任，在英国创造了5.1万个就业机会，投资30亿美元。华为是5G技术的领军者，英国电信企业都欢迎华为。当然也有一些杂音，有些国家不愿看到华为在欧洲的发展，向欧洲国家施加巨大压力，我就不点这个国家的名了。截至目前，英国、德国、法国等欧洲国家对此仍存在不同意见，仍在进行讨论，政府尚未做出最后决定。

我们理解一些国家的安全关切，华为对此也理解，而且正在努力解决这些安全关切。华为成立了完全由英国人组成的网络安全评估中心，出资请专家来监测、分析华为的设备是否存在安全隐患和问题。因此，华为是非常公开透明的，它希望能成为很好的合作伙伴。正如我常说的，华为将为中英、中欧5G领域合作带来"黄金"机遇，禁止华为意味着错失良机。

我衷心希望英国、德国、法国政府从自身国家利益，从发展强有力的对华伙伴关系出发，做出正确选择，而不是受冷战思维影响，更不能搞政治打压。我希望华为能在英国实现互利双赢合作。正如我刚才在演讲中所说，中国开放的大门只会越开越大，我们也希望其他国家同样保持开放，而不是对中国关上大门。

威斯巴赫： 你提到了冷战，中美之间地缘政治的紧张状态让人感受到了一丝冷战气息。欧洲因此承受压力，尚未做出决定，对此中国怎么看？

刘晓明： 我们已经说得很明确，中国无意与美国打仗，无论是冷战、热战，还是贸易战。我们希望与美国建立合作、协调、不对抗的关系。中美是世界上最大的两个经济体，中美关系是世界和平与繁荣的决定性因素。中美合则两利，斗则俱伤。因此我们对与美国开战不感兴趣。我高兴地看到，中美谈判官员正在加紧努力工作，解决贸易问题。

我们不要求欧洲国家在中美之间选边站队。英美有特殊关系，但中英也在致力于打造"黄金时代"。我们追求互利共赢，而非"零和"游戏，既不是欧洲赢、美国赢而中国输，也不是中国赢、欧洲赢而美国输。我们希望大家实现共赢，这就是我们的立场。

威斯巴赫： 我们谈谈中美贸易谈判第一阶段协议吧，协议似乎已经达成，但仍存在一些难点。中方认为症结在哪里？

刘晓明： 我认为双方正在就细节进行密集磋商。我并不了解细节，即便我了解，我也必须谨慎表态，以免干扰谈判进程。但根据我的理解，关税应该是重要议题之一。加征关税不符合自由贸易原则，"贸易战"起于加征关税，也应该以取消所有加征的关税而告终。我希望第一阶段协议能尽快顺利达成，以便能够进入第二、第三阶段。

威斯巴赫： 有人认为知识产权保护也是中美贸易谈判的一个焦点，中方在此问题上是否会有所妥协？

刘晓明： 改革开放40年来，中国在加强知识产权保护方面做出了切实的努力，取得了超乎寻常的进步，这一点毋庸置疑。首先，应该肯定中国所取得的巨大进步。其次，中国认真对待美国等国家在知识产权问题上的关切，也承认各国均需要不断改进。正如我常讲的，没有哪个国家是完美的，世界上最大的空间就是不断改进的空间。再次，我认为动辄指责、声讨毫无益处。一些西方政客指责中国"窃取"美国技术，这种说法是完全错误的。中国的发展奇迹靠的是中国人民过去70年的艰苦奋斗，不是靠"偷窃"他国知识产权。西方应该公正客观地看待这个问题，而不是指责中国"偷窃"。这样才有益于双方就这一重要议题开展合作。

威斯巴赫： 特朗普总统说过，打赢贸易战很容易。对此你怎么看？

刘晓明： 我在许多场合都讲过，贸易战没有赢家。

威斯巴赫： 关于贸易谈判进程，你认为有时间表吗？很明显，明年美国将举行大选，贸易战将与选战交织在一起，中国是否持观望立场，等着与下一届美国总统再谈？

刘晓明： 这不是中方的立场。中国持开放态度，我们希望问题解决得越早越好，因为这不仅符合中美两国的利益，也符合全世界的利益。中美贸易冲突已给世界带来许多不确定性、不可预测性，全世界都很关注，中美双方谈判官员责任重大。我认为中方不会观望，这不是我们的立场。我们希望尽快达成协议，但是"一个巴掌拍不响"，需要双方共同做出努力。

An Interview with Annette Weisbach on CNBC

On 14th November, 2019, I gave an interview on CNBC with Annette Weisbach after delivering a keynote speech at the Global Markets Conference 2019 held by BNP Paribas. I shared thoughts on Huawei, China-US relations and trade negotiations, China-UK relations, Brexit and other questions. The interview was broadcast on CNBC "*Squawk Box Europe*" the next morning, and carried on CNBC website and Twitter. The transcript is as follows.

Weisbach: There's a lot of controversy about Huawei's role in 5G network and its equipment. What is your response here? Can you assure European and also the US consumers that there won't be any sort of problems with those equipments?

Liu Xiaoming: I do not foresee a major problem between Huawei and their business partners, because Huawei is really a good company. They contribute a great deal not only in terms of telecom industry in this country, but also in terms of corporate responsibilities. They supported 51,000 jobs in the UK and have invested 3 billion US dollars in this country. And they are the leader in 5G. I think the British business partners still welcome Huawei.

There are some noises. I don't want to name the country. They do not want to see Huawei have a better presence in European countries. They twist arms of, they put pressure on, these countries. But so far, I think some European countries, like Britain, Germany, and France, have not yet made a final decision. In terms of government decision, I think it is still debated, with divided views.

We understand people might have some concerns. Huawei also understands the so-called security concern, so they try to address this concern. Huawei has set up Cyber Security Evaluation Centre staffed by British people. Huawei paid for this facility to monitor and analyze their own facilities—whether they are secure and safe, whether there's a problem. So they are very transparent. They want to be a good partner. I always say that Huawei will present golden opportunities for China and the UK and for China and European countries to collaborate in 5G. If you kick out Huawei, you really miss opportunities.

So I do hope that, the British government, German government, or French government, they will make decision based on their own national interests, based on their collaboration with China in building a strong partnership with China, but not based on some political witch hunt or, I would call, Cold War mentality. So I do hope Huawei will be here for win-win cooperation. As China will open its door wider, I do hope other countries will also open their doors and will not shut the doors to China.

Weisbach: You have said Cold War. And it feels a bit that these geopolitical tensions between United States and China do have a bit of a feel of the Cold War. And also, it feels that Europe has to make up its mind, at least the pressure is on Europe. How do you see China positioned here?

Liu Xiaoming: We make it very clear. We're not interested in any war, whether it is cold war, or hot war, or trade war with the United States. We want to build a cooperative, coordinated, a non-confrontation relationship with the United States. We believe that there will be no peace or prosperity in the world without sound relations between China and the US, the two largest economies in the world. We always believe that China and the United States will benefit from cooperation and lose from confrontation. So we are not interested in any wars with the United States. I'm very pleased that Chinese and American negotiators are working very hard to address trade issues.

With regard to Europe, we do not ask European countries to take side between China and the US. The UK has a special relationship with the US, but we're also building a "golden era" between China and the UK. So we want to work for win-win, not a zero sum game. Not Europe wins, America wins and China loses. Not China wins, Europe wins and America loses. We want win-win for all. That is our position.

Weisbach: Let's talk about this phase one deal between the US and China, and where the sticking points are, because it seems that the deal is within reach but there seems

to be some sticking points. What are they from the Chinese position?

Liu Xiaoming: I think the negotiators are still very much occupied with the details. I do not have the details. Even if I had, I would have to be cautious. I don't want to interrupt the process. But I think the tariffs might be one of the very important issues, based on my understanding of the negotiations. Because the trade war started with the tariffs, it should be ended with removing all the tariffs imposed by the other side, because it is not in the spirit of free trade. So we do hope that we can clinch the phase one deal sooner, so that we can move on to phase two and phase three.

Weisbach: What one is hearing is that intellectual property rights are also at the center of that debate or the negotiations. Would China be in a position to compromise a bit in that stance?

Liu Xiaoming: China has made great efforts in the past 40 years since the reform and opening up in terms of improving intellectual property rights. First, I would say people should recognize the tremendous progress that China has made in this respect. Number two, we also realize that we need to do more. As I always say, the largest room in the world is the room for improvement. So no country is perfect, but we are serious about addressing the concerns of other countries, including the United States. That is the second point I want to make. Third, I don't think resorting to war of words, accusing each other, is helpful at all. Some politicians criticize China for so-called "stealing technology" from the United States. I think they have a wrong impression. China's miracle is not built on theft of other countries' property. It's built by the hard working people of China in the past 70 years. So I think you really have to address this issue in sincerity and try to tackle this problem with honesty, sincerity, rather than accusing China of so called stealing. That will be helpful for the two sides to work on this important issue.

Weisbach: President Trump once said the trade war is easy to win. What would you respond to that?

Liu Xiaoming: I said on many occasions that there will be no winners in trade wars.

Weisbach: And let's talk about the further evolution of the trade negotiations. What do you think will be the timeline? Because we are clearly, next year, heading into new elections in the United States, so it could be all tied together. Would the Chinese position rather be to wait and see who will be the next president?

Liu Xiaoming: I don't think that is China's position. We are open-minded. We always want to resolve this problem sooner than later because we believe it is in the interest not only of China but also of the United States, and of the world.

The trade war between China and the United States really created a lot of uncertainties and unpredictabilities. And I think the world is watching. I think the negotiators of the two countries really have a big duty on their shoulders. I don't think it is the intention of China to wait and see. That is not our position. We want to clinch the agreement as soon as possible. But you need two to tango.

香港问题

Hong Kong

英国对中国香港特别关注。历史上，英国对香港殖民统治156年。回归前，香港问题始终是中英关系的障碍；回归后，它成为中英关系的积极因素。但是，英国总有一些人殖民心态挥之不去，他们身体进了21世纪，脑袋还停留在殖民时期，一有风吹草动，就跳出来，对香港事务指手画脚、说三道四。我使英11年，赶上香港三件大事：庆祝香港回归祖国20周年、"修例风波"、颁布实施香港国安法。围绕这三件大事，我率领中国驻英国使馆外交官，在英国这个国际舆论中心、西方舆论高地，积极开展公共外交，讲中国香港故事，讲"一国两制"故事，讲香港国安法故事。

　　"修例风波"以后，西方媒体，包括英国媒体，扮演了十分不光彩的角色，它们不仅没有公正客观地报道，而且混淆是非、颠倒黑白、误导公众：连篇累牍地渲染所谓"和平示威权利"，却对极端暴力分子破坏社会秩序、袭警伤人的违法犯罪行为熟视无睹，支持特区政府、守护香港法治的正义声音更是鲜有见报；将破坏香港法治、为非作歹的暴徒美化为"支持民主的人士"，却将特区政府和警队维护香港法治、保护市民生命财产安全的正当合法举措恶意污蔑为"镇压"。正是这些媒体的"选择性失声"和"歪曲性报道"，使错误舆论大行其道，误导了西方广大民众。针对这种情况，我多次发表演讲，接受媒体采访，在各主流大报上发表文章，先后举行4场中外记者会，100多家中外媒体、200多名记者出席。后来，英国报纸拒绝刊登我的涉港文章，称它们只能登支持所谓"民运"分子（即反中乱港分子）的文章，我就把主要精力投向广播电视媒体。仅2019年6月—2020年7月一年多的时间，我就香港问题7次接受英国各大电视台现场直播采访，分别两次上BBC旗舰栏目《安德鲁·马尔访谈》和《新闻之夜》，一次上《尖锐对话》。我利用这些上电视的机会，澄清事实，批驳谬论，揭穿谎言，为"一国两制"正名，为国安法助阵，让世界听到中国声音。

接受英国BBC广播四台《今日》栏目主持人汉弗莱斯现场直播采访

作者手记

2017年6月29日,我在BBC总部演播室接受BBC广播四台早间旗舰时政栏目《今日》(*Today*)主持人约翰·汉弗莱斯(John Humphrys)现场直播采访。

BBC广播四台是英国最具影响力、最受欢迎的广播电台,是BBC投入资源最多的旗舰电台。前文已介绍了《今日》栏目。

汉弗莱斯是英国著名记者、作家、评论员,担任《今日》栏目主持人长达22年,是BBC资历最深的主持人之一,获多项新闻大奖,曾于1972年赴华参加报道美国总统尼克松访华。他的采访风格以直率、犀利、咄咄逼人著称,一些政治人物抱怨他的采访过于尖酸、刻薄、不留情面。

这次采访正值香港回归20周年,汉弗莱斯在采访我之前放了一段短片,包括采访香港所谓"民主人士"。他上来第一个问题就是,有人说香港的制度日益成为"一国一制",这是不是事实?我向他介绍了"一国两制"在香港的成功实施,同时指出,"一国两制"是一个有机整体,有的人讲"一国两制",只谈"两制"而忽视了"一国",忘记了香港是中国的一部分,不是英国的一部分,更不是一个独立实体。

我们还讨论了中国的国际地位和朝鲜核问题。

采访实录如下:

汉弗莱斯: 刘大使,早上好。有人说香港的制度日益成为了"一国一制",这是不是事实?

刘晓明: 这不是事实。"一国两制"在香港得到了成功实施。在我之前你们采访的人说,中国中央政府没有兑现承诺。我不同意这种观点。事实是,中国中央政府完全兑现了"一国两制"的承诺。我认为,按照《基本法》和"一国两制"原则,香港的社会制度、经济制度、生活方式、法律制度保持稳定。与20年前相比,香港变得更好了,此时此刻的确值得我们隆重庆祝。

20年来,我们看到香港经济繁荣,社会稳定,GDP翻番,外汇储备增长了3倍多。香港继续保持国际金融、贸易、航运中心地位,香港人均寿命大幅增加,超过许多发达国家,民众生活幸福。

汉弗莱斯: 没有人怀疑香港的经济繁荣,这是公认的,但给人的印象是,中央政府很显然决心收紧对香港的管控。对此你怎么看?

刘晓明： 我不这么认为，我也不同意这种说法。我认为，人们只需要把香港20年前和现在的政治管理、民主政治做一番比较，就可以得出结论。

汉弗莱斯： 民主政治？

刘晓明： 对，民主政治。

汉弗莱斯： 真是这样吗？

刘晓明： 20年前，香港有选举吗？港督是选出来的吗？

汉弗莱斯： 没有人质疑这个，因为那时候香港还是殖民地，有港督很正常。

刘晓明： 但在过去的20年，香港举行了5次特区行政长官选举。

汉弗莱斯： 但香港新任特首仅得到了选举委员会的777票，这一数字仅代表了0.03%的香港民众，听起来不太令人信服。

刘晓明： 数字并不能说明一切。

汉弗莱斯： 但数字在民主体制中很说明问题。

刘晓明： 如果拿数字说事，那么英国国家领导人选举又是如何呢？ 6500

万人口的国家领导人只是在其几万人的选区内以微弱多数取胜，人们可以提出异议，这是不是就不能代表整个国家人民的意志？！

汉弗莱斯： 英国首相得到的选票最终还是超过了0.03%。这件事就不说了。

刘晓明： 我想强调的是，香港特首的选举是严格按照《基本法》和香港特区有关选举法律进行的。

汉弗莱斯： 但需要得到批准……

刘晓明： 民主选举进程是一个不断发展、渐进的过程。俗话说"罗马不是一天建成的"，我也可以说伦敦不是一天建成的，香港也不是一天建成的。

汉弗莱斯： 2016年2月，英国外交部发表了《香港问题半年报告》，外交大臣约翰逊发表了一个讲话，说中国严重违背了《中英联合声明》，破坏了"一国两制"的原则，也就是说，英国政府不愿看到的事情却发生了。

刘晓明： 关于这个报告，首先，我们反对英国政府每年发表两次所谓香港问题报告的做法。香港是中国不可分割的一部分，香港事务纯属中国内部事务，不容任何外部势力干涉。然而，即使在这样的报告中，英国政府也赞赏中国政府执行"一国两制"政策，承认香港"一国两制"实践取得巨大成功。虽然中英之间存在一些分歧，但是双方都认为，香港长期繁荣和稳定不仅符合中国的利益，而且符合英国的利益，同时也符合国际社会的利益。

汉弗莱斯： 在外人看来，香港的选举受到操纵，示威者被关押，民主被削弱而不是加强。现在你告诉我，香港是"我们国家"的。

刘晓明： 有些人讲"一国两制"，忘记了这是一个有机整体，忘记了香港是中国的一部分，而不是英国的一部分，更不是一个独立实体。

汉弗莱斯： 那就是"一种制度"了？

刘晓明： 是两种制度。采访前你告诉我，你是12年前去的中国。你应该再去中国看看，去香港看看，看看发生的变化。即便我们之间在诸如"民主"等概念上看法有差异，我们也应该把今天的香港和20年前的香港，和两年前甚至一年前的香港对比着来看。

汉弗莱斯： 我们来谈谈中国在世界的地位，你是否认为中国取代美国成为世界第一"超级大国"指日可待？

刘晓明： 我不认为中国在可预见的将来会成为"超级大国"，我认为中国仍然是一个发展中国家。

汉弗莱斯： 中国如果成为最大的经济体，还是发展中国家吗？

刘晓明： 即使有一天中国经济总量达到世界第一，中国要成为所谓"超级大国"的路还很长，中国地域辽阔，地区发展差异很大。我在担任驻埃及大使后，曾经在中国西部最贫困的省份之一甘肃省工作过，比当年美国"不发达的西部"还落后。

汉弗莱斯： 中国现在是第二大经济体，很可能很快发展成为第一大经济体，中国要怎样做才能成为"超级大国"？

刘晓明： 我们对成为"超级大国"不感兴趣。我们感兴趣的是改善中国人民的生活，解决地区发展不平衡等问题。许多外国人只看到北京、上海、广东和东部沿海地区，这些地区的确比较发达。比如广东省经济规模相当于西班牙，在世界上可以排第十五位，但是中国西部的甘肃、宁夏等省区经济还是很落后的。

汉弗莱斯： 最后谈谈朝鲜对世界和平的潜在威胁。朝鲜给中国造成的干扰要达到什么样的程度，中国才会说：够了，我们要采取行动了，要介入了。

刘晓明： 我认为中国为缓和朝鲜半岛局势已经做了大量工作。你知道，我来英国之前曾在中国驻朝鲜大使的岗位上工作了三年半。实际上，中国一直在积极做朝鲜工作，竭力说服朝鲜坚持半岛无核化方向。

汉弗莱斯： 但这些努力都失败了？

刘晓明： 不能说失败了，有时候"进两步退一步"，有时候"进一步退两步"。朝核问题十分复杂，需要综合施策，采取综合全面的措施是必要的，所以我们提出了"双暂停"倡议和"双轨"并进思路。也就是说：一方面采取制裁措施，说服朝鲜坚持半岛无核化方向；另一方面……

汉弗莱斯： 如果你们失败，美国就介入……

刘晓明： 另一方面，美国和韩国也应该采取措施，暂停军事演习。记得当年，我每次劝说朝鲜坚持半岛无核化方向，朝鲜方面就会说，他们受到了美国这个"超级大国"及其盟友的威胁，他们的军事演习直接针对朝鲜。所以我们呼吁"双暂停"，即朝鲜停止核导活动，美国及其盟友停止军事演习。然后大家回到谈判桌上来，通过对话解决问题，并行推进实现半岛无核化和建立半岛和平机制，这就是我们所说的"双轨"并进思路。

汉弗莱斯： 好的，大使先生，非常感谢你今天接受采访。

刘晓明： 感谢邀请。

A Live Interview with John Humphrys on BBC Radio 4 *Today* Programme

On 29th June 2017, I gave a live interview on the *Today* programme of BBC Radio 4 hosted by John Humphrys, in which I shared my views on the progress and achievement of Hong Kong Special Administrative Region since its establishment 20 years ago and the success of "one country, two systems" policy. I also answered questions about Hong Kong's political reform, China's place in the world and the DPRK nuclear issue.

The transcript of the interview is as follows:

Humphrys: I am joined in the studio by the Chinese Ambassador to this country, Liu Xiaoming. Good morning to you.

Liu Xiaoming: Good morning.

Humphrys: Isn't it the reality that it is "one country" that is increasingly "one system"?

Liu Xiaoming: No. I think "one country, two systems" has been implemented with great success. I can't agree with some of the interviews aired just before me saying that China did not deliver its promises. As a matter of fact, the Central Government of China delivered everything it promises, that is "one country, two systems". I think that basically Hong Kong has maintained its social, economic system, way of life, rule of law, and I think Hong Kong now is much better placed compared with 20 years ago. So this is really an occasion for us to have a grand celebration.

I think in the past 20 years we've seen Hong Kong maintaining prosperity and stability, the GDP doubled, and foreign exchange reserve quadrupled. Hong Kong still remains a global centre of finance, trade and shipping. The life expectancy of its people increased tremendously. They are ahead of many developed countries. So I would say people in Hong Kong are now living longer and living happier.

Humphrys: Nobody I think would argue that there has been economic prosperity in Hong Kong. That is accepted. But the impression we get is that China is determined to tighten its grip, and there is clear evidence for that, isn't there?

Liu Xiaoming: I don't think so. I don't agree with her. I think if people compare the political governance of Hong Kong today, including democratic governance of Hong Kong today with what was 20 years ago ...

Humphrys: A democratic government?

Liu Xiaoming: Democratic governance.

Humphrys: Really?

Liu Xiaoming: Let me say: 20 years ago, did you have election in Hong Kong? Who elected the governor of Hong Kong?

Humphrys: It was a colony. Nobody would argue other than that. It was a colony and there was a governor there and it was fine.

Liu Xiaoming: In the past 20 years there were 5 elections in Hong Kong.

Humphrys: And the last leader was elected with 777 votes, 0.03 percent of the registered electors. That doesn't sound very convincing.

Liu Xiaoming: Number does not tell you everything.

Humphrys: It tells you a lot in a democratic system.

Liu Xiaoming: What about here in the UK? What about UK's national leader? You have 65 million people and your national leaders get elected from their constituency of tens of thousands of voters, by a small majority. People can challenge that it doesn't represent the population of the entire country.

Humphrys: The number of people who voted for the British Prime Minister ultimately was more than 0.03 percent and there we go. All right, let's ...

Liu Xiaoming: Hong Kong's chief executive is elected according to the Basic Law, according to the Election Law in Hong Kong ...

Humphrys: But it has to be approved ...

Liu Xiaoming: You have to achieve this through incremental, gradual process and step-by-step. As we say, Rome or maybe London is not built overnight and Hong Kong is not built overnight.

Humphrys: Why do you think that the foreign office says ... You know there was a report by the foreign office in February 2016 and Boris Johnson, our present Foreign Secretary, has said seriously breached the *Sino-British Joint Declaration* by undermining the "one country, two systems" principle. And that is what the British Government fears has happened, that is, the principle has been undermined.

Liu Xiaoming: First of all, we disagree with this so-called report on Hong Kong, which is published twice a year. Hong Kong is an integral part of China, and Hong Kong's affairs are internal affairs of China. It's not for foreign governments to interfere. Having said that, even with this report, the British Government commends the Chinese Government for implementing "one country, two systems" and they believe "one country, two systems" is a great success. There are some differences between China and the UK but on the whole we all believe that the long-term stability and long-term prosperity in Hong Kong are not only in the interest of China but also in the interest of Britain and the international community.

Humphrys: And many people looking at your country from the outside believe that the facts are the elections are orchestrated, the protesters are locked up and democracy is being weakened rather than strengthened and your response now, in the end, is to say that it's our country.

Liu Xiaoming: When you say "one country, two systems", I think some people forget that this is one framework. You have to remember that Hong Kong is part of China, not part of UK, and not a so-called independent entity.

Humphrys: And therefore it has to be a single system?

Liu Xiaoming: Two systems. You told me your last visit to China was 12 years ago. You need to go to Hong Kong, to go to China, to see the changes. Even in the area where we have a difference, on democracy, you have to compare Hong Kong today with Hong Kong 20 years ago. You have to compare Hong Kong now with Hong Kong one year, two years ago.

Humphrys: Can we talk about China's place in the world at large? Do you see the day, perhaps not very far away, when China will be the world's great superpower instead of the United States, as it is today?

Liu Xiaoming: I do not foresee that China will become a superpower in the foreseeable future. I believe China is still a developing country.

Humphrys: Even when China becomes the largest economy in the world?

Liu Xiaoming: Even when China becomes the largest economy in the world, it will take a long way for China to become so-called superpower. China is a large country, and there are great differences between regions. After serving as Ambassador in Egypt, I was seconded to one of the poorest provinces in China, Gansu. It is very poor, poorer than, the Americans used to call their west "Wild West".

Humphrys: So what will it take, as you've said, you are the second largest economy, you may very well very soon become the largest in the world, so what will it take for you to be the world's superpower?

Liu Xiaoming: We are not interested in becoming a superpower ...

Humphrys: Oh you are not ...

Liu Xiaoming: We are interested in improving the livelihood of the people, and addressing the disparity between regions. When people look at China, they like to focus on the coastal region, the eastern part of China — Beijing, Shanghai, Guangdong. They are very much developed. For example Guandong is the 15th largest economy in the world. It's about the size of Spain. But if you look at other provinces — Gansu, Ningxia, they are rather backward ...

Humphrys: Just a final thought about North Korea and its threat to, potentially, world peace. What would it take for North Korea to so disturb you in Beijing that you will take action against the North Korean regime? What would they have to do for you to say, enough, we are now going to intervene?

Liu Xiaoming: China has done a lot. Before I came here I was Ambassador there — I'd been there for three and a half years. China actively engaged with the DPRK . We tried to persuade them to be committed to denuclearization.

Humphrys: And it's failed?

Liu Xiaoming: No, I can't say it's failed. Sometimes we make two steps forward, one step backward, and one step forward, two steps backward. But the DPRK nuclear programme is a complicated issue. It has to be addressed comprehensively. A comprehensive approach is necessary. That's why China proposed to have this "dual suspension", "double track" approach. That means, on the one hand, we should keep sanctions in place, we should persuade the DPRK to be committed to denuclearization and on the other hand ...

Humphrys: And if you fail, the United State will intervene ...

Liu Xiaoming: On the other hand, the United States, the ROK and other countries should also take steps. They should suspend their military exercises. Each time I tried to persuade the DPRK to be committed to denuclearization, they would say, we are threatened by big superpower, the States, joined by their allies. The US and its allies have done many military exercises directed at the DPRK .

So we are calling for "dual suspension": the DPRK suspend their nuclear and missile activities; Americans, the ROK, their allies suspend their military exercises. Then we return to the negotiation table and start talks to find solution for a nuclear-free Korean Peninsula and a mechanism for lasting peace. We call it "dual track".

Humphrys: Alright, Ambassador, many thanks for joining us.

Liu Xiaoming: Thank you for having me.

John Humprys was the main presenter for the *Nine O'Clock News*, the flafship BBC News television programme from 1981 to 1987, and from 1987 to 2019 he presented on the BBC Radio 4 *Today* programme.

接受英国BBC《新闻之夜》栏目主持人厄本现场直播采访

作者手记

2019年6月12日，我接受英国BBC旗舰访谈栏目《新闻之夜》(*News night*)主持人马克·厄本(Mark Urban)现场直播采访。

厄本是作家、记者，担任BBC外交编辑，兼任《新闻之夜》栏目主持人。他又是一位历史学家，著有10多本历史专著。

这次采访正值"修例风波"演变成大规模暴乱。厄本一上来就质问，中国是否依然遵守《中英联合声明》？我告诉他，香港回归后，《中英联合声明》就完成了它的使命。如果说《中英联合声明》今天还有什么作用的话，那就是为国际社会提供了国家之间通过和平方式解决争端的一个典范。但《中英联合声明》没有使英国政府对香港拥有任何权力，无主权、无治权、无干涉内政的权力。我们还谈了新疆和华为问题。

采访实录如下：

厄本： 今天来到我们演播室的是2010年起即担任中国驻英国大使的刘晓明。刘大使，你常驻英国的时间真是不短。我们先谈谈《中英联合声明》，中国是否依然承诺遵守这个条约？

刘晓明： 中国承诺在香港实行"一国两制"，这不仅是对世界的承诺，也是对包括香港同胞在内的全体中国人民的承诺。香港回归后，《中英联合声明》就完成了它的使命。"一国两制"在香港的实践非常成功。

厄本： 你说《中英联合声明》完成了它的使命，而两年前中国外交部发言人称，《中英联合声明》已经不具有现实意义了，它只是一个历史文件。

刘晓明： 它是一个历史文件，已经完成了其使命。

厄本： 它与今天已经无关了吗？

刘晓明： 《中英联合声明》今天的作用是为国际社会提供了国家之间通过和平方式解决争端的一个典范，国际社会仍可以参照这个很好的成功模式。但《中英联合声明》没有使英国政府对香港拥有任何权力，英国无主权、无治权、无干涉内政的权力。

厄本： 英国对香港的主权1997年就结束了，这是明确的。但是香港成千上万的民众依然认为英国根据《中英联合声明》有责任捍卫他们的权利。

刘晓明： 英国政府有义务保护自己的公民，但并没有保护香港人的义务，香港是中国的一部分，根据《基本法》，港人管理自己的事务，他们有权保持与中国内地不一样的社会制度。但这与英国政府无关。

厄本： 姑且不说英国政府。你可以看看香港民意，数以万计的香港人，有人说香港人口的1/10，他们走上街头，他们感到不满，他们认为北京不尊重他们选择体制的权利。

刘晓明： 这是错误的，整个事件被歪曲了，香港修订条例是为了完善法律，堵塞现行法律体系的漏洞。

厄本： 是谁在歪曲事实？

刘晓明： 一些媒体，我认为，包括BBC。BBC把事件曲解成香港特区政府修例是受中央政府指使的。事实上，中央从未指示香港修例，此次修例是香港特区政府自己发起的，起因是一起发生在中国台湾的凶杀案……

厄本： 对不起，鉴于争议很大，你是否建议香港特区政府放弃修例？

刘晓明： 我们为什么要要求香港特区政府放弃修例呢？

厄本： 你也看到，刚才节目中甚至有立法会成员说，警察把市民打得要离开香港。

刘晓明： 你应该记得，开始时是和平游行，但后来变得很恶劣，袭击警察，警察也要自卫，警方必须维持秩序，你不能责备警察。我认为，香港内部和外部的一些势力在利用此事来挑起事端。让我再接着讲……

厄本： 但这是香港草根民众自发的运动。

刘晓明： 事实上，100万的数字被夸大了，警方的估计大约有20万人。而且你们忽视了有80万人签名支持修例。在英国，BBC并未报道那些支持修例的沉默大多数。

厄本： 你说得有道理。

刘晓明： 香港特区政府就修例征求了民众的意见和建议，收到的4500份反馈中，3000份支持修例，只有1500份反对。

厄本： 我们再谈一两个其他问题。中国对待新疆维吾尔族的方式，对港人会产生什么影响？估计有100万穆斯林受到不公正待遇。

刘晓明： 你又在夸大其词，不知你哪来的100万。

厄本： 这是联合国的估算。

刘晓明： 联合国从来没有这样的报告。新疆为了帮助受极端思想蛊惑的群众回归社会，获得谋生技能，设立了职业技能教育培训中心，提供职业技能和语言技能培训，还提供法律知识教育，帮助学员维护自己的权益。

厄本： 我们能去培训中心看看吗？能看看里面到底什么情况吗？

刘晓明： 当然可以，我们邀请了记者和外交官去参访。

厄本： 但是有报道说那里面的穆斯林信仰得不到尊重。

刘晓明： 这种说法是完全错误的。

厄本： 还有报道说，不允许他们祷告，还说他们的信仰落后，等等。

刘晓明： 这完全是歪曲捏造，是假新闻。中国尊重公民的信仰自由，人民有信仰宗教的权利。问题的关键是，你忽视了大局。教培中心设立的初衷是教育年轻人，清除极端主义流毒。新疆采取相关措施以来，已经连续3年没有发生极端主义事件，这正说明相关措施是成功的。

厄本： 我认为任何人都能理解中国防范恐怖主义和去极端化的初衷，在这一点上中国与世界上其他政府和社会有着共同之处。但是仍不断有报告称，教培中心规模巨大，人数非常多，大约有100万，听起来很恐怖。

刘晓明： 我真不知道你哪来的100万这个数字。

厄本： 你估计有多少人?

刘晓明： 教培中心的学员有进有出，具体人数随时变化，很难统计，关键是要认识到中心设立的目的。设立中心不是为了拘押，而是为了帮助年轻人通过接受教育和培训过上更好的生活。

厄本： 你是说目的不是消灭宗教?

刘晓明： 绝对不是。

厄本： 华为，这是一个大问题，我想也是你作为驻英国大使非常关心的问题。英国政府暂时决定在5G网络建设中使用部分华为设备。你也知道，美国对此施加了很大的压力，要求不使用华为的任何设备。从中方的立场看，如果英国决定不使用华为设备，会面临什么样的后果?

刘晓明： 首先，我认为华为是一家好企业，是5G技术领军者。华为与英国企业开展互利合作，不仅对英国的电信业做出了巨大贡献，而且创造了5.1万个就业机会。从双赢角度来看，如果英国选择与华为合作，双方都将有一个十分光明的前景。

厄本： 华为的技术非常先进，没有人对此抱有怀疑。但如果英国不选择使用华为会有什么后果呢?

刘晓明: 我认为这将向华为和其他中国企业释放一个非常糟糕的信号。如果这样,英国还能保持开放吗?英国还能为中国企业提供友善的营商环境吗?这将是非常负面的信号。

厄本: 对贸易会产生消极影响吗?

刘晓明: 是的,不仅对贸易,对投资也会造成不好的影响。过去5年,中国对英国投资数量超过了此前30年对英国投资的总量。中国对英国的投资正在快速增长,去年增长了14%。如果英国对华为关门,必将向其他中国企业释放非常糟糕的负面信号。

厄本: 好的,大使,非常感谢你接受今天的采访。

刘晓明: 不客气。

A Live Interview with Mark Urban on BBC *Newsnight*

On 12th June 2019, I gave a live interview to BBC *Newsnight* hosted by Mark Urban. I talked about China's position on issues relating to Hong Kong, Xinjiang and Huawei, and answered questions. The transcript is as follows:

Urban: We are joined by Ambassador Liu Xiaoming, who's been the Chinese Ambassador to the UK since 2010. Quite a period! Ambassador, let's start with the Joint Declaration. That treaty. Is China still committed to upholding it?

Liu Xiaoming: We are upholding the principle of one country, two systems. This promise has been made not only to the world, but also to the Chinese people, including those in Hong Kong. The Joint Declaration has completed its mission after Hong Kong's handover. And now, I think the "one country, two systems" has been very successful in Hong Kong.

Urban: You say it has completed its mission, I want to put to you something your foreign ministry spokesman said two years ago, that the Declaration no longer has realistic meaning, it is purely a historic document.

Liu Xiaoming: It is a historic document. It completed its mission.

Urban: So it's irrelevant?

Liu Xiaoming: It's relevant in that it sets a good example for the international community to settle a dispute between nations by peaceful means, so it's still a shining, successful example for people to follow. But that Declaration gives British

Government no sovereignty, no right, no legitimacy to interfere in the internal affairs of Hong Kong.

Urban: No sovereignty that is clear. That ended in 1997, but still an interest and a feeling on the part of hundreds of thousands of people in Hong Kong that Britain has a duty to protect their rights, under the terms of that promise.

Liu Xiaoming: The British government has a duty to protect your own citizens but not the people of Hong Kong. The citizens of Hong Kong are, you know, they are part of China now, and according to the basic law, Hong Kong people will run their own affairs and they are entitled to implementing their social system different from the mainland. But it has nothing to do with the British government.

Urban: I am sure you can see, putting the British Government to one side now, just the feeling of the people in Hong Kong, hundreds of thousands, some say 10% of the entire population have come out on the streets, a nerve has been touched that Beijing is not respecting their right to a separate system ...

Liu Xiaoming: This is not correct. The whole story has been distorted. This case is about rectifying the deficiencies, plugging the loopholes of the existing legal system.

Urban: Who is distorting this?

Liu Xiaoming: The media, including the BBC, I think. You portrayed the story as the Hong Kong government making this amendment at the instruction of the Central Government. As a matter of fact, the Central Government gave no instruction, no order about making amendment. This amendment was initiated by the Hong Kong government. It is prompted by a murder case happened in Taiwan and this ...

Urban: Sorry. Excuse me, would you advise the Hong Kong government then to drop it, given how controversial…

Liu Xiaoming: Why should we ask them to drop it?

Urban: You can see what people, even the legislators, say. One man said "you are beating people out of Hong Kong" to the police. That is the scene we are seeing in the territory now as a result of this ...

Liu Xiaoming: But you have to remember that at the very beginning it has been a peaceful demonstration, but it has become ugly afterwards. A policeman was beaten, and the police had to defend themselves. They had to put the order in place, so you can't blame the policemen. I think there are always the forces inside and outside Hong Kong that try to take advantage of things, to stir up trouble. Let me come back to the ...

Urban: But this is a domestic, grass roots movement of people in Hong Kong.

Liu Xiaoming: But, you know, it has been exaggerated to one million. As a matter of fact, according to police count, it is about 200, 000 people. But you ignore 800, 000 people who signed up to support the amendment. This silent majority has not been reported in this country by the BBC.

Urban: Well, you are making the case now.

Liu Xiaoming: And also the Hong Kong government invited the Hong Kong public for suggestion, opinion, and they received 4, 500 replies, 3, 000 supported the amendment and only 1, 500 opposed the amendment.

Urban: I want to move onto one or two of my other issues. What effect do you think it has on people in Hong Kong when they see the treatment of Uighurs in Xinjiang. An estimated one million people, Muslims minorities…

Liu Xiaoming: Again you are exaggerating. I don't know where you get this "one million people".

Urban: It is a UN estimate.

Liu Xiaoming: I don't think the UN has any report on this. There are education and training centres to help people who have been brainwashed by extremists to return to society, to earn their living, to train them on skills, language and the knowledge of the law, so they can protect their own interests.

Urban: Can we have access, can we see what is going on?

Liu Xiaoming: Of course, we invited journalists and diplomats to visit.

Urban: But we are hearing reports that what happens in there is an assault on their Muslim faith ...

Liu Xiaoming: That is completely wrong.

Urban: ... that they are prevented from praying, they are told that as a backward religion ...

Liu Xiaoming: These are all distortions, it is all made up, fake news, I would say. We respect people's freedom of religion. People are entitled to have their religion. And the important thing is, you are missing the big picture. The reason for these centres is to educate those young people who have been intoxicated by extremist ideas. And ever since these measures, there have been no extremist violent incidents in Xinjiang for the past three years, which means these measures have been successful.

Urban: I think anyone might understand why you want to prevent terrorist acts or have de-radicalisation. I think that is because you might have in common with many other governments and societies around the world. But what we hear are persistent reports of a very large number of people, up to a million, involved in this re-education process which sounds frankly sinister.

Liu Xiaoming: I don't know where you get this number, one million.

Urban: What would your estimate be?

Liu Xiaoming: It is difficult to give a number because there are those going in, going out. The number changes from time to time, but the important thing to focus on here is the purpose of the centre. It is not to round up people. The purpose is to help these young people to have a better life after education and training.

Urban: You are saying the purpose is not to eradicate the religion among these people, it is not the aim of this exercise?

Liu Xiaoming: Not at all.

Urban: Huawei. It's a big subject, I am sure, for you in your post in London. It's something you care a lot about. The British Government has been in a position where it seems to make an interim decision or advise to use some elements of Huawei's technology in its 5G network. Now as you know, quite a lot of pressure from the United States not to do so at all. Will there be consequences, do you think, from the Chinese point of view, if Britain decides not to use it at all?

Liu Xiaoming: First of all, I would say Huawei is a good company. It is a leader in 5G. They are here for win-win cooperation with their British counterparts. And they contribute tremendously not only to telecom industry in this country, but also they supported 51,000 jobs. In terms of win-win collaboration, if the UK collaborates with Huawei, there will be promising future for both sides.

Urban: They have got advanced technology, no one doubts about it. But what if the UK chooses not to?

Liu Xiaoming: I think it would send a very bad message not only to Huawei but also to Chinese businesses. Will the UK remain open? Will the UK still be a business friendly environment for Chinese companies? It would send a very bad signal.

Urban: Negative effects on trade?

Liu Xiaoming: Yes, bad. Not just on trade but also on investment. For the past 5 years, the investment from China exceeded the total investment in the previous 30 years. So, Chinese investments are booming in this country. Last year it increased by 14%, but if you shut the door for Huawei, it will send a very bad and negative message to other Chinese businesses.

Urban: On that note, Ambassador, thank you very much for joining us.

Liu Xiaoming: My pleasure.

> Mark Urban is a British journalist, historian, and broadcaster, and is currently the Diplomatic Editor and occasional presenter for BBC 2's *Newsnight*.

接受英国BBC世界新闻台
主持人霍金斯现场直播采访

作者手记

　　2019年6月13日，我接受英国BBC世界新闻台（World News）主持人露西·霍金斯（Lucy Hockings）现场直播采访，就中国香港"修例风波"阐述中方立场。

　　世界新闻台是BBC 24小时向全球200多个国家和地区滚动播放的新闻频道，受众近1亿人。霍金斯是记者、制片人、媒体培训师，担任世界新闻台主持人10余年。

　　采访中，她反复纠缠为什么要修例。我告诉她，中国香港特区政府为的是解决现行法律体系中的缺陷，使香港免于成为"避罪天堂"，使香港变得更好。她借"修例风波"质疑中国的司法制度。我强调中国是法治社会，法律体系在不断完善，特别是中国在人权保护方面取得巨大进步。针对她怀疑中国是否遵守"一国两制"，我指出，我们严格遵守"一国两制"。香港回归以来，"一国两制"取得巨大成功，香港20年来保持了繁荣和稳定。

　　采访实录如下：

霍金斯： 关于香港问题，我们请中国驻英国大使刘晓明谈谈中国政府的看法。谢谢刘大使来到我们演播室。

我们看到成千上万香港人走上街头，他们中间有专业人士，还有律师，都在反对香港特区政府修例。为什么中国要修例？

刘晓明： 并不是所有人都反对。还有80多万香港人签名支持香港特区政府对条例进行修订。

霍金斯： 中国中央政府支持修例吗？

刘晓明： 我们当然支持。香港特区政府的这些努力是为了解决现行法律体系中的缺陷，使香港免于成为"避罪天堂"，使香港变得更好，为什么不支持？

霍金斯： 走上街头的那些人不反对把香港变得更好，但是他们担心如果向中国内地移交政治犯，那么异见活动分子、人权律师、记者、社工等将面临安全风险，你能否解决他们的关切？中国中央政府能否承诺不会发生这样的事？

刘晓明： 这种说法是完全错误的。事实上，涉及移交的37项罪行与新闻、言论、结社、出版自由等完全无关，还特别规定涉及政治等罪行不会移交，而且相关罪行必须是香港和有关司法管辖区两地法律均认定为犯罪的。最重要的是，修例不是向中国内地移交罪犯，而是面向所有尚未与香港签订移交逃犯长期安排的国家和地区建立特别移交安排。

霍金斯： 但是，你能保证修例不会被当作对付政治对手的工具吗？

刘晓明： 绝对不会。这不是修例的目的。我认为事情被歪曲了，有人怀着不可告人、别有用心的目的。

霍金斯： 谁怀着不可告人的目的？

刘晓明： 那些不愿看到香港繁荣稳定的势力。

霍金斯： 他们是谁？

刘晓明： 对香港满怀敌意的势力。

霍金斯： 是外国势力，还是香港内部势力？

刘晓明： 有的外国势力对香港的游行示威表示支持，对修例表达所谓的关切。人们有理由质疑其背后的动机。

霍金斯： 外界以及其他国家之所以关心这个问题，是因为中国内地司法体系被指责存在诸如酷刑、强迫认罪、任意逮捕等严重缺陷，令人担心如果被移交到中国内地将不会得到公正的审判。

刘晓明： 我断然拒绝这些毫无根据的指责。中国是法治社会，法律体系在不断完善，我们也在不断改革。

霍金斯： 但是大使先生，中国定罪率高达几乎100%。

刘晓明： 我不同意这种说法。这是对中国法律体系的错误描述。我觉得你真应该好好看看、认真了解中国每天都在进步，特别是中国在人权保护方面取得了巨大进步，正在努力建设一个健全的法律体系。我认为在背后挑起事端的势力，不光企图诋毁香港特区政府，同时也想诋毁中国内地的司法体系。这就是我说的"别有用心"。

霍金斯： 就是说在中国内地可以得到公正的审判。

刘晓明： 当然是，这是肯定的。

霍金斯： 世界上很多人可能不这么认为。最近新西兰法官就不想把嫌犯交还给中国。我们继续探讨下一个问题。许多示威者称，香港的体制被侵蚀，你是否承诺中国仍然遵守"一国两制"？

刘晓明： 我们严格遵守"一国两制"。香港回归以来，"一国两制"取得了巨大成功，香港20年来保持了繁荣和稳定。这个政策也保障了港人示威的权利。在修例问题上应当进行文明协商、文明辩论，应给立法会时间来进行讨论。街头暴力不利于建设香港文明社会。

霍金斯： 修例让许多商界领袖担心，投资者的信心将受到影响，许多跨国公司担心在香港的经营。

刘晓明： 我觉得恰恰相反。如果香港继续成为一个"避罪天堂"，你认为那就安全了？那能确保香港繁荣吗？我听到一些外国企业家……

霍金斯： 人们真正的担忧是，如果有人在香港做了中国政府不喜欢的事情，可能会被移送到中国内地，面临不公平司法体系的审判。

刘晓明： 这完全是曲解。我告诉你一些数字。过去20年里，香港只对外移交了100名罪犯，也就是说，每年5起移交逃犯案件。还有一个数据，自2006年以来，内地向香港移送了248名罪犯，而香港没有向内地移送任何罪犯。你认为这种关系可持续吗？内地提出了移交请求，但是因为这种安排上的缺陷和漏洞，没有一名逃犯被移交到内地。

霍金斯： 目前，街头示威群众和各种请愿给了林郑月娥特首前所未有的压力，示威者说他们大约有100万人。

刘晓明： 你的数字不对。按照警方统计，人数约为20万。过去4个月左右，香港特区政府就修例法案征询公众意见，收到的4500份书面意见中，其中3000份支持修例，只有1500份反对。

霍金斯： 我们掌握的数字确实不一样。但我们都看到了，上街的人出乎想象的多，他们来自社会各界。

刘晓明： 你们媒体的问题在于只关注那些上街的人，而忘记了沉默的大多数。

霍金斯： 所以我们要请你来告诉我们故事的另一面。

刘晓明： 是的，我来这儿的目的之一，就是要告诉人们故事的另一面。

霍金斯： 我一直在关注新华社今天的报道，作为国家媒体的新华社对香港的情况没有报道。为什么不报道？

刘晓明： 我昨晚刚刚接受了BBC《新闻之夜》的采访，中国各大网站广泛刊发了这次采访的全部内容。

霍金斯： 我想请你看一下屏幕。这是新华社网站，首页没有香港的消息。

刘晓明： 我不评价新闻通讯社自己的报道政策。但我要说……

霍金斯： 中国人，特别是内地的中国人，对香港修例了解多少？

刘晓明： 人们认为，香港特区政府修例是正确的行动，香港特区政府正在努力采取措施使香港成为"正义天堂"，而不是"避罪天堂"。这将为香港繁荣发展提供保障，中国中央政府坚决、全力支持香港特区政府。

霍金斯： 感谢刘大使接受BBC世界新闻台的采访。

刘晓明： 不客气。

A Live Interview with Lucy Hockings on BBC World News

On 13th June 2019, I gave a live interview to BBC World News hosted by Lucy Hockings, in which I talked about China's position on issues relating to Hong Kong. The transcript is as follows:

Hockings: Let's talk about the view from Beijing. With us is the Chinese Ambassador to the UK, Liu Xiaoming, who is with me now. Thank you for joining us.

We've seen hundreds of thousands of people out on the streets of Hong Kong, professionals, lawyers as well, all objecting to this bill. Why does China want it?

Liu Xiaoming: Not all are protesting. I think 800, 000 people signed up to support the Hong Kong government's move to amend these ordinances through a bill.

Hockings: Does China want this bill?

Liu Xiaoming: Of course, we support this, because this effort by the Hong Kong government will address the discrepancies of the existing system so that Hong Kong will not continue to be a safe haven for fugitive criminals. So this will make Hong Kong a better place. Why should we not support it?

Hockings: The people on the streets are not objecting to that. But can you address these concerns that this is going to put people at risk to extradition to China for political crimes. That suggest no one is going to be safe, activists, human rights lawyers, journalists, and social workers? Is there commitment from Beijing this will not happen?

Liu Xiaoming: This is totally wrong! In fact, there are 37 crimes listed in the ordinance and none of them has to do with any freedom of expression, freedom of assembly, freedom of speech, freedom of publication, and there is special mention that no offence will be related to political issues. And it has to be crimes in the laws of both places — both Hong Kong and the other jurisdiction. The important thing one has to realize is it's not about extradition to China. It's about special arrangements with all judicial parties of those who do not have a mutual assistance agreement…

Hockings: But you can assure us that this bill will not be used as a tool against political opponents?

Liu Xiaoming: Not at all. It's not the purpose of this bill. I think this has been distorted. I think there is someone with ulterior motives to make it…

Hockings: Who has ulterior motives?

Liu Xiaoming: Those forces who are not happy with stability and prosperity in Hong Kong.

Hockings: What forces?

Liu Xiaoming: Hostile forces that do not want to see Hong Kong…

Hockings: Are you talking about foreign powers, or forces inside Hong Kong?

Liu Xiaoming: You heard some foreign powers express support for the demonstrators, express so-called concerns about these amendments. People have a reason to be concerned about the motives behind it.

Hockings: One of the reasons that people are concerned, and foreign countries are concerned, is because China has a deeply flawed judicial system. There are allegations of torture, forced confessions, arbitrary detentions. There is the concern that when someone is extradited to mainland China, they will not get a fair trial.

Liu Xiaoming: No. I totally reject these allegations. China is a country ruled by law.

The legal system is improving. The reform is going on.

Hockings: But Ambassador, there is almost a 100% conviction rate in China.

Liu Xiaoming: No, I don't think so. I don't think this is a correct description of the law system in China. I think you really have to look at how China is changing with each passing day. Especially, China has made great progress in terms of protection of human rights, in terms of building a sound legal system. I think that one of the forces behind this, sterring up the trouble, not only trying to demonize the HK government but also try to demonize the judicial system in China. So that is the ulterior motive I am talking about.

Hockings: So people in China get a fair trial.

Liu Xiaoming: Yes, of course. Definitely.

Hockings: Many people would dispute that, the world over. We've just even seen the judge in New Zealand not wanting to send someone back to China. But if we can move on from that, could you also reassure people perhaps about the commitment to the One Country Two Systems, because so many of those protesters up there say that they are seeing the system eroded? Is that something that China is still committed to?

Liu Xiaoming: We are very committed to One Country Two Systems. The One Country Two Systems has been very successful. That's why you can have prosperity and stability in Hong Kong in the past 20 years. If it were not for this policy, you would not have this demonstration, I would say. So I am calling for a civilized discussion on this amendment, or a civilized debate. Give the legislative council the time to debate. So I don't think this violence, the riots in Hong Kong in the streets, are in the interest of building a civilized society in Hong Kong.

Hockings: Many leaders of business are also concerned this is going to undermine investors' confidence in Hong Kong, that multinationals will be worried about working there.

Liu Xiaoming: I think it's just the opposite. If Hong Kong continues to be a haven for criminals, you think that was safe? And that will ensure prosperity? I heard that some foreign...

Hockings: The genuine worry is that if someone does something that Chinese government doesn't like in Hong Kong, they may find themselves in a court and an unfair system in mainland China.

Liu Xiaoming: That's a complete distortion of the picture. Let me give you a figure. In the past 20 years, there are only 100 criminals being surrendered by Hong Kong government. That means five cases a year. And I will also give you another example. Since 2006, 248 criminals have been handed over from mainland to Hong Kong. Yet, none has been handed over to mainland. Do you think this relationship could be sustainable? You know, we made requests, but because of this arrangement, this discrepancy, the gap, no surrender of any criminals, no fugitive criminals have been handed over to mainland.

Hockings: There is unprecedented pressure on Carrie Lam right now from the people on the streets and from petitions. The protestors said about a million people are out on the street.

Liu Xiaoming: No, no. According to police accounts, it's 200, 000 people. And, in the past four months or so, Hong Kong government invited opinions. And they received 4, 500 written replies: 3, 000 supporting the amendment and only 1, 500 ...

Hockings: I think we will have to agree that some of the figures are in dispute. Well, you see some of the pictures of people on the streets. There are an incredible amount of people, from right across the society... in the UK.

Liu Xiaoming: The problem of your media is you only focus on the people in the street. You forget the silent majority.

Hockings: That is why you are with us to tell us about that side.

Liu Xiaoming: Yes, that's one of my purposes to share with you the other side of the story.

Hockings: Can I show you, I have been having a look at Xinhua today, the state News Agency in China. There is absolutely no mention of what is happening in Hong Kong on state media in China. Why are you not reporting this in China?

Liu Xiaoming: I just did an interview, before I came here, last night on BBC *Newsnight*. The whole interview was published on the website in China. It was broadcasted broadly.

Hockings: But can I draw your attention to the screen here. This is Xinhua right now. There is no mention of Hong Kong on the front page of the website.

Liu Xiaoming: I would not make comment about the news agency's policies. But I would say….

Hockings: What are people in China being told about what is happening in Hong Kong?

Liu Xiaoming: This is a good move, a good action by the Hong Kong government to turn Hong Kong into a "heaven for justice" instead of "haven for fugitives". It will ensure the prosperity of Hong Kong, and Hong Kong government has the full and resolute support of the Central Government.

Hockings: Ambassador Liu Xiaoming, it was good to have you with us. Thank you very much for joining us here on BBC World News.

Liu Xiaoming: My pleasure.

BBC World News claims to be watched by a weekly audience of 74 million in over 200 countries and territories worldwide. Lucy Hockings is a New Zealand news presenter for the BBC, moderator, events host, and media trainer. Her roles include anchoring *Live with Lucy Hockings* on BBC World News.

接受英国BBC《安德鲁·马尔访谈》栏目主持人马尔现场直播采访

作者手记

2019年7月7日，我在英国BBC总部演播室，接受英国BBC旗舰高端访谈栏目《安德鲁·马尔访谈》（*The Andrew Marr Show*）主持人安德鲁·马尔（Andrew Marr）现场直播采访。

采访主要围绕三个问题：香港"修例风波"、华为、新疆。他问我如何评价英国外交大臣同情香港示威者，提出所谓华为设备安全风险，称新疆到处都是"集中营"，并突然插播一段视频让我评价。

我指出，英国外交大臣威胁要对中国实施制裁，这完全是冷战思维；华为是一家优秀的企业，拒绝华为只会让英国错失巨大机遇；所谓新疆问题，完全是西方媒体对新疆真实情况的歪曲报道。

采访实录如下：

马尔： 最近，围绕香港修例引发的示威游行，中英之间发生了外交争论。示威者认为修例是对人权的侵蚀，英国外交大臣亨特对示威者表示同情。中国驻英国大使刘晓明罕见地举行了记者会，对英方干涉中国内政表示强烈谴责。今天我邀请刘晓明大使做客访谈节目，这是他自记者会后首次接受采访。欢迎大使先生！记者会上，你确实感到十分愤怒吧？

刘晓明： 是的，中方坚决反对英方干涉香港内部事务。我们认为，修例决定是合理的，香港特区行政长官和政府为的是使香港成为更好、更安全的地方，而不是"避罪天堂"。然而，英国政府高官却支持示威者。更恶劣的是，当发生暴力事件时，英方依然表示支持，不仅不谴责暴力冲击立法会的行动，反而批评香港特区政府处置暴力事件。

马尔： 亨特外交大臣只是表示"心与示威者同在"，但并不赞同暴力行动。很多人认为，香港回归中国时，中方承诺对香港政策将保持50年不变，但修例将侵蚀这一承诺。在他们看来，如果香港人能够轻易被移交到中国内地，那么很多人就不敢随便说话了，言论自由将被逐渐压制，这意味着"一国两制"开始走向终结。

刘晓明： 安德鲁，看来你对修例的实际内容缺乏了解，有关条例并不只是要把罪犯从香港移交到内地。香港与30个国家签订了刑事司法协助协定，但香港与超过170个国家或地区还没有签订相关协定。如果有人在香港以外地方犯罪，逃到香港，香港就无法对其依法惩治。修例就是为了堵住漏洞。一些人有意利用此事在香港民众中煽动恐慌。

马尔： 北京需要移交罪犯的权力，是吗？

刘晓明： 我不这么认为。修例的提议由特区政府发起，正如行政长官所说，特区政府从未收到来自中央政府的指示或命令，这完全是特区政府的提议，是为了完善香港的法律体系。

马尔： 我们都看到了立法会受冲击的视频，香港警方似乎无法阻挡抗议的示威者。如果中方认为形势失控、特区政府无法控局，中国中央政府会直接介入吗？

刘晓明： 你提到了"一国两制"50年不变，我们完全遵守这项承诺，这是毫无疑问的。从这件事开始一直到现在，中国中央政府从未进行任何干预，每个阶段都是特区政府在处理。相反，英国政府却在干涉，一开始对示威者表示支持。当暴徒冲击立法会时，它又声称不能以暴力事件为借口进行镇压，它企图破坏香港法治。对你的问题，我的回答十分明确，我们对特区政府有信心，而且事实已经证明它有能力应对事态。

马尔： 无论如何，修例将使向内地移交罪犯变得更加容易。末任港督彭定康称，事态正在逐步恶化，持有不同观点的人不能参加政治活动，媒体和大学言论自由被削弱。一些人在香港被劫持，然后被带回内地。

刘晓明： 我断然拒绝彭定康的指责。作为香港末任港督，他身体已经进入21世纪，但脑袋却仍留在旧殖民时代。修例并不会使从香港移交罪犯变得更容易，修例有保障条款，37种罪行以外的不属于移交范围。比如，涉及宗教和政治类的不在移交之列，而且罪行必须在香港、内地两地都成立。假设一个极端的例子，如果谋杀在香港不构成刑事犯罪，那么杀人犯就不会被移交。

马尔： 近期中英之间争吵十分激烈。亨特甚至威胁要对中国实施制裁，中英关系出现危机了吗？

刘晓明： 我不这样认为。我们对与英国进行外交争论不感兴趣，中方仍致力于与英国发展强劲有力的伙伴关系。我还记得上次接受你的专访，是在习近平主席2015年对英国进行国事访问前夕，那次访问开启了中英关系"黄金时代"。

马尔： 我当然记得。

刘晓明： 中方一直致力于推进中英关系"黄金时代"。但我不同意英国某些政客所谓对华保持"战略模糊"的说法，它不属于中英关系的词汇，而完全是冷战思维语境。

马尔： 英中关系另外一个争议很大的话题，就是华为参与英国5G电信网络建设。我想问的是，中国会允许西方国家，比如英国或美国的企业直接参与你们的安全领域基础设施建设吗？

刘晓明： 中国仍在不断发展中。对你的问题，简而言之，我不认为华为会直接参与涉及英国安全的基础设施建设。

马尔: 华为将能够监听涉及英国人民日常生活的方方面面。中国的法律也规定了，企业有义务配合政府，提供政府需要的信息，这是让人们最为担心的事情。

刘晓明: 绝对不会发生这样的事情。首先，华为不存在任何"后门"。其次，还有很多其他的安全措施。

马尔: 你可以在我的节目上向所有观众保证，即使华为拥有进入英国5G网络的全部权限，华为也不会将有关信息传递给中国政府吗？

刘晓明: 我可以保证，这样的事绝不会发生！华为是一家优秀的企业，是5G建设中的领军者。拒绝华为只会让英国错失巨大机遇。华为来英国是为了互利合作，而不是为了监听任何人。

马尔: 好吧，让我们转到两国关系中另一个具有争议的话题，即中国西北的维吾尔族受到的待遇。据报道，那里到处都是"集中营"。根据联合国统计数据，近100万人被关押。BBC也报道了儿童被迫与家人分开，被送到专门的"儿童营地"。那里究竟发生了什么？

刘晓明: 我认为这是你们的媒体对新疆真实情况的歪曲报道。在中国，新疆经济发展相对落后，全国30多个省级行政区中，新疆地区国内生产总值（GDP）排名位列第二十六名。自20世纪90年代以来，新疆遭受了恐怖主义、分裂主义和极端主义"三股势力"的严重破坏。10年前的7月5日，新疆发生了非常严重的暴力恐怖袭击事件，197人遇难。

马尔： 但"培训营"不是解决问题的答案。英国在北爱尔兰使用过类似方法，用铁丝网围起来，不允许人员自由离开。这种做法损害了英国的形象。

刘晓明： 没有什么"培训营"，我们称为"职业技能教育培训中心"。极端思想在贫困地区更易传播渗透，要使人们摆脱极端思想的毒害，就要使贫困地区的人民脱贫。

马尔： 那为何中国政府否认它们的存在？

刘晓明： 我们从未否认它们的存在，我们甚至邀请外国外交官和包括BBC在内的外国媒体去参访，BBC记者与学员见面并采访了他们。我认为，人们应该从积极的角度看待这件事，设立职业教培中心的目的就是预防恐怖活动，从源头上消除恐怖极端思想的侵害。自从这项措施实施以来，新疆已有3年未发生恐袭事件。

马尔： 不管怎么说，这也是严格管理的地方。在这些"集中营"，人员不能离开，是吗？

刘晓明： 他们当然能离开，他们能自由会见他们的家人亲属，这绝不是所谓"监狱"或"集中营"。

马尔： BBC采访了一些在土耳其的新疆人，他们称自己的孩子被迫与他们分开，他们表示很担心。我可以放一段视频，让我们听听他们说了什么。这些孩子现在在哪里？（马尔播放视频）

刘晓明： 我们先来谈谈这些人是什么人。这些人都是反对中国政府的，你期待他们会说中国政府的好话吗？教培中心学员的孩子们得到政府精心照顾。

马尔： 在新疆，他们的孩子被迫与他们分离？

刘晓明： 绝不是这样。这些人如果想见自己的孩子，完全可以回中国。

马尔： 所以这些都是谎言吗？

刘晓明： 当然是谎言。根本没有所谓"强制父母和孩子分离"的情况。

马尔： BBC记者去新疆采访了一次，称有400个家庭的孩子失踪。

刘晓明： 你可以把失踪孩子的家庭具体信息告诉我。关于人员失踪，有许多信息是错误的，我们需要甄别处理。比如，某国称新疆一位维吾尔族音乐家被杀害，但这位音乐家很快公开露面，活得好好的。如果你掌握所谓失踪孩子的信息，请你告诉我，我们会尽力帮助寻找，我们会告诉你，他们是谁，他们现在在干什么。

马尔： 大使先生，谢谢你接受我的采访。

刘晓明： 不客气。

A Live Interview
on BBC *The Andrew Marr Show*

On 7th July 2019, I gave a live interview on BBC *The Andrew Marr Show* about issues of Hong Kong, Huawei and Xinjiang. The full text is as follows:

Marr: Now, most diplomatic arguments are restrained muttering affairs, not so the row going on between Britain and China over protests in Hong Kong about a new extradition bill which many people there fear will shred their human rights. Jeremy Hunt, the Foreign Secretary, sympathized with the protesters. The Chinese Ambassador then held a rather rare press conference in which he angrily condemned the UK government for interfering in Chinese internal affairs. He is with me now for his first interview since then. Welcome, Mr. Ambassador. You were quite angry, weren't you?

Liu Xiaoming: Yes, very much so. We are strongly opposed to British intervention in Hong Kong's internal affairs. We believe that this amendment of ordinance has a good reasons because the Chief Executive and Hong Kong SAR government want to make Hong Kong a better and safer place, rather than a safe haven for fugitive criminals. But yet, the British government, senior officials, seemed to voice support for the demonstrators. What makes it even worse is that when the violence happened, instead of condemning the storming of the Legislative Council, they criticized the Hong Kong SAR government for the handling of the situation.

Marr: Jeremy Hunt just said that his heart went out to the protesters and he didn't approve of the violence. A lot of people thought there was a 50-year guarantee that not much would change in Hong Kong when handover happened, and that this is being eroded by this new law, because once you can extradite somebody very easily from Hong Kong to the mainland, then lots of people would stop saying what they would have said and free speech would be slowly silenced. And people do feel this is the beginning of the end of "One Country, Two Systems" agreement.

Liu Xiaoming: Andrew, that shows your lack of understanding of what this bill is about. It is not about extraditing people from Hong Kong to the mainland. Hong Kong has mutual assistance agreements with 30 countries, yet they do not have this similar agreement with more than 170 other countries and regions. So that means if some people committed a crime outside Hong Kong and returned to Hong Kong, Hong Kong cannot punish them. This bill will plug the loopholes. I think some people are trying to use it to scare the Hong Kong people.

Marr: These are powers that Beijing wants?

Liu Xiaoming: I don't think so. The whole thing was started by the Hong Kong SAR government. Just as the Chief Executive said, she received no instruction from Beijing. She received no order from Beijing. It is completely the initiative of Hong Kong SAR government to make Hong Kong system more perfect, to improve the legal system.

Marr: We've seen all the scenes in LegCo in Hong Kong recently. There seemed to be the case that the police there couldn't hold back the protesters. If you feel the situation is getting out of control and the Hong Kong authorities can't control things, does China interfere directly in Hong Kong?

Liu Xiaoming: You mentioned "One China, Two Systems" for 50 years. We are fully committed to this promise. There is no question about that. So you can see that from day one till now, the central government has not interfered at all. Every step of the way, we let the Hong Kong SAR government handle this. Instead, it is the British government that was trying to interfere, voicing support for the demonstrators. When the rioters stormed the Legislative Council, they then said that you can't use this violence as a pretext for repression. So they tried to obstruct the legal process. To answer your question in a simple way, we have full confidence in Hong Kong SAR government. And it shows that they are capable of handling the situation.

Marr: Nevertheless, this law would make it easier to extradite people to China. Chris Patten, the last governor, said, things have gone from bad to very bad to even worse. People with the wrong views have been banned from political activity. Freedom of speech has been whittled away in the media and in the universities. Beijing has even abducted individuals from Hong Kong and taken them back to the mainland.

Liu Xiaoming: I totally reject the accusation of Chris Patten. As the last governor of Hong Kong, his body is in the 21st century, but his head remains in the old colonial days. This bill won't make it easier for Hong Kong to extradite people to the mainland. There are many safeguards. You know, first of all, there are 37 clauses as safeguards in this Bill. That means, no people would be extradited to mainland because of their religious or political beliefs. And the crime has to be punishable in both places. That means, to make an extreme case, if murder was not regarded as a crime in Hong Kong, then people who committed murder would not be extradited to the mainland.

Marr: There has been a very, very angry row by diplomatic standards. Jeremy Hunt is still threatening further, possibly, sanctions and so forth against China if it goes on. Is this a moment when British-Chinese relations are in real crisis?

Liu Xiaoming: I don't think so. We are not interested in a diplomatic row with the UK. We are still committed to building a stronger relationship, a partnership, the "Golden Era" started by President Xi. I still remember the last time you interviewed me was before President Xi's visit in 2015.

Marr: I remember that.

Liu Xiaoming: We are still committed to this "Golden Era" between our two countries. But I cannot agree with some British politicians' description of the relationship. They even use this so-called "strategic ambiguity". I think this language does not belong to the vocabulary between China and the UK. It is a Cold War language.

Marr: Another big row between Britain and China potentially is over the role of Huawei in the 5G electronic communications network. Can I put it to you that there is no way at all that the People's Republic of China would allow Western or British or

American companies direct access to your security infrastructure?

Liu Xiaoming: You know, China is developing. To answer your question directly, I don't think Huawei would have access to your security infrastructure.

Marr: But it will be able to eavesdrop on lots of aspects of British life. And the law currently says it is obliged to hand over information the Chinese government wants and that's what scares people.

Liu Xiaoming: No. It will not happen at all. First of all, there is no back door, and also there are a lot of safeguards.

Marr: Can you promise people on this programme that if Huawei has complete access to our 5G network, information will not be passed back to the government in Beijing by Huawei?

Liu Xiaoming: I can promise that, a hundred percent. I think Huawei is a good company. It is the leader of 5G. I think if you reject Huawei, you will miss enormous opportunities. They are here for win-win cooperation. They are not here to spy on people.

Marr: All right. Let's turn to another big element of difficulties between the two countries, which is the treatment of the Uyghur people in northwest China. Now, there are camps all across that part of China. Up to a million people, according to the United Nations, have been interned in these camps, and BBC has reported on the separation of children from their families, going into camps for children. What is going on?

Liu Xiaoming: I think the BBC have made a distorted picture of what is going on in Xinjiang. Xinjiang is a relatively poor area in China. In terms of GDP, it ranks about 26th in the whole country. There are more than 30 provinces in China. In the past, since 1990s, Xinjiang had been severely hit by terrorism, separatism and extremism. Just ten years and two days ago, on the 5th of July, there was a very serious terrorist incident.197 people got killed.

Marr: Can I just put it to you that internment camps are not the answer? We tried them in Northern Ireland and it did not go well for Britain in Northern Ireland. These are camps with razor wire around them, people cannot leave them.

Liu Xiaoming: There is no camp. It is a vocational education and training centre. You know that extremist ideas have easy penetration to the poorer areas. The idea is to help the people, to lift them out of poverty.

Marr: If these camps are only about that, if they are so innocent, why did the Chinese government deny for so long that they existed?

Liu Xiaoming: We didn't deny. We invited journalists and diplomats to visit. That is why BBC has access to interview people over there. I think you need to look at this from the positive perspective. It is for the purpose of early prevention of terrorism. And since the measure was introduced, there has been no terrorist incident for three years.

Marr: Nonetheless, these are quite difficult areas, these camps. They are internment camps and people cannot leave them, can they?

Liu Xiaoming: They can go, of course. They can leave freely. They can visit their relatives. It is not a prison. It is not a camp.

Marr: The BBC talked to some of the parents of Uyghur children who are now in Turkey and they are really upset about the fact that they have been separated from their children and they don't know where they are. I can show you a little clip of it so we can hear what they say. So where are these children? (Video is played)

Liu Xiaoming: Let's first talk about these people. They are anti-government people. You cannot expect a good word about the Chinese government. The children, you know, the government takes good care of the children.

Marr: Are they separating forcibly, parents from their children, in Xinjiang?

Liu Xiaoming: No. If they want to visit their children, they can come back to China.

Marr: So these are all just lies?

Liu Xiaoming: Definitely. There is no forcible separation of children from their parents at all.

Marr: The BBC has been to one town in the province where, in just one town, 400 families lost their children.

Liu Xiaoming: You just give me the names of the families who have lost their children. There is a lot of misinformation about people gone missing. We handled many cases like this. Some said a musician got killed and the other day he emerged alive and happy. If you have people whose children are lost, you give me the names and we will try to locate them and let you know who they are and what they are doing.

Marr: Mr. Ambassador, thank you very much indeed for talking to us.

Liu Xiaoming: My pleasure.

接受英国天空新闻台《今夜天空新闻》栏目主持人莫纳罕现场直播采访

作者手记

2019年10月1日，我在英国天空新闻台演播室，接受该台旗舰栏目《今夜天空新闻》(*Sky News Tonight*)主持人德莫特·莫纳罕(Dermot Murnaghan)现场直播采访。

《今夜天空新闻》是天空新闻台旗舰新闻访谈栏目。莫纳罕是该台资深主持人，2011—2016年曾创办、主持天空新闻台《莫纳罕访谈》栏目，2016年起主持周一至周四的《今夜天空新闻》栏目。2015年10月，习近平主席对英国国事访问前夕，我曾接受莫纳罕的采访，我们算是"老相识"了。

采访当天正值中华人民共和国成立70周年，莫纳罕的第一个问题就是，中国在阅兵式上展示包括洲际弹道导弹在内的先进军事装备，是否会让世界感觉受到威胁？接着，他问中国是否希望在未来70年取得世界主导地位？我告诉他，中国无意主导世界。中国仍然是一个发展中国家。我们还讨论了中国香港、新疆、华为问题。

采访实录如下：

莫纳罕：　今天，我邀请中国驻英国大使刘晓明来到天空新闻台。大使先生，很高兴见到你。我们首先来看今天在北京举行的中华人民共和国成立70周年的庆祝活动。我们看到中国展示了包括洲际弹道导弹在内的先进军事装备，以及成千上万的军队。习近平主席说，没有任何力量能够阻挡中国的前进步伐。世界是否应该感觉受到一些威胁？

刘晓明：　绝对不会。习近平主席在讲话中强调，中国将坚持和平发展道路。我们愿与世界各国分享中国的发展机遇。我认为，外界特别是英国媒体在谈到中华人民共和国成立70周年庆典时，只关注阅兵，阅兵只是庆祝活动的一部分。今年参加庆祝活动的既有1.5万名各军种官兵，也有10多万名普通民众，还有70组彩车组成的方阵，展示了中华人民共和国成立70年来的发展成就。

莫纳罕：　中国从农业经济发展成为世界最先进的经济体之一，成就确实十分震撼。

刘晓明：　不仅仅是农业经济的变迁。中华人民共和国成立之初，中国刚经历了100多年的战乱（**莫纳罕**：确实是。）和外来侵略与欺凌。

莫纳罕：　大使，我想问一下，中国经历了外国欺凌、占领及其引发的战争历史，这让中国对于未来的态度会产生什么样的影响？中国下一个70年的目标是什么？有人说，中国不仅要求得到世界的尊重，而且希望在未来70年取得世界主导地位。

刘晓明： 完全不是这样。中国无意主导世界。中国仍然是一个发展中国家，中国的发展仍然面临严峻挑战。因此，习近平主席说，要把我们的人民共和国巩固好、发展好，这是中国领导人和中国人民面临的最根本的任务。正如我所说，中国曾饱受外来侵略、欺凌、羞辱，因此永远不会将之施加给其他国家。

莫纳罕： 刚才我们报道了今天香港的局势，一位示威者被近距离射中胸部，人们认为中国的镇压是对民主权利的不尊重。

刘晓明： 我不能同意你的说法，香港的情况根本不是镇压。我们强烈谴责暴徒的暴力行径。香港的暴力活动已经持续了数月，严重挑战了"一国两制"的底线，严重破坏了香港法治，严重威胁到香港安全……

莫纳罕： 香港特区政府为什么不就示威者提出的民主诉求进行接触、展开对话？

刘晓明： 你应该将和平示威者和暴徒区别开来。你谈到警察使用真枪实弹，因为他们的生命受到了严重威胁。那名左肩受到枪击的暴徒，当时正用铁棒攻击警察。我想问的是，如果同样的事发生在英国会怎样？英国警察会如何应对这样的暴徒和暴行？

莫纳罕： 那也不会用实弹射击未携枪支的示威者。

刘晓明： 如果你的生命都受到严重威胁呢？

莫纳罕： 英国警察是不带枪的。

刘晓明： 我认为你说的不是事实。假如英国议会大厦被一群暴徒冲击，英国警察会如何应对？我们应该谴责这些暴行。香港是建立在法治基础上的，法治和"一国两制"是香港未来繁荣稳定的保障。

莫纳罕： 你能告诉我，如果抗议示威持续下去，双方暴力继续升级，香港特区政府会使用更多实弹吗？

刘晓明： 我希望事态会逐渐平息。

莫纳罕： 如果不能平息会怎样？

刘晓明： 我不回答假设性问题。过去几周，香港局势已有所好转，特别是林郑月娥特首开始与各界人士进行真诚对话，还成立对话办公室。民众应给予香港特区政府机会来解决他们的关切。我们承认，香港存在一些根本的、深层次的问题，如住房、年轻人就业机会等，但示威特别是暴力活动不可能解决这些深层次问题。

莫纳罕： 我想问一下新疆维吾尔族的问题。天空新闻台记者车德明报道，有数百万维吾尔族人被关押在"集中营"。

刘晓明： 这不是事实。新疆是中国最大的省级行政区，经济发展迅速。

莫纳罕： 但新疆有许多人被关进"集中营"。

刘晓明： 那不是"集中营"，正确的说法是职业技能教育培训中心。这项措施主要是为了预防恐怖主义，过去20多年新疆深受恐怖主义之害。

莫纳罕： 我们看到视频中这些人被捆绑双手、蒙着眼睛，被警察押送。他们是自愿被送进培训中心的吗？

刘晓明： 这是完全不同的两回事。视频中是押送服刑人员的正常司法活动，一些媒体有意炒作。这与教培中心没有任何关系。我们采取的措施是为了新疆绝大多数人的安全，是对联合国《防止暴力极端主义行动计划》的具体落实。

莫纳罕： 教培中心学员完成培训后，可以自由离开吗？

刘晓明： 当然可以。培训的基本目的是教育年轻人，帮助他们消除恐怖极端主义思想、学习谋生技能，避免受到极端主义思想的毒害。

莫纳罕： 最后，我想问关于华为的问题。包括美国在内的许多国家都认为华为与中国政府关系密切，所以美方禁止华为参与其网络建设。但华为仍在参与英国的5G网络建设。我们今天刚采访了美国商务部部长罗斯，他说英国应对华为保持高度警惕。如果英国也禁止华为，中国会持什么态度？

刘晓明： 首先，我完全拒绝针对华为的所谓指控。华为是一家很好的公司，是一家民营企业，与中国政府没有关系。华为是5G技术的领军者，它到英国来是为了与英国合作伙伴实现双赢，它为英国电信行业发展做出了贡献。我希望英国政府根据自身国家利益做出明智抉择。

莫纳罕： 我们都知道，美国特朗普政府给英国约翰逊政府施加了很大压力，英美就华为问题进行了讨论。如果英国真的禁止华为，那么在英国脱欧后与中国签自贸协定时，中国将采取什么态度？

刘晓明： 我认为，如果英国政府禁止华为，会发出非常错误、消极的信号。英国一直被认为是非常开放、宜商的国家，禁止华为会向世界发出消极信号，也将向中国企业发出错误信号，影响中国对英国投资。因此我希望，英国政府能根据自身国家利益和中英合作的共同利益做出决定。

莫纳罕： 谢谢刘大使。

刘晓明： 不客气。

A Live Interview with Dermot Murnaghan on *Sky News Tonight*

On 1st October 2019, I gave a live interview on *Sky News Tonight* with Dermot Murnaghan on China's development and issues of Hong Kong, Xinjiang and Huawei. The full text is as follows:

Murnaghan: With me is the Chinese Ambassador to the UK, Liu Xiaoming. Very good to see you, Ambassador. Can I start with those celebrations in Beijing of the 70 years of foundation of the state? We saw the-state-of-the-art military hardware, inter-continental ballistic missiles, thousands of troops and the President say no force can stop China marching forward. Should the world feel a little bit threatened by all that?

Liu Xiaoming: Not at all. In the President's speech, he said that China will continue to follow the path of peaceful development, and we would like to share the opportunities of China's development with the rest of the world. I think people, especially the media here, when they talk about the celebration, they only focus on the military parade. In fact, military parade is only part of the celebration. There are 15, 000 military personnel participating in the military parade, but there are 100, 000 ordinary citizens participating in the parade. There are about 70 floats describing the great achievements China has made in the past 70 years.

Murnaghan: It is an amazing achievement: from basically a peasant society to a most advanced economy in the world.

Liu Xiaoming: Not just peasant economy! The People's Republic of China was established after 100 years of countless wars —

Murnaghan: Indeed.

Liu Xiaoming: and foreign aggression, bullying ......

Murnaghan: I want to ask you, Ambassador, about how that history forms China's attitude to the future, particularly the foreign bullying, foreign occupations and foreign induced wars. What does China want for the next 70 years? Some analysis is that China wants respect but it does want domination over the next 70 years.

Liu Xiaoming: Not at all. China has no intention to dominate the world. China is still a developing country. We have daunting challenges in developing our country. Like President Xi said, we should consolidate our achievements and we should develop our country well. That is the fundamental task before the Chinese leaders and the Chinese people. China was a victim of foreign invasion, aggression, bullying and humiliation, and we certainly will never ever transfer this to other countries.

Murnaghan: When we see these things in Hong Kong today, one of the protesters was shot at very close range in the chest. People are saying, well, this Chinese crackdown isn't showing a respect for civil rights.

Liu Xiaoming: I cannot agree with you describing what happened in Hong Kong as crackdown at all. We strongly condemn the violent rioters. The violence has been going on for several months. It challenged the bottom line of the "One Country Two Systems", it challenged the rule of law in Hong Kong, and it brought damages to the security ...

Murnaghan: Why not engage and hold talks to discuss some of the democratic demands of the protesters?

Liu Xiaoming: You have to separate peaceful demonstration from violent rioters. You talk about the police using live ammunition. It is because their life was in serious threat. The rioter who had been shot on his left shoulder was the one who was using an iron club to attack the police. So, I would ask what would happen if the same thing happened in the UK. What will be the response of the British police to such rioters?

Murnaghan: They wouldn't shoot an unarmed protester with a weapon.

Liu Xiaoming: If their lives were in serious danger?

Murnaghan: The British police are not armed.

Liu Xiaoming: I don't think so. How would the British police respond if the Westminster Hall were stormed by the rioters? I think we should condemn this violence. Hong Kong is based on the rule of law. I think rule of law and "One Country Two Systems" can ensure the future of Hong Kong.

Murnaghan: Can you tell me if these protests continue and they continue to escalate in terms of the violence — there is no doubt there is extreme violence on both sides — then more fire arms will be used by the authorities?

Liu Xiaoming: I do hope things will calm down.

Murnaghan: What if not?

Liu Xiaoming: I would not answer hypothetic questions. I think things have been improving somewhat in the past few weeks since the Chief Executive started conversation with various sectors. And she also set up a dialogue office and engaged sincerely with people from all walks of life. I think people should give an opportunity to Hong Kong SAR government to address their concerns. We acknowledge there are some deep-seated problems, like housing and opportunities for the young people. But demonstration or violence offers no solution to these deep-seated problems.

Murnaghan: Can I ask you about the plight of the Uygur people in Xinjiang? Our correspondent, Tom Cheshire, has been there recently. He reported from there recently about hundreds of thousands of or millions of people being held in prison camps there.

Liu Xiaoming: That is not true. You know, Xinjiang is the largest province in China. It enjoys prosperity.

Murnaghan: How many people are held in those camps?

Liu Xiaoming: They are not prison camps. They are vocational education and training centres. The measure being taken is for the prevention of terrorism. Xinjiang has been a victim of terrorism and extremism for the past twenty years.

Murnaghan: If you just look at those pictures, you say they are re-education centres, are these people going there voluntarily? They are bound, blindfolded and being marched by police. Are they going into these re-education camps voluntarily?

Liu Xiaoming: No, that is a different story. This is transfer of inmates. The media pick up some clips, but this has nothing to do with the education training centre. The measures were taken exactly for the safety of the majority of Xinjiang people. They are part of the UN early prevention action to prevent terrorism.

Murnaghan: So when they are re-educated, are they free to leave?

Liu Xiaoming: Of course. The basic purpose is to educate these young people so that they could get rid of the extremist ideas. They will learn some skills and they can earn their living. They can earn a living by commanding a skill. On the whole, they will not be intoxicated by the extremist ideas.

Murnaghan: Lastly, Mr. Ambassador, can I ask you about the issue of Huawei? As you know, many nations, including the United States, believe that Huawei has very close links with the Chinese government, so much so the US is banning Huawei's involvement in developments of many of its networks. In the UK, it's still involved in our 5G network. But we've just done an interview today with the US Secretary of Commerce Wilbur Rose who says that the United Kingdom should be very wary of Huawei. If the UK pulls out, what would Chinese attitude be?

Liu Xiaoming: First, I would reject totally the accusation against Huawei. This is a good company. It is a private company. It has nothing to do with the Chinese government. It is a leader in 5G telecommunications. I think they are here for win-win collaboration with British counterparts. They are contributing to the development of telecommunication industry in the UK. I do hope that the UK government will make a wise decision based on the national interest of the UK.

Murnaghan: But President Trump is putting a lot of pressure on Boris Johnson. We know they talked about it together. If the UK did ban Huawei, what would China's attitude be, for instance, to a trade deal with the UK post Brexit?

Liu Xiaoming: I think if UK got rid of Huawei, it would send a very bad, negative message. UK is regarded as a most open, business friendly country. But if Huawei were shut out of it, this would send a negative message worldwide. It would also send a bad message to Chinese businesses, Chinese investments, here in this country. So I do hope that the UK government will make its decision based on UK national interests and the interests of China-UK collaboration.

Murnaghan: Ambassador, thank you very much indeed.

Liu Xiaoming: My pleasure.

接受英国BBC《新闻之夜》栏目
主持人沃克现场直播采访

作者手记

　　2019年10月4日，我接受英国BBC旗舰栏目《新闻之夜》（*Newsnight*）主持人柯丝蒂·沃克（Kirsty Wark）现场直播采访。

　　沃克1976年进入BBC，1993年加入《新闻之夜》栏目团队，是该栏目任职时间最长的主持人；曾获多项新闻大奖，包括英国电影和电视艺术学院奖。

　　采访正值中国香港"修例风波"演变成社会动乱，沃克指责香港警察对示威者使用真枪实弹，并问如果香港的暴力活动升级失控，中央政府会怎么办。她还借香港动乱指责中国在新疆的政策。我阐述了中方原则立场，并批驳BBC和西方媒体对新疆问题的歪曲报道。

　　采访实录如下：

沃克：　　我们邀请中国驻英国大使刘晓明来到节目。欢迎你，大使先生。首先，今晚香港局势再次升级，有更多的香港人佩戴面罩，你是否对这种公然违抗禁令的行为感到震惊？

刘晓明： 完全没有。我认为《禁止蒙面规例》的出台十分及时而且非常必要。这项禁令的目的是制止暴力、恢复秩序以及震慑新的暴力行为。

沃克： 可是从今天晚上看，禁令并未奏效。

刘晓明： 现在下结论还太早。禁令生效才刚刚几小时，现在就说禁令未奏效为时过早。香港特区政府决心要止暴制乱。

沃克： 但是自香港特区政府宣布禁令以来，香港民众的反应是，我们不会容忍这些，我们还是要上街，还是要戴面罩，我们不需要谁告诉我们该怎么做。

刘晓明： 我认为你确实需要将和平示威者和凶恶暴徒区别开来。特区政府之所以要订立规例，是因为形势已经升级到了危险的程度。正如林郑月娥特首所说，到了需要颁布禁令的时候了。

沃克： 林郑月娥是否已对局势失去了控制？

刘晓明： 我不这么认为，我认为局势仍然可控。我们对此充满信心。

沃克： 可是形势看上去并不可控。

刘晓明： 如果林郑月娥特首已对局势失去控制，她怎么能宣布禁令？

沃克： 香港警察开始使用实弹，又有一个青少年被打中腿部，之前还发生枪击事件，看上去政府已不能掌控局面。

刘晓明： 警察之所以开枪是因为他们的生命受到严重威胁。让我们来看看英国警察是如何应对类似情况的。英国首席警监西蒙·彻斯特曼称，"训练有素的武装警察可以开枪，以消除威胁，保护公众和警察自身安全"。

沃克： 可是公众就是街上的示威者。我想问的是，你是否仍对林郑月娥有完全的信任？

刘晓明： 是的，对此我非常肯定。

沃克： BBC记者刚才说，根据路透社的报道，中国人民武装警察部队人数已从3000~5000名增加到1万~1.2万名，这是否属实？如果香港的暴力活动升级，超出林郑月娥的控制，中国中央政府是否还将增加部队人数？

刘晓明： 我们当然希望情况会好转，但我们也要做最坏的打算。正如我在记者会上所说，如果事态发展到特区政府无法控制的地步，中央政府不会坐视不管。这仍是我们的立场。

沃克： 但你们会怎么做？路透社报道说，香港有1万~1.2万名武警部队，比之前翻了一番，你能证实吗？

刘晓明： 我能证实的是，现在事态仍然可控。我们对特区政府和林郑月娥特首完全有信心。

沃克： 但如果本周末出现更多的示威者，数千人上街呢？是否会达到临界点？

刘晓明： 我们应该给特首时间来实施"面罩禁令"。现在下结论还为时过早。

沃克： 你们会部署更多的部队吗？

刘晓明： 如果事态发展到特区政府无法控制的地步，我们不会坐视不管。正如林郑月娥特首所说，她的政府不会让事态一直恶化下去。

沃克： 但总不能把所有香港人都关起来吧？

刘晓明： 我对特区政府有信心。我相信这项禁令可以有助于改善香港局势。我希望香港大多数民众能对特区政府的努力做出积极反应。

沃克： 但整个夏天事态都在发酵，你们还会容忍多久？如果到圣诞节还控制不住抗议活动，你们会怎么应对？

刘晓明： 如果你将现在与几个月前做对比，就应看到香港局势整体呈转稳趋缓态势。英国乃至西方媒体的问题在于，你们只关注暴徒和暴力。

沃克： 我们关注的是街头发生的事。如果林郑月娥为平息街头抗议而取消"面罩禁令"，你会支持吗？

刘晓明： 我认为，她决心实施禁令。我们尊重林郑月娥特首和特区政府。我们理解和支持她的决定。我们对她应对事态完全有信心。

沃克： 香港示威者称他们是在为生存而战，因为当他们看到你们如何对待内地的新疆维吾尔族人时，比如"再教育中心"等，他们担心香港也会那样。

刘晓明： 我认为这是你们媒体捏造的故事。

沃克： 怎么捏造？

刘晓明： 中国新疆的职业技能教育培训中心是为了预防恐怖主义而设立的，此项措施实施3年以来，新疆没有发生过一起恐怖事件。此前的20多年里，新疆发生过数千起令人发指的恐怖事件，我们没有看到BBC和西方媒体对此有任何报道。请你告诉我，新疆发生恐怖事件的时候，你们在哪里？！

沃克： 刘大使，你说到中国在新疆实施反恐措施，而进驻香港的中国武警也具有这样的职能。

刘晓明： 你是在混淆视听！香港没有中国武警，目前香港的局势是由香港警方处理的。

沃克： 我们知道中国在香港派驻了武警，而且数量在增加。

刘晓明： 这不是事实。

沃克： 港人因此感到恐惧，他们没有别的选择，他们想要林郑月娥特首下台，要求调查警方暴力执法，还要求实行普选。香港能实现普选吗？

刘晓明： 中国坚定奉行"一国两制"。习近平主席在庆祝中华人民共和国成立70周年招待会上强调，中国政府将继续全面准确贯彻"一国两制"、"港人治港"、高度自治的方针，这是中国政府坚定不移的政策。

沃克： 这是否意味着中国中央政府绝对不会介入并接管香港？

刘晓明： "一国两制"50年不变，我们会坚定奉行这一政策。

沃克： 非常感谢大使。

刘晓明： 不客气。

A Live Interview with Kirsty Wark on BBC *Newsnight*

On 4th October 2019, I gave a live interview on BBC *Newsnight* hosted by Kirsty Wark to explain China's position on the situation in Hong Kong and the Prohibition on Face Covering Regulation. The full text is as follows:

Wark: I'm now indeed joined by the Chinese Ambassador, Liu Xiaoming. Thank you very much for coming in, Ambassador. First of all, real escalation tonight. More people wear face masks. Are you shocked at the defiance?

Liu Xiaoming: No, not at all. I think the ban is timely and necessary. The purpose of this face mask ban is to stop the violence, to restore order, and to deter further violence.

Wark: But it hasn't worked tonight.

Liu Xiaoming: It's still too early to tell. You know it's just a few hours. We will see. it's too early to tell the result of this ban. I think the Special Administrative Region Government is determined to stop violence and restore order.

Wark: It hasn't been able to restore order so far. And the ban has had, it seems, it has had the impact of saying to people, you know, we're not going to stand for this. We are gonna come out. We're gonna wear a face mask. We are not going to be told what to do.

Liu Xiaoming: I think you really need to separate peaceful demonstrators from die-hard radicals. I think the Special Administrative Region Government decided to introduce the ban because the situation has escalated to a dangerous level. So, according to the Chief Executive, it's time to introduce a ban.

Wark: Has Carrie Lam lost control?

Liu Xiaoming: I don't think so. I think the situation is still under control and we have full confidence.

Wark: It doesn't look like under control.

Liu Xiaoming: If she lost control, how could she try to introduce this ban?

Wark: But the problem is that the police are firing live rounds. A young boy had, you know, a shot in the leg. So we've seen shooting before. This is not the look of an authority in control.

Liu Xiaoming: The reason why police shot is because their lives were under a serious threat. Let us see how your British police would have handled the situation. I quote, according to Simon Chesterman, the Chief Constable of the British police, "Armed police officers are highly trained to shoot to neutralise the threat in order to protect the public, their colleagues or themselves. "

Wark: But the public themselves are on the streets. Do you still have full confidence in Carrie Lam?

Liu Xiaoming: Yes, I can say that in a very resolute term.

Wark: You heard Gabriel Gatehouse saying there, and the Reuters reported that the People's Armed Police have already had 3, 000 to 5, 000 paramilitary police and now it's between 10,000 to 12, 000. Is that correct? And will you keep putting more paramilitaries in if you don't think Carrie Lam can deal with this?

Liu Xiaoming: We certainly hope the situation would improve, but we have to prepare for the worst. As I said during my press conference: If the situation in Hong

Kong becomes uncontrollable for the Hong Kong SAR Government and the Central Government will not sit on their hands and watch. I still stand by my statement.

Wark: But what will you do? The Reuters report says there are 10,000 to 12, 000 paramilitaries in just now. That's a doubling of what there was. Can you confirm that, first of all?

Liu Xiaoming: I will say, I can confirm the situation is still under control, and we have full trust in the Hong Kong SAR Government and its Chief Executive.

Wark: But you say that there will come a point — you know, if over this weekend, there are more demonstrations in the thousands and thousands in the street – there'll come a point where your Government really needs to make a decision.

Liu Xiaoming: I think you need to give time to Chief Executive to implement the ban.

Wark: But will you put more troops if you have to?

Liu Xiaoming: If the situation becomes uncontrollable, we certainly would not sit on our hands and watch. Just as the Chief Executive said, her Administration would not allow the situation to get worse and worse.

Wark: You cannot lock up the whole of Hong Kong.

Liu Xiaoming: I have confidence in the Hong Kong SAR Government. I believe this ban will help to improve the situation, and I hope the majority of Hong Kong people will respond to the efforts made by the Special Administration Region and communicate with them.

Wark: But it's been going on all summer. How long will you give it? If Carrie Lam is still, at Christmas, battling protesters, are you not going to do something about that?

Liu Xiaoming: If you compare the situation now with the situation a few months ago, I think things improved somewhat after Carrie Lam withdrew the bill. I think, the problem with the British media, and Western media as a whole, is that you only focus on the rioters and only focus on the violence.

Wark: We are focusing on what we see on the streets. And I wonder if Carrie Lam will have your backing if she has to withdraw this ban in order to restore peace?

Liu Xiaoming: I think she will be determined to implement the ban. And we certainly respect Carrie Lam and her Administration, and we understand her decision, and we show our support for her decision. And we have full trust in her Administration to handle the situation.

Wark: Ambassador, you hear Hong Kongers say they feel they're fighting for their lives, because when they look at the way that you are dealing with the Uygurs on the mainland, the re-education camps, or whatever, and they think this is what lies ahead for them.

Liu Xiaoming: I think this is a made-up story by your media.

Wark: How is it made up?

Liu Xiaoming: What you are talking about is the vocational training and education centre in Xinjiang. That is for the prevention of terrorism. Since this measure was introduced in Xinjiang, there has been no single terrorist case in the past three years. And before that, for twenty years, there were thousands of terrorist activities. We haven't seen any coverage by BBC or any Western media. Where are you? Where were you then? Tell me!

Wark: Ambassador, as you said, you put in anti-terrorist forces to deal with Uygurs. These paramilitaries that are in Hong Kong are of the same stripe.

Liu Xiaoming: Not in Hong Kong. You mixed up things. They are inside in China. In Hong Kong, it is the Hong Kong police that's handling the situation.

Wark: But we know that there are paramilitaries in Hong Kong at the moment. And according to Reuters, they are increasing.

Liu Xiaoming: No! Not at all.

Wark: So, my point is that people fear for their lives. They feel this is the only alternative they have. Because what they want is: they want Carrie Lam gone, they want an inquiry into the police brutality, and they also want universal suffrage. Are they ever going to get universal suffrage?

Liu Xiaoming: The Central Government has reaffirmed our commitment to "One Country, Two Systems". President Xi Jinping repeated this commitment on the eve of Chinese National Day that we are committed to "One Country, Two Systems". We will continue to let Hong Kong people administer Hong Kong, and Hong Kong will continue to enjoy a high degree of autonomy. That's a very firm commitment.

Wark: So did you have a commitment that the mainland Chinese Government will never step in and take over Hong Kong ever?

Liu Xiaoming: That commitment has been made for fifty years and the policy will remain for fifty years and we are committed to it.

Wark: Thank you very much, Ambassador.

Liu Xiaoming: My pleasure.

Kirsty Wark is *Newsnight*'s longest-serving presenter, having joined the programme in 1993. She was named journalist of the year by BAFTA Scotland in 1993 and Best Television Presenter in 1997.

接受英国BBC《尖锐对话》栏目主持人萨克现场直播采访

作者手记

2019年11月26日，我在英国BBC总部演播室，接受BBC旗舰访谈栏目《尖锐对话》(*HARDtalk*)主持人斯蒂芬·萨克(Stephen Sackur)现场直播采访。

《尖锐对话》是BBC旗舰访谈栏目，聚焦国内外热议、敏感话题，邀请各国政要、商界领袖、社会名流、知识精英与主持人进行一对一的"尖锐对话"。栏目以深度挖掘、唇枪舌剑、激烈交锋、充满火药味著称。节目通过BBC新闻频道、世界新闻台、国际广播电台等平台，向全球200多个国家和地区播放，受众达4亿多人次。

萨克是BBC著名节目主持人，曾担任BBC外事记者，常驻中东和北美。他主持过广播四台和世界新闻台等，担任《尖锐对话》主持人7年多，曾采访过多国总统和总理，获多项新闻大奖，包括"国际电视年度人物"。他的采访风格以直率、敏锐、犀利、执着著称，提问刁钻、尖锐、咄咄逼人，曾引起一些被采访者的抱怨。他的一句名言是："好的采访，从深度调研开始，通过激烈交锋，达到揭示真相。"

这次采访聚焦中国香港暴乱。刚好12天前，习近平主席在巴西出席金砖国家领导人会议期间就香港问题发表讲话。我在第一时间通过英国电视台向世界解读习主席的重要讲话，指出这是中国政府发出的最权威的声音，那就是，止暴制乱、恢复秩序是香港当前最紧迫的任务。

我们谈到香港的民主、自由、普选，谈了中国的发展、法制、人权、新疆、中国的战略目标等问题。

采访实录如下：

萨克： 刘晓明大使，欢迎来到《尖锐对话》栏目。

刘晓明： 谢谢！

萨克： 很高兴你能接受我们栏目的邀请。让我们从香港问题开始。香港持续动乱，这是否是习近平主席就职7年以来面临的最大挑战？

刘晓明： 中国政府的立场十分清楚。12天前，习近平主席出席金砖国家领导人会议期间发出最权威的声音，那就是，止暴制乱、恢复秩序是香港当前最紧迫的任务。

萨克： 中方几个月来一直在讲这些话，但香港的暴力局面从初夏开始到现在仍在持续。除了暴力局面，还有上周日香港区议会选举结果所体现的民众普遍的政治呼声。香港民众投票让民主派取得绝对多数席位，明确表达了对香港特区政府和中央政府的严重不满。

刘晓明： 首先，我认为你需要将和平示威者与暴力犯罪分子区别开来。你提到最近区议会选举，这正说明习近平主席阐述的严正立场产生了积极影响。只有在和平的环境下，民众才能行使民主权利。

萨克： 那么这次选举的结果意味着什么？候选人中既有很多是建制派，也有不少是代表反对派和街头民主抗议者的观点，选民们是可以选择的。此次选举投票率高达70%。结果是，反对派赢得452个议席中的400个，取得压倒性多数，在18个区议会中，17个被他们控制。

刘晓明： 首先，我认为你不应过度解读所谓反对派取得"压倒性多数"胜利。虽然看上去反对派赢得18个区议会中的17个，但从得票率上看，是60%比40%，40%的选民没有把选票投给反对派。其次，在任何国家包括在西方国家选举中，在暴乱、动乱和经济放缓等背景下，当政者总是容易失去更多选票。而这些正是暴力犯罪分子造成的，他们给香港带来了巨大麻烦。

萨克： 可是，刘大使，你和许多中国官员这几个月来一直在对我们说，香港"沉默的大多数"并不支持民主抗议示威，他们拥护中央政府。我们现在知道事实并非如此。

刘晓明： 我认为目前下结论还为时过早。我刚说了40%的选民没有把选票投给反对派。根据媒体报道，建制派候选人受到骚扰、干扰、威胁，一些人甚至遇刺，比如何君尧先生。这些暴力极端分子制造恐怖气氛，让一些选民无法前往投票站投票，我称之为"黑色恐怖"。

萨克： 大使先生，你和我一样在电视上看到了香港发生的一切，香港警察近几个月来对抗议示威者实施了野蛮的暴力"镇压"，但未奏效。林郑月娥行政长官最终代表的是中国中央政府的利益。她开始的应对策略是用撤销修例平息民主抗议，但不管用。之后，她明确指示警察要更强硬，但也不管用。中央政府现在要做什么？

刘晓明： 我认为你没能看到事情的全貌。问题不在于香港警察。我认为香港警察是世界上纪律最严明、最专业、最文明的警队。如果和英国做一个比较，你认为如果类似的暴力事态发生在英国会持续多久？

萨克： 但你看到警察近距离向抗议者开枪的画面了吗？

刘晓明： 警察开枪是为了自卫，是为了维护法治。我在接受BBC《新闻之夜》栏目采访时曾引述英国首席警监西蒙·彻斯特曼的话，他说"训练有素的武装警察可以开枪，以消除威胁，保护公众和警察自身安全"。英国媒体的问题是，你们只盯着警察的应对行动，而对暴徒的暴力行径视而不见。这些暴徒向一位持不同意见的香港市民泼洒易燃液体并对他纵火焚烧，你们仍然称暴徒为抗议者。

萨克： 刘大使，我们也采访了抗议活动的头目，就他们使用的一些暴力策略提问，包括为什么使用汽油弹和其他武器，这些问题我们都提了。但现在的问题是，中国政府面临巨大的困境，暴力和动荡仍在继续，林郑月娥的策略失败了。下一步，比较现实的策略是是否让林郑月娥下台？

刘晓明： 首先我要说，林郑月娥特首工作做得很好。她的政府和管治团队仍然获得中央政府的全力支持。

萨克： 这可太有意思了，林郑月娥过去半年来的执政状况很失败。

刘晓明： 我不这样认为。我有许多理由。如果外部势力不在幕后操纵，激进的暴徒不破坏特区政府与民众的对话，她就不会失败。林郑月娥特首和她的团队做了许多努力，他们以开放的态度与民众接触、沟通。自"修例风波"发生5个多月以来，林郑月娥特首和特区政府与民众进行了100多场对话交流，但极端分子不给他们机会。

萨克： 你是位资深大使，你知道外交如何运作取舍。林郑月娥现在可以做出选择。她可以让步，成立真正独立的调查委员会，对警方近几个月的行为进行调查；她也可以推动下届特首选举实现全民普选。否则，香港警察将没有能力重建秩序，特首将不得不依靠1.2万驻军实施更加严厉的镇压。你有没有认真考虑过这种前景？

刘晓明： 林郑月娥特首及其团队为解决问题竭尽全力。一开始，她搁置了逃犯条例修订草案，后来撤销了草案。她还提出4项行动，包括与民众进行100多次沟通。全民普选不可能一蹴而就，需要经过法律程序。中央政府致力于在香港实现普选。如果反对派在2015年没有投票否决普选方案，早在2017年就可以实现普选。

萨克：　行政长官这样关键岗位的选举并不是普选。行政长官候选人由北京提名，由约千人组成的选委会来选。我认为，中国内地同胞正在密切关注香港人追求真正的自由民主最终会得到什么样的结果，这才是你们担心的事。

刘晓明：　你又忽略了另一个更大的问题。你提及的问题太多，让我一个一个解释。首先是全民普选，如果反对派在2015年没有投票否决普选方案，2017年就可以实现特区行政长官普选。虽然那不是百分之百的全民普选，但是全民普选要一步一步来。

萨克：　大使先生，你是一位外交官，不应粉饰普选。

刘晓明：　全民普选涉及两个选举：一个是特区行政长官，另一个是香港立法会。如果反对派没有否决2015年普选方案，明年的香港立法会选举将是全民普选，700万人一人一票。

萨克：　这些都不会发生，香港没有全民普选。不久前北京宣布香港高等法院有关《禁止蒙面规例》不符合《基本法》的判决无效，这是在侵蚀"一国两制"的基础。

刘晓明： 你的说法是完全错误的。你没有给我时间回答你提出的问题。你谈到中国的根本性问题，你还说中国担心香港事态泛滥影响内地。事实并非如此。如你所知，我们刚刚庆祝了中华人民共和国成立70周年，你应该看到中国在过去70年取得了怎样巨大的成就。中国人民的生活更加美好，更加幸福，寿命也更长。70年来，中国人民预期寿命从35岁提升至77岁。请你告诉我，世界上哪个国家取得了这样的成就？改革开放40多年来，中国从世界经济排名第十一位跃居第二大经济体，7亿人实现脱贫。中国人民热爱中国共产党，中国共产党是中国的脊梁！你说香港事态会在中国其他地方引起外溢效应，引发大规模示威，这样的情况根本不存在。

萨克： 你描绘了一幅美妙的画卷。

刘晓明： 我没有做任何粉饰，这些都是事实。

萨克： 你的话题已脱离香港，我们可以讨论。

刘晓明： 是你把我带入香港以外的话题。

萨克： 没有人怀疑中国政府过去几十年来取得的惊人经济成就。如果你坚持认为中国人民的生活非常幸福，那中国政府为何如此害怕不同意见？

刘晓明： 我们不害怕任何不同意见。

萨克： 中国有多少政治犯?

刘晓明： 中国没有政治犯。

萨克： 大使先生，这不是事实。

刘晓明： 没有人是因为不同政见入狱。入狱服刑者都是因为违反了中国法律。

萨克： 中国的法律事实上阻止政治反对派存在，谁不和党保持一致，就是违法。

刘晓明： 根本不存在你说的情况。

萨克： 不仅如此，过去两三年，中国加大了对社会各种思想、行动的监控。

刘晓明： 我来问问你，英国有多少监控探头?

萨克： 没有中国那么多。

刘晓明： 但人均……

萨克： 英国并不是世界上拥有监控探头最多的国家。

刘晓明： 你怎么解释英国人均监控探头数量非常多这种情况?

萨克： 我可以解释，但中国……

刘晓明： 我在问为什么英国有这么多监控探头。

萨克： 我想说，中国监控探头数量达到每两人一个，中国人口有14亿，这是一个难以想象的被监控的社会。为什么要进行监控？

刘晓明： 你去过中国吗？

萨克： 去过。

刘晓明： 最近一次去中国是什么时候？

萨克： 大约3年前。

刘晓明： 在中国，你会感到人们是很自由、很幸福的。难道你没有感受到吗？你认为中国人民处于被压迫、被恐吓的状态并且有很多不满吗？在中国，你到处都能看到人们的笑脸。当然，任何社会都会有人有不满，但中国人民有表达意见的渠道。我们有人民代表大会和政治协商制度。你认为中国没有街头政治，所以中国就没有民主。但是，中国的民主是中国特色的民主。你们不能用自己的标准去评判别的国家，就像我们不用自己的标准来评判你们。

萨克： 我们讨论一下中国西部的自治区新疆。

刘晓明： 你去过新疆吗？

萨克： 还没有。如果中方邀请，我很乐意去。

刘晓明： 当然可以。中国有句话：不到新疆，不知道中国之大；不到新疆，不知道中国之美。新疆是和睦、繁荣的好地方，但自20世纪90年代—2016年，发生了很多让人不愿看到的事情，新疆某种程度上变成了"战场"，发生了数千起恐怖袭击事件，成千无辜群众遇难。仅2014年，每3天就发生2起恐袭事件。民众无法安全出行，纷纷呼吁政府采取应对措施。所以，政府依法设立了"职业技能教育培训中心"，目的是去极端化。

萨克： 大使先生，你们的确遇到了问题。我们刚才讨论了香港局势和新疆问题。美国国会刚刚通过了《香港人权与民主法案》，准备制裁带头镇压示威者的香港官员。你本人也被英国外交大臣拉布"召见"了。中国处于守势，是否反映出你们的外交面临巨大压力？

刘晓明： 我不这样认为。相反，我认为西方国家应该为干涉中国内政而感到巨大压力。如果中国全国人大通过一项与英国某地方有关的法律，表达我们的关切并制裁你们的政客，你们会怎么想？现在是21世纪，不是"炮舰外交"时代。中国不会再任人欺凌。

萨克： 你认为西方国家政府是任意欺凌中国吗？你担任大使时间很久了，不久前，你和英国政府还常常提到中英关系"黄金时代"。

而现在，英国外交大臣告诉你，英国政府对英国驻香港总领事馆雇员郑文杰被逮捕并遭酷刑感到震惊和震怒，对中国在香港和新疆的做法提出批评和谴责。美国联邦调查局负责人称，"中国的目标看起来是要取代美国成为世界头号超级大国，为此不惜违反法律"。中英关系"黄金时代"是否已因互相谴责和竞争而不复存在？

刘晓明： 现在该轮到我讲话了？

萨克： 是的。

刘晓明： 希望你不要再打断我的讲话。你们的《尖锐对话》栏目应该是话题尖锐，而不是你总一个人讲，不让别人讲。首先，关于英国外交大臣拉布和我的会见，他的确提到郑文杰案，但并没有谈及新疆问题。是我向他指出，中国对英国干涉中国内政、干涉香港事务表示坚决反对。关于郑文杰案，郑因涉嫌嫖娼违反了中国法律，他对违法事实供认不讳。

萨克： 他在警方酷刑下当然会认罪。

刘晓明： 请你不要总打断我。你提了很多问题，我需逐一回答。关于所谓中国警方对郑使用"酷刑"，我们完全拒绝这种无理指责。我们已经对英国外交部做出了回应，我们绝不接受英方指责，郑没有遭受所谓"酷刑"，他在被收押和被释放时均接受了体检，身体状况很好，没有任何问题。这只能说，你们对中国充满偏见。

萨克： 大使先生，你已讲清楚了你的观点。我们剩下的时间不多了。还有一个大问题。美国一位高级官员称，"中国的目标是取代美国成为头号超级大国"。美国和英国现在都持这种观点。这是北京的终极战略目标吗？

刘晓明： 绝对不是。我们根本没有兴趣取代谁，也没有兴趣挑战谁。尽管中国是世界第二大经济体，但是我们依然是一个发展中国家，人均GDP不到1万美元，在世界上排名靠后。这是我第三次担任驻外大使，在我担任驻埃及大使后，我曾到中国西北部贫穷省份甘肃挂职。在偏僻的西北地区，人们连喝水都很困难，要靠挖水窖收集雨水、净化雨水，人畜都得依靠这种净化窖水。对于中国政府和中国领导人来说，解决这些问题都是很艰巨的任务。对内，我们要保障中国人民的温饱，使中国人民更幸福、更长寿；对外，中国奉行和平发展的外交政策。

萨克： 邓小平有句名言：中国的战略是"韬光养晦、绝不当头"。这显然不是习近平的战略。

刘晓明： 中国坚持奉行和平发展战略，因为我们从和平发展中受益。中国40多年发展的奇迹是在和平的环境中取得的，只有继续努力营造和平环境，才能取得更大发展。这就是为什么习近平主席提出构建人类命运共同体的倡议。这是我们的目标，是我们坚定不移的目标。

萨克： 刘晓明大使，非常感谢接受《尖锐对话》的采访。

刘晓明： 不客气。

A Live Interview with Stephen Sackur on BBC *HARDtalk*

On 26th November 2019, I gave an interview on BBC's *HARDtalk* hosted by Stephen Sackur to expound China's position on Hong Kong, Xinjiang and China's peaceful development. The full transcript is as follows:

Sackur: Ambassador Liu Xiaoming, welcome to *HARDtalk*.

Liu Xiaoming: Thank you for having me.

Sackur: It's a pleasure to have you here. Let us start with Hong Kong. President Xi Jinping has been in power for 7 years. Would you accept that the prolonged unrest and instability in Hong Kong is the greatest challenge he has faced in his presidency?

Liu Xiaoming: I think our government's policy is clear. Twelve days ago, President Xi made a very authoritative statement when he attended the BRICS summit. He said the top priority for Hong Kong is to end violence and restore order.

Sackur: With respect, he's been saying that for months. The violence began in early summer and violence continues. Not just the violence. We also have the massive political expression represented by the results of last Sunday's Council elections. The people of Hong Kong have squarely, by an overwhelming majority, expressed their grave dissatisfaction with the Hong Kong and Beijing authorities.

Liu Xiaoming: First thing first. I think you have to separate the peaceful demonstrators from the violent rioters. You mentioned the latest Council elections. That exactly shows that President Xi's message, loud and clear, has been well received, that you can only exercise the right for democracy in a peaceful environment.

Sackur: If I may just continue with the story about what the Council elections tell us. They had a choice. They had a lot of pro-Beijing candidates. They had a lot of candidates expressing views of the opposition and the protestors, pro-democracy protesters, on the streets. And the overwhelming majority, almost 400 out of the 452 seats, went to those opposition figures. The figures are actually extraordinary, 70% of turnout, 17 of 18 Councils now controlled by the pro-democracy political movement.

Liu Xiaoming: I don't think you should have an over interpretation of the so-called "landslide" victory of the opposition. Though it's 17 out of 18 Councils, in terms of votes, it's 40% versus 60%. So 40% of the voters voted against the opposition. Secondly, like in any country, even in Western culture, incumbents tend to lose votes, if there is a riot, if there is violence, if there is slowdown of economy. That is caused by the violent law-breakers. They cause the big trouble in Hong Kong.

Sackur: But if I may say so, Ambassador, you and many of the Chinese officials have been saying to people like me for months that the silent majority of people in Hong Kong are not with the pro-democracy protesters and demonstrators. They are with Beijing. That's not true and we now know that.

Liu Xiaoming: I think it's still too early to tell. I said 40%, OK. According to some reports, pro-establishment candidates have been harassed, interrupted, threatened and there was even an attempted assassination of one of them, Mr. Ho Kwan-yiu. These violent radicals created terror. I called it "black terror". So that really prevented people from going to the poll.

Sackur: Ambassador, you watched events in Hong Kong from afar like I do on television and you see just as I do the brutal crackdown that Hong Kong police have been implementing against the protesters for months now. The point is that it hasn't worked. Carrie Lam's strategy – she is of course Chief Executive of Hong Kong, representing the interests of Beijing ultimately – she began with a strategy which was built on withdrawing the extradition bill, hoping that would quell the pro-democracy protesters. That didn't work. She then clearly instructed the police to get tough. We've seen that doesn't work. What's Beijing gonna do now?

Liu Xiaoming: I think you missed the whole picture. The problem is not the Hong Kong police. I think the Hong Kong police is the most disciplined, professional and civilized police force in the world. If you compare what is going on in Hong Kong with what is going on in the United Kingdom, do you think the similar situation will go on and on in the UK?

Sackur: Have you seen the picture of a policeman opening fire on the protesters at point blank range?

Liu Xiaoming: The police opened fire in self-defense. They need to safeguard rule of law. Even here in the UK, I think in the *Newsnight* program, I quoted Simon Chesterman, Chief Constable of the British police. He said that armed police are trained to shoot to protect themselves and to protect lives of their colleagues and public order. You know the problem with the British media is that you only focus on the police reaction. You did not focus on the violent rioters. And you still call these rioters who tossed flammable liquid onto an onlooker who disagreed with them, disapproved their vandalism, and set fire on him — you still say these are protesters.

Sackur: Ambassador, if I may say so, we've interviewed leaders of the protest movement, too and we've asked them about some of the violent tactics that they've employed including the use of petrol bombs and other missiles. So we have questioned them precisely on that basis. But the point for you is that your government is now in a very big hole. The violence continues. The instability continues. Carrie Lam's strategy has failed. Is the next realistic move you have to make to get rid of the Chief Executive, Carrie Lam?

Liu Xiaoming: First, I would say Chief Executive Carrie Lam did a good job. Her team and her administration enjoy full support.

Sackur: That is fascinating. For six months she has failed.

Liu Xiaoming: No, I wouldn't say that she had failed. There are many reasons. She wouldn't if there were no foreign forces behind it, if there were no radical, violent rioters who blocked and sabotaged the conversation. Carrie Lam and her team made many efforts to communicate, to reach out to the public. Since this happened in the past five months, Carrie Lam and her team have conducted more than 100 events to communicate with the local people, but the radicals do not give them the chance or opportunity.

Sackur: You're a veteran ambassador. You know how diplomacy works. I mean, she's got a choice now. She can either make some concessions – that is, establish a truly independent inquiry into the police actions of recent months and make moves towards universal suffrage for the election of the next chief executive – she can either choose to do that or there's gonna have to be a much more serious crackdown, and that crackdown if I may say so is going to have to come not from the Hong Kong police who clearly are not capable of restoring order, but it's going to have to come from the Chinese military, 12, 000 of whom are currently based in barracks in Hong Kong. Is that something that you could contemplate?

Liu Xiaoming: I think Carrie Lam and her team made every effort to address the problem. Firstly, she suspended the extradition bill and then she withdrew it. And she also, made what she called four major actions, including more than 100 engagements with local people. But universal suffrage is not something that will come at just a blink of the eye. You know that you, have to go through a legal process. The Central Government is committed to universal suffrage. If it had not been for the opposition to veto the political reform plan in 2015, there would have already been universal suffrage by 2017.

Sackur: There isn't anything like universal suffrage for the key post of Chief Executive. That is ultimately a choice that is based upon nominees selected from Beijing and ultimately voted upon by about 1, 000 people. That is very far from universal suffrage. What seems to me is that in the end, Beijing is scared about what is happening in Hong Kong because you fear that the rest of your population in the rest of your nation is watching very carefully to see what happens to this call for genuine, genuine freedom and democracy in Hong Kong.

Liu Xiaoming: I think you missed another big picture. You know, you raised so many topics, so many issues. Let's go one by one. Firstly, about the universal suffrage, as I said, if it had not been for the veto of the opposition to the political reform programme in 2015, by 2017, two years ago, the chief executive would have been selected by universal suffrage. Yes, it's not a hundred percent universal suffrage, but it has to go step by step.

Sackur: Ambassador, you are still a diplomat. You can't dress up ...

Liu Xiaoming: You know, when we talk about universal suffrage, there are two areas. One is chief executive and the other is legislative council. So if it had not been for the blocking by the opposition, next year, legislative election will be universal suffrage – one man one vote in Hong Kong for 7 million people.

Sackur: It's not going to be. There isn't universal suffrage. We've just seen the Communist Party in Beijing declared that a decision taken by the High Court in Hong Kong to disregard Carrie Lam's ban on face mask, according to Beijing, according to your Party, is now null and void. So you are now intruding on the fundamental principle of "One Country, Two Systems".

Liu Xiaoming: No, not at all. I think you gave me no opportunity to answer all your questions. You talked about the fundamental question, about the situation in China. You said that people are concerned about what is going on that might spill over to China. That is not the case. You know, we just celebrated 70th anniversary of the founding of the People's Republic of China. So you have to realize what achievements China has made in the past 70 years. People are living better, happier and longer. So within 70 years, we elevated people's life expectancy from 35 to 77. You tell me which country has this achievement. In the past 40 years since reform and opening up, China's status in terms of the world ranking rose from the 11th to the second largest economy. And we have elevated 700 million people out of poverty. So people love the Communist Party of China, and the Communist Party of China is the backbone of the country. So there will be no such thing as you talk about, that what happened to

Hong Kong will spill over or cause some huge demonstration in China.

Sackur: You painted a fascinating picture.

Liu Xiaoming: I didn't paint a fascinating picture. It's the fact.

Sackur: Let us explore what you just said, because you're taking it beyond Hong Kong.

Liu Xiaoming: You are taking me beyond Hong Kong.

Sackur: Nobody would doubt the incredible economic achievements of the Chinese government over decades. If you are so insistent that the people of your country are so very happy, why is your government apparently so frightened of dissent inside your country?

Liu Xiaoming: We're not frightened of any dissent.

Sackur: How many political prisoners are there in China?

Liu Xiaoming: There is no political prisoners in China.

Sackur: Ambassador, that's not true.

Liu Xiaoming: The people will not be put behind the bars because of their thoughts. The people are put behind the bar because they have violated the law in China.

Sackur: But your laws preclude genuine political opposition. If people are dissenting from the party line, they will very quickly find themselves contravening your laws.

Liu Xiaoming: No.

Sackur: Not only that, we have seen in the last two or three years, the creation of a surveillance society in China, where every thought and every move made by your population is surveilled.

Liu Xiaoming: Can I ask you a question? How many surveillance CCTVs are there here in the UK?

Sackur: Not as many as in China.

Liu Xiaoming: But in per capita…

Sackur: We are not one of the highest …

Liu Xiaoming: So how would you explain this situation?

Sackur: I would explain the situation by pointing out that in China …

Liu Xiaoming: But I am asking you about the CCTV in the UK.

Sackur: In China, there will be one CCTV camera for every two people. You have 1.4 billion people. That is an unimaginable surveillance society. What's it for?

Liu Xiaoming: Have you been to China?

Sackur: I have been to China.

Liu Xiaoming: When was your last visit to China?

Sackur: It was probably about three years ago.

Liu Xiaoming: I think in China, you will feel that people are very free and very happy. You can't feel it? You feel people are under harassment, people are threatened, and they have a lot of complaints? You can see smiling face on the Chinese people. Yes, people have some complaints. In any society people will have complaints. But people have their channels to make their complaints known. We have the National People's Congress and National Committee of the Chinese

People's Political Consultative Conference. You feel China has no street politics, so China has no democracy. But China's democracy is of Chinese characteristic. You can't use your standard to judge other country, just like we would not judge you based on our standard.

Sackur: Let's then talk about Xinjiang, one of the provinces in western China.

Liu Xiaoming: Have you been to Xinjiang yourself?

Sackur: No, I haven't. I would love to go and if you're prepared to invite me to travel.

Liu Xiaoming: Definitely. We have a saying, if you do not go to Xinjiang, you do not know how vast China is and how beautiful China is. This place used to be very peaceful and very prosperous. But between 1990s and 2016, it was not the scene we'd like to see. It became a battleground. There were thousands of terrorist attacks. Thousands of innocent people got killed or injured. In 2014 alone, there were two terrorist attack cases every three days. People cannot walk safely in the street during those days. So people call for the government to take actions. The government, according to law, set up the vocational education and training centres. The purpose is to de-radicalize some young people especially.

Sackur: But you have a problem here, Ambassador. We talked about Hong Kong. We talked about what you're doing to the Uyghurs in the west of your country. The United States Congress has just passed a new round of targeted sanctions against officials in Hong Kong who are leading the crackdown against the protesters. Your diplomatic position, and you know it well yourself because you've just been hauled over by Dominic Raab, the Foreign Secretary in London. You know that your diplomatic position as the Chinese government defends what is happening is coming under enormous pressure.

Liu Xiaoming: I don't think so. I think the Western countries are under enormous pressure for interfering in China's internal affairs. Let me say this. What if China's National People's Congress passed a law concerning a region in the United Kingdom to express our concern and to impose sanction on your politicians if you do not follow the law, what do you think about that? We are in the 21st Century. We are not in the age of the gunboat diplomacy. China is not a country you can kick around.

Sackur: Do you really think that governments in the West in particular are trying to kick you around? You are a long-serving Ambassador. Not so long ago, you and the British government were talking about the "Golden Era" in relations. Now, you've just come back from the foreign office with the Foreign Secretary describing himself as shocked and appalled by the arrest of a former employee in the UK consulate in Hong Kong who was tortured in China. The British government is furious about it. They're just criticizing and condemning your actions in Hong Kong, and in Xinjiang as well. The United States is now saying, and I'm quoting the head of the FBI, "China's goal, it seems, is to replace the US as the world's leading superpower, and they're prepared to break the law to get there". This "Golden Era" has collapsed into recrimination and rivalry.

Liu Xiaoming: So it's my turn to talk?

Sackur: It is.

Liu Xiaoming: I hope you will not interrupt me. I know your *HARDtalk* is about hard subjects. It is not about you talking all the time. First, about Raab's meeting with me. Yes, he did raise this case of Simon Cheng. He didn't mention Xinjiang. Let me tell you this, it is me who expressed our strong opposition to UK interference into China's internal affair, that is, Hong Kong. With regard to Simon Cheng, you know, he violated the law in China for soliciting prostitution. And he confessed all his wrongdoings.

Sackur: I'm sure he did after the usual Chinese torture tactics.

Liu Xiaoming: Would you give me some time to explain before you can interrupt me? You know, you covered so many subjects. I need to come back to you one by one. His so-called charges against China's police are totally rejected. We already made our response to the Foreign Office. We cannot accept the so-called "torture" claim. There's no torture at all. When he was arrested and when he was released, he had physical examinations. His condition was perfect. No problem at all.

Sackur: Ambassador, you have made your points. The bigger point I want to make is…

Liu Xiaoming: So that shows you had such a bias against China.

Sackur: Forgive me. We are almost out of time, so I just want to go to this big point. The US and the UK appear convinced now that, as I just quoted a senior US official, "China's goal is to replace the US as the world's leading superpower". Is that ultimately the strategy in Beijing?

Liu Xiaoming: No, not at all. We're not interested in replacing anyone or challenging anyone. You know, we are still a developing country though we are the second largest economy. In per capita income, we are way behind. You know, it's just less than ten thousand US dollars. This is my third ambassadorship. After my ambassadorship in Egypt, I was seconded to Gansu, one of the poorest provinces in west China. People there did not even have access to drinkable water, you know. They had to build cellars to catch rainwater and then to purify it. Both human being and livestock have to depend on this purified rain water. So it's an enormous challenge for the Chinese government, for the Chinese leaders: How to feed the Chinese population, how to make the Chinese people even happier, live longer. China follows the foreign policy of peaceful development.

Sackur: But you know, Deng Xiaoping famously said China's strategy was to hide the strength, bide your time, never take the lead. That clearly is not the strategy of Xi Jinping.

Liu Xiaoming: Peaceful development is still our strategy, because we benefit from it. People talk about 40 years of miracle in China. We can achieve this because we are in a peaceful environment. We can only have more success by having, and continuing to build, a peaceful environment. So that's why President Xi Jinping calls for building a shared future for mankind. That is our goal and continues to be our goal.

Sackur: Ambassador Liu Xiaoming, thank you very much for being on *HARDtalk*.

Liu Xiaoming: My pleasure.

HARDtalk is a BBC television and radio programme broadcast on the BBC News Channel, on BBC World News, and on the BBC World Service. *HARDtalk* has interviewed many public figures of historical significance. Stephen Sackur is the main presenter. For fifteen years, he was a BBC foreign correspondent and a regular contributor to BBC 4 and a number of newspapers and magazines. He was the moderator of BBC's worldwide broadcast of a debate on climate change with a panel of world leaders.

接受英国BBC《安德鲁·马尔访谈》栏目主持人马尔现场直播采访

作者手记

2020年7月19日，我在英国BBC总部演播室，接受BBC旗舰访谈栏目《安德鲁·马尔访谈》(*The Andrew Marr Show*)主持人安德鲁·马尔(Andrew Marr)现场直播采访。

这是我在英国11年期间第四次，也是最后一次接受马尔的采访。当时,《香港国安法》刚刚颁布实施，我们围绕中国香港、华为、新疆等问题进行了激烈的辩论。

马尔一上来就指责《香港国安法》违反了中国关于"一国两制"的承诺，他还质问香港人是否有自由。

关于华为，他问英国政府将为禁用华为设备付出什么代价。

关于新疆问题，马尔使用他的惯用伎俩，当场播放一段囚犯被押上列车的视频。

我阐述了中方在香港问题上的原则立场，批驳了西方情报机构和媒体关于新疆的虚假信息。关于华为问题，我提及英国历史学家雅克的一段话，即乾隆皇帝在1793年告诉英国国王，"天朝物产丰盈"，不稀罕英国的东西。结果这成了中国此后150年衰落的开端。我说，227年后的今天，英国对中国说，"我们不需要你们的5G技术"。我真不知道接下来的150年将会发生什么。

访谈节目播出后，一些英国友人来信祝贺，称中国大使给英国大牌主持人、历史学家上了一堂生动的历史课。

采访实录如下：

马尔： 欢迎大使先生。我想首先谈谈中国香港的情况，在香港，表达不同意见的权利和言论自由是否仍然得到尊重？

刘晓明： 完全得到尊重。有人拿《香港国安法》说事，事实上，《香港国安法》旨在恢复香港的正常社会秩序，保护的是绝大多数人的权利，针对的是极少数危害国家安全的犯罪分子。

马尔： 我想提醒观众《香港国安法》实际上说了些什么。它说：什么行为属于违法将由北京而不是香港决定，抗议者仅因使用标语牌就可能被捕，警方无须搜查令即可进入建筑物进行搜查，审判可以在没有陪审团的情况下秘密进行。这些法律条款显然违反了中国"一国两制"的承诺。

刘晓明： 这些信息是完全错误的。我不知道你是否读过《香港国安法》。首先，《香港国安法》开宗明义指出，中国将坚定不移并全面准确贯彻"一国两制"、"港人治港"、高度自治方针。为什么要实施国家安全法?《基本法》第二十三条授权香港特区就维护国家安全自行立法,即我们常说的第二十三条立法。但23年来,由于反对派的干扰和麻烦制造者的恐吓,相关立法迟迟未能完成。维护国家安全历来是中央政府的职责所在。

马尔: 你提到麻烦制造者,但是根据我们节目观众所尊重的"大赦国际"组织称,随着香港当局逐步采用中国内地模糊且包罗万象的国家安全定义,香港人享有的和平集会、言论、结社自由的权利迅速受到侵蚀。

刘晓明: "大赦国际"没有任何信誉可言,因为它制造了大量污蔑中国的不实之词,对中国从来没有说过一句好话,从来没有一句客观的评论。这就是它的问题。去年我曾和你讨论过香港形势,面对当时的动荡和暴乱,任何负责任的政府都必须采取措施予以制止。

马尔: 香港现有的法律相当有力了,难道还不够吗?如果真的有人在香港制造麻烦、扰乱香港,可以用现有法律对付他们。

刘晓明: 这恰恰就是为什么香港需要一部国家安全法。现有的法律不足以遏制打砸抢烧以及冲击立法会等暴力行为。这种行为就如同冲击英国议会。过去23年,香港始终没有一部维护国家安全的法律。

马尔: 真正的问题是,你们不希望香港人谈论民主,不是吗?特朗普总统说过，香港人的自由和权利已被剥夺；没有特殊待遇，就没有香港，因为香港将无力与任何自由市场进行竞争。很多人会离开香港，前往澳大利亚、美国和英国。这些人可以自由离开吗？

刘晓明： 人们当然可以自由进出。回归祖国23年来，香港人享受到前所未有的自由。回归前，他们有什么自由？他们可以自由选举港督吗？末任港督还是英国政府任命的。但过去23年中，香港人已经自由选举了5任行政长官。

马尔： 一个根本性的事实是，在你们新领导人的领导下，中国更具民族主义倾向，更加咄咄逼人。中国还能否与世界上的自由市场国家建立一种完全开放的关系？这是真正的问题所在，而香港是问题的"震中"。

刘晓明： 我认为，你们对中国真实情况的认识是非常错误的。我可以给你提供最新情况。你们常常不相信中国的表态，认为那是一种宣传。你们更相信美国人，认为他们的话不是宣传。那么好，我可以告诉你美国人如何看中国。最近，哈佛大学肯尼迪政府学院发布了一份报告，这份报告涵盖了过去13年的调查，结论是，中国民众对中国共产党和中国政府的满意度高达93%，远远高于任何西方政府和任何西方国家领导人。这才是中国的真实情况。

马尔： 下周，英国政府将就香港问题做出反应，据报道，英国政府很可能会采取类似《马格尼茨基法案》的措施，禁止中国某些个人入境英国，也可能废除英国和香港之间的移交逃犯协议。如果真是那样，中国将如何回应？

刘晓明： 那将是完全错误的。我们历来反对单边制裁。只有联合国才有权力实施制裁。如果英国政府走出对中国任何个人实行制裁这一步，中国必将做出坚决有力的回击。你已经看到中美之间的情况。美国制裁中国官员，中国就制裁美国参议员和官员。我不愿看到这种针锋相对的情况发生在中英之间。英国应该有独立自主的外交政策，而不是随美起舞，就像对待华为问题一样。

马尔： 说到针锋相对或是报复措施，我们来谈谈华为。在有关华为的决定宣布后，中国外交部称此举将严重削弱互信，要付出代价。请问是什么代价？

刘晓明： 英国的决定是一个非常错误的决定。我们正在评估其影响和后果。在这一决定宣布那天，我说这对华为是黑暗的一天，对中英关系也是黑暗的一天，对英国则是更黑暗的一天，因为英国失去了成为5G领军者的机会。我和英国历史学家马丁·雅克的看法不约而同。

马尔： 他很了解中国。

刘晓明： 他是很了解中国，写了一本名为《当中国统治世界》的书。他有一段精辟论述：中国的乾隆皇帝在1793年告诉英国国王"天朝物产丰盈，无所不有，原不籍外夷货物以通有无"。结果这成了中国此后150年衰落的开端。历史总在轮回。227年后的今天，2020年，英国对中国说，"我们不需要你们的5G技术"。我真不知道接下来的150年将会发生什么。

马尔： 有媒体报道，抖音近日做出搁置在英国设立全球总部的决定。中国政府是否会对捷豹路虎等在华经营的英国企业进行惩罚？

刘晓明： 我们无意将经济问题政治化。这种做法是十分错误的。英国迫于美国的压力对中国企业采取歧视性措施是十分错误的。有些人大谈所谓"国家安全风险"，却拿不出华为对英国构成"风险"的确凿证据。华为已在英国经营20年，它不仅为英国电信产业发展做出了巨大贡献，而且认真履行企业社会责任，助力英国发展。约翰逊首相制订了雄心勃勃的计划，要在2025年实现全英5G网络覆盖。华为有实力，本可以大力相助，但英国现在却要把华为"踢出去"，用你们媒体的话，是在美国的压力下"清理门户"。美国领导人近日表示，这都是他们的功劳。

马尔： 让我们谈谈新冠疫苗研发。现在，英国指责俄罗斯试图窃取英国疫苗研发机密。我采访与特朗普总统关系非常密切的美国佛罗里达州联邦参议员里克·斯科特时，斯科特说美国情报机构有证据表明，中国正试图破坏或迟滞美国疫苗研发。你对此怎么回应？

刘晓明： 这些"逢中必反者"对中国的无端指责数不胜数。我不想浪费我们的时间去驳斥他们的无端指责。中国在疫苗研发上非常开放，包括正与英国在内的各国科学家开展研发合作。习近平主席在第七十三届世界卫生大会上明确表示，中国新冠疫苗研发完成并投入使用后，将作为全球公共产品，特别是要实现非洲最贫穷国家等发展中国家的可及性和可担负性。

马尔： 让我们谈谈中国维吾尔族的境况，这也是目前中国和西方国家之间最大的问题。首先，让我们看一段无人机拍摄画面。这段非常令人不安的视频已在世界各地广泛传播，几乎可以肯定发生在中国新疆。你能告诉我们视频里是什么情况吗？（马尔播放视频）

刘晓明： 我不同意你的观点。这已不是你第一次给我播放视频，我记得去年你采访我时也播放过所谓新疆情况视频。你本人去过新疆吗？

马尔： 没有，我从未去过新疆。

刘晓明： 新疆被认为是中国最美丽的地方。中国有句俗语：不到新疆，不知道中国之大；不到新疆，不知道中国之美。

马尔： 大使先生，这个视频可是一点也不美。

刘晓明： 这正是我要告诉你的。自1990年以来，新疆共发生数千起恐怖袭击事件，人们无法……

马尔： 那是10年前的事了。我想问，在中国北方地区为什么有人跪在地上、被蒙上眼睛、剃光须发、被带上火车？那里到底发生了什么事？

刘晓明： 我不知道你从哪里得到这段视频。要知道，不论哪个国家，都有需要正常转移监狱囚犯的时候。

马尔： 但是大使，这视频里到底发生了什么事？

刘晓明： 我不知道你从哪里得到这段视频。

马尔： 这段视频已经传遍全球。西方情报机构和澳大利亚专家都已确认其真实性。澳大利亚专家说这是维吾尔族人被带上即将出发的火车。

刘晓明： 西方情报机构不断对中国进行虚假指控。他们诬称有100万人或更多的维吾尔族人遭到迫害。新疆维吾尔族有多少人口？ 40年前，新疆维吾尔族人口为400万~500万人，现在是1100万人。这些人谎称，我们搞"种族清洗"，但40年间新疆维吾尔族人口翻了一番……

马尔： 抱歉打断你。根据中国地方政府的统计数据，2015—2018年间，新疆维吾尔族聚居区的人口增长率下降了84%。

刘晓明： 这个数据不对。我以中国大使的身份给你最权威的官方数据：过去40年新疆维吾尔族人口翻了一番。没有所谓人口控制，也没有所谓强制绝育。

马尔： 但是从中国逃出来的人说，目前新疆正在实施强迫维吾尔族妇女绝育的政策，这一政策已经实施很长时间。一位勇敢的女士在BBC《新闻之夜》栏目上公开做证。你可以看看视频，的确有人在中国经历了强制绝育。（马尔播放所谓维吾尔族妇女视频）

刘晓明： 这种污蔑指控不值一驳。一小撮反华分子和组织不遗余力地从事损害中国利益的活动。但是大多数新疆人民对新疆的发展变化感到满意。过去3年多，新疆没有发生过一起恐怖袭击。包括维吾尔族在内的新疆人民享受和谐生活，各民族和平、和谐地共处。维吾尔族仅占中国人口的一小部分，即使在穆斯林中也是如此。他们与其他民族幸福、和平、和谐共处。中国的民族政策非常成功，各民族一律平等。（马尔重播所谓维吾尔族妇女视频）
首先，不存在所谓针对维吾尔族的大规模强制绝育，这绝非事实。其次，中国政府的政策是，坚决反对这种做法。但个别违反政策的情况不能排除，这在任何国家都是如此。

马尔： 你不能完全排除个案，但总的看法是……

刘晓明： 总的看法是这绝不是中国政府的政策，在中国各民族一律平等。

马尔： 西方民众收看这个采访，看到人们被蒙上眼睛押解到火车上，送往"再教育营"的视频，就会想起20世纪三四十年代的德国。

刘晓明： 这种说法是完全错误的。正如我过去向你指出，新疆没有所谓"集中营"。现在我们已进入信息时代，反华势力可以用各种手段编造各种污蔑中国的虚假信息。

马尔： 我读一段联合国《防止及惩治灭绝种族罪公约》的内容。公约说，种族灭绝行为包括：杀害该团体的成员；致使该团体的成员在身体上或精神上遭受严重伤害；故意使该团体处于某种生活状况下，以毁灭其全部或局部的生命；强制施行办法，意图防止该团体内的生育；强迫转移该团体的儿童至另一团体。据称，中国存在所有这些情况，将在联合国面临指控。

刘晓明： 这不是事实。恰恰相反，新疆人民享受着幸福生活，他们要求在新疆恢复良好的社会秩序。中国坚决反对酷刑以及迫害、歧视任何少数民族。中国不存在这样的情况。如我所说，中国政府的政策是，每一个少数民族在中国都得到平等对待，这是中国少数民族政策的成功所在。

马尔： 对于西方国家来说，还有没有可能与一个笃信民族主义、由共产党领导的国家打交道？

刘晓明： 你对中国的描述是不对的，中国并没有变得"更加民族主义"，这种说法大错特错。中国没有变，是以美国为首的西方国家对中国发起了所谓"新冷战"，制裁、抹黑、污名化中国。以新冠肺炎疫情为例，这些人仍将新冠病毒称为"中国病毒""武汉病毒"。对这种非常错误的言行，我们必须做出回应。我们从不惹事，但也不怕事。如果有人挑衅，我们必须回击。

马尔： 刘大使，非常感谢你参加我们今天的访谈节目。

刘晓明： 不客气。

A Live Interview
on BBC *The Andrew Marr Show*

On 19th July 2020, I gave a live interview on BBC *The Andrew Marr Show* about Hong Kong, Huawei, and Xinjiang. The full text is as follows:

Marr: Ambassador, welcome. Can I, first of all, ask you about Hong Kong? Are rights of dissent and freedom of speech still valued in Hong Kong?

Liu Xiaoming: Fully respected. I think people talk about this National Security Law. National Security Law is about restoring order and protecting the rights of the majority of people. It's targeted on a very small group of criminals who intend to endanger the national security.

Marr: But let me remind people what the National Security Law actually says. It says that Beijing now decides what breaks the law, not Hong Kong itself. Protesters can be arrested just for using placards. Police can search buildings without warrants and trials can be held in secret without a jury. Surely those laws break that "One Country, Two Systems" promise China originally made.

Liu Xiaoming: That is wrong information. I don't know if you have read the National Security Law yet. First, I would say, the Law begins with the statement that China will continue to implement "One Country, Two Systems" and Hong Kong people will administer their affairs with a high degree of autonomy.
The reason why this National Security Law was enacted is that in the past 23 years, although Hong Kong Special Administration Region government is entitled to enact its own law, according to Article 23 of the Basic Law, to protect the national security, because of the opposition — because of these troublemakers' scaremongering — the SAR government failed to enact it. But it is the Central Government's responsibility to

take care of national security.

Marr: You said trouble makers. But Amnesty International, which is an organization much respected by many people watching this program, says there was a rapid deterioration in the rights to freedom of peaceful assembly, expression, and association as the Hong Kong authorities increasingly adopted mainland China's vague and all-encompassing definition of national security.

Liu Xiaoming: The Amnesty International is not respected in China because it has made numerous false accusations against China. Never said a nice word, and has never been objective about China. That's the problem of them. We talked about Hong Kong situation last year, this turbulence and riots. Any responsible government has to take measures to address this situation.

Marr: Why couldn't the existing laws be enough to do that, because there are quite strong existing laws? If they are really causing trouble, really trying to cause disruption in Hong Kong, they could have been dealt with by existing laws.

Liu Xiaoming: That is exactly the reason why there should be a national security law, because the existing laws fail to contain this violence, looting, smashing, and storming the legislative council — just imagine if people stormed the British parliament! But that was possible in Hong Kong because there's no law governing national security in Hong Kong for the past 23 years.

Marr: Isn't the real problem that you don't want people in Hong Kong to talk about democracy in Hong Kong. President Trump said this. He says their freedom has been taken away. Their rights have been taken away. No special privileges, and with it goes Hong Kong, he said, because it will no longer be able to compete with free markets. A lot of people will be leaving Hong Kong. They are leaving Hong Kong for Australia, the United States, and for the UK. Will they be free to leave?

Liu Xiaoming: Certainly, they are free to leave. Hong Kong people enjoy unprecedented freedom after the handover for the past 23 years. Before the handover, what kind of freedom did they have? Did they have the freedom to elect their governor? The last governor was appointed by British government. But for the past 23 years, there were five Chief Executives elected by the Hong Kong people.

Marr: Surely the fundamental truth is that under your new leader, you have a nationalistic, more assertive regime in Beijing. And the real question is whether that regime can have a completely open relationship with free markets around the world. And Hong Kong is the epicenter for that.

Liu Xiaoming: I think you have a very wrong impression about what is going on in China. Let me give you an update. You don't trust our statement. You always regard it as propaganda. But it seems to me you trust Americans more. You don't regard them as propaganda. The Harvard University's Kennedy School of Government just issued a report. They did this report covering last 13 years. They did polling. The conclusion is, the Chinese people's rating of satisfaction for Chinese Communist Party and Chinese government is 93%, much higher than any western government, western leadership. So that's the fact about what is going on in China.

Marr: We are going to get a response from the British government this coming week over Hong Kong, and there are reports that, for instance, the Magnitsky Act might be used to ban individual Chinese people from British territory. And also that the extradition agreement is going to be torn up. What would be China's reaction if that's the case?

Liu Xiaoming: That is totally wrong. We never believe in unilateral sanction. We believe that the UN has the authority to impose sanctions. If the UK government goes as far as to impose sanctions on any individual in China, China will certainly make resolute response to it. You've seen what happened between China and the United States. They sanctioned Chinese officials. We sanctioned their senators and officials. I do not want to see this tit-for-tat between China and the US happen in China-UK relations. I think the UK should have its own independent foreign policy rather than to dance to the tune of Americans, like what happened to Huawei.

Marr: You've talked about the possibility of tit-for-tat or reprisals. Let me ask about Huawei because when the Huawei decision was announced, the Chinese foreign ministry said that it would severely undermine mutual trust and come at a cost. Can I ask you what the cost is?

Liu Xiaoming: We are still evaluating the consequences. This is a very bad decision. When this decision was announced, I said, this is a dark day for Huawei. It's a dark day for China-UK relations. It's an even darker day for the United Kingdom, because you will miss the opportunity to be a leading country. I happen to agree with Martin Jacques who is a British scholar and historian.

Marr: He knows China well.

Liu Xiaoming: He knows China well. He wrote a book entitled *When China Rules the World*. He has this good line: In 1793, the Chinese emperor Qianlong told the English King "We have not the slightest need of your country's manufactures", and that marked the start of 150-year decline of China. History turns full cycle. 227 years later, in 2020, the UK told China, "We do not have the slightest need of your 5G technology". So I do not know what will happen in the next 150 years.

Marr: Is China—looking at the TikTok's decision as well—is China going to punish British companies like for instance Jaguar Land Rover which is operating in China as part of the response?

Liu Xiaoming: We do not want to politicize the economy. That is wrong. It's wrong for the United Kingdom to discriminate against Chinese companies because of pressure from the United States. Some people are talking about "national security risk". There is no hard, solid evidence to say Huawei is a risk to the UK. They've been here for 20 years. They have made a huge contribution not only to the telecom industry of this country. They have fulfilled their corporate responsibility. They have helped the UK to develop. Prime Minister Boris Johnson has an ambitious plan to have full coverage of 5G by 2025. I think Huawei can deliver that. Huawei can be a big help. But now it seems to me the UK just kicks them out and, to use the media words, to purge them under the pressure from the United States. The US leaders have claimed credit for this.

Marr: Let's turn to vaccine development. Now, Britain has accused Russia of trying to steal vaccine secrets. And when I had Rick Scott, the American senator from Florida, very, very close to Donald Trump on this program, he accused China of much the same thing. He said we have evidence — that's the United States — that China is trying to sabotage or slow down our ability to get this vaccine done. It came through our intelligence community. What's your response?

Liu Xiaoming: Those China bashers have made countless accusations. I don't think I should spend time refuting their accusation against China. China is very open and China is working also with the UK scientists on vaccine. And President Xi made it very clear at the World Health Assembly that we'll make it a public good when it's ready. We want to make it accessible, especially in the poorest countries in Africa.

Marr: Let's turn to the single biggest problem at the moment between China and the West, which is the treatment of the Uighur people in north China. Let's look at some very disturbing drone footage that has been widely shared around the world. This is almost certainly over northern China, over Xinjiang. Can you tell us what is happening here?（Video is played）

Liu Xiaoming: I cannot see this as you do. This is not the first time you showed me a video. I still remember last year, you showed me what you thought was happening in Xinjiang. Let me tell you this about, Xinjiang…Have you been to Xinjiang yourself?

Marr: No, I never have.

Liu Xiaoming: Xinjiang is regarded as the most beautiful place in China? There's a Chinese saying you do not know how big China is until you visited Xinjiang ……

Marr: Ambassador, that is not a beautiful coverage however, is it?

Liu Xiaoming: That is exactly what I'm going to tell you. Since 1990, Xinjiang has come under a challenge because of the thousands of terrorist attacks. People cannot ...

Marr: That was 10 years ago. Can I ask you why people are kneeling, blindfolded and shaven, and being led to trains in northern China? What is going on there?

Liu Xiaoming: I do not know where you get this video tape. Sometimes you need to transfer prisoners, you know, in any country.

Marr: But just what is happening here, Ambassador?

Liu Xiaoming: I do not know where you got these video clips.

Marr: These have been going around the world. They've been authenticated by western intelligence agencies and by Australian experts who say these are Uyghur people being pushed on the train and then taken off to ...

Liu Xiaoming: Let me tell you this. The so-called Western intelligence agencies keep making up false accusations against China. They said one million or more Uyghur have been persecuted. What is the population of Xinjiang? Forty years ago, its population was about 4 to 5 million. Now it's 11 million. And people say we have ethnic cleansing. But the population has been doubled in 40 years.

Marr: I'm so sorry to interrupt. But according to your own local government's statistics, the population growth in Uyghur jurisdictions in that area has fallen by 84 percent between 2015 and 2018.

Liu Xiaoming: That's not right. I give you an official figure. I give you this figure as a Chinese ambassador. This is a very authoritative figure. In the past 40 years, the population in Xinjiang has doubled. So there's no so-called the restriction of population and there is no so-called forced abortion, and so on.

Marr: But there is a program of forced sterilization being imposed on Uyghur women at the moment. It's gone on for a long time. And people, who are finally coming out of China, are talking about it. And I've got the witness statement from a woman who's on *Newsnight*, a brave woman who talked about it openly. You can now watch. Here is somebody who went through the forcible sterilization program in China. (Video is played)

Liu Xiaoming: I can easily refute this accusation. There are some small groups of anti-Chinese people working against the interests of China. But the majority of Xinjiang people are happy with what is going on in Xinjiang.

In the past three years, there's no single terrorist attack in Xinjiang. Uyghur People enjoy harmonious life and peaceful, harmonious coexistence with people of other ethnic groups. Uyghur people are just one small portion of the Chinese population and even the Muslims in China. The majority of them are living happily, peacefully and harmoniously with other ethnic groups. We have a very successful ethnic policy. We treat every ethnic group as equal. (Video is played)

Liu Xiaoming: First of all, there's no so-called pervasive, massive, forced sterilization of Uyghur people in China. This is totally against the truth. Secondly, the government policy is strongly opposed to this kind of practice. I cannot rule out single cases. For any country, single cases exits.

Marr: You cannot rule out at all, but the general view...

Liu Xiaoming: The general view is that it is not a government policy and we treat every ethnic group in China as equal.

Marr: When we see interviews like that and we see people blindfolded and led off to trains to be taken to re-education camps. It reminds people in the West what was going on in Germany in the 1930s and 1940s.

Liu Xiaoming: That's completely wrong. There is no such thing as a "concentration camp" in Xinjiang. I think we discussed that before. With regard to that video clip, I will get back to you. Your know, even if we are in the information age, there are all kinds of fake accusations against China.

Marr: Let me remind you what the UN Convention on the Prevention and Punishment of the Crime of Genocide says. It says the genocide is killing people, causing serious bodily or mental harm, deliberately inflicting conditions of life calculated to bring about a group's physical destruction, imposing measures intended to prevent births, and forcibly transferring children to another group. All of those things, it is alleged to have been happening in China and China is going to face accusations at the United Nations about this.

Liu Xiaoming: This is not true. The fact just shows the opposite. People in Xinjiang enjoy happy life. They call for order to be restored in Xinjiang. China is strongly opposed to any torture, persecution and discrimination of people of any ethnic group. This is not the case in China. The policy of the Chinese government is, as I said, every ethnic group in China is treated equal. That's the success story of Chinese ethnic policy.

Marr: Is it any longer possible for the West to deal with the country which is so nationalistic and so much under the thumb of the Communist Party leadership?

Liu Xiaoming: I do not agree with your description of China. It is not China that becomes "so nationalistic". People say China is becoming very nationalistic. That's totally wrong. China has not changed. It's the Western countries headed by the United States. They started this so-called "new cold war" on China. They have this sanction, they have this smearing and name-calling. Take what happened with this coronavirus. They still keep calling it "China virus" and "Wuhan virus". It's totally wrong, but we have to make a response. We do not provoke. But once we were provoked, we have to make a response.

Marr: Ambassador, thanks very much indeed for coming to talk to us today. Much appreciated.

Liu Xiaoming: My pleasure.

新冠肺炎疫情

Covid-19

新冠肺炎疫情是百年来全球发生的最严重的传染病大流行，也是中华人民共和国成立以来我国遭遇的传播速度最快、感染范围最广、防控难度最大的重大突发公共卫生事件。在以习近平同志为核心的党中央坚强领导下，我国迅速打响疫情防控的人民战争，夺取了全国抗疫斗争的重大战略成果。我们同时与世界各国携手合作、共克时艰，第一时间向世界卫生组织、有关国家和地区组织主动通报疫情信息，第一时间发布新冠病毒基因序列等信息，第一时间公布诊疗方案和防控方案，同许多国家、国际和地区组织开展疫情防控交流活动，毫无保留地同各方分享防控和救治经验。我们以实际行动帮助挽救了全球成千上万人的生命，彰显了中国推动构建人类命运共同体的真诚愿望。

然而，一些西方国家自己疫情防控不力，却将矛头指向中国，极力污名化中国，甚至要求中国"道歉"和"赔偿"，以此"甩锅"，逃避责任和转移视线。一些西方媒体也罔顾事实，颠倒是非、混淆黑白，炒作各种"阴谋论"。

面对这种恶劣的舆论环境，我不惧风险挑战，迎难而上，利用各种机会发表演讲，在英国主流大报上发表文章，接受各大电视台采访，包括上BBC的直播访谈栏目《安德鲁·马尔访谈》和《尖锐对话》，澄清事实，说明真相，戳穿谎言，批驳谬论，激浊扬清，大讲中国抗疫故事，大讲中外合作抗疫故事，向世界展示中国人民和中华民族的伟大力量，展现中国负责任大国的贡献和担当。

接受英国BBC《安德鲁·马尔访谈》栏目主持人马尔现场直播采访

作者手记

2020年2月9日，我就抗击新冠肺炎疫情接受英国BBC旗舰访谈栏目《安德鲁·马尔访谈》(*The Andrew Marr Show*)主持人安德鲁·马尔(Andrew Marr)现场直播采访。

我介绍了中国的抗疫情况，指出中国政府已经采取了最全面、最严格的防控措施。中国人民不仅是在保护自身的生命安全和健康，也是在为保护世界人民的生命安全和健康做出贡献。

我们还讨论华为问题，马尔称，美国对英国施加了巨大压力。我说，"不列颠"只有坚持独立自主的外交政策，才能成为"大不列颠"。我希望英国政府能坚持接受华为的决定，这符合英国的利益，也有利于中英合作，更重要的是，有利于维护英国全球最开放、最自由的市场经济形象。

采访实录如下：

马尔： 刘大使，欢迎你。首先，可否请你介绍一下最新的病毒感染病例的数据，包括不幸病亡的病例数字？

刘晓明： 根据最新数据，截至北京时间2月8日24时，死亡病例811例，治愈病例2649例，治愈病例数是死亡病例数的3倍多，这是令人鼓舞的，说明治疗是有效的。此外，确诊病例数首次超过疑似病例数，说明医院的收治率在上升。你也看到我们用10天时间新建的两家医院已投入使用，有效地提升了收治率和医疗救治能力。

马尔： 同时给人的印象是感染率仍在上升？

刘晓明： 是有新的感染，但我认为没有必要恐慌。可以比较一下，这次病毒的致死率是2%左右，与埃博拉的40%、SARS的10%相比低得多，因此没有必要恐慌。中国政府已经采取了最全面、最严格的非常规防控措施。

马尔： 中国政府采取了不同寻常的措施，在城市周围设置路障，实际上是对整个城市实施了防疫隔离。隔离期间大部分的交通关闭，经济活动暂停。这种状态还要持续多久？

刘晓明： 目前很难预测拐点何时到来，我们当然希望能早点到来。隔离防疫措施是非常有效的，目前大部分的病例仍集中在湖北和武汉。湖北的面积相当于英格兰加上苏格兰，人口相当于英格兰加上威尔士，涉及相当大的范围。

马尔： 受到影响的大约共有 6500 万人吧？

刘晓明： 是 5900 万人，但中方采取的措施是有效的，否则病毒很容易扩散到中国其他地区。中国人民不仅是在保护自身的生命安全和健康，也是在为保护世界人民的生命安全和健康做出贡献。

马尔： 的确如此。中国政府是否准备在中国其他地区和城市实施同样的隔离措施？

刘晓明： 这要视情况而定。湖北以外的中国其他地区也在采取防控措施。中国各地情况不同，虽然 80% 的感染病例发生在湖北省内，但全国人民都要提高警惕，所以其他地区也采取了相关预防性的防控措施。

马尔： 关于年轻医生李文亮，他是最先对未知新病毒可能带来的威胁发出警告的人。然而中国政府逮捕了他，对他进行了严厉警告，称他要是不悔改、继续从事非法活动，他将受到法律的制裁。然后，令人悲伤的是，他去世了。你是否认为中国政府在这件事上做得不对？

刘晓明： 我要纠正你的说法，不是中国政府，是地方政府相关部门。事实上，国家监察委员会已派出调查组赴湖北省武汉市，就群众反映的涉及李文亮医生的有关问题进行全面调查。人们对李医生的去世感到悲痛，我也通过推特表示哀悼和致敬。李医生是位英雄，人们会永远记住他的勇气和他为抗击疫情做出的贡献。我们还有成千上万的医护工作者，李文亮是他们中间的一员，他们都将生死置之度外，战斗在抗疫第一线。

马尔：　他们中的很多人都是英雄，但是李医生公开谈及信息公开的必要性。此时此刻中国政府是否已经意识到，面对这样的形势，中国需要信息更开放、反应更迅速？

刘晓明：　我们非常开放，我们分享了所有的信息，包括治疗情况、病例情况，同时我们也欢迎国际合作。我们认为这次的病毒是人类共同的敌人，全世界应该并肩作战。同时，我们与英方也正在进行良好合作。中国驻英国使馆正在尽我们所能，协助中英两国科学家合作研发治疗药物和疫苗。

马尔：　如果以中国的实力和所采取的所有措施，依然无法阻止病毒——现在中国以外已经有感染病例，疫情是否将蔓延到全世界所有地区？

刘晓明：　我们会竭尽全力，但是我仍然要提醒人们不要恐慌。我们认为，病毒是可防、可控、可治的。我们相信，有中国中央政府的坚强领导，有全国人民众志成城，有国际社会广泛支持，我们一定能战胜疫情，打赢疫情防控阻击战。

马尔：　你也知道，中国对世界经济至关重要。包括苹果、汽车制造商、时尚产业在内的许多公司已经面临供应链的问题，这些公司关心的是工厂何时重新开工。

刘晓明：　经济当然会受到一定影响，但我认为影响是暂时和短期的，中国政府正在采取措施，推动企业复工复产。你在节目开始时也提到，中国正在打一场"人民战争"，举国上下都动员起来了。我认为，对中国经济应该保持信心，因为中国经济的基本面依然良好。世界银行、国际货币基金组织及国际知名经济学家普遍认为，长期看，中国经济仍极具韧性。

马尔：　　但是短期影响将是非常严重的。很多公司都在担心，希望知道中国的工厂何时复工。什么时候能恢复生产苹果手机。

刘晓明：　我不能替苹果公司回答这个问题，但据我所知，华为手机的生产仍在加班加点。我知道，你可能还要问关于华为的问题，它现在在中国做得很好。中国有句话……你会说中文吗？

马尔：　　你可能已经注意到，我不会说中文。

刘晓明：　在中文里，"危机"是由"危"和"机"两个字组成的。我们始终认为，危机里面蕴含着机遇，因此我们正努力化危为机。

马尔：　　说到机遇，我想问个问题。疫情最初暴发时，就有人说中国政府试图隐瞒，他们对中国政府释放的种种信息表示高度怀疑。那么，中国共产党和中国人民看到当前的情况，是否意识到中国需要比以往更加开放，到了该改变的时候了？

刘晓明： 我们没有任何隐瞒。世界卫生组织（WHO）总干事谭德塞高度评价中方的应对行动。我们与WHO以及包括英国在内的相关国家和地区分享信息，它们对中国体现出的开放和透明给予了高度评价。

马尔： 我打断一下，1月22日，约2000万人在得到疫情暴发的消息后离开了湖北。换句话说，在疫情暴发初期，地方政府反应并不迅速，却对李医生采取了行动。地方政府是否会因此受到惩罚？

刘晓明： 这是一种新病毒，我们对它并不十分了解，认识它需要一个过程。但一旦意识到它的危害和风险，人们就会迅速动员起来，采取正确的措施。李医生做得很好，人们向他表示敬意。我刚才说了，中央政府已经派出工作组进行调查。有了调查结果之后，我会向你反馈。在对此事的处理中，任何人有任何不当行为都将承担后果并受到惩罚。

马尔： 大使先生，你说我会问关于华为的问题。是的，我是一定要问的。现在有5位保守党重量级议员在英国议会呼吁撤销英国政府的相关决定，确保华为被排除在英国5G网络之外。他们认为华为毫无疑问与中国政府有着紧密的联系，在数据传输问题上是不可信赖的。他们说，5G网络是关系到国家安全的基础设施，中国政府同样绝对不会允许任何英国公司参与其国家安全基础设施核心建设。

刘晓明： 这些议员的说法是完全错误的，这与中世纪欧洲的"猎巫行动"如出一辙，可谓"欲加之罪，何患无辞"。华为是一家民营企业，与中国政府没有任何关系。它唯一的"问题"就是它是一家中国公司。改革开放以来，中国越来越开放。中国现在实行市场经济，民营企业在国民经济中占1/3，外资和中外合资企业占1/3。华为是完全独立的公司，它是电信领域的领军者。英国首相之所以选择华为，是因为他对英国的发展有雄心勃勃的计划，希望在2025年前在英国实现5G网络全覆盖，而华为可以为之做出重要贡献。

马尔： 这一决定的代价就是，美国总统特朗普火冒三丈、暴跳如雷，对约翰逊首相大发雷霆，对此你怎么看？对首相站到中方一边，你是否感到满意？

刘晓明： 英国首相和特朗普总统之间的事还是交给首相去处理吧。正如我常说，"不列颠"只有坚持独立自主的外交政策，才能成为"大不列颠"。我希望约翰逊首相能坚持他的决定，这符合英国的利益，也有利于中英合作，更重要的是，有利于维护英国全球最开放、最自由的市场经济形象。当然，我们对英方决定并非100%满意，因为英方给华为设定了35%的市场份额上限，这不符合英国自由经济和自由竞争的原则，但英方的决定仍是值得欢迎的。

马尔： 非常感谢刘大使接受我们的采访。

刘晓明： 不客气。

A Live Interview
on BBC *The Andrew Marr Show*

On 9th February 2020, I gave a live interview on BBC *Andrew Marr Show* about China's fight against the novel coronavirus epidemic. The full text is as follows:

Marr: The Chinese Ambassador Liu Xiaoming is joining me now.

Liu Xiaoming: Thanks for having me.

Marr: Ambassador, welcome. Can I ask you first of all to update us on the number of people infected in China so far as you know and sadly, the number of people who have died?

Liu Xiaoming: According to the latest figures by midnight Beijing time, the number of death cases is 811 and cured cases is 2, 649. That is very encouraging. That means the number of cured cases is three times the death cases. That shows the effectiveness of the treatment. And also, we have seen that the confirmed cases for the first time exceed the suspected cases. That means the hospitalization rate is coming up. You know, we built two hospitals within ten days. These figures show the improvement of the treatment and hospitalization.

Marr: Is it the impression that the rate of infection, however, is still increasing?

Liu Xiaoming: Yes, the rate is increasing. But I think people should not panic. If you compare the fatality rate, —currently, it is 2%, much lower than the Ebola which is 40%, and even lower than SARS which is 10%. So there is no reason to panic. The Chinese government has adopted the most comprehensive and strict, unconventional

control measures.

Marr: You've done some extraordinary things as a government. You have effectively quarantined, you put a roadblock as it were around whole cities. And big parts of the transport system and the economy have closed down while this is going on. Can I ask you, how long is this going to have to go on for?

Liu Xiaoming: At this moment, it is very difficult to predict when we are going to have the inflection point. We certainly hope it will come sooner. But the isolation and quarantine measures have been very effective. So far, the most cases are concentrated in Hubei and Wuhan. Hubei is about the size of England plus Scotland, and the population is about England plus Wales. So this is such a large area.

Marr: 65 million people, therefore, around about that?

Liu Xiaoming: It's 59 million. The measure has been effective. Otherwise, it will spread out to the other parts of China. And also, I think the Chinese people are making a contribution not only for the safety of life and health of ourselves but also to that of the world people.

Marr: Indeed. Is the Chinese government ready to take the same kind of measures in other places in China, other cities?

Liu Xiaoming: It depends. I think there are some prevention and control measures taken in other parts of China. But, you know, China itself is different.80% of the cases are concentrated in Hubei province. But people have to be cautious. So there are prevention and control measures taken in other parts of China.

Marr: There was the very difficult case of the young doctor Li Wenliang, who was the first person who alerted people that there was something strange going on, a new virus that was worrying and unknown. And the Chinese authorities arrested him and gave him a notice of admonishment and they were very, very tough with him. They said if you are stubborn, refused to repent and continue to carry out illegal activities, you will be punished by the law. And then sadly, he died. Do you think the Chinese state has made a mistake in that case?

Liu Xiaoming: I would correct you here. It's not Chinese authorities. It is local authorities. Chinese authorities as a matter of fact, we have a supervision committee. It has sent an investigation team down to Wuhan to find out what was really going on. People feel very sad. I tweeted to express my condolences and paid tribute to Dr. Li. He will be remembered as a hero. He will be remembered for his bravery and contribution to the fight of this disease. But he is one of the millions of the Chinese medical doctors and nurses. We have so many of them on the forefront of this battle.

Marr: Many of them are being heroic at the moment. But nonetheless, he was very open about the need for openness. Is this the moment where the Chinese state looks into the situation and says, we need to be more open and move more quickly when it comes to this kind of situation.

Liu Xiaoming: We are open. We shared all the information about the practice, the cases of disease. We welcome international cooperation as well. We believe this virus is the enemy of mankind. So people of all countries should work together to fight against the common enemy. And also, we work very hard with British scientists. So my Embassy tries very hard to facilitate Chinese scientists working with the British scientists to develop medicine and vaccine.

Marr: A very simple question is that if the Chinese state, with all its power and the way it operates, can't stop this from spreading — now it's out of China, it's going to spread everywhere, isn't it?

Liu Xiaoming: We will try our best. But I still want to caution people: don't panic. We believe this virus is controllable, preventable and curable. So we are confident that with the strong leadership of the central government of China, with the people of China united behind the government and with the broad support of the international community, we can beat this virus and win the battle.

Marr: You also know of course that China is very, very important in the entire world economy. Lots and lots of companies, from Apple, making iPhones, to car-makers and fashion companies, are already seeing problems in the supply chain and they are asking — I'll put this brutally and simply — when will the factories reopen?

Liu Xiaoming: Certainly, there is an impact on the economy. But I think the impact is temporary and short-term. The government now works very hard to encourage people to restore production. You said at the very beginning that we have waged a people's war. So the whole country has been mobilized. And I think you have to keep the confidence in Chinese economy, because the fundamentals of the economy are still sound. The IMF, the World Bank and many respected economists in the world believe that the long-term Chinese economy is very resilient.

Marr: There is going to be a very, very acute short-term hit to the economy. Lots and lots of companies are worried. I will ask again, do you know when Chinese factories will reopen? When will iPhones be manufactured again?

Liu Xiaoming: I can't answer for iPhone. But I think the big smart phone producer Huawei is working round clock. I know you will ask me about Huawei. But they are doing very well in China. In China, we have a saying. Do you speak Chinese?

Marr: I speak no Chinese, as you may have noticed.

Liu Xiaoming: The Chinese word for "crisis" is the combination of two words, crisis and opportunities. We always believe there are opportunities in crisis. So we will try our best to turn crisis into opportunities.

Marr: Let me ask you about the opportunities here. As I said right at the beginning, there is a sense the Chinese state was hiding things and a lot of people were highly skeptical about the Chinese state when it said this or that. And I ask again, is this a moment when the Chinese Communist Party and the people within China look at the situation and think we need to be a much more open society than we have been? This is a moment of change in turn?

Liu Xiaoming: We didn't hide anything. If you talk to the WHO Director-General Dr. Tedros, he spoke highly of the efforts made by China. We shared information with the

WHO, shared information with countries like the UK and other relevant countries and regions. They all spoke highly of China's transparency and openness.

Marr: And if I may just interrupt for a second. In Wuhan, about 20 million people were in and left the province after it was known that this virus was out on 22 January. In other words, right at the beginning there was not enough speed and the local authority did crack down on Dr. Li. Are they going to be punished for that?

Liu Xiaoming: You know, this is a new virus. People do not know it well. It will take some time for people to understand it. But once people realize the risk and danger, people will be mobilized. You have to adopt a reasonable approach. Dr. Li, as I said just a moment ago, he did a marvelous job. People paid tribute to him. And the central authorities sent an investigation team to find out what was really happening. I will get back to you if you would like to have a conclusion to find out what really happened. Those who had misconduct will be made accountable for their conduct, to be held responsible for the handling of this case.

Marr: Ambassador, you said I was going to raise Huawei and I am, absolutely. Because there are five leading conservative MPs who are competing with other conservative MPs to reverse the decision to ensure Huawei is kept out of the system, because they see Huawei as, first of all, absolutely connected to the Chinese state and being unreliable when it comes to transmissions and secrecy. This is part of our national infrastructure, they say, and there's no way China would allow a British company to be absolutely at the centre of their national infrastructure in the same way.

Liu Xiaoming: I think they are totally wrong. What they are doing is a kind of witch-hunt. Number one, Huawei is a privately owned company having nothing to do with the Chinese government. The only problem they have is that they are a Chinese company, and that's the problem. China is more open, as we get back to your original argument. Since the reform and opening up, China has run a market orientated economy, and one third of Chinese economy is privately owned. The other one third is owned by foreign and joint ventures. So Huawei is an independent company and the leader in this area. I think the reason why the Prime Minister decided to keep Huawei

is he has a very ambitious plan for the UK. He wants to have 5G coverage in the UK by 2025. Huawei can be of great help.

Marr: But the price he paid for that was the incandescent anger of Donald Trump. How do you respond when you heard Donald Trump absolutely blasting Boris Johnson? Were you pleased when he jumped to your side of the fence?

Liu Xiaoming: I will leave the Prime Minister to deal with President Trump. I always say, Great Britain can only be great when it has its own independent foreign policy. So I do hope that the Prime Minister will stay with his decision, because I think it is in the interest of the UK. It's also in the interest of China-UK cooperation. The important thing is that it is in the interest of maintaining British image as the most open and free market economy in the world. Although we are not 100% satisfied — the 35% percent cap does not show your principle of free economy and free competition — I think it's a good decision.

Marr: Ambassador, thanks very much indeed for talking to us.

Liu Xiaoming: My pleasure.

接受英国天空新闻台外事
编辑海恩斯采访

作者手记

　　2020年2月18日，我接受英国天空新闻台（Sky News）外事和国防编辑黛博拉·海恩斯（Deborah Haynes）采访。

　　采访当天，习近平主席与英国首相约翰逊通了电话。我重点阐述了两国领导人通电话的重要意义，介绍了中国抗击新冠肺炎疫情的最新进展和相关国际合作。

　　这次采访在天空新闻台《晚间新闻》（*Nightly News*）栏目和《10点新闻》（*Sky News at Ten*)栏目播出，并在该台整点新闻时段滚动播放。该台网站和推特对采访进行了报道。

　　采访实录如下：

海恩斯：　刘大使，你有消息要跟我们分享？

刘晓明：　是的，是一个好消息。习近平主席刚刚同约翰逊首相通了电话，这是约翰逊首相连任后中英两国领导人首次通话。两国领导人谈得非常好，讨论了中国抗击新冠肺炎疫情的最新进展情况。习主席强调，中方已经采取了最全面、最严格的防控措施，全国上下都动员起来，我们的措施已开始显现积极成效。我们有信心、有能力打赢这场疫情防控阻击战。约翰逊首相高度肯定中方的努力和贡献，对中方反应的迅速和措施的全面、有力、高效表示赞赏。双方表示中英应"肩并肩"共克时艰。

习主席表示，中方始终坚持公开、透明的态度，与包括英国在内的国际社会保持密切合作。中国政府不仅对中国人民的健康与生命安全负责——这是政府工作的首要任务，而且也正在为保护全世界人民的生命安全和健康、维护全球公共卫生做出贡献。我们对英方的支持表示感谢，约翰逊首相表示英国愿进一步提供帮助。

通话中，两国领导人还谈及引领中英全面战略伙伴关系新的10年再出发，进一步推进中英关系"黄金时代"，双方达成广泛共识。约翰逊首相向习主席表示，他喜欢中国，他和他领导的英国政府愿与中方共同努力，将中英关系推向更高水平。习主席也重申了中方重视发展中英关系，中英同为具有全球影响力的国家，都是联合国安理会常任理事国，两国在双边和多边事务上拥有巨大共同利益。约翰逊首相还提到《生物多样性公约》第十五次缔约国会议（COP15）和《联合国气候变化框架公约》第二十六次缔约国会议（COP26），认为中英面临诸多机遇，应该合作推进全球事务，应对包括气候变化在内的全球性挑战。在当前关键时期，两国领导人通话不仅为中英关系定了调，也为两国关系未来发展指明了方向。这就是我想第一时间向你传递的好消息。

海恩斯： 谢谢！通话时有没有谈及何时能够谈判达成英中自由贸易协定？

刘晓明： 通话涉及广泛议题。在自贸协定问题上，中方的态度是开放的。英国离开欧盟后，希望与中国达成新的自贸协定，我们也始终持开放态度，中英已成立工作组进行可行性研究。英国政府去年专注于脱欧，今年成功脱欧，首要任务当然还是与欧盟贸易伙伴谈判。中方也已做好准备，争取与英方达成自贸协定。

海恩斯： 由于脱欧等原因，去年工作组暂停工作，目前有没有恢复？

刘晓明： 我们随时准备好与英国合作。英方仍处于政策调整之中，政府也刚刚重新组阁，尚不知谁是负责双边贸易的国务大臣。我们准备好进行接触，英方表态也很积极。但目前中方正在全力抗击疫情，仍需要一些时间，我们才能开始讨论具体问题。双方都有进一步加强接触的积极意愿。

海恩斯： 两位领导人是否谈到安全、华为、5G等问题？

刘晓明： 我尚未掌握更具体的信息。习主席指出，中英应相互尊重，重视彼此的核心利益和重大关切。双方应合作建设开放经济，坚持自由贸易和多边主义。我认为中方传递的信息是清晰的。

海恩斯： 坦率地说，如果英国政府没有做出允许华为参与英国5G网络建设的决定，是不是就不会有这次通话？

刘晓明： 不能将这次通话与某个具体问题联系起来。此次通话涉及广泛议题。我认为约翰逊首相希望直接向习主席了解中国抗击疫情的情况，相信他听了习主席的介绍，对中国防控举措取得的积极成效更有信心了。我想，天空新闻台的广大观众也希望了解疫情防控最新积极进展。根据我刚刚收到的数据，今天我们实现了"三个首次"：全国新增确诊病例首次降至2000人以内；全国新增死亡病例首次降至100人以内；湖北省以外新增确诊病例首次降至100人以内，这些数字说明隔离防控举措取得了良好效果。通话还谈及中英双方如何合作应对疫情。用首相的话说，要"肩并肩"抗击疫情。此次疫情对中国和整个世界都是一次严峻挑战，所以国际社会应团结应对。英方向中方提供了援助，并表示愿继续帮助中国。我们对此表示感谢。我想强调，华为只是中英关系的一个议题、一个局部。

海恩斯： 英国能在哪些具体方面向中国提供帮助？

刘晓明： 首先，我们感谢英国人民给予的同情和支持。女王陛下通过约克公爵安德鲁王子向习主席和中国人民转达了慰问，习主席在通话中对此表示感谢。约翰逊首相也向李克强总理致信表达同情和支持。我们收到了英国工商界乃至普通民众的捐赠，特别是最急需的医疗物资。许多英国普通民众也致信我们使馆表达慰问或提供捐款，我们十分感谢。英国政府还向中方援助了两批医疗物资，我们对此表示感谢。

海恩斯： 你认为中国的感染病例已经达到峰值了吗？

刘晓明： 我很难确定地说已经达到峰值。每天还有新增确诊病例和死亡病例，但数量已经明显下降。17日，湖北以外其他省市新增死亡病例只有5例，目前绝大多数死亡病例还是集中在湖北。治愈病例大幅增加，现在治愈病例数是死亡病例数的7倍，证明我们对患者的治疗是有效的。我无法预测何时出现拐点，希望拐点尽快到来。但我想，如果我们继续采用这些有效做法，疫情就能达到峰值，就能尽早实现死亡病例的大幅减少。

海恩斯： 中国政府是否行动太慢，在初期试图掩盖真相？

刘晓明： 不存在这个问题。中国中央政府十分重视疫情防控。习主席强调，始终要把人民的生命安全放在政府工作的第一位，他3次主持召开中共中央政治局常务委员会会议，部署防疫工作。中央成立应对疫情工作领导小组，领导全国防控工作，军队也动员起来了。但这是一种新病毒，一开始人们并不了解。世界卫生组织最近才正式命名了这种病毒，这说明认识和应对它需要一个过程。约翰逊首相赞赏中国防控措施的速度和效果。我可以十分肯定地说，中国政府全力以赴应对疫情，同时坚持做到公开透明，并与世界卫生组织和包括英国在内的相关国家分享信息。中国和英国科学家还在合力研制治疗药物和疫苗，希望他们早日取得成功。

海恩斯： 关于疫情对中国经济的影响，你在不久前的中外记者会上提到，疫情虽对交通运输、旅游等行业影响较大，但未对中国经济产生严重负面影响。近日，韩国政府表示疫情可能对今年韩国经济发展产生连带不利影响。苹果等大型跨国企业也表示在华业务受到影响。关于疫情对中国经济的负面影响，你能否提供更多信息？比如影响到底有多严重？是否会给世界经济带来风险？

刘晓明： 短期内会有一些影响。近日，BBC或天空新闻台的电视节目也谈到中国来英国的游客减少，不少商店、购物村被迫关闭，景区游客也不多。但我想强调，这种影响只是短期的、暂时的，中国经济韧性强劲，基本面是好的。中国全面深化改革、扩大对外开放的步伐并未停滞。今年1月1日，《中华人民共和国外商投资法》正式生效。当前，中国政府正一面抗击疫情，一面领导各行业复工复产。整个国家都被动员起来，全力完成这两大任务。中国经济长期向好的基本面并未改变，正如习主席在同约翰逊首相通话时指出的，我们有信心、有能力实现今年经济社会发展目标。今年是中国发展的关键一年，我们将实现第一个"百年目标"，全面建成小康社会，完成脱贫攻坚。

海恩斯： 对近期有关新疆的"泄密文件"，你有何评论？

刘晓明： 有关报道纯属捏造。我曾多次指出，新疆问题的实质不是人权问题，更不是什么民族、宗教问题，而是防范打击宗教极端主义和恐怖主义的问题。新疆人民享有充分的宗教信仰自由，并受到法律的保护，各族人民安居乐业。

海恩斯： 谢谢刘大使接受我的采访。

刘晓明： 不客气。

An Interview with Deborah Haynes on Sky News

On 18th February 2020, I gave an interview to Deborah Haynes, Foreign Editor of Sky News, on the telephone conversation between President Xi Jinping and Prime Minister Boris Johnson. I also answered questions about China's fight against the COVID-19 epidemic and other issues. The contents of the interview were aired on Sky News "*Nightly News*" and every hour. The transcript is as follows:

Haynes: Ambassador, have you something you want to share?

Liu Xiaoming: Yes, very good news. President Xi Jinping and Prime Minister Boris Johnson just had a telephone conversation. This is the first conversation between the two leaders after Prime Minister Johnson got reelected. They had a very good conversation. They talked about China's battle against COVID-19 and President Xi emphasized that China has taken very comprehensive, strict and thorough prevention and control measures. The whole country has been mobilized and our methods are showing positive effect. We are confident that we have the capability to win the battle against the virus. The Prime Minister spoke highly of China's efforts, China's contribution, and appreciated highly the speed and effectiveness of the measures taken by China. They also talked about how China and UK can collaborate to fight shoulder to shoulder against the virus.

President Xi also said that we are open and transparent in terms of collaboration with the international community, including the UK. We are responsible not only for the health and safety of the Chinese people, which is the top priority of the government work. We are also making contribution to safety and health of all people of the world people by contributing to global public health. We appreciate the support given by the

British side. Prime Minister Johnson also expressed readiness to assist further.

They also talked about how the two countries will strengthen China-UK relationship for the next ten years. Prime Minister Johnson also mentioned the "Golden Era" and they've reached broad consensus.

Talking about the relationship, the Prime Minister told President Xi that he loves China, and he and his administration want to work with China to elevate the relationship to a new level. President Xi also expressed our commitment to the relationship. China and UK are both countries of global influence and permanent members of the UN Security Council. There are enormous common interests between our two countries not only on bilateral issues but also on multilateral agenda. The Prime Minister mentioned the COP15 (the 15th Meeting of the Conference of the Parties of the Convention on Biological Diversity) and COP26 (the 26h Meeting of the Conference of the Parties of the UN Convention on Climate Change) . He believed that there are lots of opportunities between China and UK to work on the global agenda and address the global challenges, like climate change. It's a very good conversation, which not only set the tone but also set the new direction for China-UK relations at this critical moment between China and UK. That's basically the good news I want to let you know, first hand.

Haynes: Thank you. And in the conversation, did they talk about a trade deal and the timeline, when that would be achieved?

Liu Xiaoming: They covered broad issues. When it comes to the trade deal, we are open. Once UK leaves EU, you'll have a new free trade agreement with China and we are open to that. Last year, the two countries set up a working team to carry out feasibility studies on the trade deal. But last year the British government was so focused on Brexit. This year after you have Brexit done, I think your top priority is still negotiating with your EU partners. China is open and ready to engage with UK to reach a new agreement on trade.

Haynes: Those working groups paused, as I understand, last year because of the Brexit, in part. Have they restarted?

Liu Xiaoming: We are ready to work with British colleagues at any time. I think UK is still in a process of making adjustments: you just had a new administration, a new reshuffle. We do not know who will be the minister responsible for bilateral trade. We are ready to engage with each other, and the British side has already expressed willingness as well. But because now we are focusing on the battle against the virus, it will probably still take some time for the two sides to get into the details. I think both sides have the willingness to engage with each other more positively.

Haynes: Did the two leaders talk about security, and Huawei and 5G?

Liu Xiaoming: I don't have the specific information. But the President mentioned that we hope that the two countries should show respect for each other and attach importance to the main concerns and core interests. Both sides will work together to build open economic relations and to be committed to free trade and multilateralism. I think the messages are very clear.

Haynes: Do you think that frankly speaking, if Britain hadn't made that decision to choose Huawei to be part of the network, this telephone call wouldn't have happened?

Liu Xiaoming: I would not link the telephone call with one specific case. Because this telephone call is about a much bigger picture. Prime Minister Johnson would like to know first hand from the President how things are going on in China. From the President's remarks, the Prime Minister would feel much more confident that the virus is under control and China's measures are showing positive effects. In fact, I think your audience might be interested in the most recent positive signs in our work. I just received the figures which show "three firsts". As of today, it is the first time that the confirmed cases were brought down to less than 2,000, the death cases were brought down to less than 100, and the confirmed cases outside Hubei were brought down to less than 100. That shows the quarantine efforts and measures are taking very good effect. Also it's about how China and UK can work together, to use the Prime Minister's term, "shoulder to shoulder", to fight against this virus. This virus is not only a challenge to the Chinese government, but also a challenge to the whole world. So the international community has to work together. The UK has offered its assistance and expressed willingness to help China. We highly appreciate that. And also about the big picture of China-UK relations, Huawei is just one of the issues or maybe one part of China-UK relations.

Haynes: How can UK help China deal with the virus? What are the specifics?

Liu Xiaoming: First, we appreciate the sympathy and support expressed by the British people from all walks of life. Her Majesty the Queen passed on the message through the Duke of York to President Xi and the Chinese people. The President highly appreciated that. Prime Minister Johnson also wrote a letter to Premier Li Keqiang to show support and sympathy. We received many donations from British businesses, both in terms of medical supplies badly needed in China and also from students, even ordinary people, average citizens. Here at the Embassy we received letters showing their sympathy, support and donations. We highly appreciate it. The British government sent two shipments of medical supplies to China, which is also highly appreciated.

Haynes: Do you believe the peak has been reached now in China?

Liu Xiaoming: I cannot say for sure that we have reached the peak because there are still new confirmed cases and fatality cases every day, though they have been brought down tremendously. Yesterday the death cases outside Hubei was only 5, and most death cases are happening in Hubei. The cured cases are increasing tremendously. Now they are about seven times the number of death cases. That shows the effectiveness of the medical treatment of the patients. I can't say when we are going to have the inflection point. I do hope that we will get there sooner. But I think, with these effective measures, and if we keep working, we will reach the peak. I hope we will see the absolute reduction of death cases sooner.

Haynes: Do you think the authority reacted too slowly and tried to cover up the obvious in the early days?

Liu Xiaoming: I don't think so. I think the central government attached great importance to this. As the President emphasized, the life and safety of the people is the top priority of the government work, and he called 3 meetings of the top leadership, that is, the Standing Committee of the Political Bureau of the CPC, to map out emergency measures. The central government set up a task force to lead the efforts of the whole country. The military has been mobilized. But this virus is really something very new. People do not understand it. In recent days, it got a new name from the World Health Organization. So people should understand that it will take time for people to understand and to respond. As I said, Prime Minister Johnson appreciated the speed and effectiveness of the measures taken by the Chinese government. So I can say with certainty that the government has made every effort to address this challenge. The government has also tried every effort to be transparent, to share all the information with the WHO and also with relevant countries including the UK. Chinese scientists and British scientists are working together on the drug and vaccine. I do hope scientists will make early success on this.

Haynes: You said at your press conference that you didn't think the Chinese economy will be too badly affected in areas obviously like tourism and travel. And yet we're hearing that South Korea express concern of the knock-on effect on its economic prospects. And big companies like Apple too are saying that their profits are going to be affected. Can you say now, with a better picture of what's going on, how grave the effect the epidemic is having on the Chinese economy, and potentially the world economy?

Liu Xiaoming: I would say there will be impacts on the economy. Even here— I watched the television the other day—I'm not sure it was Sky News or BBC— people are talking about the reduction of tourism and Chinese shoppers, and at the Bicester Village, many shops are closed, and some tourist attractions do not have any more Chinese tourists. Yes, there will be some impacts. But I think the impacts are short-term and temporary, because the fundamentals of the Chinese economy are still good. The Chinese economy is still very resilient. The reform and opening-up will continue and China will open wider. Starting from this year, on January 1, the Foreign Investment Law took effect. The Chinese government puts emphasis on two fronts: one is the battle against the virus, and the other is the resumption of production. You can see the country mobilized to fight the two battles. I think in the long term, the Chinese economy is still good and President Xi Jinping also told Prime Minister Johnson that we are confident that we will reach the target of our economic development this year. This year is a very important year for China— we'll achieve our centenary goal, that is, to complete the building of a moderately prosperous society in all aspects and to eliminate extreme poverty in China.

Haynes: Do you have a statement too about the Xinjiang-related leaks?

Liu Xiaoming: That is totally a rumor and made-up story. I said on many occasions that Xinjiang is not about human rights, not about religion. It's about anti-terrorism. And the rights of religious freedom are fully protected in Xinjiang, and people enjoy happy life. Thank you.

Haynes: Thank you, Ambassador.

Liu Xiaoming: My pleasure.

接受英国BBC《尖锐对话》栏目
主持人萨克在线直播采访

作者手记

2020年4月28日，我接受英国BBC旗舰访谈栏目《尖锐对话》（*HARDtalk*）主持人斯蒂芬·萨克（Stephen Sackur）在线直播采访。

这是我第二次上《尖锐对话》栏目接受萨克的采访。采访主要围绕新冠肺炎疫情展开。我重点介绍了中国抗疫情况，批驳了美西方对中国的污蔑不实之词。

BBC《尖锐对话》栏目团队称，这次采访非常成功，有助于人们，特别是西方公众全面、准确了解中国的抗疫情况和中国政府的基本立场。BBC在线直播此次采访后，又在新闻频道向英国国内播放2次，通过世界新闻台和国际广播电台等平台，向全球200多个国家和地区播放5次，受众达4亿多人。BBC还在黄金时段新闻节目滚动播放采访片段，并通过BBC网站和新媒体平台进行了延伸报道。

采访实录如下：

萨克：　　刘晓明大使，欢迎来到《尖锐对话》。

刘晓明：　谢谢！很高兴再次接受你的采访。

萨克：　　很高兴你能在这艰难时期接受我们的采访。先问一个简单、直接的问题：你是否同意新冠肺炎病毒源自中国？

刘晓明：　武汉最早报告病毒，但不能说病毒起源于武汉。根据多方信息，包括BBC的报道，病毒可能源自任何地方，在航空母舰甚至潜艇中可以找到，在一些与中国很少联系的国家中也可以找到，在从未去过中国的人群中也可以找到。所以我们不能说它源自中国。

萨克：　　这个回答让我有些困惑。显然这是一种新病毒，它起源于某个地方。根据免疫学家和病毒学家的说法，病毒由动物传播给人类，先出现一个病例，然后迅速传播。毫无疑问，第一起病例发生在中国。你刚才说，病毒传播到了世界各地，一些从未到过中国的人也被感染，显然病毒已引发全球大流行病，但至关重要的问题是，它最初来自何处？

刘晓明：　我认为这个问题应交由科学家来解答。据我了解，中国的首起病例是由张继先医生于2019年12月27日向中国地方卫生主管部门报告的。我还看到报道，称中国以外有些病例甚至远早于此。昨天英国报纸上的报道称，英国的科学家、医学专家在去年早些时候就曾警告政府，可能存在一种未知病毒。因此，我只能说中国第一例报告的病例于2019年12月27日发生在武汉。

萨克：　我认为不容置疑的是，专家们确信在武汉及其周边地区发现了首例确诊病例。你是否也认为我们必须搞清楚疫情暴发初期到底发生了什么，以及哪些地方做得不对、哪些步骤走错了，才导致病毒演变成全球大流行？

刘晓明：　争论了半天，我们只能各持己见。我还要强调，病毒是在中国武汉首次报告的，但不能说它起源于武汉。让我给你介绍一下中国抗疫时间表。张继先医生首先于2019年12月27日上报了不明原因肺炎病例。中国卫生部门和疾控中心在4天后，也就是12月31日，以最短的时间通知了世界卫生组织并与其他国家共享信息。中国还第一时间同世界卫生组织分享病原体，在第一时间同世界卫生组织和其他国家分享病毒基因序列。

萨克：　大使先生，让我打断一下，你忽视了非常重要的一点。12月30日，武汉医生李文亮在微信群里告诉他的同事，武汉出现了一种非常令人担忧的新疾病，建议他的同事们必须穿防护服，以避免被感染。几天后，他被公安局传唤并被迫供认散播虚假信息、严重干扰社会秩序。从那以后一直到1月份，中国政府一直在试图掩盖真相。

刘晓明：　现在我明白为什么一些人要鼓吹进行所谓独立调查了，其实就是试图罗织借口来指责中国掩盖真相。但事实是，李文亮医生不是

"吹哨者"，如我刚才说的，张继先医生比李医生早3天向卫生部门报告，武汉市卫生部门随即向中央政府报告。4天后，也就是李医生发出微信信息后一天，中国政府与世界卫生组织及其他国家共享了这一信息。完全不存在所谓掩盖事实。

萨克： 大使先生，实际上中方共享的信息非常有限。根据《华盛顿邮报》和美联社获得的内部信息，中国国家卫生健康委员会主任马晓伟曾在2020年1月14日的内部会议中对形势做出了非常严峻的评估，他说复杂、聚集案例表明病毒正在"人传人"。但是第二天，中国疾病预防控制中心对外称持续"人传人"的风险很低，疫情是可防可控的。因此，我再次强调，有充足的证据表明中国在好几个星期内没有说实话。

刘晓明： 你都没有给我足够的时间回答问题，我还没有说完关于李文亮的问题。你所谓"掩盖事实"是不存在的。张继先医生通过正常渠道向卫生部门报告，但李文亮则在朋友圈传播相关信息。在任何国家，如果出现极其危险的未知病毒等情况，都可能引起恐慌。我认为警方传唤李医生，向他提出警告，要求他停止网上传播，这不能称为"隐瞒"。疫情已经通过正规渠道上报，这种情况下要尽量避免恐慌。目前，英国政府也在打击利用假消息制造恐慌以达到个人目的的做法。有关李文亮医生的事已经有结论，中国中央政府接到报告后，即向武汉派出调查组，武汉市公安局决定撤销对李医生的训诫书。李医生被追认为烈士，被授予很高的荣誉。

萨克： 李医生去世的时候的确被中国人民视为英雄。

刘晓明： 不仅是中国人民，中国政府也是一样，你不能将两者分开。

萨克： 我认为中国人民很清楚，政府对他们和世界其他国家并不坦率。1月14日，中国卫健委的内部文件称存在人传人、聚集性感染的证据，形势严峻复杂，并要求有关内容不公开、不上网。对此你如何解释？

刘晓明： 我想你们的所有信息都来自《华盛顿邮报》，你们过于依赖美国媒体。我真希望你们能采纳世界卫生组织的信息。我们与世界卫生组织分享了所有信息。我看了你对世界卫生组织新冠特使大卫·纳巴罗（David Nabarro）博士的采访，中国始终坚持公开、透明，第一时间与世界卫生组织分享信息。一方面在中国国内，我们必须保持高度警惕，采取最严格的防控措施，当时对这个病毒并不十分了解。另一方面我们与世界卫生组织和其他国家分享了信息和我们对病毒的认知。

萨克： 刘大使，你是一位资深外交官，应该了解目前世界上很多人并不相信中国的故事版本。几个小时前，特朗普称对中国的立场并不满意，说中国完全可以把疫情控制在源头，他还说美国正在进行彻底调查。美国副总统彭斯也列出一系列理由证明，中国没有对世界说实话，应对疫情在全世界蔓延并造成大规模死亡和经济损失负有责任，中国现在面临巨大的问题。

刘晓明： 我不同意这种说法。这只是一些西方国家的说法。疫情发生后，中国第一时间与世界卫生组织和其他国家通力合作，我们派出技术援助和医疗专家组，并向150多个国家提供医疗物资援助，受到这些国家的高度评价。我认为，美国不能代表全世界，即使不少西方国家，包括英国、法国、德国，也对中国表示赞赏。你引用了特朗普总统的表态，我也想引用几句他有关中国的表态。1月24日，在中国通报疫情大约1个月之后，特朗普总统说，"美国高度赞赏中国的努力和透明度"。6天后，他表示"中国正全力以赴抗疫，美国与中国进行了紧密合作"。2月初，他又表示"习近平主席工作出色，疫情处理得很好"。

萨克： 自1月底以来，情况发生了很多变化。中国说，我们做了很多好事，向世界各国提供了医疗物资援助，但在外界眼里则是中国最近几周正在全世界掀起一场假消息和宣传攻势。中国外交部官员在社交媒体上散布"阴谋论"，称美国军人将病毒偷带到中国。为什么中国要掀起假消息攻势？

刘晓明： 我认为你选错了目标。不是中国散布假消息，如果将中国领导人、中国外交官和中国大使的表态与美国领导人、美国外交官和美国大使做一个比较，你就会发现谁在散布假消息。

萨克： 你同意赵立坚关于"美国军人将新冠病毒偷带到中国"的说法吗？你相信吗？

刘晓明： 赵立坚是转推一些媒体的报道。我不明白你为什么抓住中国某个个人的言论，却对美国国家领导人、高级官员，特别是美国最高级别外交官、国务卿发布的假消息视而不见？只要这位国务卿谈到中国，就没有一句好话；中国在抗疫斗争中向美国伸出援手，却成了恶人。我实在不能理解。

萨克： 你认为，目前由于疫情引起的各种指责给中美关系带来的外交危机有多严重？

刘晓明： 我们当然希望与美国保持良好关系。我曾两次常驻美国，我始终认为中美和则两利、斗则俱伤，我们有充分的理由与美国保持良好关系，但这应该建立在相互信任、合作而不对抗的基础上，双方需要相向而行。疫情发生以来，习近平主席和特朗普总统保持了密切沟通，通了两次电话，讨论抗疫合作。正如习主席与约翰逊首相通电话一样，中国致力于与国际社会一道，携手战胜疫情。我在此特别要告诉美国人，中国不是美国的敌人，美国的敌人是新冠病毒，美国应该找对目标。

萨克： 你发出了非常重要的信息。那么针对美国以及澳大利亚、英国等许多国家提出的中方应永久，而不是临时关闭从事野生动物交易的"湿货市场"的要求，中方是否将做出一些积极姿态，从而改善与这些国家的关系？

刘晓明： 首先，我不同意你关于中国与许多国家关系出现问题的说法，中

尖锐对话
Sharp Dialogue

国的朋友多，对手少，敌人更少。正如我所说，少数西方国家不能代表整个世界。中国拥有良好的对外关系，正在积极推动国际抗疫合作。正如习主席所说，团结合作是国际社会战胜疫情最有力的武器。我现在回答你所谓"湿货市场"问题。

萨克： 大使先生，我们时间不多了，你能不能就"湿货市场"问题给出具体明确的回答？市场是关了还是没关？

刘晓明： 事实上，在中国根本不存在所谓"湿货市场"，这个说法对很多中国人都很陌生，是西方、外来的说法。人们常说的是农贸市场和"生鲜"市场，主要销售新鲜的蔬菜、海鲜等农副产品，也有极少数市场销售活禽。我想，你所谈到的应该是非法销售野生动物的市场，这类市场已经被彻底禁止。中国全国人大已经通过决定，全面禁止非法野生动物交易。

萨克： 这是否意味着中国政府已经意识到这些野生动物市场的危险性，即它们确实造成病毒从动物传给人类？

刘晓明： 我们终于达成了一项一致。请注意，这里所说的是非法野生动物市场已完全被禁止，在中国猎捕、交易、食用野生动物都是非法的。

萨克： 如果中国能在新冠病毒蔓延之前早点下达禁令，就不会给世界造成这么大的伤害。中国是否将为此表示歉意？

刘晓明： 你又回到了采访开始时的问题。我要说，不能因为疫情在中国发现就指责中国，这是错误的。中国发现了疫情，在很多与中国毫无联系的地方也发现了疫情。不能因为中国暴发疫情就指责中国，要看到中国正在竭尽全力抗击疫情。中国是病毒受害者，中国不是病毒制造者，中国也不是病毒源头。对于这一点，必须明确。

萨克： 但一些英国政界要员称中国应为疫情负责，比如，议会下院外委会主席表示，中国政府实行的是苏联式、有害的体制，这种体制损害中国人民的健康和福祉，背叛了中国人民，也背叛了世界。他们呼吁英国、美国和其他一些国家切断与中国的紧密经济联系。在英国，这一问题的核心是，华为不应被继续允许参与英国5G网络建设。作为中国驻英国大使，你是否担心对华经济脱钩？

刘晓明： 既担心，也不担心。你所谈到的那位政界要员，他的观点并不能代表英国政府的官方立场。我相信，在约翰逊首相领导下，英国政府仍致力于发展强劲的中英关系。在与习主席的两次通话中，约翰逊首相重申将致力于推进中英关系"黄金时代"。疫情期间，中英除了紧密沟通之外，还积极开展合作。我出任中国驻英国大使10年了，从未见到两国领导人和高层保持如此密切的联系，除了习主席与约翰逊首相两次通话外，中央外事工作委员会办公室主任杨洁篪、国务委员兼外长王毅同英国首相国家安全事务顾问塞德维尔、外交大臣拉布也保持着密切沟通。在伦敦，我也与外交大臣拉布，卫生大臣汉考克，商业、能源和产业战略大臣夏尔马保持着密切接触，中英关系十分强劲。至于你提到有人将中国比作苏联，这完全是"冷战"思维。我们已经生活在21世纪第三个10年，而这些人还停留在过去"冷战"时期。中国不是前苏联。中英之间的共同利益远大于分歧，我对中英关系充满信心。

萨克： 刘大使，今天的采访只能到此结束。我再次对你在这样一个艰难时刻做客《尖锐对话》表示真诚的谢意。

刘晓明： 不必客气。

A Live Interview with Stephen Sackur on BBC *HARDtalk*

On 28th April, 2020, I gave an interview on BBC's *HARDtalk* hosted by Stephen Sackur, where I shared the timeline of China's efforts to contain the spread of Covid-19 and gave an update on what China is doing to join the international cooperation in response to the pandemic. The full transcript is as follows:

Sackur: Ambassador Liu Xiaoming, welcome to *HARDtalk*.

Liu Xiaoming: Thank you. Good to be with you again.

Sackur: We are delighted to have you on our program in this difficult time. Let me start actually with a very simple direct question: Do you accept that Covid-19 has its origins in China?

Liu Xiaoming: It was first reported in Wuhan, but I can't say it's originated from Wuhan. According to many reports including BBC reports, it can be anywhere. It is found on aircraft carriers. It is even found in the submarine. It is found in some countries with very little connection with China and also found in groups of people who have never been to China. So we cannot say it's originated from China.

Sackur: I'm a little confused by that answer. Clearly, it is a new virus. It originated somewhere. It seems, according to all of the immunologists and virologists, the virus crossed from animals to humans. And there was a first case and then it spread. There is no doubt that the first case was in China. I'm wondering why you are telling me that it spread all over the world and people who caught it had never been to China. That is clear because it's become a pandemic. But the question that matters so much is:

Where did it start?

Liu Xiaoming: I think this question is still up for scientists to decide. I read the report that the first case in China was reported on the 27th December by Dr. Zhang Jixian to Chinese local health authorities. But I also read reports that some of the cases were found to be much earlier than that. We read even the report by your newspapers yesterday that your scientists, medical advisers, even warned your government that there might be a virus unknown to us, much earlier, last year. So all I can say is that the first reported case in China was on 27th of December in Wuhan.

Sackur: I think there's no doubt experts believe the origin of the first outbreak, first examples of this Covid-19 virus to be found in human beings, came from Wuhan and the surrounding area in China. I just wonder whether you accept that it is very important that we understand exactly what happened at the beginning of this outbreak, that we understand frankly what mistakes and missteps were made, which allowed the first outbreak to become a global pandemic.

Liu Xiaoming: I think it is still debatable. I think we have to agree to disagree. I think it was first reported in Wuhan, China, but I can't say it originated from Wuhan. Let me tell you the timeline of China's fight against this virus. It was first reported on the 27th of December by Dr. Zhang, and then Chinese health authorities and CDC notified the WHO four days later, on 31st December, in the shortest possible time, and then shared this information with other countries. China also shared the discovery of the pathogen with the WHO in the shortest possible time, and also shared the information about the genetic sequence of the virus in the shortest possible time.

Sackur: Ambassador, let me just interrupt you on this question of timeline because you missed out one very important point. On December 30th, a doctor in Wuhan, Li Wenliang, used his chat group online to tell fellow doctors that there was a new and very worrying disease in Wuhan. He advised his colleagues that they must wear protective clothing to avoid this new infection. And just a couple of days later, he was summoned to the public security bureau. He was made to sign a letter in which he confessed to making false statements that had severely disturbed the social order. That was the beginning of an official cover-up, which continued through the month of January.

Liu Xiaoming: As I said earlier, now I understand why there's a so-called call for independent investigation. They try to find excuse for them to criticize China for cover-up. But the fact is that Li Wenliang was not the first one who discovered this virus. As I told you, it was Dr. Zhang Jixian, and she reported 3 days earlier than Li Wenliang to the health authorities. Then, the health authorities in Wuhan reported to the central government, and then four days later, that means one day after Li Wenliang spread the word, the Chinese authorities shared the information with the WHO and other countries. No cover-up at all.

Sackur: With respect, Mr. Ambassador, the information that was shared was actually extremely limited, because on January 14th, we now know this from leaks that have been given to the *Washington Post* and the Associated Press, we know that internally China's national health commission head, Mr. Ma Xiaowei, laid out a very grim assessment of what was happening. He said that the situation was severe. Complex, clustered cases suggest human to human transmission is happening, the memo said. The risk of transmission and spread is high, but in public, that was internal, but in public, the head of China's disease control emergency center, the very next day, said the risk of sustained human-to-human transmission is low, that it was preventable and controllable. So, I put it to you again, there is compelling evidence that China for weeks did not tell the truth.

Liu Xiaoming: You give me not enough time to answer your question. I haven't answered the question with regard to Li Wenliang. You talk about cover-up. That's not true. Dr. Zhang reported through a normal channel to health authorities, but Li spread this word among his friends. In any country when you have something like the virus which is dangerous to people's health, when there is something unknown, there might be a panic. So I think the police authority summoned Li to warn him not to do it. You can't say this is a cover-up, since we reported through the normal channel. But on this, we need to make sure that there should be no panic. Even today, in the UK, I think your government is fighting misinformation. Some people try to use this to create panic for their own gain.

I think Li's case is closed. After it's reported to the central authorities, the government sent investigation team down to Wuhan and find out that Li did the right thing and the police reprimand has been revoked. And Li was made a martyr and given the highest honor for his contribution.

Sackur: Dr. Li was in deed regarded by the Chinese people as a hero when he died.

Liu Xiaoming: Not only by the Chinese people, but also regarded by the Chinese government. You cannot separate ...

Sackur: With respect, I think the people of China are very aware, and I come back to it, that the Chinese government wasn't straight with them, nor with the outside world. Just tell me, if you can one more time, why on January 14 the national health commission document — that was an internal document — was labeled not to be spread on the internet, not to be publicly disclosed, in which they said that there was evidence of human-to-human transmission, clustered cases, severe and complex problem?

Liu Xiaoming: I think all your information is coming from *Washington Post*. I think you depend too much on American media. I really hope you will depend on the WHO for information. We share all the information with the WHO. I saw your interview with Mr. David Nabarro, and I think China has been straightforward, transparent, and swift in terms of sharing information with the WHO. Of course, inside China, we have to take cautious measures. We have to take strict measures to fight this virus. The virus was still unknown then. So people did not know what will happen, what this virus was about. But on the one hand, we share our knowledge, our understanding, with the WHO, with the other countries.

Sackur: But Ambassador, with all respect, your problem is — you're a very senior diplomat and you know this is a problem — that many people around the world simply don't believe the Chinese version of events. Donald Trump, only a few hours ago, said that he is not happy at all with China's stance. They could have stopped the virus at the source, he said, we are undertaking a thorough investigation. And the Vice President Mike Pence has listed a whole host of reasons why the United States believes that China was not straight with the world and is therefore culpable for the fact this pandemic is now causing so much death and so much economic damage right around the world. You have, as China, a massive problem now.

Liu Xiaoming: I don't think so. When you say that China has a massive problem, I think you're talking more about the Western world. Since the outbreak, China has had very strong cooperation with the WHO and with many other countries. We sent technical assistance and experts to and provide medical supplies for more than 150 countries. All of them spoke highly of Chinese efforts. So I can't say the United States represents the world. And even in the Western world, we've been receiving appreciation from the countries like United Kingdom, from France, from Germany.

You quote President Trump. Let me also quote his comments about China. On 24th of January, that was almost one month after we reported this virus. He said, United States greatly appreciates China's efforts and transparency. Six days later and he said, they are working very hard, and we are working very closely with China. In early February, he said, President Xi is doing a great job, he handles it well.

Sackur: Things have changed a great deal since the end of January. You say, look at what we've done to deliver medical assistance and equipment around the world. What many people see is China running a campaign of disinformation and propaganda around the world in recent weeks. Your colleague in the Foreign Ministry use social media to promote the conspiracy theory that the US military has smuggled coronavirus into China. Why is your country running this disinformation campaign?

Liu Xiaoming: I think you've picked a wrong target. It's not China who started this campaign of disinformation. If you could compare China's statements and comments by Chinese leaders, Chinese diplomats, Chinese Ambassadors, with their American counterparts, you will know who is spreading disinformation.

Sackur: Do you agree with Zhao Lijian, the Foreign Ministry Spokesman who did put up the link suggesting that the US military has smuggled coronavirus into China? Is that something that you also believe?

Liu Xiaoming: I think what you're saying is that Mr. Zhao retweeted some media report. I do not know why you focus on some comments by individuals in China but miss the disinformation by senior officials, even the national leaders, of the United

States who started this campaign of disinformation, especially by the top diplomat, the secretary of state? When it comes to China, there's no any good word about China. And China is really regarded as an evil force, not as a country which has been lending a helping hand to America in the fight against this virus. I do not quite understand.

Sackur: In your view, Ambassador, how deep is the crisis with the United States right now, that has been sparked by all of the accusations that have arisen from the coronavirus? How deep is the diplomatic crisis?

Liu Xiaoming: We certainly want to have good relations with the United States. I've been posted twice to Washington, DC. I always believe that China and the United States will gain from cooperation and lose from confrontation. And we have every reason to have a good relationship with the United States. But it has to be based on mutual trust, coordination and non-confrontation. But you need two to tango.

Since the outbreak, President Xi and President Trump have kept very close contact. They had two telephone conversations and compared notes, just as President Xi had two telephone conversations with Prime Minister Johnson. We want to build international response to this virus.

I just want to let Americans know that China is not an enemy of the United States. It's the virus that is the enemy of the United States. They need to find the right target.

Sackur: It's a very important message you're sending. Maybe China could consider some gestures that would improve relations with not just the United States but many other countries, including Australia and the UK who've made the same point to your government.

One, will you now categorically guarantee to close down the so-called "wet markets", that there will no longer be the sale of these live wild animals in the food markets that are known as the "wet markets"? Is that now something that has been banned, not just short term, but absolutely banned forever in China?

Liu Xiaoming: First, on your first point about "many countries", I cannot agree with you that China has a problem with many countries. I would say we have more friends than opponents or enemies. A few Western countries do not represent the world. I think China enjoys good relationships. with many and I think we are building an international response to the virus. As President Xi said, solidarity and cooperation are the most powerful weapons to fight the pandemic. I will come back to the "wet market".

Sackur: Ambassador, we are short of time. I just need specific answer on the "wet markets". Are they right now closed for good, yes or no?

Liu Xiaoming: There's no such a thing as a "wet market". This is a Western, a foreign, notion to many Chinese. We do have fresh food markets where fresh vegetables, fresh seafood, fish, are sold, and some live poultry. I think you are talking about the so-called illegal market for selling wildlife. That has been totally banned. The law has been passed and it will be banned permanently.

Sackur: That is therefore a recognition — I just want to be clear — a recognition on your government's part that the dangers of those markets, where live wild animals were sold alongside other food stuff, they were dangers that did cause the spread coronavirus from animals to humans.

Liu Xiaoming: I agree with that. Finally, we have a few points to agree on. I'm very pleased with that. That's why this market, we're talking about, illegal wildlife market, is totally banned. It's illegal to hunt, to trade, to eat wild animals.

Sackur: So people watching this will only wish that you had made that ban real before coronavirus spread and cause such terrible damage around the world. Are you in any way prepared to say sorry for what has happened?

Liu Xiaoming: So you come to your first point again. You can't blame China for coronavirus. That's the problem of this argument. It was found in China. It was found in many other places that have no connection with China at all. So you can't point your fingers at China for the outbreak, and we have done our best.
China is a victim of the coronavirus, but China is not a source of this problem. China

is not the producer of this epidemic, and that is something we have to come clean about.

Sackur: China is seen, for example, by leading politicians in this country, like the Chairman of the Parliamentary Foreign Affairs Select Committee, as very much the cause. He's talked about a soviet style system, a toxic system, inside your government, inside your regime, which he says has been responsible not just for betraying the Chinese people and their health or wellbeing, but betraying the wider world as well. And there are now calls in the United Kingdom, and also calls in the United States and other countries, for a disengagement from close economic ties with China. In Britain, it's of course centered on Huawei, your telephones giant's activities in the 5G sector. People say that should no longer be tolerated in the United Kingdom. As the Ambassador in the UK, are you worried that there is going to be now an economic disengagement?

Liu Xiaoming: Yes and no. I think you talk about this person as a very senior politician, but I don't think this view represents the official position of the UK government.

I think the UK government under Prime Minister Johnson is still committed to stronger partnership with China. In his two telephone conversations with President Xi, he reaffirmed UK's commitment to building a Golden Era with China. And we do have very good cooperation with the UK side throughout this outbreak, in addition to intensive communication. I've been here for 10 years as a Chinese Ambassador. I have never seen that our top leaders have such an intensive communications between them.

And also at the ministerial level, we have our State Counselor and Foreign Minister Wang Yi having telephone conversation with Secretary Raab, and Yang Jiechi, Director of the Office of the Central Commission for Foreign Affairs, having close contact with the Sir Mark Sedwill. Here in London, I have very close contact with the government secretaries, including Secretaries Mat Hancock and Alok Sharma, and Foreign Secretary Raab. We have a very strong, robust relationship.

And you quote those people using Soviet example. I think this is a totally Cold War mentality. We are living in the third decade of the 21st century, but those people still live in the old days when they were fighting cold war. China is not former Soviet Union. I think China and the UK are united by common interests rather than divided by our

differences. So I'm very confident about this relationship.

Sackur: All right, Ambassador, we have to end there. But I do thank you very much indeed for joining me on *HARDtalk* at this difficult time. Liu Xiaoming, thank you very much indeed.

Liu Xiaoming: My pleasure.

接受英国天空新闻台《新闻时间》栏目主持人奥斯汀在线直播采访

作者手记

2020年5月14日，我接受英国天空新闻台《新闻时间》(*The News Hour*)栏目主持人马克·奥斯汀 (Mark Austin)在线直播采访。

《新闻时间》是英国天空新闻台旗舰栏目，时长两小时，包括滚动新闻、一对一访谈和专家分析评论，在每天17—19点黄金时段播出。

奥斯汀是英国著名记者、时事评论员，曾担任英国独立电视台旗舰栏目《十点新闻》主持人，2018年9月起担任《新闻时间》栏目主持人。曾获多项新闻大奖，包括英国电影和电视艺术学院奖和国际艾美奖。

采访的主题是新冠肺炎疫情。针对奥斯汀的提问，如"国际社会"似乎不相信中国关于新冠病毒的解释、中国为什么拒绝国际独立调查、中国的数据是否真实、英国抗疫的问题出在哪里等，我介绍了中国的抗疫情况及与世界卫生组织和相关国家的合作，批驳了美国等少数西方国家对中国的毫无根据的指责。

采访实录如下：

奥斯汀： 数月来，全世界越来越多的人呼吁中国就新冠病毒的蔓延做出解释。大多数科学家都认为病毒最早在武汉开始扩散，包括美国总统在内的一些人认为病毒源于实验室泄漏而非自然界。到今天，中国仍拒绝邀请来自世界卫生组织的科学家参加对该病毒来源的调查。问题还有很多，今天我们有难得的机会向中国驻英国大使刘晓明提出这些问题。大使先生，晚上好，感谢你接受采访。

刘晓明： 晚上好！感谢邀请。

奥斯汀： 首先，你是否同意中国面临信任危机？就目前来看，全世界似乎并不信任中国。

刘晓明： 我认为并非如此。中国做得很好。中国是首个报告该病毒的国家，在第一时间甄别出病原体，并在第一时间与世界卫生组织及其他国家分享病毒基因序列资料。你提到全世界不信任中国，我不同意你的看法。我认为只有少数几个国家在对中国进行毫无根据的指责和挑衅。

奥斯汀： 我们从头梳理一下为何一些国家不信任中国。据新华社报道，张继先医生于2019年12月27日向中国地方卫生主管部门报告了其接诊3例不明原因肺炎患者的情况，她怀疑存在"人传人"，一对夫妇传给其子。但直到1月22日，即近4个星期之后，中国才向世界卫生组织通报了病毒的人际传播。为何会有这样的延迟？

刘晓明： 这不是事实。张继先医生于12月27日向当地卫生部门报告。4天后，中国卫生部门即通知世界卫生组织驻华代表处。1月3日，即7天后，中国政府卫生主管部门国家卫健委正式通知世界卫生组织。这是一种新病毒，不论是对世界还是对中国，这都是未知病毒，我们必须采取谨慎、负责任的态度，全力以赴应对。因此，在11天后，我们甄别出病原体，并与世界卫生组织及其他国家分享病毒基因序列资料。所以我认为上述指责是不公平的。

奥斯汀： 但是世界卫生组织的时间线清楚地表明，中国卫生部门于1月22日才通告称有证据表明病毒存在人际传播。张继先医生告诉新华社："一家人病状基本相同，可以确定是人传人了。"她于12月27日上报了武汉当局，为何直到次年1月22日，世界卫生组织才确认病毒的人际传播。

刘晓明： 正如我所说，这需要过程。即使这样，我们在获知了病毒人际传播的风险后没有丝毫延误就通知了世界卫生组织。钟南山院士是这一领域的权威。他在1月20日的发布会上表示，目前非常肯定地证实出现了人传人现象，这比你说的时间线要早。那时，中国仅有不到200个确诊病例。对任何国家而言，确定某种传染病都需要一定程序和时间，这才是负责任的处理方式。

奥斯汀： 可以理解。但为什么李文亮医生在社交媒体上表达了对疫情扩散的担忧之后就被警方逮捕并被噤声呢？

刘晓明： 首先，李医生没有被捕，媒体报道有误。他是被警方传唤训诫。对任何国家包括英国来说，给传染病定性都必须谨慎、负责，不能引发恐慌。李医生在网上发帖的3天前，张继先医生已经向当地卫生部门报告了不明原因肺炎病例，当地卫生部门立即向中央政府报告了情况，中方随后也就是李医生在网上发帖的第四天就向世界卫生组织通报了，所以中方不存在任何隐瞒。中央政府对李文亮一事十分关注和重视，派调查组到武汉了解实际情况。最后李文亮被追认为烈士，被确认为英雄。

奥斯汀： 我们谈一下国际社会不相信中国的另一个原因。美国国务卿蓬佩奥称，中国未能及时分享疫情信息，特朗普总统说有大量证据显示病毒源于武汉实验室，中方犯了错并试图隐瞒。我想问，中方犯了什么错误，是否存在隐瞒？

刘晓明： 根本不存在任何隐瞒。中方及时与世界卫生组织和国际社会分享了疫情信息，并早在1月3日通报了美方。此后，中美双方疾控部门均就疫情信息保持日常沟通。美国领导人和首席外交官的有关说法根本代表不了国际社会。要说特朗普总统说了些什么，让我告诉你，3月27日特朗普总统与习近平主席通话后，对外表示："我们了解中国为抗疫做出的巨大努力，美中双方一直保持密切沟通，中方向我们提供了很多资料，美方获取了全部信息，中国的经验对美国很有启发。"而现在你引述的特朗普的表态与那时截然不同。

奥斯汀： 国际社会不信任中国还有一个原因是中国拒绝国际独立调查。如果没有隐瞒的话，中国为什么不允许国际社会对武汉的实验室、"湿货市场"进行调查？

刘晓明： 这种国际调查不应含有政治目的。首先，当前国际社会的首要任务是抗击疫情。我同意英国卫生大臣所说，目前国际社会应全力合作应对疫情。其次，中国是开放的、透明的，没有任何隐瞒，也没有什么好怕的。我们支持在适当时候对疫情进行回顾和总结，但必须由世界卫生组织牵头开展，必须是国际性的。

奥斯汀： 中国同意由世界卫生组织牵头组织各国科学家到中国进行调查吗？

刘晓明： 是总结和评估，但应该在适当的时候，而不是现在。评估的目的是进行科学分析、总结经验，在应对下次大流行病时怎么能做得更好。这才是评估目的，而不是指责中国。

奥斯汀： 恕我直言，源自中国武汉的病毒已导致全世界450万人感染，近30万人死亡，这是一场全球性悲剧，难道不应该由世界知名科学家尽快开展全球调查吗？

刘晓明： 目前，中国、美国、英国的科学家和专家们正在努力工作，寻找病毒源头。疫情暴发，中国是第一个报告病例的国家，但不能说中国就是病毒的源头。这应该由科学家来决定，不是你，也不是我。

奥斯汀： 我使用"源头"一词是因为中国发现了第一起病例。这不是第一次了，之前的SARS，这次的冠状病毒，我们不能允许这种情况再次发生。

刘晓明： 当然不能。但科学家尚未弄清病毒的源头，因此不能指责中国，中国是受害者，不是肇事者。病毒不是人为制造的，而是源自自然。我们应该坚持科学的态度，而不是像个别美国政客一样，对中国污名化、利用假消息无端抹黑。

奥斯汀： 那就让科学家们进去调查，他们会发现真相。大多数发达、公正、公开和负责任的国家都会允许国际科学家尽快进去调查。

刘晓明： 毫无疑问，我们与国际社会的科学家密切合作，但是这应与背后有政治动机的所谓"独立调查"区分开来。当你说世界各国呼吁进行独立调查，那只是个别国家，美国、澳大利亚，你能说出10个国家吗？我认为许多国家呼吁的是全球团结合作抗疫，而不是相互指责。当今的主题是聚焦如何战胜病毒、挽救生命，而不是玩指责、甩锅游戏。

奥斯汀： 根据情报机构所说，中国支持黑客组织窃取英美科学家关于新冠病毒的研究资料。中国为什么要这么做？

刘晓明： 这种指控从何而来？你们有证据吗？

奥斯汀： 美国联邦调查局声称"调查发现黑客组织试图窃取公共卫生数据"。

刘晓明： 这已经不是美国第一次对中国污蔑抹黑，美国的企图就是阻挠国际社会合作研发疫苗。疫苗是战胜疫情的最终解决办法。中国科学家正在争分夺秒地工作，一是靠我们自己的努力，二是进行国际合作，包括与美国科学家的合作。中英在疫苗研发方面也紧密合作，两国领导人，习主席和约翰逊首相对两国科学家的合作给予了大力支持。

奥斯汀： 谈到疫苗，如果中国比其他国家先研发出疫苗，中国会遵循"全球疫苗免疫联盟"的原则，公平、公正地分享疫苗吗？

刘晓明： 中国当然愿意分享疫苗，我们视之为全球科学家共同努力的结果，将助力全球抗疫，因此我们积极地与各国开展科研合作。

奥斯汀： 根据"全球疫苗免疫联盟"的原则，疫苗将首先提供给疫情暴发的中心地区，无论是在世界哪个地方，之后再提供给世界各地的医护人员。中国会同意这一原则吗？

刘晓明： 我认为现在提这样的问题为时尚早，因为各国尚未研发出新冠疫苗。现在讨论疫苗如何使用，似乎也有些超前。但正如我此前所讲，中方本着一贯原则，愿同其他国家分享相关科研成果和疫情防控经验，不论是急需这些信息的国家，还是那些身处抗疫一线的医护工作者。我们已向包括英国在内的150多个国家和地区援助医疗物资，这些物资大部分被分配至一线医护工作者手中。我们还向英方捐赠最急需的医疗物资，协助英国政府在中国采购呼吸机等设备。这些物资均已在英国抗疫中有效发挥作用。

奥斯汀：　好。你刚才谈到中国是开放的，那咱们再来谈谈"开放"这个话题。我的第一个问题是，中国为何要驱逐13名美国记者？要知道他们中很多人曾尝试在中国调查新冠病毒来源问题。此外，在中国疫情初期曾发布相关视频的当地记者陈秋实、方斌为何会失踪？他们人在何处？

刘晓明：　你应该首先问美国政府，为何要驱逐60名中国记者？你还应该问，为何中方为美国记者在华采访提供了更多便利？由于美方驱逐中国记者在先，中方被迫采取了反制措施，这与新冠肺炎疫情无关。正如我所讲，中国疫情防控是开放的、透明的……

奥斯汀：　大使先生，据我所知，美国并未监禁记者，但中国去年拘押了48名记者，这个数字比世界其他任何国家都要多。你怎么解释中国的所谓"开放"？

刘晓明：　在中国，没有人因为从事记者工作被拘押，有些人被拘押是因为从事了违法活动。在中国，没有人能凌驾于法律之上，法律面前人人平等。任何人不能以记者身份为掩护从事违法活动，回答就是这样简单。

奥斯汀： 下一个问题，中国人口超过10亿人，但你们官方公布的因新冠病毒死亡人数不到5000人，这在很多人看来难以置信。这个数据是真实的吗？

刘晓明： 这是因为疫情发生以来中国采取了最全面、最严格、最彻底的防控举措。我们愿同世界其他国家分享这些经验。武汉在面积上是伦敦的5倍，人口有1100万人，超过伦敦和北爱尔兰人口的总和。这座城市封城76天，当地民众为此做出了巨大牺牲。但新冠病毒具有很强的人与人之间的传染性，因此封城对防控病毒传播是一种非常有效的手段。此外，我们采取了"四早"方针——"早发现、早报告、早隔离、早治疗"。这些举措都被证明是十分有效的。因此，不能因为中国死亡人数较少，就指责中国"掩盖数据"或"隐瞒事实"。

奥斯汀： 大使先生，我并未指责中国。我想再谈最后一个问题，英国人口比中国少得多，但疫情导致的死亡人数却超过3万人。你认为英国的问题出在哪里？

刘晓明： 我无意批评英国的防疫政策。我想说，我们愿同英方分享、交流疫情防控经验。我在这里向你提供一条第一手新闻：明天，中国卫健委主任马晓伟及中方专家将与英国卫生大臣汉考克及英方专家举行视频会议，会议预计持续两个多小时，双方届时将就疫情防控进行深入交流。我认为，这才是我们现在要做的事情。我们需要认识到新冠病毒是人类共同的敌人，我们需要加强团结合作，携手应对风险挑战，共同抗击疫情，直至最后胜利。正如习主席所说，团结合作是国际社会战胜疫情的最有力武器。

奥斯汀： 很好。刘大使，谢谢你。无论对病毒来源的国际调查何时开展，我都十分期待。再次感谢你今晚做客我们的栏目，回答我们的问题。

刘晓明： 不客气。

A Live Interview with Mark Austin on Sky News *News Hour*

On 14th May 2020, I gave an online live interview via zoom on Sky News *News Hour* with Mark Austin regarding China's fight against the Covid-19 outbreak. The full transcript is as follows:

Austin: For months now, there have been growing calls around the world for China to come clean about just how the spread of the coronavirus began. China says and most scientists accept that it began in the city of Wuhan. But some, including the US president, say it may not have been spread naturally, but escaped from a laboratory. China has so far refused to invite scientists from the World Health Organization to join in its internal investigation into the source of the virus. There remain many questions, and today we have a rare opportunity to put some of them to China's Ambassador to the UK. Liu Xiaoming joins us now from his Embassy in central London. Good evening to you, Mr Ambassador. Thank you for agreeing to answer questions.

Liu Xiaoming: Good evening. Thank you for having me.

Austin: First of all, do you accept that China has a problem with trust? The world, simply at the moment, doesn't seem to trust China.

Liu Xiaoming: I don't think so. I think we have a good record. China was the first country to report the virus, the first to identify the pathogen, and the first to share the genetic sequence with the WHO and many other countries in a record time. When you said the world, I can't agree with you. I think there are only a few countries that challenge and make some accusations with no grounds at all.

Austin: Let's look at why some of the world may not trust China. Let's go to the

beginning and according to your own state news agency, Doctor Zhang Jixian reported her suspicions of the virus to the authorities on 27 December. She suspected human to human transmission because she treated a couple in Wuhan and then their son. But it was not until 22 January, nearly four weeks later that China through the WHO confirmed human to human transmission. Why was there such a delay?

Liu Xiaoming: That's not true. Doctor Zhang Jixian reported to the local health authority on 27 December. Then four days later, Chinese health authorities notified the WHO office in Beijing. That was four days later. Then on 3 January, that was seven days later, the National Health Commission, the highest Chinese central government authority for health, notified the WHO officially. Since this is a new virus — it is unknown not only to the world but also to China — we have to be responsible. We have adopted a cautious approach, tried our very best. So eleven days later, we identified the pathogen and shared the genetic sequence without delay at all. So I think it's unfair.

Austin: But the WHO timeline says clearly that it was on 22 January that they confirmed human to human transmission. And this doctor told Xinhua, your news agency, and I quote, it is unlikely that all three members of a family caught the same disease at the same time unless it is an infectious disease. On 27 December, she knew and the authorities in Wuhan knew, but it wasn't until the 22 January that the WHO confirmed it was human to human transmission.

Liu Xiaoming: As I said, it will take some process. Even so, we have lost no time in informing the WHO, once we knew there was a risk of transmission from human to human. Doctor Zhong Nanshan is the most authoritative in this field. He said at the briefing on 20 January, earlier than your timeline, that there is a high risk of transmission from people to people. By that time, there were about less than 200 cases in China. It takes time. For any country, there's a certain procedure in terms of determining the infectious disease. That is the responsible way to handle this case.

Austin: I understand that. Why was Doctor Li Wenliang arrested and silenced when he wrote on social media about his fears about the spread of the disease?

Liu Xiaoming: First, Li was never arrested as some media reported. He was summoned to a police station and got a reprimand. As I said, when you have some infectious disease, in any country including the UK, you have to be careful and responsible. You do not want to create panic. But as I said, three days before Li, Doctor Zhang reported to the health authorities. Then the local health authorities reported to the central government. Then the central government notified the WHO. That was four days later and one day after Li wrote on social media. So there was no cover-up. And the government took care and attached importance to this complaint and sent an investigation team down to Wuhan to find out what was really going on. Li was made as a martyr and a hero.

Austin: Let's look at another reason why the world may not trust China. Mike Pompeo, the US Secretary of State, says you failed to share information about the virus. Donald Trump says he has seen a report saying there is enormous evidence that Covid-19 began in the Wuhan laboratory, and he said they made a mistake and they tried to cover it up. So my question is, was it a mistake? And did you try to cover it up?

Liu Xiaoming: As I said, there's no cover-up at all. We shared information with the WHO and the world without delay. We notified the United States at the very beginning, on 3 January. When we notified the WHO, we also notified the CDC of the United States. Since then, there's communication and daily briefing between the Chinese CDC and American CDC. When you said the world, I don't think what the United States says, either their national leaders or top diplomat, represents the world. That's not true. As for Donald Trump, he had a comment on China. On 27 March, after his telephone conversation with President Xi, he said, "We learned quite a lot and China had a very tough experience. We have a good communication and they sent a lot of data. We are getting all that information." Now, Donald Trump was really different from then and where you quoted him.

Austin: Then let me look at another reason why the world may not trust China. You're refusing to open up for a full investigation, an international investigation by scientists. If you have nothing to hide, and as you say, there's no cover-up, why not allow an international investigation of the lab and the wet market or other places?

Liu Xiaoming: I think this investigation should not be politically motivated. I think first of all, the top priority for the international community is to focus on fighting the virus. I happen to agree with your Health Secretary when he said a hundred percent of the focus should be on working together to fight against the virus. Secondly, we are open, we are transparent, and we have nothing to hide and nothing to fear. We welcome international independent review, but it has to be organized by the WHO. It should be international.

Austin: Would you agree to the WHO organizing international scientists from across the world to come into China to investigate?

Liu Xiaoming: Yes, of course, at a proper time. Not now. The purpose of this review is to compare notes, to summarize, to learn experience: how we can do better for future pandemic. That's the purpose, not to accuse China.

Austin: With respect, 4.5 million people have been infected by this virus and nearly 300, 000 people have died as a result of this virus which you can see probably came from Wuhan in your country. It is a global tragedy that has been caused here. Doesn't it need a global investigation now as soon as possible with the world's renowned scientists?

Liu Xiaoming: I think scientists and experts are working. Even now, the scientists from China, from the US, from the UK are working to find the origin. When you say the outbreak happened in China, China is the first to report the cases. You can't say the virus originated from China. It is still up to the scientists, not up to you, not up to me.

Austin: I am using the word "origin" as the first case was in China. It is not the first time. It happened with SARS. It happened with Covid. It cannot be allowed to happen again.

Liu Xiaoming: Definitely. It cannot be allowed to happen again. But this is still unknown to many scientists, right? So you can't blame China. China is a victim. China is not the culprit of this virus. It's not a man-made virus but natural in origin. So we have to adopt the scientific approach. You can't have this campaign of stigmization, disinformation and smearing against China, as some American politicians are doing.

Austin: Then allow scientists in and they would find out the truth. Most modern, fair-minded, open and responsible countries would let international scientists in very quickly.

Liu Xiaoming: We are working with scientists from the international community. There is no doubt about that. But you have to separate it from the politically motivated so-called "independent investigation". When you say the world, they are just a few countries. The United States. Australia. Can you give me ten countries who call for the so-called independent investigation? I think many countries call for global response, solidarity and constructive cooperation, not criticism. The theme of today is to focus on fighting this virus and saving lives instead of playing the game of blaming and scapegoating.

Austin: Why is China or Chinese backed groups trying to steal coronavirus research according to the intelligence agencies? They say you are hacking British and American scientists working on Covid programmes. Why would you want to do that?

Liu Xiaoming: Where did you get these charges? Do you have a proof?

Austin: The FBI said "the hackings have been observed attempting to obtain illicitly public health data".

Liu Xiaoming: This is not the first time that the United States made such a false accusation against China. This is only their attempt to undermine the international collaboration on working together to find the vaccine. A vaccine will be the final solution to the problem. Chinese scientists are working around the clock, first on their own, then engaging collaboration even with scientists from the US. China and the UK are also working very closely. Both our top leaders, President Xi and Prime Minister Johnson, give their support to the scientists to find the vaccine.

Austin: Ambassador, talking about the vaccine, if China discovers the vaccine before other countries, do you agree to distribute it equitably and fairly along the line of advice by the Vaccine Alliance?

Liu Xiaoming: Yes, we certainly would like to share. We regard it as the joint efforts of the international scientists. We would share this to enhance the global response to the virus. That's why we are engaging with other countries in collaboration on science.

Austin: That policy is that it goes first to those at the heart of the outbreak wherever it is in the world, and then it goes to health workers around the world. China will agree to that, will it?

Liu Xiaoming: I think it's still too early to say something in specific terms on this question, because we haven't made the vaccine yet. So you are asking the question of vaccine use in much advance. But as I said, in principle we would like to share what we have achieved with other countries, either with the most needed countries or with the very front line workers, just as what we have done to provide medical supplies to about 150 countries. I think most of these medical supplies have been used on the front line medical workers, including here in the UK. We are donating the most needed supplies, and helping the UK government procure ventilators. I think they have all been put to good use.

Austin: OK. You talked about openness, and let's just talk about that. Why have you expelled 13 American journalists out of China, many of whom were trying to investigate the origin of the virus? That's point one. And why have two citizen journalists who put out videos at the very beginning of this epidemic, Chen Qiushi and Fang Bin, disappeared? Where are they?

Liu Xiaoming: You should ask why the United States expelled 60 Chinese journalists? And you should ask why we have given more preferential treatment to American journalists? We are forced to take counter-measures. That's nothing to do with COVID-19. As I said, China has been open and transparent …

Austin: Mr Ambassador, as far as I know, America doesn't imprison journalists, but you imprisoned 48 in the last year — more than any other country. How was that? How was that "openness"?

Liu Xiaoming: No journalist has been put behind bars because of what he or she had been doing as a journalist. Some people have been put behind bars because they have violated the law. Nobody is above the law, and everybody is treated equally in front of the law. Nobody can use journalism as a cover to do anything that violates the law. The answer is simple.

Austin: OK. You are a country with more than a billion people, and yet you have fewer than 5, 000 official deaths. To many that number seems unbelievable. Is it true?

Liu Xiaoming: That's because we have adopted the most strict, comprehensive and vigorous measures in containing the virus. We want to share this with other countries. Wuhan is a city five times larger than London in area, with a population of 11 million which is bigger than that of London and Northern Ireland put together. The city was locked down for 76 days. The local people made huge sacrifice. But the virus can transmit from people to people, so the lockdown has been a very effective measure. And we also have the effective measures that we call the "four earlies" — early dignosis, early reporting, early quarantine, and early treatment. All these have turned out to be very effective. So you cannot blame China for "cover-up" just because we have a low number of death cases.

Austin: I'm not blaming you, Mr. Ambassador, for anything. I'm just making a point Finally, I've got to ask you, in the UK, we have over 30, 000 deaths with an obviously much smaller population. Where do you think Britain went wrong?

Liu Xiaoming: I do not want to be critical of the UK policy. What I want to say is that we would like to share our experience, and compare notes with our British colleagues. I just want to give you first-hand information: Tomorrow Secretary Matt Hancock, together with British scientists and experts, will have an on-line meeting with the Chinese health minister. It'll be more than two hours' discussion to compare notes and exchange experience. I think that is what we need now. We need to enhance collaboration. We have to know the virus is our common enemy. We need to pull together, and we should come to the aid of each other to win the final battle against the virus. As President Xi Jinping said, solidarity and cooperation are the most powerful weapons for the international community to combat Covid-19.

Austin: OK, Mr Ambassador, I appreciate your time. And I look forward to the international investigation whenever it happens. Thank you very much indeed for joining us this evening and answering our questions. Thank you.

Liu Xiaoming: My pleasure.

Mark Austin is an English journalist and television presenter, currently working for Sky News. He has won six BAFTA awards.

参加英国天空新闻台《疫情后我们的新世界》特别节目在线直播访谈

作者手记

2020年6月1日，我应邀参加英国天空新闻台特别节目《疫情后我们的新世界》(*Live Panel Discussion—After the Pandemic: Our New World*)在线直播访谈，与爱尔兰前总统玛丽·罗宾逊、英国前外交大臣戴维·米利班德、美国历史学家尼尔·弗格森就疫情的全球影响、中国抗疫表现、涉疫情独立调查、新冠疫苗研发、世界卫生组织改革、气候变化、中国香港局势等展开讨论，并回答在线观众的提问。英国天空新闻台著名主持人德莫特·莫纳罕(Dermot Murnaghan)主持访谈节目。该台电视、网站、新媒体全平台进行直播。

采访实录如下：

莫纳罕： 首先请嘉宾们谈一谈我们的世界面临的机遇与挑战？

刘晓明： 疫情将带来什么样的影响？世界是将走向团结，还是更加分裂？

围绕这一问题，有很多的讨论。我认为，疫情会使世界更加团结。疫情再次证明人类生活在一个地球村。正如习近平主席所说，我们应努力构建人类命运共同体。我认为，疫情再次说明，国际社会应该加强合作。事实证明，凡是携手抗疫、支持世界卫生组织、听取世界卫生组织建议、支持多边主义的国家，疫情都有效得到了控制；凡是拒绝国际合作、排斥世界卫生组织建议的国家，则付出了沉重代价。疫情证明，再强大的国家也不可能独善其身，也不可能对病毒"免疫"，因为病毒不分国界、不分种族。

莫纳罕： 谈到国际调查，核心问题是：中国是否为这次危机承担责任？是否接受独立调查人员进入中国领土进行实地调查？

刘晓明： 我们当然欢迎国际审议。但审议的目的不是给哪个国家贴标签，审议应覆盖所有与疫情密切相关的国家。在世界卫生大会上，我们与世界卫生组织的120个成员国共同支持国际社会在合适的时机对本次疫情进行审议，审议的目的是总结经验教训，以便今后更好地应对重大传染性疾病。审议必须是独立的，排除各种政治干扰，应该是以科学为依据，由科学家主导。

莫纳罕： 中国认为应该由谁领导这一审议？

刘晓明： 应该由世界卫生组织主导。所有国家都应该参与，特别是主要国家。我不同意弗格森刚才的说法。他批评中国反应缓慢，这不是事实。弗格森讲的许多信息都是错误的，包括他说武汉封城期间，仍有很多航班从武汉飞到其他国家。这不是事实。1月23日武汉封城后，所有航班都停飞了。没有航班，也没有火车，没有任何对外交通。中国是第一个向世界卫生组织报告疫情的国家，第一个分离出病原体，第一个与世界卫生组织和其他国家分享病毒全基因序列。中国没有浪费任何时间与各国分享信息和防控经验。

莫纳罕： 武汉封城后还有许多中国航班没有停飞，导致疫情传播到很多国家，这不是一个很严重的问题吗？

刘晓明： 你的信息完全不对。武汉封城后根本没有任何航班飞行，已经与外部断绝了联系。我很遗憾在这里听到弗格森的许多冷战言论，我与弗格森相识，但不知道他为何对与中国进行冷战这么感兴趣。中国不是前苏联。作为历史学家，你应该认真研究中国的历史。中方编写了一份关于疫情的24个谎言与真相的材料，我可以寄给你看看。世界卫生组织赞赏中国的抗疫努力，不应因此就贬低世界卫生组织的作用。世界卫生组织是一个重要的国际组织，有194个成员国。

莫纳罕： 中国是不是对疫情负有责任？中国在很长一段时间里否认病毒从动物传染给人、否认人之间的传染，你们并没有及时告诉世界真相。

刘晓明： 我已经明确告诉你，中国第一时间向世界卫生组织进行了通报，没有任何延误。新冠病毒是一种全新的病毒。面对未知的全新病毒，我们必须采取负责任的态度，这需要科学家进行认真、负责任的研究。中国在发现首个病例11天后，就完成了病毒鉴定，并立即向世界卫生组织通报，同时与有关国家分享信息。中国没有任何隐瞒，也没有任何延误。中国抗疫记录清清楚楚、一目了然，经得起时间和历史的检验。我还要指出，中国首先报告疫情，并不意味着病毒起源于中国。病毒的源头问题需要科学家去研究探索。随着形势的发展，我们看到一些报道，美国、意大利等国发现了比中国更早的病例。因此，对待病毒溯源问题应当采取科学的态度。

莫纳罕： 中国会同意对世界卫生组织进行改革吗？

刘晓明： 当然。在这次疫情应对中，反映出世界卫生组织的一些不足，包括应对能力和资源不足，如何更快、更有效地应对，以及如何帮助最贫困和缺乏能力的国家抗疫。改革可以在我们战胜疫情之后进行。当前，疫情仍在全球蔓延，当务之急是团结合作，支持世界卫生组织领导抗疫斗争。

莫纳罕： 作为世界上最大的碳排放国，中国将采取什么举措，以保持目前疫情期间排放暂时减少的局面？

刘晓明： 中国坚定支持《巴黎协定》，认真履行义务。中国提前3年完成降低碳排放计划，2018年碳排放强度比2005年累计下降45.8%。2019年中国单位GDP能耗同比下降2.6%。中国是全球新能源和可再生能源最大投资国。中国始终致力于应对气候变化。中国原定于今年年底前举办《生物多样性公约》第十五次缔约方大会（COP15）。

莫纳罕： COP15还开吗？中国计划何时举行？

刘晓明： 因为疫情，具体时间尚未最后确定。今年本应是中英环境保护合作之年。英国已将第二十六届联合国气候变化大会（COP26）会期调整至明年11月，但我们仍与英国同事们在线上保持密切联系，交流沟通，确保两场会议均取得成功。

莫纳罕： 我想问一个关于重建信任和新冠疫苗研发竞赛的问题。我们看到中国和一些国家正领先疫苗的研发。如果中国研制出有效疫苗，从重建信任的角度，中国是否愿意将疫苗以尽可能低的价格与全世界分享？

刘晓明： 当然。习近平主席在世界卫生大会上庄严宣布，中国新冠疫苗研发完成并投入使用后，将作为全球公共产品，特别是要实现疫苗在发展中国家的可及性和可担负性。中国在疫苗研发上居于世界领先行列，我们有5支疫苗已进入二期临床试验，我们愿与世界各国分享。中国同时也在与包括英国、美国在内的各国科学家开展研发合作。

刚才，你展示了一个图表，显示所谓"中国的声誉已经受损"，我不同意这个结论。这要看你从哪儿获得信息。我可以向你提供一些信息。今年初，全球最大的独立公关公司爱德曼根据它发布的《全球信任度调查报告（Trust Barometer）》显示，中国民众对政府的信任指数高达82%，在所有被调查的国家中高居榜首。还有，根据近期新加坡独立民调机构"黑箱研究"（Blackbox Research）民调公司对全球23个经济体所做的调查，中国民众对政府的满意度最高，以综合得分85%再次位居榜首。

莫纳罕： 我们剩下的时间不多了。最后，我想问一下刘大使关于民众，特别是年青一代对政府缺乏信任的问题。在香港街头可以看到这种情况：中国政府镇压要求民主的抗议者。

刘晓明： 香港事态根本不是什么"中国政府镇压民主抗议者"，香港街头上演的是持续不断的违法暴力活动。这些活动危害中国国家安全。这些暴力激进分子冲击香港立法会，甚至放火烧伤无辜民众。请问，如果同样的事情发生在伦敦街头，如果暴徒冲击英国议会，英国将做何反应？难道英国政府和警方会坐视不管、听之任之吗？我认为，任何一个负责任的政府都会采取行动。另一方面，人们应当看到，香港回归23年来，"一国两制"在香港取得巨大成功。

莫纳罕： 对不起，我们时间到了。我要感谢所有嘉宾。谢谢你，刘大使。

刘晓明： 不客气。

Sky News *Live Panel Discussion — After the Pandemic: Our New World* with Dermot Murnaghan

On 1st June 2020, I attended a live panel discussion hosted by Dermot Murnaghan on Sky News' special programme *After the Pandemic: Our New World* with Mary Robinson, former president of Ireland, David Miliband, former British foreign secretary and historian Niall Ferguson. The following is a transcript of my Q&A session:

Murnaghan: Let's get the initial thoughts from our panelists on the opportunities and challenges facing our world today.

Liu Xiaoming: I think there's a lot of debate these days about the consequences of this pandemic — whether the pandemic will unite the world or make the world more divided. I tend to believe it makes the world more united. I think this pandemic really shows us again that we all belong to this global village. Just as President Xi said, we should all try to build this Community with a Shared Future for Mankind. I think this pandemic shows us that the international community should cooperate. It shows that those countries who supported each other, who supported WHO in playing a leading role, who supported multilateralism and who listened to the advice of WHO have been able to put the virus under control. But those countries who rejected international corporation, who rejected WHO advice have paid a high price. I think no country, no matter how strong you are, can be immune. You cannot be insulated from this pandemic. Viruses respect no borders, no races.

Murnaghan: When investigations are underway, the core question to China is: Does China accept its culpability and responsibilities during this crisis? Let me ask you straight up: Will you allow independent investigators onto Chinese soil to work out what happened?

Liu Xiaoming: We certainly welcome international review. But the purpose is not to label any country. All the countries should be covered. Together with 120 member states during the World Health Assembly, we supported the international community to carry out a review of the pandemic at a proper time. The purpose is to sum up experience and get better prepared for future pandemics. And this review, firstly, should be independent, free from politicization. It should be based on science, that is, let the scientists take the lead.

Murnaghan: Who do you accept leading it? Who would you like to oversee it?

Liu Xiaoming: The WHO should lead this independent review. All countries should get involved, especially the major players. I found I have differences with Niall. He blamed China for slow reaction. That is not true. I think Niall got a lot of wrong information. He said during the lockdown, there were still many flights going to other countries. That is not true. That's false information. When Wuhan was locked down, starting from 23rd of January, there were no flights at all. No flights, no trains, not at all. With regard to how China reacted to this pandemic, China was the first country to report the virus to the WHO, first to identify the pathogen and first to share the genetic sequence with the WHO and other countries. China wasted no time in sharing information and experience in containing the virus.

Murnaghan: During the pandemic, there were hundreds of flights out of China as a whole, and the virus surely started circulating in the world like that. You've got to admit that, have you, before the world's gonna take you seriously?

Liu Xiaoming: Your information is totally wrong. As I said earlier, when Wuhan went into lockdown, there was no flights at all, no connection with the outside world. I am sorry to hear so much cold-war rhetoric from Niall. We knew each other before, but I do not know why he is so interested in having a cold war with China. I just want to let you know that China is not the former Soviet Union. You, being a historian, should have a serious study about China. I can provide you with more information and facts about that. We have a "Reality Checks" of 24 allegations and I will mail it to you. I just want to say that we should not talk down the role played by the WHO just because the WHO spoke positively about the efforts of China. The WHO is a very important international organization. It has 194 members.

Murnaghan: Let's talk about China's responsibilities. Undoubtedly, China was in denial about COVID-19 for so long, about animal to human transition and about human to human transition. You did not tell the world soon enough.

Liu Xiaoming: As I told you, we lost no time in informing the WHO. This is a new virus, you have to be responsible. It was unknown to all of us. You need the scientists to study in a responsible way and seriously. When we identified the virus 11 days after the first report, we immediately reported to the WHO and shared the information with relevant countries. There was no cover-up. There was no delay. China's record is clean. It can stand the test of time and history. What I am also saying is that China first reported the virus, but it does not mean the virus originated from China. In terms of the origin, I think it's up to the scientists to decide. As the situation unfolds, we hear reports that there were some cases in the United States, in Italy, that were much earlier than China. You know, we need to adopt a scientific approach about this matter.

Murnaghan: What about the question of reform of the World Health Organization? China will accept that?

Liu Xiaoming: Yes. The pandemic really shows the weakness of WHO, both in terms of its capabilities and resources, and how WHO could respond more quickly and more effectively, especially taking care of the poorest and the weak countries. I think it needs reform. We can do this after we claim the final victory over the virus. The top priority now is to pull together and to support WHO to lead this battle. We have not put the virus under control yet.

Murnaghan: As the world's biggest emitter, what's China's commitment to keeping up this temporary fall in emissions during the pandemic?

Liu Xiaoming: China is very much committed to the Paris Agreement. China has fulfilled its obligations three years ahead of plan. In 2018, we had brought down the carbon intensity by 45.8% from 2005. We have also brought down the consumption of carbon per unit GDP by 2.6%. China is now the largest investor in new energy and

renewable energy, and China is very much committed to mitigation of climate change. According to the original plan. China will also hold the Conference of the Parties to the Convention on Biological Diversity by the end of the year.

Murnaghan: Is it going to go ahead? You are still planning to do it?

Liu Xiaoming: It has not yet been finalized because of the pandemic. So it's still open. This year is supposed to be the year of collaboration between China and the UK in environmental protection. Now UK has rescheduled COP26 to November next year. But we are still keeping very close contact on line with my British colleagues to compare notes on how to make the conferences successful.

Murnaghan: I want to ask you specifically about rebuilding trust, about the race to develop a vaccine for Covid-19. We noticed the advances China and some other countries are making. But if China were to develop an effective vaccine, would it be willing — and this is in terms of rebuilding trust I suppose — will it be willing to share that vaccine with the planet as cheap as possible?

Liu Xiaoming: Definitely. President Xi made firm commitment during the World Health Assembly that once the vaccine is available, China wants to make it a public good and make it especially accessible and available to developing countries. China is now among the most advanced countries in terms of vaccine research. Now we are in phase II, we already have five clinical trials and we want to share with the rest of the world. China is working with scientists from the UK and other countries including the United States on the vaccine.

I can't agree with the table you just showed that China's reputation has been damaged. It depends on where you get this information. According to the information I have by an independent PR company in United States, the Edelman Trust Barometer of 2020, Chinese government enjoys the highest support among its people. It's about 82%,that is top of all countries. And also according to a Singapore public opinion company Black Box Research, they did a survey of 23 countries, China again tops the rest 22 countries.The Chinese government enjoys more than 85% of public support.

Murnaghan: We are running short of time, I am going to ask the Ambassador finally on this lack of trust, particularly with the younger generation. Well you are seeing that on the streets of Hong Kong: the Chinese state's repression of those protesters — the seekers after democracy.

Liu Xiaoming: No, it's not "Chinese repression". What is going on in Hong Kong is violence. It's a risk to the national security. Those perpetrators stormed the Legislative Council, and they even set fire to innocent people. If the same thing happens on the streets of London, if the rioters stormed the UK Parliament, what would be the UK's reaction? The UK government and police will sit back and let these things go on? I think any responsible government has to take measures. Some people do not realise that "One Country, Two Systems" has achieved great success since Hong Kong returned to China twenty-three years ago.

Murnaghan: We are running out of time. I want to say thank you to our panelists. Thank you, Ambassador Liu.

Liu Xiaoming: My pleasure.

中日关系

China-Japan Relations

2013年12月26日，日本首相安倍晋三冒天下之大不韪，悍然参拜供奉有14名二战甲级战犯的靖国神社。这一事件引发中国、韩国等亚洲国家和国际社会的严厉谴责。7天后，即2014年1月2日，英国主流大报《每日电讯报》在社论评论版刊登我题为《拒不反省侵略历史的日本必将对世界和平构成严重威胁》的署名文章。我在文章中把日本军国主义比作英国家喻户晓的小说《哈利·波特》中的反面人物"伏地魔"。我说，伏地魔把自己的灵魂分藏在7个"魂器"中，消灭伏地魔的唯一方法是把7个"魂器"全部摧毁。如果把军国主义比作日本的"伏地魔"，靖国神社无疑是藏匿这个国家灵魂最黑暗部分的"魂器"。

　　我在文章中指出，靖国神社100多年来一直是日本军国主义对外发动侵略战争的精神工具和象征，至今仍供奉着对亚洲受害国人民犯下滔天罪行的二战甲级战犯。日本领导人参拜靖国神社这一问题绝不是日本内政问题和个人问题，也不仅仅是中日、韩日关系问题，它的实质是日本领导人能否正确认识和深刻反省其军国主义对外侵略和殖民统治历史，日本是否遵守《联合国宪章》的宗旨和原则、走和平道路的根本方向问题，是关乎侵略与反侵略、正义与邪恶、光明与黑暗的大是大非问题。

　　文章发表后在英国和国际上引起很大反响，英国各大报，以及美国《纽约时报》《华尔街日报》等主流报纸，路透社、美联社、法新社、合众社等西方四大通讯社，英国各大电视台、电台和美国有线电视新闻网（CNN），纷纷报道和引用。英国电视台和电台也提出采访我。对此，我来者不拒，并主动出击。10天内，我对英国各大电视台和电台全覆盖，其中1天接受2次现场直播采访。英国和西方主流媒体把我这一系列撰文和采访称为"中国大使在伦敦发起强大攻势，狠批日本军国主义"。还有英国评论说，"伏地魔"这个比喻通俗易懂，既鲜明表达了中国的立场，也易于被西方民众接受。

接受英国独立电视台《十点新闻》栏目
高级外事记者庄锐采访

作者手记

2014年1月3日，我接受英国独立电视台《十点新闻》(ITV NEWS AT TEN) 栏目高级外事记者庄锐（John Ray）采访，揭批安倍企图复辟日本军国主义的本质，阐述中方在钓鱼岛及其附属岛屿问题上的严正立场，呼吁国际社会共同努力制止日本军国主义复活，维护地区稳定与世界和平。

庄锐曾任英国天空电视台政治记者，2000年加入独立电视台任高级外事记者，曾在中国、中东、非洲常驻，获多项新闻大奖，包括国际艾美奖、英国电影和电视艺术学院奖。

独立电视台在当晚黄金时段播放了此次采访的主要内容，并在该台网站播放了采访实录视频。

采访实录如下：

庄锐： 能否先从"伏地魔"谈起。你在《每日电讯报》上使用的这个比喻非常生动。为什么把日本比作"伏地魔"这样一个邪恶角色？

刘晓明： 我认为日本军国主义与"伏地魔"有一些共同之处。消灭"伏地魔"的唯一方法是把7个"魂器"全部摧毁。只要靖国神社还留存在日本人民的记忆之中，军国主义就始终阴魂不散。一些人认为中国在参拜靖国神社这个问题上小题大做。但是日本领导人参拜的是一个供奉战争罪犯，特别是有14名二战甲级战犯的神社。这些战犯给各国人民，包括英国人民带来重大伤亡和损失。东条英机是14名二战甲级战犯之首。他不仅对中国发起战争，而且对美国、英国和荷兰开战。所以日本领导人参拜靖国神社是一个关乎日本未来发展方向的重大问题，是关乎和平与战争、正义与邪恶、光明与黑暗的大是大非问题。鉴于上述原因，中国对日本领导人参拜靖国神社提出强烈抗议。

庄锐： 你认为日本什么是邪恶的？是日本军国主义吗？

刘晓明： 确实如此。我们对日本领导人背离和平的言论深感忧虑。你知道，安倍甚至否认日本发动过侵略战争，鼓吹所谓"侵略未定论"。日本副首相麻生太郎甚至扬言"日本可以学习纳粹德国修宪的做法"。他们还蓄意煽动所谓"中国威胁论"，制造地区紧张，为扩充军备寻找借口。我们对安倍复辟军国主义的企图表示严重担忧。今天的日本和二战前的德国有不少相似之处，对此我们深感忧虑。

庄锐： 在日本看来，过去20年来中国不断扩充军备，正成为地区新兴大国，日本需要防御中国这个新的超级大国。中国军费在过去25年中一直保持两位数增长。

刘晓明：　实际情况不是这样。中国国防支出近年虽有所增加，但是中国的人均军费和美国、英国、日本相比都是最低的。中国是一个拥有13亿多人口的大国，拥有2.2万公里陆地边界线和3.2万公里海岸线，国防任务十分繁重。中国的国防费用占GDP和财政总支出比重近年来不断下降。美国、英国、日本的人均军费分别是中国的22倍、9倍和5倍。最重要的是中国国防政策的性质，中国奉行的是防御性国防政策。中国从没有侵占过别国一寸土地。事实上，中国百年近代史是被外国列强侵略瓜分的历史，而日本恰恰相反。

庄锐：　但从另一个角度来说，中国是侵略者而不是日本。比如钓鱼岛，中国划设东海防空识别区，但国际法认定钓鱼岛属于日本，不是吗？而中国却在宣誓主权，看上去是中国存在领土野心。

刘晓明：　这种观点是完全错误的。钓鱼岛自古以来就是中国的领土。1895年中日甲午战争后，钓鱼岛才被日本非法侵占。根据中、英、美三国首脑发表的《开罗宣言》，日本必须向中国归还所有通过战争窃取的领土，包括台湾及其周边岛屿，当然也包括钓鱼岛。二战结束后，美国在冷战中支持日本，向其移交岛屿行政管辖权。中国从未承认美日这种私相授受并提出多次抗议。然而即便是美国，在钓鱼岛的主权问题上也保持中立。

钓鱼岛一直是中日之间的争议问题。中日邦交正常化时，两国领导人达成谅解，同意将钓鱼岛问题放一放，留待以后解决。1978
年，中国领导人邓小平访问日本时，一位日本记者向他提出钓鱼岛
问题。邓小平回答说：这个问题我们同日本有争议，可以把它放一
放，也许下一代人比我们更聪明些，会找到实际解决的方法。

庄锐： 但从目前看来，中国在钓鱼岛问题上似乎不会妥协，坚持认为岛
屿是中国领土，归中国所有。

刘晓明： 现在的问题是，日本主动挑起了争端。日本右翼势力和日本政府
制造了将钓鱼岛"国有化"的闹剧，才引起领土争端紧张，中国
不得不做出反应。中方一直在被迫回应日本的挑衅。中国是一个
爱好和平的国家。但我们也是讲原则的：人不犯我，我不犯人；
人若犯我，我必犯人。

庄锐： 在外人看来，目前局势令人担忧。我想问你，局势将向什么方向
发展？人们将中日争议视为可能引发战争的"火药桶"。你是否
有同样的担心？

刘晓明： 我们同样感到担心。但我想强调，中国希望与日本发展睦邻友好
关系。42年前中日邦交正常化时，两国领导人宣布"中日永不再
战"。中日同为亚洲重要国家，中日关系对亚太地区和平至关重
要。但日本右翼势力及军国主义蠢蠢欲动、再次抬头，形势的发
展并不取决于中国。这也是我为什么把日本军国主义比作"伏地
魔"。只有制止日本军国主义，才能确保地区和平与稳定，避免

战争。因此我们呼吁安倍政府不要在错误的道路上越走越远。

庄锐： 在电影结尾，"伏地魔"最终被消灭了。

刘晓明： 要想保证亚太地区的和平与繁荣，就必须消灭日本军国主义。

庄锐： 中国政府表示中国不会允许日本重新走上扩充军备之路，这是否意味中国将采取防御性军事行动来阻止日本？

刘晓明： 正如我刚才所说，中国从不挑衅，但会反击。我们对外阐明我们的立场，是希望引起国际社会的警觉。我在《每日电讯报》上发表文章正是希望英国民众了解我们的担忧。我们看重中英关系，也看重英方如何看待这件事。英国在维护欧洲及世界和平与稳定上发挥着重要作用。中英既是二战盟友，也是战争受害者，两国应与国际社会一道共同承担起维护战后秩序的责任。这一秩序带来了战后70年的和平与稳定。明年将迎来世界反法西斯战争胜利70周年。我们在庆祝胜利的同时，也应关注二战历史是否会重演。如不制止日本军国主义复活，另一场世界大战的可能性就不能完全排除。我们希望以和平的方式解决问题，但也要做最坏的打算。因此，最好的办法是国际社会共同努力。我高兴地看到，不仅中国抗议安倍参拜靖国神社，韩国、美国等国家也表达了严重关切和失望。我们希望国际社会共同制止日本军国主义复辟。

庄锐： 我们知道，日本侵华战争给中国人民造成了巨大的伤害，中国人民是否能够原谅日本，还是在70年后的今天仍然怀有仇恨？

刘晓明： 日本侵华战争给中国人民带来了巨大灾难，造成了3500多万人伤亡，直接和间接经济损失达6000多亿美元。我们希望弥合战争造成的伤痛，因此中日邦交正常化时，中国政府决定放弃对日本战争索赔。因为我们认为，犯下战争罪行的是日本军国主义者，不是日本普通百姓。我们也不希望今天的日本年轻人为父辈曾经犯下的罪行承担责任。中国希望与日本和平相处。但日本领导人通过参拜靖国神社、改写历史、篡改教科书、拒绝忏悔，不断挑起新的仇恨。日本当局不希望向下一代讲述侵略历史。日本和德国在对待历史问题上采取了截然不同的态度。德国时任总理勃兰特在犹太人纪念碑前下跪谢罪，现任总理默克尔访问纳粹集中营凭吊遇难者。而日本领导人从未做出类似政治姿态，甚至连向中国人民道歉的话都没有，怎么让中国人民忘记历史？日本政府和领导人的态度非常重要，我们希望他们改弦易辙，向中国、亚洲和所有遭受日本侵略战争苦难的人民真诚道歉、忏悔，从而翻开新的一页。问题是，日本战争罪行从未得到彻底清算，因此军国主义在日本总是蠢蠢欲动，国际社会应对日本军国主义的危险动向保持警惕。

An Interview with John Ray on ITV *News at Ten*

On 3rd January 2014, I talked to ITV diplomatic correspondent John Ray during ITV *News at Ten* programme. I criticised Japanese Prime Minister Shinzo Abe's attempt to revive militarism in Japan, elaborated on China's solemn stand concerning the issue of the Diaoyu Islands, and called on the international community to stop the rise of Japanese militarism, with a view to safeguarding regional stability and world peace. The full text of the interview is as follows:

Ray: Can I start with Lord Voldemort? This is a very vivid language that you've used. Why compare Japan to a character who is pure evil?

Liu Xiaoming: I think there are some similarities between the two because Lord Voldemort will not be destroyed if you don't destroy all the seven horcruxes. And I made the comparison because militarism has not been completely destroyed, and because the Yakusuni Shrine is always alive in the memory of the Japanese people. Some people think China makes a big fuss about this visit. But I do think the visit is a big deal because it is by Japanese leaders, especially national leaders, to pay respect to a shrine which honours war criminals, especially 14 Class A war criminals who inflicted enormous casualties and damages on the people who suffered from that war, including British people. In fact, Hideki Tojo, the top war criminal among the 14, not only started the war against China, but also declared war on America, on Britain and on the Netherlands. So we believe this is really a matter concerning which way Japan is heading. This is really a choice between peace and war, between right and wrong, between light and darkness. So that's why we made a very strong representation about Japanese leaders visiting this shrine.

Ray: So where from your point of view is the pure evil in Japan? Is it what you perceive as their militarism?

Liu Xiaoming: I think that's very much so. We are very concerned about Japanese leaders' anti-peace rhetoric. As you know, Prime Minster Abe even refuses to recognize that Japan started this war of aggression. He even challenges the definition of aggression. The deputy prime minister even tries to, in his word, learn from Nazi Germany to amend the pacifist constitution. And they also play up the so-called "China Threat" in order to create regional tensions to make excuse for Japanese military expansion. So we are very concerned about the spectre of militarism that Abe is trying to raise again. We found some similarities between today's Japan and Germany before the WWII. So we are very concerned about that.

Ray: From the Japanese perspective, you might look at the buildup of Chinese military forces over the past 20 years and say here is a big power emerging in the region. We need to defend ourselves against this new superpower. You have been increasing defence spending by double digit numbers for the past 25 years.

Liu Xiaoming: That's not right. We did see some increase in China's military spending. But if you compare China's per capita military expenditure with that of America, Britain, Japan, China is still the lowest. China is a large country. We are much bigger than Britain and Japan. We have more than 1.3 billion people. We have 22, 000 km of land borders and 32, 000 km of coastal lines. China is a large country to defend. And if you look at the military budget-to-GDP ratio, and its percentage in China's total fiscal expenditure, the figures are decreasing year-on-year. In per capita terms, the US is 22 times that of China. Even Britain is 9 times that of China, and Japan's military spending is five times that of China. And what is important is the nature of China's defence policy. Chinese defence policy is defensive in nature. You have never seen China occupy a single inch of other country's territory. As a matter of fact, in the past hundred years or so, China has been a victim of foreign aggression and occupation. But if you look at Japan, it is a completely different story.

Ray: When you look at it from a different perspective, you might see not Japan as the aggressor but China as the aggressor. Take for example the Diaoyu Islands.

You've declared a sort of defensive zone over there. They belong, according to the international law, to Japan. Do they not? You're claiming them. So it looks as if it is China that has the territorial ambitions there.

Liu Xiaoming: That is not right. In fact, Diaoyu Dao has been China's territory since ancient times. It was not until China-Japan War about 120 years ago that Japan had seized it illegally. According to the Cairo Declaration reached by the Chinese, British and American leaders, Japan must return all the territories it had seized illegally as a result of that war, including Taiwan and the surrounding islands. But after the Second World War, the Cold War ensued. The Americans tried to support Japan. Instead of returning the Diaoyu Islands to China, they transferred the administrative power of the Diaoyu Islands to Japan. We never recognized that. We launched protests against this. But still, Americans do not recognize Japan's sovereignty over the islands. When it comes to sovereignty, they take a neutral position. Diaoyu Dao has always been a dispute between China and Japan. And we had proposed, before the events in the past few years, to shelve the dispute. When Deng Xiaoping visited Japan, he was asked a question at a news conference about the future of Diaoyu Dao. He said we have a dispute with Japan over the Islands. We may shelve the dispute for the time being. Maybe the future generation would be wiser than us today to find a solution to this disputed territory.

Ray: But at the moment, it looks like that China on the islands is not going to compromise, that it is your territory. And you should have it.

Liu Xiaoming: The problem is it is the Japanese who have provoked all this. First of all, a group of right-wing forces in Japan tried to nationalize these islands. So the Japanese government wanted to take it over. This raised the tension over the disputed territory. We had to make a response. China in fact has been passive in making response to Japanese provocations. According to Chinese philosophy, we will never attack others. We are a very pacifist country. But we will make a counter-attack when we are attacked.

Ray: If you watch this from the outside, it's quite alarming. I want to ask you where you think or where you fear all this is heading? When people talk about potential flashpoints for war, they look at this dispute between China and Japan. Do you share that worry?

Liu Xiaoming: We are concerned, I would say. First of all, I would stress that we want to have good relations with Japan. We want to live peacefully with them. In fact, when we normalized relations with Japan about 42 years ago, the leaders of the two countries all proclaimed that there would be no war for ever between China and Japan. We all know that you can not have a peaceful Asia and Pacific without good relations between China and Japan, such two important countries. But it's not really very much up to China when you have these right-wing forces and militarist forces working and getting momentum in Japan. So we are very concerned. That's why I made a comparison of Lord Voldemort and militarism in Japan. So the only way to maintain peace and stability, to ensure there will be no war, is to stop the militarism in Japan. That's why we call on Mr. Abe and his government to stop it before it's too late.

Ray: At the end of the movie, Lord Voldemort is destroyed.

Liu Xiaoming: Militarism should be destroyed in order to maintain peace and prosperity of the Asia-Pacific.

Ray: Chinese authorities have said, when they are talking about Japan re-arming, that you will not allow it to happen. What does that mean? Does that mean that you will take defensive military action to stop Japan?

Liu Xiaoming: As I said, China will never provoke. China will only make counter-attack. We want to draw the attention, and the alert of the international community, so that's why I wrote this article. I want to share my concern with the British public. In Britain, we attach great importance not only to our relations, but also to how you see this. Britain has played an important role in the past and still has a role to play today in maintaining peace and stability not only in Europe but also in the world. So that's why I'm calling on China and Britain, not only as the victims of the Second World War, but also as victors of the Second World War, to take on our common responsibility. We should work with the international community to ensure that post-war order will be maintained. Because this post-war order really has ensured peace and stability for the world for the past 70 years. Next year will be the 70th anniversary of the end of the Second World War. I think we really have to celebrate it not only with some joy but also with some concerns about whether the history of the Second World War will be repeated. If the militarism in Japan is not to be stopped, we can not rule out the recurrence of another world war. So that's why we are really concerned about this. We want it to work out in a very peaceful way, but sometimes you have to prepare for the worst. So the best way to do it is to resolve it with the efforts of the international community. So I'm very pleased that not only China has lodged strong protests, but also South Korea and America have expressed deep concern and disappointment. Some other countries have done the same. So we do hope that the international community will join force to stop the development of the militarism in Japan.

Ray: Can I ask you a question that I asked you earlier on. We know that Chinese people suffered terribly from the invasion of the Japanese in the 1930s. Has that wound that was inflicted ever been forgiven? Has it ever healed? Or the Chinese people feel as strongly now, as hurt and as angry now as it did 70 years ago.

Liu Xiaoming: I think you are right. The war really inflicted an enormous wound and casualties on the Chinese people. It caused 35 million casualties, and direct or indirect economic losses of $600 billion. We want to see the wound healed, so that's why when China and Japan normalized relations, the Chinese Government and Chinese leaders decided that we were not going to seek war reparations from Japan. We believed it was the war criminals, it was the leaders of Japan who started the war should be held accountable, not the average Japanese people. So we do not want the young people of Japan today to bear the cost, to bear the responsibility of their fathers or grandfathers who committed this crime. So we want to live peacefully with Japan. But it was always the Japanese leaders who always open this wound of hatred between China and Japan. In addition to visiting the war shrine, they tried to rewrite the history, refuse to show remorse of their aggressive past, and even tries to alter the text book. They do not want to teach the children about their aggressive past. So it's quite different if you compare Japan with Germany on how they did with their past. For example, you see German Chancellor Brandt kneeling down in front of the tomb of the Jews, and you see Mrs. Merkel showing respect to those dead in Nazi concentration camps. But you have never seen the same political gesture, not even a word of apology to Chinese people from Japanese leaders. So how could you make sure Chinese people would forget this past? So it's very important that the attitude of Japanese leaders and Japanese government really makes a big difference. We do hope that they will change their course, show remorse and make apology not only to Chinese people, but also to Asian people, to all the peoples they have caused casualties and damages, and to start a new life, a new Japan. So I don't think the issue of Japanese war criminal has been thoroughly settled. Therefore, you see the spectre of militarism rising from time to time. So the international community really should be alert about this dangerous direction where Japan is heading.

ITV is the second largest public broadcaster in the UK after the BBC. *News at Ten* is ITV's flagship news programme and one of the most watched evening news programmes in the UK with an audience of 4 million. John Ray is an international, award-winning British television journalist for ITV News, currently based in London.

接受英国BBC国际广播电台《周末》栏目
主持人沃里克现场直播采访

作者手记

　　2014年1月5日，我接受英国BBC国际广播电台（BBC World Service）《周末》（*Weekend*）栏目主持人朱利安·沃里克（Julian Worricker）现场直播采访，阐述中国在日本侵略历史、钓鱼岛主权等问题上的严正立场，揭批安倍复辟军国主义企图，呼吁国际社会对此保持高度警惕。

　　BBC国际广播电台用40多种语言向200多个国家和地区广播，听众达2.1亿人次。《周末》是该台品牌栏目，聚焦一周重大事件，邀请英国和外国政要、社会名流、各界精英与主持人一对一对话。沃里克于1985年加入BBC，先后任记者、编辑，在BBC多个频道担任主持人，创办《沃里克星期日访谈》栏目，是《周末》栏目资深主持人。

　　在这次采访中，沃里克还邀请英国《金融时报》政治编辑乔治·帕克和远在新德里的印度记者乔蒂·马豪特拉参加讨论。

　　采访实录如下：

沃里克： 日本首相安倍晋三参拜靖国神社的理由遭到中国政府的驳斥。中国驻英国大使刘晓明呼吁英国和国际社会对日本军国主义复辟保持高度警惕。今天，刘大使来到了我们的演播室。大使先生，早上好。

刘晓明： 早上好，朱利安。

沃里克： 中国对安倍参拜靖国神社的具体关切是什么？

刘晓明： 我们对安倍参拜靖国神社表示严重关切。靖国神社一直是日本军国主义对外发动侵略战争和殖民统治的精神工具和象征，至今仍供奉着包括东条英机在内的14名二战甲级战犯。东条英机不仅对中国发起战争，而且偷袭珍珠港，对美国、英国和荷兰开战。这是一个双手沾满了数百万中国人民鲜血的战犯。

沃里克： 我理解中国人民为何对安倍参拜如此愤怒。但这归根到底不是日本的内政吗？

刘晓明： 这当然不是日本的内政问题。我们关注的不仅是日本领导人如何对待这些战犯和历史，更关注他们对未来的态度。

沃里克： 你认为日本政府是什么态度？

刘晓明： 日本领导人参拜战犯，显示他们对日本侵略和殖民统治历史毫无忏悔之意。日本副首相麻生太郎甚至扬言"日本可以学习纳粹德国修宪的做法"。安倍本人也鼓吹所谓"侵略未定论"。

沃里克： 我想进一步探讨一下这个问题。中国也在不断加大军费开支，中国新一届领导人表示还将继续加大军费投入。你们批评日本，这不是双重标准吗？

刘晓明： 我不同意你的看法。我愿谈谈中国的军费开支。中国是一个大国。中国的国土面积是日本的25倍，人口是日本的10倍，但日本的人均军费开支是中国的5倍。就国防费在GDP中的比重而言，日本与中国差不多。

沃里克： 但中国将会加大军费投入，我想我们应该明确这一点。

刘晓明： 那是因为中国经济在不断增长，中国的国防任务十分繁重。正如我刚才所说，中国有幅员辽阔的国土需要保卫。我们有14个陆上邻国和7个海上邻国，拥有2.2万公里陆地边界线和3.2万公里海岸线。

沃里克： 我想讨论一下中日在东海一些无人居住岛屿的争端问题。中日都表示拥有这些岛屿的主权。作为争端的一方，中国单方面宣布在该地区划设防空识别区。日本不可避免地会将这种行为视为"侵略"。

刘晓明： 我们把这些岛屿称作钓鱼岛。钓鱼岛及其附属岛屿自古以来就是中国的领土。

沃里克： 你知道日本对此有不同看法。

刘晓明： 它会有不同看法，但我说的是事实。1895年中国在甲午战争战败后，钓鱼岛被日本非法侵占。根据二战期间中、英、美三国首脑发表的《开罗宣言》，日本必须向中国归还所有窃取之领土，包括台湾及其周边岛屿，当然也包括钓鱼岛。20世纪50年代初，美国"接管"钓鱼岛。由于冷战的原因，美国未向中国移交钓鱼岛及其附属岛屿，因为美国需要日本。70年代，美国向日本"移交"钓鱼岛"行政管辖权"。但美国在钓鱼岛的主权问题上保持中立，并未承认日本对钓鱼岛拥有主权。

沃里克： 除了加剧本已紧张的争端外，你认为中方单方面划设防空识别区能达到什么目的？

刘晓明： 请让我把关于钓鱼岛的话说完。20世纪70年代中日实现关系正常化，两国领导人达成谅解，同意将钓鱼岛问题先放一放，留待以后解决。1978年，中国领导人邓小平访问日本时曾被问到钓鱼岛的归属问题。邓小平回答说：这个问题我们同日本有争议，可以把它放一放，也许下一代人比我们更聪明些，会找到实际解决的方法。因此两国领导人决定搁置争议。但近年来，日本多次单方面采取行动，发起了挑衅性的行为，制造了"购岛"闹剧，企图将钓鱼岛进行所谓"国有化"。中国被迫对此做出反应。

沃里克： 你们用这来证明划设东海防空识别区的合法性？

刘晓明： 划设防空识别区是国际通行的做法。

沃里克： 但在某种程度上，双方都必须从各自的立场上后退。

刘晓明： 你说的是划设东海防空识别区问题吗？

沃里克： 我指的是更广泛意义上的。

刘晓明： 应当指出，日本早在45年前就已在该地区划设防空识别区。过去45年里，它不断扩大防空识别区范围，甚至划到离中国领空仅有130公里。

沃里克： 我想邀请一位嘉宾乔治·帕克在线加入，他想问你一个问题。乔治，你一直在认真倾听。

帕克： 非常认真地听。大使先生，我完全理解中日之间那段痛苦的历史，以及你对安倍参拜靖国神社的愤怒。但如果对比一下中日的军事实力，中国已远远超过日本。你仍然认为中国面临日本的军事威胁吗？

刘晓明： 你说的是包括军费开支在内的一系列数字。但你忽略了一个事实：日本也在增加军费开支。未来5年，日本的军费开支将增长5%。目前日本的军费开支已达18年来历史新高。美国的国防预算比中国多4倍，人均国防开支是中国的22倍。即便英国，人均军费开支也是中国的9倍。这只是其一。其二，军费开支是衡量一国军力的重要因素，但更重要的是看一个国家的国防政策，看它的历史。中国是一个爱好和平的国家。如果你对比一下中日的历史，就会知道日本与中国完全不同。

帕克： 你是否认为日本仍是威胁？

刘晓明： 历史上，中国曾多次遭到侵略。一战期间，日本强加给中国许多不平等条约。二战期间，日本发动了侵华战争，中国人民伤亡和损失惨重。

沃里克： 你认为日本仍然对中国构成军事威胁？

刘晓明： 当然。因为日本政府对待历史的态度，因为日本领导人仍然参拜战犯，并且企图修改"和平宪法"。这些不能不使我们感到担忧。

沃里克： 下面我们连线在新德里的印度记者乔蒂·马豪特拉。

马豪特拉： 大使先生，早上好。

刘晓明： 早上好。

马豪特拉： 很高兴在BBC节目里与你对话。我是一名驻新德里的印度记者。在印度，我们认为中国是一个有着悠久历史文明的伟大国家。中国很快就会成为世界第一大经济体。但为什么中国与包括印度在内的邻国有着如此多的争端？中印争端的历史可以追溯到印度独立之前，双方对一段长达4000公里的边境线存在不同看法。你刚才说中国是一个爱好和平的国家，但就在几个月前，中国军队越过实际控制线进入印度领土，并在那里停留了3周时间。这是为什么？

刘晓明： 我想强调的是，我们希望与所有邻国发展睦邻友好关系。关于边界争端问题，需要说明的是，中国曾长期遭受帝国主义列强侵略。中国与一些邻国的边界问题许多都是外国殖民者遗留下来的。但我们真诚地愿意与争议有关各方，包括印度，坐下来进行认真的谈判。我高兴地看到中印关于边界问题的谈判取得了积极进展。

马豪特拉： 大使先生，中印曾在2005年就解决边界问题达成过协议。但几年后，中国单方面退出该协议。目前两国之间在边界问题上不存在谅解。

刘晓明： 我不同意你的说法。我今天主要是谈中日关系问题。说到争端，你不能只听一面之词。我们对印度方面的一些行动也是不满的。但今天我不想与你争论这个问题。我想强调的是，我们真诚希望双方通过谈判找到解决办法。

沃里克： 大使先生，非常感谢你参加本期节目。

刘晓明： 不客气。

A Live Interview with Julian Worricker on BBC World Service *Weekend*

On 5th January 2014, I gave a live interview on BBC World Service *Weekend* programme. I elaborated on China's solemn stands on Japan's aggressive past and on the Diaoyu Islands, exposing the Japanese Prime Minister Shinzo Abe's attempt to revive militarism in Japan and calling on the international community to keep on high alert. The full text of the interview is as follows:

Worricker: Mr. Abe's claim has been brushed aside by the Chinese leadership. And now Chinese Ambassador to London Liu Xiaoming has called on Britain and the United Nations to be on high alert against what he describes as Japan's growing militarism. Ambassador Liu is with us in the studio. Good morning.

Liu Xiaoming: Good morning, Julian.

Worricker: What is your specific concern here?

Liu Xiaoming: We are very much concerned about this visit. Because, as you said, Yasukuni Shrine has long been the spiritual symbol and instruments used by Japanese militarists for their war efforts, in their war of aggression and colonial rule. The Japanese national leaders pay respect to this shrine which today still honors 14 class A war criminals including Hideki Tojo, who was responsible not only for launching a war against China but also for attacking the Pearl Harbor, for declaring war on the United States, on Britain and the Netherlands. This is a man whose hands were stained with the blood of millions of Chinese people.

Worricker: I can see why the Chinese would be angry about it, but ultimately, is it not

an internal Japanese matter?

Liu Xiaoming: It is not an internal Japanese matter. It's not only that we care about how Japanese leaders treat these war criminals. It's not only about their attitude toward the past. It's also about their attitude toward the future.

Worricker: And what do you say their attitude is?

Liu Xiaoming: By paying respect to war criminals, they show no signs of repentance for the past aggression and colonial rule. And also it shows that they want even to, as their deputy Prime Minister asserted, that Japan would like to learn from Nazi Germany to revise the Japanese Constitution. And Abe himself challenged the definition of "aggression of Japan".

Worricker: Let's explore that for a moment, because you are saying this from the point of view representing a country that spends massively on its military, that has a relatively new President who says he wants to spend more on its military. Therefore for you to criticize the Japanese for even contemplating what you have just alluded to, it's surely double-standard.

Liu Xiaoming: I don't agree with you. Let's talk about China's defense. First of all, China is a large country. China's territory is about 25 times that of Japan and the Chinese population is ten times that of Japan. Yet by per capita military expenditure, Japan is 5 times that of China. Also, in terms of the share of military expenditure in GDP, Japan and China are about the same.

Worricker: But China wants to spend more, let's just be clear on that.

Liu Xiaoming: Yes, because of the growth of the economy and because of enormous mission of China's defense. As I said, China is a large country to defend. We have 14 neighbors on land, 7 neighbors on sea. We have 22, 000 km of borderlines and 32, 000 km of coastallines.

Worricker: I want to talk as well about the current dispute which I referred to at the top of the hour over a group of islands in the East China Sea, uninhabited islands, both China and Japan claim them. As part of that dispute, China has unilaterally declared air defense identification zone over a large part of that area. Inevitably, the Japanese will view that, will they not, as an act of aggression.

Liu Xiaoming: We call them Diaoyu Islands. It is a long story. The Diaoyu Island and its adjacent islands have long been China's territory since ancient times.

Worricker: You know the Japanese would dispute that.

Liu Xiaoming: They would dispute but I can talk about the fact. The fact is fact. It was not until 1895 when China lost war to Japan that Japan illegally seized it. As a result of Second World War, as a result of the Cairo Declaration agreed to by British, Chinese and American leaders that Japan had to return these territories, including Taiwan and Diaoyu Island to China. But in early 1950s, Americans took it over. It was not delivered because of the Cold War. The US needed Japan. And in the 1970s, they transferred administrative power of Diaoyu Island to Japan. But, America still did not recognize sovereignty claimed by Japan. They still remain neutral.

Worricker: In which case, what does this unilateral declaration of air defense identification zone achieve from your point of view other than make the dispute more acute than it is already?

Liu Xiaoming: Let me finish on the Diaoyu Islands. It was not until the recent past when China and Japan normalized relations in early 1970s, both leaders agreed to shelve the dispute. To use Deng Xiaoping's words when he visited Japan, he was asked about Diaoyu Islands, Deng said, I think our future generations will be wiser to find a solution. So they shelved this dispute. But in the recent past, Japanese took a lot of unilateral measures. It was Japan who took provocative actions. They wanted to purchase the islands. They wanted to nationalize the islands. We've been put into a position where we have to make response to what they are doing.

Worricker: That's what you would use as a justification for declaring this unilateral air identification zone.

Liu Xiaoming: This is a normal procedure.

Worricker: But at some point, either side has got to pull back from the situation.

Liu Xiaoming: You are talking about this air defense identification zone.

Worricker: Well, more broadly.

Liu Xiaoming: I want to point out, Japan has established this kind of zone 45 years ago. They have been keeping expanding this zone over the past 45 years. And their so-called zone even got as close as kilome ters from China's coastal line.

Worricker: I want to bring a guest in because I knew he is very keen to ask you a question. George Parker (political editor of Financial Times), you've been listening with interest.

Parker: Very much so. And I totally understand the painful history between your two countries and the upset you felt about Prime Minister Abe going to Yasukuni Shrine. But now you look at military levels in China versus military might of Japan. And China far out-muscles Japan. Are you saying that you still feel some kind of military threat from Japan?

Liu Xiaoming: You are talking about the figures of military expenditure. You ignored the fact that Japan is also expanding their defense budget. In the next 5 years, Japan's military expenditure will increase by 5%. And their military expenditure now is at a historical high over the past 18 years. America's military budget is much bigger than China. It is four times bigger and also in terms of per capita military expenditure, 22 times of China. Even Britain is 9 times that of China. That's number one. Number two. Military expenditure is an important factor to analyze the defense posture of a country. What is more important is the strategy of a country. China is a pacifist country. If you look at the record of China, if you compare the record of China with Japan, you will see Japan is quite a different country.

Parker: But do you still feel a military threat from Japan?

Liu Xiaoming: Because we've been attacked and we've been invaded in history. In the First World War, Japan imposed a lot of unequal treaties on China. In the Second World War, the Chinese people suffered dearly at the hands of Japanese aggressors.

Worricker: Do you still feel that military threat now is the question?

Liu Xiaoming: Of course. Because of the way they treat history, because they still respect the war criminals, because they want to revise the pacifist parts of the Japanese Constitution. So we are very concerned about that.

Worricker: Let me bring in Jyoti Malhotra from Delhi.

Malhotra: Good morning Ambassador.

Liu Xiaoming: Good morning.

Malhotra: Good to talk to you through the BBC. I am an Indian journalist based in Delhi. And I just wanted to say that in India we look at China as a great country and an ancient civilization. You're well on your way to becoming the world's number one economic power. But having said that, I'm just wondering why is that China has so many disputes with its neighbors, including with India. Our disputes of course go back to independence. And we have different views of our border, which is about 4, 000 km long. You just talked about China being a pacifist country and yet only a few months ago, the Chinese PLA crossed the line of actual control and came into India. And China was there for 3 weeks at the Depsang plateau. Why?

Liu Xiaoming: First of all, I would say that we would like to have good relations with all our neighboring countries. We enjoy good relations with most of our neighbors. When it comes to a border dispute, we all have to recognize that China has been a victim of imperial power and suffered dearly from foreign aggression. I think most of these border disputes are legacies left by the colonial rulers. Having said that, we are very sincere in sitting down to have sincere, serious discussions and negotiations with our neighboring countries on these disputes, including with the Indian people. I am very pleased to see there has been progress in the negotiations between China and

India in terms of boundary issues.

Malhotra: Mr Ambassador, there was an agreement between India and China in 2005 on the border. The agreement talked about the border disputes. But a couple of years later, China unilaterally withdrew from that understanding. And now there is no understanding at all.

Liu Xiaoming: I don't agree with you. You know, I'm here to talk about China-Japan relations. When it comes to dispute, you can't listen to just one side's story. We also have complaints about the conduct, about the actions from the Indian side. But I do not want to debate with you today on this issue. All I want to say is we are sincere in negotiating solutions acceptable to both sides.

Worricker: Mr Ambassador, we do appreciate your coming in this morning. Thank you very much indeed for your time.

Liu Xiaoming: My pleasure.

The BBC World Service is broadcast to 200 countries and regions around the world with an international audience of about 210 million. Julian Worricker is an English journalist, currently working as one of the main presenters of *Weekend* on the BBC World Service.

接受英国BBC世界新闻台
主持人库马拉萨米现场直播采访

作者手记

2014年1月5日，我在英国BBC总部演播室，接受BBC世界新闻台主持人詹姆斯·库马拉萨米（James Coomarasamy）现场直播采访。

库马拉萨米曾任BBC外事记者，常驻苏联、波兰、法国、美国，在BBC多个栏目担任主持人。

我在采访中揭批了日本首相安倍复辟军国主义企图，阐述了中方在划设东海防空识别区、中国军费等问题上的立场。

采访内容除在BBC世界新闻台现场直播外，还在该台向全球100多个国家和地区滚动播放，受众近1亿人次。

采访实录如下：

库马拉萨米： 中国提醒国际社会对日本军国主义保持警惕，中国的主要关切是什么？

刘晓明： 我们对安倍参拜靖国神社表示严重关切。靖国神社一直是日本军国主义对外发动侵略战争和殖民统治的精神工具和象征，至今仍供奉着包括东条英机在内的14名二战甲级战犯。东条英机不仅对中国发起战争，而且偷袭珍珠港，对英国、美国和荷兰开战。日本领导人参拜这些战犯，我们不能不对此感到担忧。

库马拉萨米： 你认为靖国神社所象征的意义将把日本引向何方？

刘晓明： 这正是我们所担忧的。日本领导人参拜靖国神社并不是一个孤立事件，而是挑起地区紧张局势的一系列行动的一部分。安倍上台以来，鼓吹所谓"侵略未定论"。他不承认日本是侵略者，甚至认为日本是战争的受害者。日本副首相麻生太郎还扬言"日本可以学习纳粹德国修宪的做法"。与此同时，日本不断增加军费。未来5年，日本军费开支将增长5%。这应引起我们的警惕。

库马拉萨米： 中国单方面划设东海防空识别区，也引起了邻国担忧，这是否也是一种"侵略"行为？

刘晓明： 我完全不同意你的说法。划设防空识别区是主权国家的通行做法。英国、美国等许多国家都设有防空识别区。事实上，日本早在45年前就设立了防空识别区，并且不断扩大，离中国海岸线最近距离仅130公里。

库马拉萨米： 但中国在当前局势下宣布划设防空识别区，使紧张局势升级，这难道不是"侵略"行为吗?

刘晓明： 我完全不同意你所谓中方"侵略"的说法。我想强调的是，东海防空识别区的划设完全是为了防御。它不是禁飞区，不会影响他国航空器依国际法享有的飞越自由，只需向中方通报即可。自中国设立东海防空识别区以来，识别区内从未发生过冲突，一直保持着和平。中国的做法完全符合国际法和国际惯例。

库马拉萨米： 中国在外交层面将采取什么行动缓解两国紧张关系？缓解紧张局势也符合中国利益。

刘晓明： 是日本挑衅在先。当务之急是制止日本军国主义复辟企图。我们要动员国际社会的力量，共同阻止日本在错误的道路上越走越远。安倍参拜靖国神社后，不仅中国、韩国表达了强烈愤怒，美国也表示失望。我们只有建立国际统一阵线，共同防止日本重走军国主义扩张的老路，战后国际秩序才能得以维护。

库马拉萨米： 你刚才说美国也对安倍参拜靖国神社表示失望，但这还不够。因为这未能阻止日本领导人参拜靖国神社。我们是否需要外部干预？

刘晓明： 日本侵华战争造成中国3500多万人伤亡，直接和间接经济损失达6000多亿美元。韩国也在日本侵略战争中遭受惨痛损失。

事实上，英国人民也是日本侵略战争的受害者。

库马拉萨米： 如果当前紧张局势无法缓解，会导致什么后果？

刘晓明： 我们希望日本领导人能倾听国际社会的声音，改弦更张，回到中日两国领导人达成的共识和中日关系4个政治文件上来，对历史罪行进行深刻反省和真诚忏悔。事实上，日本战争罪行从未得到彻底清算，因此军国主义势力总是蠢蠢欲动。我们决不能让日本军国主义再度复活。

库马拉萨米： 但中国也在增加军费开支，在地区部署航母，这不是对外发出错误信号吗？

刘晓明： 中日两国不能相提并论。中国是一个幅员辽阔的大国。中国人口是日本的10倍，国土面积是日本的25倍，但日本的人均军费开支却是中国的5倍。而且，中国的国防费用占GDP和财政总支出比重近年来不断下降。更重要的是，中国是爱好和平的国家，从未发动过侵略战争，相反却屡遭外国列强侵略。而日本则完全不同，在历史上多次发动对外侵略战争，包括侵华战争。

库马拉萨米： 谢谢刘大使。

刘晓明： 不客气。

A Live Interview with James Coomarasamy on BBC World News

On 5th January, 2014, I gave a live interview on BBC World News to presenter James Coomarasamy. During the interview, I analyzed the Japanese Prime Minister Shinzo Abe's attempt to revive militarism in Japan, and elaborated on China's stance on the Air Defense Identification Zone in the East China Sea and China's military expenditure. The full text of the interview is as follows:

Coomarasamy: China reminds the international community to be vigilant against Japanese militarism. What is your main concern here?

Liu Xiaoming: We are very much concerned about Shinzo Abe's visit to the war-linked Yasukuni Shrine, because the Yasukuni Shrine has long been the spiritual symbol and instrument used by Japanese militarists in their wars of aggression and colonial rule. The Shrine today still honors 14 Class A war criminals including Hideki Tojo, who was responsible not only for launching a war against China but also for attacking the Pearl Harbor and for declaring war on the United States, Britain and the Netherlands. We have to express concern about the Japanese Prime Minister paying homage to war criminals.

Coomarasamy: In your opinion, where will Japan be led to by what Yasukuni Shrine symbolizes?

Liu Xiaoming: That is what we are concerned about. The Japanese leaders'visit to Yasukuni Shrine was not an isolated event, but a part of a series of actions that provoked regional tensions. Since Abe came to power, he has challenged the definition of "Japanese aggression". Instead of admitting that Japan was an aggressor, he regarded Japan as a victim of war. The Deputy Prime Minister Taro Aso asserted that Japan would like to learn from Nazi Germany to revise Japan's pacificist Constitution. Meanwhile, Japan is also increasing its defense budget. In the next 5 years, Japan's military expenditure will increase by 5%. This should put us on alert.

Coomarasamy: China has unilaterally declared an Air Defense Identification Zone over the East China Sea, and this has caused more worries among its neighbors. Is this also an act of "aggression"?

Liu Xiaoming: I totally disagree with you. The establishment of air defense identification zones is a common practice of sovereign states. Britain, the United States and many other countries have their own air defense identification zones. In fact, Japan had established such a kind of zone 45 years ago and has kept expanding it ever since. And this Japanese ADIZ is only 130 kilometers from China's coastal line at the closest point.

Coomarasamy: But China's declaration of its air defense identification zone in the current situation has escalated the tensions. Is this not an act of "aggression"?

Liu Xiaoming: I totally disagree with what you termed as Chinese "aggression". What I would like to stress is that the East China Sea Air Defense Identification Zone has been designed solely for defense. It is not a no-fly zone, and it will not affect other countries' freedom of overflight according to the international law, so long as they inform us. Since its establishment, there has never been a conflict in the area, and peace has been maintained. What China did was in full compliance with the international law and international common practice.

Coomarasamy: What action will China take at the diplomatic level to ease the tensions between the two countries? Relieving tensions is also in the interests of China.

Liu Xiaoming: It was Japan who committed provocation first. It is imperative to stop Japan's attempt to revive militarism. We should mobilize the international community to work together to prevent Japan from going farther down the wrong path. After Abe's visit to Yasukuni Shrine, China and Korea expressed their strong indignation, and the United States also expressed its disappointment. The postwar international order can be maintained only if we form an international united front to prevent Japan from taking the old path of militarism.

Coomarasamy: You just said that the United States also expressed its disappointment over Abe's visit to Yasukuni Shrine, but that was not enough, because it failed to stop Japan from visiting Yasukuni Shrine. Do we need external intervention?

Liu Xiaoming: Japan's war of aggression against China caused more than 35 million casualties in China, and direct and indirect economic losses of more than 600 billion US dollars. Korea also suffered a painful loss from Japan's aggression. In fact, the British people are victims as well.

Coomarasamy: What can be the consequences if the current tensions cannot be alleviated?

Liu Xiaoming: We hope that the Japanese leaders will hear the voice of the international community, change its current course and come back to consensus reached by the leaders of China and Japan and the four political documents on Sino-Japanese relations, and reflect and repent deeply over their historical crimes. In fact, the Japanese war crimes have never been fully and completely acknowledged by the militarist forces in Japan who are always ready to make trouble. We must not let anyone raise the spectre of Japanese militarism again.

Coomarasamy: But China is also increasing military spending and deploying an aircraft carrier in the region. Are you sending a wrong signal?

Liu Xiaoming: China and Japan should not be mentioned in the same breath. China is a large country. China's population is ten times that of Japan, and the land area is about 25 times that of Japan. Yet Japan's military spending per capita is 5 times that of China. And if you look at China's military budget-to-GDP ratio and the percentage of China's defense budget against its total fiscal expenditure, the figures are decreasing year-on-year. More importantly, China is a pacifist country and has never waged wars of aggression. Instead, we have been repeatedly invaded by foreign

powers. But Japan is quite a different country. In history, it has launched many wars of aggression against foreign countries, including the war of aggression against China.

Coomarasamy: Thank you very much.

Liu Xiaoming: My pleasure.

BBC World News is broadcasted to more than 100 countries and regions around the world, with an audience of 100 million per week. James Coomarasamy is a British presenter of the BBC Radio 4 evening programme *The World Tonight* and the flagship *Newshour* programme on the BBC World Service.

接受英国BBC《新闻之夜》栏目
主持人帕克斯曼现场直播采访

作者手记

2014年1月8日，我在英国BBC旗舰栏目《新闻之夜》（Newsnight）演播室，接受该栏目主持人杰里米·帕克斯曼（Jeremy Paxman）现场直播采访。

我在英国《每日电讯报》上发表文章，揭批日本首相安倍参拜靖国神社，并把日本军国主义比作"伏地魔"后，日本驻英大使紧接着在同一报纸发表文章，狂妄地也把中国比作"伏地魔"。中日驻英大使在英国报纸上的公开论战，引起英国媒体极大关注。BBC第一个提出，大牌主持人帕克斯曼希望邀请两国大使做客《新闻之夜》，就双方各自立场进行辩论。我表示，没有问题，愿意赴约。然而，日本驻英国使馆回绝了BBC，说日本驻英国大使林景一可以接受帕克斯曼单独采访，但不与中国大使同台辩论。

英国是一个不愁创意的国度。BBC并没有因为日方的回绝而放弃，它提出能否请两国大使同时做客《新闻之夜》演播室，可以不面对面地辩论，由帕克斯曼分别采访。BBC告之，《新闻之夜》演播室有两个演播台，两国大使可分坐两个不同的演播台，相距

10米，可以看到听到，不必打招呼。帕克斯曼将分别采访两位大使。采访为现场直播，时长8分钟，每位大使4分钟。我方表示没有问题，可以接受。但既然是同时到场，分别接受采访，就有一个谁先谁后问题。为了掌握主动，我方提出后接受采访。日方也要求后接受采访。

英国也是一个讲规矩的国度。BBC说，英方提出两国大使同台辩论，中方同意，日方不干，英方依了日方。现在中日双方都要求后接受采访，英方必须照顾中方，这才公平。

于是，1月8日，我和日本大使林景一同时步入BBC《新闻之夜》演播室，分别在两个演播台坐下。帕克斯曼先采访林景一，一连串的问题让他招架不住。我在10米外静听，摩拳擦掌，准备逐一批驳他的谬论。4分钟后，帕克斯曼移步我的演播台。这是他第二次采访我，俗话说，"一回生，二回熟"，我们也算是"熟人"了。一见面，我们互致问候，气氛与第一次采访大不相同。我们谈了安倍参拜靖国神社、钓鱼岛等问题，我阐述了中方在这些问题上的严正立场，揭批安倍企图复辟日本军国主义的行径。

这场中日大使交锋被媒体称为"舆论甲午战争"，还有的媒体将两位大使的表现做比较：日本大使语焉不详，前后矛盾，被动招架；中国大使慷慨陈词，有理有据，始终处于主动，可谓"完胜"。这一幕也被定格在6集大型政论专题片《大国外交》中。

采访实录如下：

帕克斯曼： 大使先生，你好！非常感谢前来接受采访。

刘晓明： 你好！杰里米，很高兴再次见面。

帕克斯曼： 我也很高兴见到你。你认为安倍参拜靖国神社问题有多严重？

刘晓明： 非常严重。这是一个大是大非的问题。它事关日本如何看待其侵略历史，温斯顿·丘吉尔曾经说过，"不从历史中吸取教训的人注定重蹈覆辙"。如果日本不能正视其侵略历史，人们不能不担心日本今后将走什么道路。

帕克斯曼： 你提到参拜靖国神社的问题。二战以来，日本首相参拜靖国神社共60多次，但中国对其中20多次都没有表示反对。

刘晓明： 这种说法是不对的。我知道这是日本驻英大使提供的数字。但事实是，1978年以后靖国神社才移入14名二战甲级战犯的牌位。1985年，日本时任首相率领全体内阁成员参拜靖国神社，中国当即表示强烈抗议。此后，中国对日本领导人的参拜行为不断提出严正抗议。

帕克斯曼： 让我们谈谈钓鱼岛问题。为什么中国突然宣布对该岛屿空域的控制？为什么中国突然采取行动？

刘晓明： 这个问题问得很好。过去40年来钓鱼岛问题一直平静，为什么近来突然升温呢？首先，我想强调钓鱼岛及其附属岛屿自古以来就是中国的固有领土，1895年中国在甲午战争战败后，日本将其非法侵占。根据《开罗宣言》和《波茨坦公告》，日本必须向中国归还所有非法窃取之领土。这是中、英、美三国首脑共同达成的国际文件。

帕克斯曼： 对不起，我不熟悉《开罗宣言》，请问那是什么时候？

刘晓明： 1943年。

帕克斯曼： 好的。你认为目前的问题与钓鱼岛及其海域蕴藏丰富的自然资源是否有关？

刘晓明： 这一问题事关国家主权，事关领土完整。让我继续说明这一问题为何突然升温。1972年中日实现关系正常化，两国领导人达成谅解，同意将钓鱼岛问题先放一放，留待以后解决。1978年，中国领导人邓小平访问日本时曾被问及钓鱼岛归属问题。邓小平回答说：这个问题我们同日本有争议，可以把它放一放，也许下一代人比我们更聪明些，会找到解决的方法。因此两国领导人决定搁置争议。但近年来日本不断单方面采取行动，企图改变现状，制造了"购岛"闹剧，企图将钓鱼岛进行所谓"国有化"，迫使中国不得不做出反应。

帕克斯曼： 对这一争议，中国准备走多远？

刘晓明： 首先，日本要承认双方在钓鱼岛问题上存在争议。日本甚至拒绝承认存在争议。

帕克斯曼： 就在几秒钟前，坐在那里的日本大使说有必要进行对话，这不是暗示承认存在分歧吗？

刘晓明： 事实上，是安倍破坏了中日关系的政治基础，是安倍关闭了中日对话的大门。安倍拒绝就日本军国主义向中国人民犯下的战争罪行表示真诚忏悔，在这种情况下怎么可能要求中国同意与他对话！而且不仅中国表达了这一立场，韩国总统也因为安倍在历史问题上的言行拒绝与他会见。

帕克斯曼： 非常感谢你接受采访。

刘晓明： 不客气！

A Live Interview with Jeremy Paxman on BBC *Newsnight*

On 8th January 2014, I gave a live interview to Jeremy Paxman on BBC 2 *Newsnight* programme. I elaborated on China's solemn stands on Abe's visit to the Yakusuni Shrine and the Diaoyu Islands. The transcript of the interview goes as follows:

Paxman: How are you? Thank you very much for coming in.

Liu Xiaoming: Fine. Jeremy, nice to see you again.

Paxman: Nice to see you. How serious do you think this is?

Liu Xiaoming: Very serious. This is a very serious issue. Japanese prime minister's visit to the Yakusuni Shrine, in our view, is not a small matter. It concerns how Japanese face up to their history of aggression. I would quote Winston Churchill's words, "Those who fail to learn from history are doomed to repeat it". So we are concerned that if they do not face up to their disgraceful record of aggression, what will happen for the future?

Paxman: You raised the question of this visit to the Shrine. There have been over 60 prime ministerial visits to that Shrine since the Second World War, and to 20-something of them the Chinese raised no objection at all?

Liu Xiaoming: That was not right. I know this was the Japanese Ambassador's figure. You know it was not until 1978 that the 14 Class A war criminals had been moved in. And then in 1985, the Japanese prime minister, together with the whole cabinet, visited the shrine. We lodged a strong protest. So since then, we made countless protests against it.

Paxman: But let's look at these islands. Why have you suddenly asserted control of the air, for example, above them. Why have you suddenly done that?

Liu Xiaoming: That was a good question. Why has this matter cropped up so suddenly? It has been very peaceful for the past 40 years. First of all, I would say these islands have been part of the Chinese territory since ancient times. It was in 1895 when China lost the war with Japan that they had been seized illegally. But according to the *Cairo Declaration* and *Potsdam Proclamation*, all the territories seized illegally by Japan should be returned to China. That is an international document agreed by the British, American and Chinese leaders.

Paxman: Sorry, I am not familiar with the Cairo Declaration. When was that?

Liu Xiaoming: 1943.

Paxman: Right. Now it has nothing to do, you say then, with natural resources which may be connected with these islands or may be available from these islands?

Liu Xiaoming: It is about sovereignty. It is about territorial integrity. Let me finish about why it came up. When we normalized relations in 1972, both leaders agreed that there was a dispute over the islands. We should shelve the difference. Deng Xiaoping, in 1978 when he visited Japan, was asked this question about Diaoyu Islands. And he said, "We have a dispute with Japan, but I think we can shelve it for the time being. The future generation will be wiser than us. " So we agreed to shelve it. But the Japanese want to change the status quo. In the past few years, you know, what did they do? They tried to "nationalize" these islands. Their government wanted to "purchase" these islands.

Paxman: How far are you prepared to take this dispute?

Liu Xiaoming: How far? First of all, they have to face up to the fact that we have a dispute over the islands. They even refuse to recognize there is a dispute between the two countries over the islands.

Paxman: Implicitly, the Japanese ambassador over there a second or two ago was talking about the need for dialogue. That is an implicit recognition that there is a disagreement over it.

Liu Xiaoming: In fact, it was Abe, the Japanese prime minister, who shut the door to dialogue between China and Japan because he overturned the political foundation of the two countries. How would you expect China would agree to talk to him when he refuses to repent on the war crimes the Japanese did to the Chinese people? This is not only a case for China. The Korean president also refused to meet Abe because of his behaviour on history issue.

Paxman: Thank you very much indeed. Thank you.

Liu Xiaoming: My pleasure.

出使英国11年，我接受了170多次采访，其中电视、电台采访53次。所有主流电视台和电台都采访过我。我被英国舆论界和外交界称为"上镜率最高""被媒体引用最多"的外国驻英使节。我离任回国后，不少朋友和同事都说，看了我在英国电视台的采访，印象深刻。他们希望我把这些采访整理一下出本书，更希望我讲讲采访背后的故事。

凡是故事，皆有源头。采访故事的源头就是我们国家的崛起。随着中国日益走近世界舞台的中央，世界更加关注我们，希望听到我们的声音，更多了解我们。与此同时，国际上的反华势力极尽造谣污蔑之能事，抹黑、诋毁中国，把西方涉华舆论环境搞得乌烟瘴气。英国拥有大量媒体资源，是国际舆论中心，也是西方舆论高地。在这样的国度工作，我深感肩上沉甸甸的担子，更感讲好中国故事，传播好中国声音，是我义不容辞的责任。正是这种责任感，使我在严峻的舆论环境面前，不畏困难，不惧挑战，敢于担当。正是这种责任感，使我充满自信，从容应对，努力展现中国大国风度，彰显中华民族志气和底气。

许多人问我与西方媒体打交道有什么经验和体会，向我讨教应对西方媒体的"秘诀"。我说，责任感和自信心是我最主要的经验和体会，也是我制胜的法宝。说到"秘诀"，我倒有"三套武器"。每次上阵前，特别是接受现场直播采访前，我都要认真仔细检查这"三套武器"。一是"长矛"，二是"盾牌"，三是"匕首"。"长矛"用来主动出击，积极阐述中国立场和内外政策，讲好中国故事，向世界展示真实、立体、全面的中国。"盾牌"用来防守，事先假设各种刁钻问题，做足功课，备好预案，从容应对。"匕首"用来反击。最好的防御是进攻。短兵相接，特别是对方纠缠不休的时候，要伺机反问，打乱对方进攻节奏，转守为攻，变被动为主动。比如2019年11月，我接受BBC《尖锐对话》栏目现场直播采访，主持人不停质问所谓中国人权问题。我问他：你去过中国吗？他说3年前去过。我接着问：难道你没有感受到中国人民是很自由、很幸福的吗？你认为中国人民处于被压迫、被恐吓的状态吗？一连串的反问使他赶紧转换话题。还是这次采访，主持人一再纠缠新疆问题，而且不停打断我，不给我介绍新疆情况的机会。我抓住机会反问：你去过新疆吗？他一下愣了，没想到我会问这个问题。他说还没有去过，如果中方邀请，他很乐意去。我表示欢迎。接着向他介绍新疆情况，告诉他中国有句俗语：不到新疆，不知道中国之大；不到新疆，不知道中国之美。但20世纪90年代至2016年，新疆变成另外一种景象，恐怖袭击事件频发，成千无辜群众遇难。中国政府对此必须采取措施，包括依法设立"职业教育技能培训中心"。有力的反问打断了对方纠缠，也为我说明新疆真相争取了机会。反击还要备足"炮弹"。也是在这次采访中，主持人反复纠缠所谓香港警察过度使用暴力"镇压"，甚至近距离向抗议者开枪。我引述英国首席警监的话："训练有素的武装警察可以开枪，以消除威胁，保护公众和警察自身安全。"主持人无言以对。

习近平总书记说，我们党带领人民经过几代人不懈奋斗，基本解决了"挨打""挨饿"问题，但"挨骂"问题还没有得到根本解决。我的体会是，解决了"挨打"问题，使中国人民站起来；解决了"挨饿"问题，使中国人民富起来；还没有根本解决"挨骂"问题，说明我们国家仍面临复杂严峻的国际舆论环境。要实现中华民族从站起来、富起来到强起来的伟大飞跃，必须要下大力气加强国际传播能力建设，解决"挨骂"问题。换句话说，解决

"挨骂"问题将伴随从站起来、富起来到强起来的全过程。这充分说明解决"挨骂"问题的长期性和艰巨性，也说明加强国际传播能力建设的重要性和必要性。在这一过程中，既要加强对国际传播理论和规律的研究，也要用好外国主流媒体的平台和渠道，"借船出海"，"借台唱戏"，努力构建对外话语体系，提升对外发声能力。北京出版集团把我使英国期间接受英美电视电台采访实录汇编成《尖锐对话》，这既是一次有益的尝试，也可谓恰逢其时。

在此，我要感谢北京出版集团董事长康伟、总编辑李清霞、副总经理赵安良，北京人民出版社总编辑吕克农、特邀译审艾玫子和责任编辑马群。由于他们的鼓励和支持，特别是他们编辑和出版团队的敬业精神和高效工作，使本书在较短的时间内顺利出版。我还要感谢外交部的同事陈雯、曾嵘和王小晶，她们参与本书的审核、校对和联络工作，提出不少宝贵意见。

最后，我要感谢为本书写推荐语的中英人士，特别是英国友人，他们中有前政府大臣、议员，有著名企业家、金融家、科学家，有知名学者、大学校长、教授，有公爵、男爵、勋爵。他们的肯定和鼓励不仅充满热情，而且充满智慧。他们是中英关系的见证者和参与者，也是中国声音的倾听者和建议者。我将珍视他们的友谊，不辜负他们的期望，接续努力，积极探索，让世界更多的人听到新时代中国声音。

刘晓明

2022年立秋

CPSIA information can be obtained
at www.ICGtesting.com
Printed in the USA
BVHW060858130223
658402BV00015B/498